STRINGS ATTACHED

ERIN THOMSON

Strings Attached

I would like to acknowledge the Wurundjeri
Woi-wurrung people as the traditional custodians of
the land I live and work on, and pay respect to the
Elders, past, present and emerging.

1

JAKE

Then

The plane touched down at JFK and I tried to squash the feeling that I shouldn't be here, that I'd be better off heading straight to Barcelona. Impatience and excitement were at war in my gut. Impatience, it would appear, was very close to winning. The prospect of spending some time with Hunter was the only thing keeping me from getting on another plane to Barcelona here and now. That, and the fact training didn't start for six weeks. So two things then. Even with a few weeks in New York I'd still be arriving in Spain early, giving myself plenty of time to settle in and acclimatize to the city. My new home. After so many years of working toward this, so many years of waiting,

A few weeks wouldn't kill me—even if right now it felt like it might.

For as long as I could remember, all I'd ever wanted to do was play soccer. From the moment I first kicked that black and white ball I was hooked. It was all I did, all I thought about, all day, everyday. I ate, slept, fucking *breathed* soccer.

It was my life. And I didn't see it changing in a hurry. In fact, it was probably about to consume me even more.

The cab made its way through the streets, and I let my gaze wander, enjoying the view—so different from California. I almost went to school on the East Coast, but a full scholarship from Stanford was hard to say no to, even if I was bailing on it now. My dad was less than thrilled at the decision, but how the hell was I supposed to turn down an opportunity to play in fucking Europe? Europe, then the EPL. That had always been the goal.

I bounded up the stoop and knocked, buzzing with this feeling like life was full of possibilities. Like I could do anything. Like everything was about to change. And I guess it was, all that separated me from my soccer career was six short weeks.

The door swung open, and I only just managed to keep my jaw from hitting my shoes. The girl standing just inside the threshold was most definitely not my cousin. No, she was a smiling package of curves and curls. And I was staring.

"You're not Hunter," I said, uselessly. I'd never been so relieved not to be related to another person in my life.

She planted one hand on her popped hip and peered up at me, recognition firing in her whiskey-colored eyes. "The cousin." Her voice was incredible. Sweet and husky, like honey over gravel.

"I am. And y—"

"The same cousin," she cut in, "who steals my friend away every summer." Those eyes made a slow journey of perusal from my feet up to my face. "I remember you being taller," she said before turning on a dime and walking deeper into the house, the neon pink of her bikini drawing my attention to her swaying hips. "You comin' California?"

I stood for a beat, mute and dumbfounded, before I scrambled inside and followed down the hall. I had the distinct feeling that my entire world had just shifted on its axis. This girl was now my gravity, and I was being pulled from a spot in the center of my chest.

"Jake!" Hunter said, clapping me on the shoulder as I stepped out the back door and onto the porch. I returned his half hug, even as my eyes sought *her*. She was on one of the two banana lounges that sat on the grass, legs outstretched, large sunglasses perched on her nose. Even with her face turned up to the sun, I could have sworn she was watching me from the corner of her eye.

"How was the flight?" My attention snapped back to Hunter.

"Good, uneventful, except for the numerous voicemails Dad left, which I am ignoring."

He laughed. "Probably wise. He's not happy?"

"You could say that."

"He'll get over it."

"I'm not sure he will, but it doesn't matter." I paused. It was true, Dad's opinion on my career no longer mattered. What the fuck did I care if he didn't support me? I'd secured a spot with Barcelona on my own, anyway. I didn't need him—not anymore. "It's really fucking good to see you," I said.

"It's really fucking good to see you, too." Another slap to my shoulder. "And you've met Harley, again." One hand waved in the direction of the banana lounge and my eyes followed. Harley. Wait, *again?*

"Ah ... perhaps not officially." I tried to sound cool, but my cracking voice probably gave me away. Were my palms sweating?

"Well then, *officially*," he started as she stood. "Jake Davenport, cousin, meet Harley O'Connell, best friend. Harley, meet Jake."

Her head tipped to one side as she extended a hand. "Jake Davenport ..." God, that voice. "Should I be offended that you don't remember me?"

My hand swallowed hers as we shook and a bolt of something ran up my arm and down my spine. "I can guarantee I won't forget you again."

Her face split into a grin that showed off pretty much all her teeth and I knew, right then and there, that I was going to marry this girl.

2

HARLEY

Now

It was a well-known fact that there was nothing more frightening than a broken coffee machine on a Monday morning. Granted, it would be a less than ideal situation any day of the week, but on a Monday, it hit just that little bit harder.

"I've tried everything!" Darcy wailed, green eyes wide and panicked as I rounded the counter and eased her out of the way. She was waving one of the group handles around like a baton, or maybe a weapon.

"Good morning to you, too, Darce. Now, when you say everything, does that include speaking in soothing tones? Because you know Edith can tell when you're all ... agitated." I gave her a pointed look.

Her answering one was flat as she slapped the group handle into my waiting palm.

"Harley, you have ten minutes to fix it or I'm calling Tommy."

"*It*, is Edith, and Tommy is not allowed to touch her again after what happened the last time." I shuddered at the memory of how she'd run after Tommy's last service. It took a week of daily tweaking before she felt right again. It was not an exaggeration to say that I would break Tommy's fingers if he touched her again.

"Ten minutes," Darcy repeated before turning on her heel and fleeing to the kitchen, the doors swaying in her wake. I stowed my bag in the cubby hole under the counter and turned my attention to my favorite coworker. Was it strange that my favorite coworker was a piece of machinery? Some might say yes, but they had not worked with Edith.

"Good morning, Miss Edith," I crooned, running a hand across her smooth chrome face. "How are you this morning, my dear? A little grumpy, by the sound of it? Now, I'm sure you didn't mean to give Darcy a hard time, but you know you need to take it easy on her—especially on a Monday." I started my usual routine, checking her over in preparation for another busy day of caffeine and advice dispensary.

God, I loved my job, even with a grumpy Edith.

It didn't take long to find the issue—a kink in one of the pipes—and it was fixed with three minutes to spare.

Darcy reappeared from the kitchen carrying a large tray of banana-coconut muffins—if you ever wondered what day of the week it was, all you needed to do was look at Darcy's muffin of the day and you would wonder no more. Monday was banana-coconut. Tuesday was double chocolate. Wednesday was blueberry streusel. Thursday was apple cinnamon. Friday was raspberry and white chocolate (my least favorite on the principle that white chocolate was the devil's handiwork and not actual chocolate). Saturday was orange and poppyseed. Finally, on Sundays was the Elvis, a glorious, salty-sweet behemoth of banana, peanut butter, and bacon. I ate three of them yesterday and regretted nothing.

"Fixed?" Darcy inquired as she unloaded the batch of muffins.

"Was there ever a doubt?"

"I'm looking into a new machine."

"You are not!" I gaped. "Darcy, Edith is an integral part of our team."

"It is a piece of machinery and one we can now afford to replace."

"She does not need to be replaced," I assured her. And it was true. Yes, she was on the older side, but the older machines were made to last. I didn't need a fully automated thing with a million buttons. Buttons meant issues, as far as I was concerned. Issues that were trickier to fix than a couple of kinked pipes. Give me analog and leave me be. Darcy was spared the rant as the door opened and Deacon, one of our regulars, entered. Judging by the look on his face, I was needed.

"I need a triple, STAT!" he said and slumped onto the counter with a dramatic flail.

I tried, and failed, to reign in my delighted smile. "Tell me everything."

We made it through the breakfast rush without further issues from Edith, which was a relief and allowed me to assure Darcy that she didn't need replacing. I really didn't want to think about adjusting to a new machine.

As the flow of people turned into a trickle, Cecilia tripped through the door guzzling the remains of a Red Bull. She was working with us for the summer before she started her junior year of high school in the fall.

"Do not bring that shit in here, Cece. It will rot your

insides." Apparently, I had turned into my high school vice principal Mrs Pruit.

"Yes, mom," she said with a wink and tossed her can in the trash behind the counter. "Sorry I'm late, I slept through my alarm." She pulled her ash blonde hair into a high ponytail. There was clearly more to it than just missing an alarm—she looked like she'd had about two hours sleep and neither of them had been restful.

Ten excruciating minutes of silent table clearing and meal delivery later my patience had officially worn out.

"Okay, come on, out with it."

"Out with what?"

"With whatever is making your ponytail all droopy. Usually it's taking out half the customers and victimizing everyone else, but right now it's barely managing a lethargic sway."

"I'm just tired."

"Uh-huh ..." I waited.

"Toby and I broke up last night. No, we didn't break up, he dumped me. Over text! Because, and I quote, 'I'm feeling really suffocated right now, Cece.' Suffocated! Because I asked him if the rumors about him and Shelley fucking at his going away party were true." She slumped onto one of the stools and let her head drop onto her arms with a sad little groan. As much as I loved being kept in the loop, sometimes this generation made me genuinely fear for the future.

"Cecilia, what have we said?" I slid a muffin across the counter.

"That Toby is a moron," she said around a mouthful of banana-coconut.

"That pretty much all boys are morons. But at least now you can enjoy your summer and kiss as many cute ones as you like."

"But Shelley Price!"

"This is on Toby, not Shelley."

"It's kind of on Shelley," she mumbled.

"Other women are not our enemies, or our competition—they are our allies, our sisters. You should know that! Isn't Shelley on your JV team?"

"Yup, I get to do six weeks of trust exercises with the girl who had sex with my boyfriend. Lucky me. Maybe I should be grateful the summer program isn't happening."

"What, why wouldn't it be happening?"

"Apparently the coach has pulled out or something. Any chance I can keep working here for the whole summer?"

"Only if you turn up on time," I said, and she poked her tongue out. "I will give you the next ten minutes to wallow about Toby and his poor decision making. After that, you're going to pick yourself up, have a triple shot and get on with your life. Deal?"

She sat up and squared her shoulders. "Deal. Can I take that triple shot now?"

"Yes, you can. And I don't think you need to worry about some drunk dipshit at a party spreading baseless rumors about your soccer training program thing. What the hell would they know anyway?"

"I think his dad is the one who's fronting the cash for it or something."

"Oh. Well, he might still be full of shit."

"I guess you're right."

"I'm always right."

"Thanks, Harley."

"You're welcome," I said, placing the triple shot in front of her, she drank it so fast it had to have scalded. "Now, get back to work."

She bounced off her stool and took the tray for table three

while I lamented the fact that girls were still being pitted against one another for male attention. Such a waste of their collective potential. But I was doing my part to educate the youth.

"The hot one with the hair is here again," Darcy whispered as she sidled up beside me. I glanced up to see Chase and Jeremy walking in. Darcy wasn't wrong, Jeremy really did have a spectacular head of hair. Even after an exercise class it still had remarkable height and looked all shiny, and not from the sweat. I also knew from experience that it felt just as silky as it looked.

Chase, on the other hand, was pink-cheeked, somewhat glassy in the eyes, and the messy knot on top of her head was listing to the left. That was a woman who'd just had her butt kicked.

I nodded for a couple of bottles of water to be taken to the table and watched as Chase guzzled down half of one as she collapsed into her seat.

"Thank you, Harley," she called across the small space and I curtsied in response.

Jeremy caught my eye as he sat and winked, a thrill danced its way down my spine. We'd been hooking up here and there since Thanksgiving and it was always a good time. But I was beginning to get the feeling that he was teetering on that edge of asking for more from our rendezvous and that just wasn't in my game plan. He was a nice guy. Great in bed. And that hair. But I was unmoved about the idea of more with him. Yes, my nipples and vagina were always happy to see him, but my heart remained untethered. Just the way I liked it.

In my defense, I had been very clear about the casual nature of our arrangement well before we got naked, and he had assured me he was fine with it. But then, like so many other (delusional) men, he seemed to think that his magic penis would change my mind and have me begging for him to put a ring on it or something.

"He's looking' at you all dreamy," Darcy said.

"Dreamy? Really?" I bumped her hip with mine. "How about you go do your job and take his order?"

"Like you are not already making his coffee."

"Because I am outstanding at my job, yes of course I am, but that doesn't mean the man isn't also hungry."

"Oh, he's hungry alright."

"I walked right into that one."

"You really did." She slapped my butt with a laugh as she walked away.

"Good morning, gorgeous," a smooth voice said from the to-go window, and I found a guy with his elbows propped on the sill. He looked way too confident in that perfectly preppy kind of way, like he'd never been shot down in his life. I suppressed my eye roll.

"Good morning, what can I get you?"

Brown eyes predictably darted down to my chest before he ordered. "An Americano and your number." And there it was.

"I can provide half that order for you." He might be cute, but I didn't like it when they assumed they could just ask for my number before they asked my name. Where was the give and take? Where was the 'will they-won't they' dance? It was never a good sign if they didn't appreciate the building of tension and anticipation. In my experience, it was a sure-fire sign that foreplay was the last thing on their mind—when it should be the first.

"So, no coffee for me today?" Hilarious.

"That'll be three-eighty," I said with a wide smile as I handed over his cup.

"No number?"

"Not this time."

He shoved a ten into the tip jar, like it would make me change my mind.

"You have a great day!" After a moment of hesitation, he stepped away, mumbling something I was sure he thought was cutting.

"Brutal," the next customer said with a low whistle. I shrugged, hands still busy with the line of waiting coffees. This guy, unlike the last one, had a little more heat about him and it wasn't just the scruffy jaw, messy man-bun, and the tips of a tattoo poking out from the top of his shirt. It was that indefinable something-something.

I smiled. "A girl's gotta have standards, and I am not about to apologize for that ... what can I get you?"

He smiled right back. "I'll take a macchiato."

"Can do."

"So, how's your morning been so far?" Small talk, not a great start but I was willing to let it slide because he had a good smile. Wide, just a little devious.

"Entertaining."

"Is that right?"

"Mm-hm." I nibbled my lip and enjoyed the way his attention followed the small movement. He didn't say anything else though, just watched me watching him. I could practically see where his mind was going. And I was not opposed. I popped the cap off one of my sharpies and scrawled my number on the side of his cup, then slid it across the counter.

"I'll be seeing you ... *Harley*," he purred as I shooed him away from the window.

"Really?" Darcy said, once again at my side.

"Really what?"

"Really, you are literally flirting with Jeremy across the room, and you still wrote your name on that guy's cup?"

"Where is the harm? For one, he probably won't even call. And two, Jeremy and I are not exclusive."

"He might like to be."

"Then I will be forced to end our naked fun times."

"Are you so opposed to dating just the one person? I thought you liked Jeremy?"

"Jeremy is great, we have fun, but it's not going further than that. And I am not opposed to exclusive dating, should the right person present themselves," I rushed to add—though it wasn't strictly true.

"And if the right person does not present themselves?" she asked as she placed another few to-go cups beside the others waiting in a patient line on top of Edith.

I was confident that Darcy believed I lived my life in direct defiance of the societal norm of seeking out *the one*. She probably didn't think I even believed in the concept. But I did. I believed—even when I thought the whole idea of only one person for everyone was absurd, cruel even. There were so many things that could stop you from meeting that one perfect person, and if you did miss them, then what? Did that mean you were going to be miserable for your entire life?

Yes, I believed that there was that one person that could set your heart and soul on fire, but that didn't mean you couldn't enjoy yourself with any number of other people. You could be wildly happy and not even realize there was anything missing. Unless you already knew what it felt like to love someone with your whole heart—*nope, not going there today*. I pulled myself up before that train of thought took me on a journey I was not in the mood for.

"There is a lot to be said for a deeper connection."

"I agree." She opened her mouth, ready to pounce, but I cut her off. "But sometimes you're not after a deeper connection and I do not see the problem in enjoying a ... diverse portfolio."

She barked out a laugh. "Diverse portfolio? I didn't realize we were talking about stocks."

"I'm just saying that if you find someone you want that deeper connection with, cool, you do that, but otherwise, why put all of your time and effort into one basket when there are so many out there? You could do with diversifying your portfolio, if you ask me."

"I am perfectly happy, thank you very much."

"*Perfectly happy* sounds a little bit like you're settling for boring dates and lackluster sex. Two iced lattes for table six." I slid the coffees across the counter before she could argue and shooed her away.

As the day wore on, my mind strayed here and there. In between the general chatter, my conversation with Darcy rolled around my head—no matter how many times I kept pushing it away.

Men were praised for dating around, encouraged even, before it was time for them to 'settle' for just the one person. Why should it be different for women? That wasn't what I was doing, I wasn't waiting for the right one. But I continued to shuffle through man after man, because I saw no need to do otherwise. I was young and enjoyed their company; each one lit me up in a slightly different way. A low, whispering voice told me that wasn't the only reason, but I shoved it aside, even as Liam's face flashed up behind my eyes, a wave of pain coming with it. I could no longer see the details I had loved the most— they were fading more with each passing day.

Yes, I believed in *the one*. I met mine when I was eighteen and he was everything. My moon. My stars. My world. My soulmate. Then he was gone. So what did that mean for me? What did that mean for my still broken heart and fractured soul? Another fifty years of this? I was sure I could make it fun, if nothing else.

Maybe I should call Mrs S, finally ask her to be my mentor and learn her ways. The only difference between us was that she had decades with Ronnie before he was gone. Decades of that bone-deep happiness, while I got less than two years. Even now, I was tempted to rage at the world, kick and scream and cry that it wasn't fair, but what would be the point? It wouldn't change the fact he was gone—that he had been gone so much longer than I knew him.

My chest got that hollow kind of ache it always did when I let myself think of Liam. What would he be like now? What would *we* be like now? What would our lives have looked like if I hadn't sent that text, if he hadn't been alone?

The burn behind my nose snapped me out of those pictures in my head, conjured so often in the quiet dark that they felt like memories. But they weren't, they were nothing but wishes —how things might have been.

I shook out my shoulders, blinked against the rising tide of emotion, and plastered on my best beaming smile. Right now, it felt like a mask, a flimsy one at that, but it didn't always. In fact, some days I could almost convince myself that this was me, that there was nothing else underneath—all that hurt, and rage belonged to someone else, a girl I used to know.

3

JAKE

The passengers in coach were clapping. I'd never understood that. The only thing pilots needed to do was fly and land the plane—and not kill everyone on board. Why did we have to clap because they'd just done their job? It made no sense to me. Ironic, I suppose, given my chosen career.

The plane landing meant we were in New York, and I would have to turn my cell phone on.

I didn't want to turn my cell phone on.

I wanted to continue to pretend I was just a normal guy—a normal guy who hadn't blown up his fucking life and ran like hell. I should have gone further away. Australia, maybe, or some island in the pacific. Somewhere with a flight time upwards of ten hours. A full twenty-four would have been ideal. The eight hours to JFK wasn't nearly far enough.

The seatbelt light clicked off and the other passengers started to move around. Pointless. They wouldn't have the doors open for at least another five minutes. I slumped lower in my seat and tapped my cell phone on my knee. It was still off. Maybe it could just stay off? Forever. Or at least another hour or two. As soon as I turned the thing on, Blair would call. My manager had a sixth sense for these things. And the number of missed calls and irate voicemails I was about to find was making me regret all those whiskeys at the start of the flight. She was going to murder me.

The notifications came rolling in as soon as I got signal. Ding-d-ding-ding-ding. One after the other after the other.

Then Blair was calling.

"Are you completely incapable of keeping your dick in your pants, Jacob!" she screeched down the line as soon as the call connected. I ducked my head as several people swiveled in my direction. Why weren't the doors open yet? When were we going to get off this fucking plane?

I willed the heat crawling up the back of my neck to subside. "Blair, I'm not in the mood. You've covered everything, more than once." In fact, I'd lost track of the number of lectures I'd received over the last few days, few weeks, few months. I was done. Which was why I was 3,500 miles away.

"Well, clearly the others haven't made enough of an impression."

"What are you talking about?" I asked while avoiding eye contact with the small, elderly woman who was standing next to my seat. Seriously, why weren't they opening the fucking doors?

"You are not this stupid. Where was it?"

"Where was what?" I pinched the bridge of my nose. I still hadn't had enough sleep to be dealing with Blair, especially not Blair on the warpath.

"The blowjob, Jake! The fucking blowjob!"

The old woman looked positively delighted at the direction of my conversation. But how the hell did Blair know about the blowjob? Granted, it had not been my finest moment, but when an enthusiastic and persistent member of the airline staff approached me in the lounge before boarding, I was just drunk enough to take her up on her offer. Was it stupid? Yes. Did I regret it? Also, yes. But how the fuck did Blair know about it?

"And, before you try to play dumb," she continued, when it was clear I was struggling for an appropriate retort, "there's a photo. Whoever she was, she took a fucking selfie while she was blowing you." Well, that explained that. And there was probably an important lesson in there somewhere. "Now, where are you?"

"I don't see how that is any of your business," I said and might have regretted it if I wasn't far enough away that she couldn't actually strangle me like I was sure she wanted to. One day she was going to tell me that no amount of money was worth dealing with my shit.

"Oh, yes, it is," she growled. "Now, you're going to tell me where you are." Today was not that day apparently.

"I'm taking some ... personal time."

Another low growl. "*Jake*, if you are on some fucking island with a bunch of fucking models—"

"No island. No models. Just me." The door finally opened, and the line of people started to file out. Thank fucking god. I jumped from my seat and pulled my bag down from the overhead locker.

"If that's true, then tell me where the fuck you are. We cannot survive another scandal. I'm working hard enough to keep your career alive as it is—please do not make my job harder."

I smiled at the flight attendant manning the door and made it into the comparatively fresher air of the tunnel.

"I'm visiting family in the U.S." I almost said I'd be back in a week, but what was the point of that? The words *indefinite suspension* rolled through my head. We were almost two months away from the start of the next season. There was no telling how long this was going to last.

"Good, great, as much as I want you to be shaking hands and kissing babies right now, I think it's probably better if you lay low for the time being." Hearing her confirm my thoughts was not the least bit encouraging.

However accustomed I'd become to seeing my face in the media, the latest drama meant it had gone well beyond saturation point.

But I guess that was going to happen when you got into a brawl with your captain in the middle of a charity event.

There wasn't even any defending it from my end. I fucked up, end of story. I would have preferred if there wasn't footage of me and Pierre's wife in the back of a cab. And it would have been even better if said footage didn't leak—while the team was at an event raising money for reducing youth violence through team sports. It was a disaster. Pierre saw red and went for me. Knowing I was in the wrong didn't stop me from taking him down and breaking his nose.

Naturally, once the media were dragging my name through the mud, every snippet of stupidity I'd been involved in over the years got trotted out, too.

It was a shitshow. *I* was a shitshow.

Despite all the coverage, I didn't grasp quite how bad it was. Not until I was hauled in front of Arturo Concella and told I was suspended, indefinitely.

"You can't afford to lose your best striker over some bad press." It was a lot more than bad press, I knew that, but I needed to pretend it didn't bother me even as I wanted to crawl out of my fucking skin.

"Get your head out of your ass, you're thirty years old"—thirty-two, actually, but I didn't correct him—"you're supposed to be a mentor to the young ones, not dragging them into god knows what off the pitch and breaking your captain's fucking nose." Six months ago I was the fucking captain, and then I was replaced by a player who'd been with the team for less than a year.

"Art, come on."

"It's not up to me." He held up a hand as I went to interrupt. "You're a good player, Davenport, a great one, even. But, right now, you're a liability. I can't have liabilities—not when they're already gutting us in the press ahead of next season."

I burst out into the bright New York sun, pulling my hat lower and willing my heart rate to slow the fuck down. A liability. A fucking liability. I wasn't a liability. There were at least three clubs I could walk into tomorrow and they'd kiss my fucking cleats in gratitude. I was not a liability; I was an all-star.

"Jake, are you listening to me?" Blair jerked my attention back to our conversation.

"Yes, listening, lay low, don't make your life harder, I got it."

My stomach rolled. For the first time since I started playing, I wasn't even sure I wanted to go back. But what the fuck else was I supposed to do? I couldn't think about it now, not when my brain felt like it was going to leak out my ears. I needed sleep. Food and sleep.

"And take care of yourself please," she added, her tone softening. She might be a hardass a lot of the time, but I knew it was because she cared, even when I made her earn that monthly retainer.

"I'll do my best, Blair."

"I'm serious, Jake, please don't do anything stupid."

"Stupidity is officially off the to-do list."

"Keep it that way." She hung up and I pocketed my cell phone, wondering if maybe I should have let Hunter know I was coming before I was literally arriving on his doorstep. It also occurred to me that I didn't know if he'd even have room for me to stay. I could find somewhere else if his place was full but, as sad as it was to admit, I wasn't sure I wanted to stay alone.

I was a grown man, and I was lonely. Fuck, that was sad, wasn't it?

The cab pulled up at Hunter's address. A red-brick building that was quintessentially New York. A fire escape ran down one side, balconies jutted out from the other, and a short stoop took you up to the front door with a panel of names and buttons. I climbed the four steps and scanned the list, finding *H Buchanan* second from the top. I pressed the button and waited.

There was no answer. I buzzed twice more. Still nothing. And this was why you should warn people you were coming, rather than just turning up on a fucking whim in the middle of an existential crisis.

"Hey man, who are you after?" I turned at the question. "A few of the buzzers are broken so—Jake?" My cousin's face was comically slack as he recognized me.

Be cool. "Hunter, hey, how are you?"

"Yeah good, man. How are you doing?" he asked as he unlocked the door and gestured for me to go in ahead.

I opened my mouth, closed it again. "I've been better."

"No shit." Of course, he was up to speed with the shit-show that was my life.

We went up three flights of stairs before he turned on the landing and down the short hall, unlocking a apple green door with a white number thirty-four painted on the front. Uncertainty rolled through me. What the fuck was I doing here? Sure, Hunter and I spoke on a semi-regular basis but that didn't mean I should be just turning up at his fucking apartment and expecting a bed to sleep in. I shouldn't be here. I should be back in London trying to fix my mess. Bile rose in my throat at the mere thought. No. London was the last place I wanted to be right now.

I followed Hunter into a bright living area and kitchen.

"So ..." he started, throwing his keys onto the kitchen counter and going to the fridge. "You want a beer or a coffee?"

"It's two in the afternoon."

"You want a beer or a coffee?" He repeated.

"Beer." What harm could it do now?

With a nod he pulled two bottles from the fridge and handed one to me. I uncapped it and took a deep pull.

"Sorry, to ah, just turn up like this. I—I got on a plane without much of a plan."

"It's cool, you need a place to crash?"

"No. No, I can find a hotel or something—"

"Jake," Hunter cut me off. "If you wanted a hotel, you would have gone to a hotel, right? But you're here."

I sipped my beer, avoiding the question for a long moment before giving a sharp nod in confirmation. He returned it and stepped out onto the balcony. I followed, letting my attention drift down to the street.

"Everything's fucked," I said, not taking my eyes off the people going about their day below us.

"Looks that way," he agreed, dropping into one of the faded deck chairs. I took the other.

"I've been suspended."

"I figured. For how long?"

"Indefinitely."

He sucked in a breath, and I inclined my head.

"What the fuck happened?" I knew he wasn't just asking about the brawl with Pierre, it was pretty obvious what happened there. He was asking what happened to *me*. Wasn't that just the million-dollar fucking question.

What happened to Europe's top striker?

What happened to the Page Six golden boy?

What happened to Jake Davenport?

I wished I had an idea of how to answer, but I didn't. I didn't have a fucking clue. All I knew was that, at some point, things started slipping away. I could feel *myself* slipping away. It was like a strand had come loose somewhere and I was slowly unraveling. And because I didn't know how, or why, or where it all started, I had no fucking idea how to stop it.

I didn't say any of that to Hunter, just shook my head and shrugged.

"Well, the spare room is yours for as long as you need it."

"Thanks, I appreciate that." My throat felt embarrassingly tight. I swallowed another couple of mouthfuls.

"Mi casa, su casa. You want the grand tour?"

"Sure." I followed him back into the living room.

"Alright, living, kitchen, and dining as you have already seen." We headed back toward the front door. "My room." It was tidier than I had been expecting—the bed was made and everything. Last time I had stayed with Hunter the guy was a complete slob; but he was eighteen, people could change a lot in twelve years.

On the other side of the living area there were two more bedrooms.

"This one is Harley's," he said, rapping on the door of the one on the left, but leaving it closed. I froze. My feet stuck fast to the floor as I stared at the closed door.

Harley. She lived here?

"And yours." He pushed open the door on the right. The bed was covered in a white comforter and more pillows than I knew what to do with. There was also a beaten-up old armchair in one corner and a dresser.

Hunter pulled his cell phone out of his pocket. "Shit. As much as I want to hang out and show you around, I've got some shit to deal with at Buck's. It'll probably be a few hours. You good?"

"Sure, I'll just get some sleep, maybe shower."

"Sounds like a plan—bathroom is here." He swung open another door. I was barely going to be able to fit in the shower, but it would do the job. Hunter was still talking. "We did have a spare key, but I'm pretty sure Harley lost it last Halloween and we never replaced it." He scratched his head. "Anyway, I'll get one cut for you."

"Harley, is she—"

He stopped. "Oh, I totally forgot you guys met! Ten years ago, right? No, it was more. We'd just finished high school and you were about to go big. Fuck, that makes me feel old. Anyway—"

"She won't mind? About me being here?" This was it. This was the sign I needed to take my ass directly to a hotel. Right now.

"Nah." He shook his head. "She'll be fine with it. I'll text her, give her the head's up, but I'm sure it won't be an issue."

I nodded once, my body and brain at complete odds. Leaving was the most rational thing to do, but I couldn't get my feet to move in the direction of the front door.

I'd been coasting on adrenaline since I packed my bag in London, and it was finally draining out of my system, leaving me with a desperate need to collapse into the closest bed. There would still be time to go to a hotel. All I needed was a little sleep and then I'd be able to make an actual decision.

Hunter said a final goodbye before the door clicked shut behind him and I soaked in the silence. My brain fought the need for rest, trying to get me to think of all the things I should be doing. But what was the point? My career was over, wasn't it? I was thirty-two. How the hell was I going to come back from an indefinite suspension? The more frightening question was, did I even want to?

4

HARLEY

By the time I walked out of Cream and Sugar, I was feeling all kinds of funky and had zero interest in working out. I turned my face up to the sun, willing it to suck the bad vibes from my pores. But it was useless, the mood had well and truly settled in.

> I'm not coming.

> How did I know you were going to text me this exact thing 20 minutes before you're supposed to be here?

> Because you've got the gift?

> Because you're a shit.

> Rude.

> At least make up an excuse… that time of the month?

My brother was a child. I was tempted to go to the gym just to slap him for the jab, but that was what he wanted. Provoke a response—that was his game plan. I knew this because it was often my game plan, too.

> Your silence is cutting. What if I said we could move it into the park?

I chewed on my lip. The idea of being out in the sun did make the prospect of the workout marginally more appealing.

> Fine, but I'm not doing burpees.

> Just get your ass over here.

"You're late," Murphy said as I approached the small park across from the gym. I attempted to wrangle my hair into submission ahead of whatever my brother had planned.

"By, like, three minutes—considering I didn't want to turn up at all, you should be grateful that I'm even here." I shot back and stretched out my quads. "My walk over here can count as a warmup if you've got somewhere to be?"

"You are not getting out of warming up."

"It's close to eighty, I am plenty warm."

"Harley, quit arguing and start moving."

I poked out my tongue but did as he asked. Despite my numerous complaints, I actually enjoyed working out. And Murphy, as an exercise physiologist, was well placed to design said workouts. I just wished he wasn't quite so smug about it when my legs wound up like jelly.

"What's up with you today? You're distracted," Murphy said as I dropped the forty-pound sandbag with a huff.

"Nothing. I mean, aside from the fact that I think you're trying to kill me, I'm fine."

"Oof, *fine*, really?"

"Alright, you asked. I've got this ... prickly feeling, like something's about to happen, but I can't quite figure out what."

Murphy rolled his eyes to the sky. "Harley, you are not psychic."

"I'm not saying that I'm psychic, *Murphy*."

He planted his hands on his hips. "You cannot, in any way, shape, or form, predict the future."

I rolled my eyes. "Such a nonbeliever. And when you accurately guessed I wanted to bail today."

"You always want to bail." He may have had a point there, but not one I was willing to acknowledge.

"Grandma Rose predicted Kennedy's assassination, the 9/11 attack, and the crash in 2008." I took a swig from my water bottle.

"Grandma Rose didn't even know her own name in 2008." God, he was being particularly infuriating today.

"What does that have to do with her ability to accurately forecast future events?"

He shook his head. "I am not psychic. And neither are you."

"I'm just saying, maybe my hair wasn't the only thing I inherited from her. I knew Mom and Dad were going to split up."

"You didn't need to be psychic to know that."

"You didn't know."

"I was 10," he said, throwing his hands up.

"I was nine. Anyway, this morning I figured it was about Edith, but once I fixed her—"

"Who's Edith? Actually, you know what, I don't want to know."

"The coffee machine," I answered anyway.

"You've named a coffee machine?"

"Why does everyone think that's so weird?"

"Because it's a coffee machine."

"She is an integral part of the team."

"She is a piece of machinery."

"*Anyway*, I thought the funky feeling was about her, but it's not gone away. I checked with Mom and Dad, they're both fine. You also seem to be your cynical self. I don't get it."

"Hunter?" he suggested.

"Ha! So, you do think I've got the gift!"

"Stop slacking and pick up the bag—and keep your steps shorter this time. You want ninety degrees with each leg."

"Yes sir."

If I was going to make it out tonight more caffeine would be required. There were no actual plans, but Monday was like my Friday, so I had two glorious days of nothingness ahead of me and that deserved to be celebrated. I also needed to get the fuck out of my head after today—and that was best done with alcohol and possibly getting naked with a stranger, if the night went well. I would make sure the night went well.

I made my way up the stairs at a snail's pace thanks to Murphy's bright idea of ending the session with jump lunges to failure—his fancy trainer way of saying *until your legs can no longer hold you up*. He was an undercover sadist, he had to be. It was why he excelled at putting together programs that made me want to cry and vomit simultaneously. My butt *was* looking particularly perky of late though.

If I was able to walk tomorrow it would be a small miracle. Thank God Odette and I hadn't planned a hike because I would definitely be canceling on her.

"Hunter, what's the plan?" I called as I kicked the door shut, only to be met with silence. I immediately started peeling off my sweat-soaked clothes. No Hunter meant naked Harley. Shoes, socks, bag and shorts were all left where they fell as I made my way through the apartment. I'd apologize if he happened to get home before I managed to pick them all up. And if I didn't, I'd just give him one of the muffins I swiped before I left Cream and Sugar. He was a sucker for anything that Darcy baked.

I fumbled with the bathroom door handle, attempting to wrestle my tank over my head at the same time, but it was stuck on one of my earrings, so I was just stumbling around blind. Once I got the door open, I walked straight into something, some*one*, with an *oof*. Only that didn't make any sense. Hunter had his own bathroom, unless he was using my body wash again, in which case he was a dead man.

"Hunter, what are you doing in my—" I freed my earring, then head and found myself staring at a broad chest. A broad chest that did not belong to my best friend and roommate.

What the fuck? Why was there a man in my bathroom?

My eyes made a swift trip upwards as panic sent my pulse into overdrive. Why was there a strange—and admittedly, ridiculously attractive, and maybe vaguely familiar?—naked man in my bathroom?

He reached a hand toward me, and my fight or flight reflex kicked in. I screamed, then slapped him so hard my palm burned, and ran. I was not going to be murdered in my own home.

I needed to call someone. But where the fuck was my phone? In my shorts? Where were my shorts? No, not shorts, it was in my bag.

"Harley, wait!"

"You had better get the fuck out of my house before I call the cops!" I would not be reduced to a name on the news, used as an example of what happened when you slept with too many strange men you met on dating apps, which yes, I did, or left your doors unlocked, which I did not. If anything, I was overly vigilant with ensuring our door was always locked. If I died right now it would be Hunter's fault, without a doubt. I skidded to a stop and rummaged for my phone, pulling it out as it dawned on me that the ridiculously attractive, mostly naked man had said my name.

Well, if he's a stalker then of course he'd know your name.

A stalker! I had a fucking stalker! Hunter had left the goddamn balcony door open again (probably) and let the guy just stroll on in and use my body wash. That was weird, why would he be using my body wash?

Because he's a stalker, they do that!

"I don't think so, *stalker*." I lunged for the knives and pointed the largest in the direction of the hall.

He came out into the living room, still only in a towel, with his hands out like he was approaching a wild animal. Why the hell wasn't he leaving? Or putting on fucking clothes, for a start! And why was part of me itching to trace the intricate tattoo that covered a decent portion of his left side? No! I didn't want that. This stalker was going to give me my towel back—although I could admit the pink and white stripes looked fetching wrapped around his cut hips—and get the fuck out of my house!

"Do not come any closer. My boyfriend will be here any minute, so you should probably get the fuck out!" I hated that I felt the need to make up a boyfriend to scare the guy, and that my hand shook as I pointed the knife at him. He didn't, however, seem particularly concerned about either the knife or the imaginary boyfriend.

"Harley, I'm sorry to startle you, it's—I'm Jake, Jake Davenport, Hunter's cousin, remember?"

I let the knife drop a fraction. Jake? I hadn't seen Hunter's cousin, my first epic crush and one-time rebound summer fling, for ... twelve years. Was it actually him? I looked a little more closely. His hair, still wet from the shower, was a wild mess and difficult to know if it was the same warm rusted brown I remembered. His eyes, however, did look like they were that impossible shade of blue-green. Twenty-year-old Jake did not have a physique like the one in front of me, which was, wow. But I wasn't willing to let my guard down just because he was inhumanely hot—which he was, even with the red, hand-shaped welt on his cheek.

"Bullshit. He lives in London." Jake the hot-hot cousin was also some uber successful soccer player, so if he was in New York, I had my doubts he'd be crashing here, rather than in some fancy penthouse in Manhattan. The stalker theory still had some merit.

"Yes, you're right, I do. I do live in London, but I'm—ah—I'm taking a vacation." Was that a wince? Who winces when they talk about being on vacation? That was weird. "I thought I'd come and see Hunter, hang out ..." He looked sincere, but I wasn't ready to believe him. Not just yet.

"Hunter has made no mention of this," I said, my voice all high and squeaky. It was Jake. I knew it. I could see it now and I had the overwhelming urge to giggle but I managed to hold it in. He was my first muse. Eleven-year-old Harley spent a month drawing pictures of the two of us together, including our wedding—my dress was epic and was paired with cowboy boots for some reason. I had perfected my signature for when we got married. Harley Davenport was scrawled *everywhere* in my room.

Then, I started junior high and there were so many boys who drew my attention that Jake slipped off my radar. Until he turned up again the summer before college and I was miserable after just being dumped by Miles King—and Jake proved to be the perfect distraction. For three weeks we hung out and fucked around in secret. He was the perfect rebound. Then I started art school and met Liam. And somewhere along the line Jake became a distant, albeit fond, memory.

Now, he was in my living room, in a towel. He took half a step forward and I raised the knife a little higher, his hands flew back up. "He didn't know until today, when I literally turned up on your doorstep. He didn't text you?"

"No, he did not text me." I narrowed my eyes. "Why here?"

"Sorry?" He blinked.

"Why. Are. You. Here? And not in some fancy hotel?" I paused, debating whether or not to drop the knife. I didn't, but I stopped pointing it right at him. "You play soccer. Aren't all soccer players rich? Why would you be staying here in a three bedroom in Greenpoint?" Our apartment was nice but not I-get-paid-millions-of-dollars-a-year-to-kick-a-ball-around nice.

His eyes darted down to the knife then back up to me. "That is a fair question."

"I thought so."

"I came here straight from the airport and Hunter said I could crash, that's honestly all there is to it."

He looked kinda sad. Also alarmed, because I'd been threatening him with a knife. *Way to make a first—third?—impression, Harley.* I didn't think it made sense that he'd be staying here when he could stay literally anywhere. But Hunter offering our spare room made total sense. Jake was, after all, his favorite cousin.

I dropped the knife on the counter with a clatter and Jake's shoulders sagged with relief. He was off the hook. Hunter, however, was not. Offering our spare room without running it past me first was bad roommate behavior.

Unfortunately, I was having trouble focusing on that—or anything, really—while staring at Jake's well-defined torso. Honestly, the man looked like he was carved from a block of marble or something. Even calling him a man felt wrong, he was more god-like. Broad, strong shoulders, smooth pecs, if I wasn't staring at him in the glorious flesh, I'd assume all those abs were photoshopped—there were goddamn shadows between them. They weren't photoshopped, though, they were real. As was the trail of hair that dipped under the edge of the towel.

How many jump lunges would he be able to do before he passed out? Two thousand, maybe. He even had nice feet, for god's sake. Who had nice feet?

I spun on my heel to stop myself staring and dialed. Not even an all-caps text was going to get the job done right now.

Hunter answered on the second ring. "Hey Harls, what's up?"

I put on my best sarcastic smile hoping he'd be able to hear it through the phone. "Oh, nothing. Just found a naked man in my bathroom. What's up with you?"

"You what—oh, fuck, I forgot to text you."

"Mmm ..." I hummed in response. Imagining the panicked look on his face eased a little of my irritation.

"I meant to, I swear, but there was this thing at Bucks—"

"I don't care about your thing, Hunter, I care about the fact that you said your cousin could stay with us without running it by me first. Without even bothering to let me know!"

"I know, I'm sorry, I fucked up. But I figured you'd be okay with it."

"On what grounds?"

"On the grounds that you're an amazing and accepting person who doesn't believe in holding grudges when your friends fuck up?"

I smiled despite myself. "I am amazing. And you're an idiot."

"I'll make it up to you."

"Yes, you will." I peeked over my shoulder as footsteps shuffled behind me. Jake was, regrettably, dressed and carrying a duffle bag. I darted around the island and blocked his path before he got to the front door.

"I'm just gonna go," he said, taking a step toward me. I shook my head.

"Is that Jake? Is he leaving? What did you do?"

I planted a hand on my hip. "Now is not the time to ask what I did, Hunter."

"Harley, what happened?"

"Nothing, nothing happened. I was startled, there may have been a knife."

"You threatened Jake with a knife?!"

"I was not expecting a naked man in my bathroom, Hunter. I was defending myself."

"Didn't you recognize him? Isn't your first crush's face supposed to be, like, burned into your brain or something?" Of course, he would bring that up now. Judging by the smile attempting to lift the corners of Jake's mouth, he'd heard. Well, he would not be seeing our wedding pictures.

"I was startled!"

"I'll be back in an hour or so," Hunter said.

"Can't wait." I hung up and went to pocket my phone, only I had no pockets. I had no pockets because I was in my underwear. Good. Great. That was exactly what I needed. I cleared my throat and straightened my shoulders, putting aside the fact I was half naked in front of young Harley's future husband, and teenage Harley's perfect summer fling rebound guy, who was now a relative stranger. Life was weird sometimes.

"You were right," Jake started, trying once again to make for the door.

I went with him. "No, I was *startled*, like you said—you caught me off guard. But you don't have to go, honestly."

"It's fine. There are lots of other places to stay in New York, I don't need to be here."

I backed up a step and flicked the deadbolt on the door. "You're right, you don't need to be here, but you obviously want to be here, or you wouldn't have made Hunter your first stop as soon as you got off the plane." I raised an eyebrow, daring him to disagree. "Don't leave because I threatened you with a knife. I promise I won't do it again, unless you deserve it."

He was still eyeing the door, but the corner of his mouth once again twitched like he might smile. He didn't.

"Look, I'm just going to take a quick shower—assuming you haven't used all the hot water—at least wait until we are both clothed. Agreed?" His eyes darted below my chin, and I regretted drawing attention to the fact that I was half naked. In a fucking sports bra—not even a cute one.

"Agreed," he said, although it was more of a grunt than a word.

"Okay." I nodded, but he wasn't making any moves to back up into the living room. It didn't bode well for him being here when I got out of the shower. "Please don't leave while I'm in there. Hunter said he'd be back soon, and he'll kill me if you leave. Just wait, please."

He eased back a step, then another, until he dropped his bag on the armchair. I took it as a win.

"Give me five minutes."

5

JAKE

The bathroom door closed, and I let out a wobbly breath. What the hell had I been thinking coming here? What the hell was I thinking, staying after I learned that Harley also occupied this space? Right now, I was pretty sure getting on a plane to New York was the worst idea I'd ever had. Okay, so maybe it was not as bad as getting naked in the back of a cab. That was a low point. This was a close second.

Harley O'Connell.

Knowing she was going to be here had not prepared me for the reality of her barging into the fucking bathroom. I hadn't seen her in over a decade, but she was always in Hunter's photos—and my sporadic memories. It should not have surprised me that neither managed to capture even a fraction of the woman in the flesh.

This was a mistake.

I thought I didn't want to be alone. Thought that, if I was, the loneliness might consume me whole. But now the idea of being in other people's space, having them in mine, made my skin prickle with unease. I didn't like people in my business, I

37

never had, so why the fuck did I think staying with another person—with two—was going to help me now?

It was stupid. And I should definitely go to some fancy hotel, like Harley said, sit alone in the dark thinking about the mess I'd made of my life. More silent, gnawing introspection was probably just what I needed.

I'd text Hunter, tell him that I found somewhere else to stay, somewhere that did not include a third person who walked around in her underwear. Admittedly, she was entitled to walk around in her underwear in her own home. The walking around in her underwear wasn't the problem. The problem was me being around to see it. It wasn't even sexy underwear, it was practical; full coverage briefs and what looked like a sports bra, but fuck if I didn't find it sexy anyway. Even when she had a knife pointed at me.

I had loved eighteen-year-old Harley's body, worshipped it even, and thirty-year-old Harley's body was something else. The lines of her waist and hips were more exaggerated, her breasts—even contained in her sports bra—looked full and round. She was a fantasy come to life. She was *my* fantasy come to life.

The fact she had a boyfriend was not in the least bit surprising. Even if she didn't, even if she was single, I wasn't interested. The last thing I needed right now was a relation-ship. Especially with the girl I left behind to pursue my career. No, I didn't leave her behind. Our time together was a three week, no strings attached arrangement. When I left, we said we'd keep in touch. We exchanged numbers and emails, and, for a few weeks, we sent texts here and there. Then I started training and got busy, and I assumed she did too, because things just petered out. And that was that.

"I thought for sure you would have left," Harley said as she came padding back into the living room—now clothed, thank

God. Not that her outfit left much to the imagination. The floral skirt hugged her curves from waist to mid-thigh, and the white tank didn't quite meet it, leaving a slice of skin exposed. Keeping my eyes away from that skin was a lesson in restraint.

"I nearly did," I confessed, running a hand through my hair. She smiled. It was unnerving how much I still liked it, how it drew me in. "Maybe I still should?" I didn't intend for it to be a question.

"No, you shouldn't," she said, turning and heading for the refrigerator. "I overreacted. Honestly, it wasn't actually about you. I had a funky day, and it was more about the fact that Hunter didn't give me the heads up than about you being here. You want a drink? Something to eat?"

I shook my head, even as my stomach let out a low rumble that I was pretty sure Harley heard but didn't comment on.

"I'm sorry again, for the whole threatening-you-with-a-knife thing," she added.

"And I'm sorry for the whole scaring-the-living-daylights-out-of-you-in-your-own-apartment thing."

Another smile, wider this time. And, hell, if that wasn't fucking deadly. "I guess that makes us even." She pulled a bottle of wine from the refrigerator. "It's a rose' kind of day, wouldn't you agree? Are you sure I can't interest you in some?"

"I'm okay, thanks."

"Well, if you change your mind, let me know." She retrieved a glass from a high cabinet, the hem of her skirt inching higher as she reached for it. I once again forced my eyes away from her smooth skin.

Despite getting some sleep before my shower, exhaustion still weighed heavily as I stood in the middle of the living room scratching my head and wondering what the fuck I should say to get out of this situation. There was something about Harley that made me think she saw too much. Her whiskey eyes watched me as she poured her wine, and I resisted the urge to squirm under her attention. I almost sagged when the connection was broken, and she turned her back to return the bottle to the refrigerator. The reprieve didn't last long.

"Are you doin' okay?" She asked as she came back to me, sipping her pink wine and rounding the kitchen island.

"Sure, why wouldn't I be?" I tried not to sound defensive, and failed.

Her lips pursed for a fraction of a second. "No reason." She took another sip, crossed the living room and pulled open the door to the small balcony. Despite wanting space from the woman, my feet followed.

She glanced over her shoulder as she leaned on the railing. "So, how long are you staying at casa H and H? And, before you assume it's because I'm keen to get you out, it's not. I'm just curious." Another smile, slower this time, tipped the corners of her lips upwards. Mischief, that's what this girl was. Just the same as before. Mischief wrapped in a sweet, innocent looking package, but mischief nonetheless.

I had no answer to her relatively simple question. There hadn't been a great deal of thought happening in the early hours of this morning—yesterday morning? I didn't understand time zones—when, after being awake for over thirty hours, I packed a bag and headed to Heathrow.

Harley's eyes swung to me again and I shifted on my feet, uncertainty about my future, my life, and my career bubbling in my gut. How did everything get so out of hand? How did I let it happen? It had been one fucked up domino after the other.

I'd been quiet too long. Harley was still watching me as she sipped her wine and part of me wondered if she could hear my thoughts. Not that anything betrayed it on her face, which remained neutral, if a little curious.

She didn't know what happened. How could she? I barely

fucking knew what happened. But those wise, assessing, mischievous eyes made me think that maybe she'd be able to shed some light on the whole clusterfuck. And, if I was curious enough, I might have started talking. But I wasn't.

"A few days," I lied. "A few days and I should be out of your hair."

Her head tipped to one side. "No, I don't think you will be," she said lightly and turned her attention back to the city.

I was alone. Finally. The apartment was quiet, and I slouched further into the couch cushions. Hunter and Harley tried to get me to go with them, wherever they were going. I politely declined, using the excuse of jetlag, which was true. I was jetlagged. I also knew that my chances of getting to sleep before dawn were slim to none. Sleep, as much as I craved it over the last few days, had all but eluded me. I didn't see tonight being any different.

My phone rang, Nico's face filling the screen, and I slumped lower. I didn't want to talk to him. I didn't want to talk to anyone. I just wanted to sit here and soak in my misery. But, if I didn't answer, the guy was persistent and annoying enough that he'd just keep calling back until I picked up.

"Where the fuck are you?" He asked as the line connected.

I smiled, despite myself. "Hey, Jake, how are you? Thanks for asking, Nico, everything is still fucked. What's up with you?"

"Why the hell would I ask that when I know full well everything is still completely fucking fucked? They roasted you on *This Morning* again. It's basically a segment at this point—*How Much Do We Hate Jake Davenport?* They're really gunning for you. The fact you're American probably isn't helping your case," he mused. Pierre wasn't English, either. And they'd all hated him when he came to the club eighteen months ago, had roasted him for months in the press. Now, though, he was their favorite fucking son, because I was the bigger—the *biggest*—asshole.

"Thank you for that update." I stood, and went to the kitchen, not actually hungry but needing to move. Even still, when I found a carton of chocolate ice cream in the freezer, I tore off the lid, found a spoon and dug in. Fuck I loved chocolate. Natalie tried to tell us that her carob alternatives tasted *just like chocolate*. And I had somehow believed her?

"Was that all you called to say?" I asked around a frozen mouthful.

He laughed and it would have been really satisfying to punch him right now. But I was still happier almost five thousand miles from London.

"I was calling to make sure you're fucking alive, you ungrateful prick. I turned up at your place to conduct a welfare check with your favorite curry from Singhs—like the outstanding friend that I am—and what do I find?"

I figured his question was rhetorical, but I answered anyway. "Nothing."

"Nothing!" He echoed. "I had to eat all that curry alone, which Natalie is going to kick my arse for, so I hope you're happy with yourself. Now, I will ask again, where the fuck are you?"

"Brooklyn."

"Brooklyn? What the fuck are you doing in Brooklyn? Wait ... is this about that model you met in Bora Bora?"

I rolled more ice cream around my mouth. "No."

"Then why Brooklyn? You know that New York has just as many cameras as London, right?"

"Yes, I'm aware of that, but they're not all pointed at me

here. I'd be surprised if many people even know who I am, let alone recognize me."

There was silence as he considered this. "You might not be completely out of your mind."

I laughed; it was bordering on hysterical. There wasn't any question that I was out of my mind. It had been a slow decline over the last six months since Celeste left, but I didn't think a person got to sleeping with a teammate's wife and then brawling with said teammate at a charity press conference without losing their mind, at least a little.

It shouldn't have come to this. I knew that. The worst part was that I didn't think I was even really in love with Celeste. We had fun together, sure, and the sex was always good, but there was always that spark of something missing. I figured it would come over time, only it never did. And then she left— with my brand-new Range Rover.

Nico was still talking. "I want to be pissed that you didn't tell me you were leaving—"

"It wasn't exactly a planned-out decision. I literally packed a bag and drove to Heathrow."

"Does that mean one of your cars is sitting at Heathrow fucking airport right now?"

"Yes, it does." As far as I was concerned, the fewer eyes there were on me the better. I didn't even go to long stay parking lot, so it was going to cost me a fucking fortune when I got back. *If you go back.* I shook off the whispered voice because of course I was going back. What else was I supposed to do with my life if it wasn't football?

"Which one?"

"Which one, what?"

"Which *car*?"

"The Aston."

"Fuck you."

"Fuck you, too."

"I'm taking the spare keys and getting it out of there."

"You are more than welcome to do that Nico." So long as he was also prepared to pick me up when—not if—I got back to London.

He was quiet for long enough that I had time to eat another mouthful of ice cream.

"Well, like I said, I want to be mad you didn't tell me, but I get it. Also, your Aston is going to be well taken care of in your absence. So, what's the plan? You take some time out and come back when things have settled down?"

"That's pretty much it," I said, even while part of me very much wondered if things would settle down. Logically, I knew it had to, every scandal was only really as long as the news cycle, which was shrinking by the day, but it felt big this time. Bigger than any of the others. Even once the media had moved on, it didn't mean my teammates would, didn't mean management would. *Indefinite suspension.* I had no one to blame but myself.

"It's solid. Add to that the distraction of a few willing women and you'll be back here before you know it."

"I don't know if Blair would sign off on that part."

"Please, what Blair doesn't know won't hurt her."

"Is there anything Blair doesn't know?" I missed his muttered response but didn't bother asking him to repeat himself. If he wanted me to hear it, I would have.

After a few more minutes of largely mindless conversation, and Nico assuring me he would take good care of the Aston, we hung up. And I was scraping the bottom of the ice cream container.

Despite the jet lag circling and making my eyes feel heavy with sleep I spent the next few hours scrolling what felt like every streaming service known to man. I almost hit play on *Ted*

Lasso no less than six times, but it was just a little too close to home. If I watched the last episode of season one, there was a good chance I'd cry like a baby when Roy went down.

Eventually, I went to the bedroom and collapsed, but still wound-up staring at the ceiling for at least an hour before sleep took me.

When I shuffled out to the bathroom the following morning, knocking twice to ensure it was vacant, I discovered a post-it note on the mirror.

You owe me a pint of double Belgian chocolate fudge.

6

HARLEY

If I was forced to take one more step, there was a very good chance I'd collapse and then roll all the way back down this motherfucking mountain. Why did I continue to agree to these hikes? I glanced six or so feet ahead of me where Odette was setting our pace. She was a touch out of breath and had this cute sheen of sweat across the back of her neck, just below her bubblegum-pink hairline. I, on the other hand, was on the brink of passing out and, if I had to guess, my face was a charming blotchy red. Maybe that was why I kept coming back, in the hopes that one day I might look as effortless as Odette while walking up a sixty-degree slope.

I had been misled, though. She assured me that today would be a chill hike, since we'd set off after work. And it had been chill—initially. There were wildflowers and cow pastures, and it was delightful. Then Odette shot me a truly terrifying smile and we started climbing.

"Need a sec," I wheezed, and Odette paused where she stood. She planted a hand on her hip and took a swig from her neon yellow water bottle.

"I feel no sympathy, because this hangover is one hundred percent self-inflicted."

I gasped, or I would have if I hadn't still been struggling to breathe. "This has ... nothing to do with my ..."—I puffed, dropping my head for a second before continuing—"hangover and everything to do with the fact you took me on an advanced trail when you know I am a beginner."

"You're not a beginner."

"I am intermediate at *best*."

"Whatever the case, your hangover is not helping." She wasn't wrong.

"Maybe, but it's not actually all my fault."

Odette smiled. "How's that?"

"Okay, so it's probably, like, sixty percent my fault."

"And who's responsible for the other forty?"

"My house guest," I growled. My too-attractive, former summer fling houseguest who kept popping up in my dreams at the most inopportune moments.

"Ah, yes, the mysterious Jake, who no one has laid eyes on and we're all starting to think is just a figment of your imagination."

I snapped up straight. "We what now? Who's we?!"

"Darcy and Jem were talking about it the other day."

Rude! "Well, I can tell you that he is most definitely not just a figment of my imagination."

Odette snorted out a laugh.

"He's not! He's an ice cream thief who has been this weird spectral presence in my apartment for a week!" A whole week and I'd not seen him more than twice, but there was evidence of him everywhere. It was driving me fucking crazy.

"What's his deal?"

I shrugged my backpack on and closed the space between us as we took off again. "I don't know, as far as I can tell he has not left the apartment since he got in last Monday. Not even to replace the entire pint of my ice cream he ate on his first night. I don't think he leaves his room unless Hunter and I are both out, which is just fucking weird, right? Why come and stay with someone if you're not going to talk to them?"

"Maybe he's not okay?"

"I mean, I don't think you fly thousands of miles only to lock yourself in a room in someone else's apartment if you're okay. Hunter said something about some drama back in London. I went to Google him but then felt kind of guilty about it, like I was invading his privacy or something. Anyway, he eats my ice cream and uses my body wash, and I don't like it." And I maybe want to see him naked again. No! Nope—there would be none of that.

"Harley, is this guy under your skin?" Odette asked with a laugh that I did not appreciate. Plus, no, obviously Jake was not under my skin. I'd barely seen him; how could he be under my skin? Guys didn't get under my skin. Not anymore. Not since Liam.

"Absolutely not," I said with confidence.

"You sure? Because you're all … antsy." That was a whole other issue.

"I haven't had sex all week."

Odette laughed again, which was irritating because I was still out of breath, and my butt was on fire. She must have a superhuman lung capacity.

"Seriously, no sex, that's your problem?"

"Yes, that is my problem!"

"Are you serious that you haven't gone longer than a week without having sex?"

"No, that's—yes, maybe. I am not going to start apologizing for my very healthy sex life."

"Nor would I expect you to. No one should have to apologize for, or feel guilty about, an outstanding sex life. Honestly, I'm totally jealous."

"Sorry, I know that. I mean not that you're jealous of my sex life—I know you weren't saying—I'm just—"

"In need of an orgasm."

"That is correct." I hadn't even used any of my favorite toys because I was feeling all weird about him hearing me. Like it was some dirty little secret. Sex and masturbation were not things to feel guilty about. I knew this. It didn't help that every time I had tried to do a little self-care, Jake's face had popped into my head, and I went all squirmy—and not in a fun way.

Yes, I was antsy and in need of orgasm good times, whether alone or assisted, but that didn't mean I needed to be a hell beast to everyone around me. And exercise endorphins were almost as good as orgasm ones, right? They didn't come (ha!) with the toe-curling full body tingles, but they were something.

"Are you giving yourself a pep talk back there?" Odette asked.

"Maybe."

Another laugh. "I'm sorry that you are orgasm-less." There was a pause before she added. "It sounds like the mysterious, ice cream eating man that's currently haunting your apartment might need a friend, or just someone to talk to."

I hated to admit that she was probably right. I was still tempted to Google the shit out of him, and there was a chance it may still happen. But, in the meantime, I would make him my friend again—because we were friends before, right? While I was making him my friend, I would attempt to coax all those deep, dark secrets out of him. For his own good, obviously, not just to satisfy my intense curiosity.

"What's with the devious look?"

"No devious look!" I said, forcing my face into a serene, if tomato red, smile.

"What are you planning?"

"I don't know what you're talking about. Come on, this mountain isn't going to hike itself!"

I set down the steaming cup of coffee, and hesitated. Was this a stupid idea? I didn't even know why I was going through with it. If the guy wanted to talk, he probably would have made an effort to leave his room, right? He wouldn't stay holed up in there unless everyone was out. But Odette's words about him needing a friend were an itch under my skin that I couldn't ignore.

Just do it.

The drumroll knock was obnoxiously loud, but I kept it up for five seconds anyway. Operation make friends with Jake was a-go. Our reunion started off on the wrong foot, what with him (and me, I guess) being mostly naked and me threatening him with a knife. That was a sure-fire way to get someone offside. The knife thing—not the naked thing. The naked thing, in my experience, was generally positive. Unless you were a highly successful athlete whose life was picked apart in the press and you were dealing with the fallout of a sex scandal, I guess—then it wasn't ideal.

Last night, while soaking in the tub, I caved and did some googling and the results were illuminating, to say the least. Among other things, I now knew how good Jake looked in his soccer jersey. Exceptionally good. I knew that there was some remarkably well-written, and filthy, fanfic dedicated to him. I got a refresher on how big his dick was thanks to one particular photo taken at what should have been an impossible angle considering how preoccupied the photographer was with Jake's dick in her mouth at the time.

And, finally, I learned why he ran from London. Naturally, I did not plan on telling him any of this. I hadn't read most of the articles, anyway. Except for the fanfic, which I bookmarked for another time.

There was shuffling behind the door as I retrieved the coffee and held it aloft just as Jake appeared. He looked understandably bemused about me standing there, so I smiled a little wider. Friendly Harley was on the hunt. He ran a hand absently through his hair, making it even more wild as my eyes drifted down to his naked chest. And my mouth went spontaneously dry. Friends. I just wanted to be friends. He was sad, and I was going to be his friend. Maybe I needed to un-bookmark that fanfic to make sure my brain stayed in the friendzone.

"Was th—"

"Hi! Good morning," I interrupted, my heart beating at an uncomfortably fast pace.

"Good morning?" he croaked. The hand that had been in his hair migrated to his jaw, and the layer of scruff that called to my inner thighs like a siren song. Friends, Harley, *friends*. Friends did not think about other friends' facial hair on their inner thighs, that was not a friendly thing to do. I cleared my throat.

"Coffee?"

"Ah—"

"I brought coffee, because I think we started things off on the wrong foot. So, think of this as a peace offering coffee?" It wasn't up to the kind of standard I'd be able to make with Edith, but it was good enough.

"Thank you, although I don't think it was necessary."

We stood there staring at one another and it occurred to me

that I probably should have made some kind of plan before all the knocking.

He went to take the coffee. "Well, thank—"

"And," I started, not relinquishing my hold on the cup. "I thought we could hang out or something." There wasn't time for him to respond, because my mouth had gone rogue. "I know this isn't your first trip to New York, obviously—" I should not have brought up his previous trip to New York. The one where we were having sex whenever and wherever possible for three weeks. Our eyes clashed, heat flaring. I plowed on, "But I thought we could—thought I could—give you a tour." Because he didn't see much of the city the first time.

"A tour."

"Yeah, you know, show you around, like a good friend." I wanted to slap myself right in the face.

"Yes ... I understand the concept of a tour, Harley, but I didn't realize we were friends." Rude of him to point that out, but I would not be deterred.

"Well, maybe not anymore, but we were once, no reason why we couldn't—"

"I think I'm okay."

"You're—"

"Thank you, for the offer." He took the cup from my hands. "And the coffee." Then he shut the door. In my face.

What. The. Actual. Fuck?

I brought coffee and a smile and an offer to show him around, to help him leave his sad, self-imposed isolation where he was probably crying into his pillow all day long or just staring at the ceiling, and all I got was a *thank you for the coffee* and a door slammed (pretty much) in my face? Seriously?

What was that?! What exactly was wrong with me as a tour guide? I was a great tour guide. I provided thoughtful, personal detail—and he would be lucky to be my friend again! Well, if he thought one little rejection was going to be enough to put me off, he had another thing coming. I'd try again tomorrow, and the day after that. Jake was going to be my friend, whether he liked it or not.

As soon as I saw Odette cross the street on Thursday morning, I threw together an iced latte, dragged Morgan in front of Edith to carry on the coffees, and bolted out the door.

"You were wrong," I said.

Odette looked over both shoulders. "Good morning to you too." She slipped inside the construction site that was almost Weston Events—and just so happened to be next door to Cream and Sugar. We both smiled at the contractor, Matt, and his assistant person who were both working away on the other side of the room.

Odette dropped her bag onto a table, grabbed the coffee from my hand and took a long sip. "Okay," she said when she was done. "What exactly was I wrong about?"

"The houseguest. He does not want a friend." But he was still going to get one.

"And you know this because ..."

"I know this because I extended a caffeinated hand of friendship to him."

"And he didn't accept it?"

"Oh, he accepted the coffee alright, then slammed his door in my face."

She didn't bother trying to hide her confusion. "He took the coffee and slammed a door in your face without a word? That— well, that is fucking rude."

"He may have said thank you, grudgingly, before slamming the door."

"Uh-huh." Another sip from her coffee. "Maybe you caught

him by surprise. You didn't, like, pounce the second he opened the door, or something did you?"

I scoffed, shaking my head. "No, no, nothing like that."

Her eyes narrowed. "You knocked on the door, didn't you?"

"I waited until after nine."

"And you did the drumroll knock."

"I may have."

"Harley!"

"What?!"

"You probably scared the shit out of him."

"And then I brought him coffee. And offered to show him around. And all he said was *I'm okay*." In that irritatingly deep and rumbly voice of his. While shirtless—and looking alarmingly lickable. I nibbled the corner of my lip.

"What just happened?" Odette waved a hand at me.

"What? Nothing. What?"

"Why did you go all glazed over for just then?"

"I didn't. There is no glazing here. I'm not glazed."

Her gray eyes held mine for a breath. "You like him!"

"I am trying to be his friend—on your suggestion."

"Have you thought about him naked?"

Should I tell her about our summer rebound? Not right now, it would undermine my argument. "He was mostly naked when I met him."

"That's a yes. You like him."

"Oh my god, I do not like him. He's rude. He eats my ice cream and doesn't replace it. He accepts coffee but not invitations to hang out. And—no—and I do not like him. Good day." I marched out onto the sidewalk and then back into Cream and Sugar. Did I just say *good day*? Like some annoyed woman in the Victorian Era? I felt like Keira Knightly in *Pride and Prejudice*. I needed a field to walk through moodily while my dress got all muddy. But Odette was out of line. I didn't like Jake. I was just trying to be a friend, which had been her idea in the first place. I didn't like him. I was capable of appreciating his spectacular bone structure, warm, tan skin, and perfectly defined torso and still try to be his friend—in a purely platonic way.

Because that worked so well the first time.

7

JAKE

I needed to leave the apartment.

If for no other reason than to get Harley off my back. I hadn't actually seen her since the unhinged knocking on Monday, or was it Tuesday? I had completely lost track of what day it was. At any rate, every day since then there had been post-it notes and snacks and coffee waiting for me. Three days of this undercover friendship.

Harley and I were not friends. Harley and I were not going to be friends. I didn't need more friends. Granted, I didn't have a huge number of them to begin with, but that suited me just fine, who needed a lot of friends? Not. Me. Especially not some curly-haired, sparkly-eyed, bouncy woman who lived in another country to the one I currently called home.

I was here until the storm in London calmed down, which, according to Nico's daily updates—via long winded voicemails because I refused to answer his calls—had not yet happened.

I shut my laptop, silencing the credits of *Avengers: Endgame*, and slumped onto my back. A shower first, and then I'd leave the apartment.

When I arrived in New York, I had not intended to lock myself away for over a week—closer to two, now. I thought maybe I would take some time to explore, see the sights, like Harley had suggested. But it hadn't happened. Not yet, anyway. So far, I'd been too busy feeling sorry for myself and working my way through the entire Marvel Cinematic Universe in order—except for *The Incredible Hulk*, because Edward Norton was a bullshit Bruce Banner.

After a quick shower, during which I used Harley's body wash because it smelled good and I knew it annoyed her (she'd left post-it notes about it), I dried off and dressed. Pulling on a shirt felt odd after laying around in shorts all week. I really needed to get outside and, as much as I knew it was going to hurt, I was going to run.

"He lives!" Hunter said as I came into the living room. If I'd known he was still home, I would have put off the run a little longer.

"Yep, I'm alive." I ran a hand through my hair before sliding on a baseball cap, tugging on the peak.

He watched me from his spot on the balcony. "I was starting to get concerned, thought you might have died in there, but Harley assured me there wasn't any stench of death wafting around and you've been eating my cereal, so I figured you were still with us."

"Thank you for your concern, I think, and I'll replace the cereal." The mention of food drew my attention to the hollow feeling in the pit of my stomach. It wasn't just about hunger, but I'd deal with food when I got back.

"I don't give a fuck about the cereal, Jake." His pause was heavy, loaded, and I braced for the inevitable questions. *What are you doing? When are you going to snap out of it? What the fuck is the matter with you?* But, instead, he asked, "Where're you off to?"

"No idea." It was an appropriate answer to pretty much everything in my life right now. I had no fucking idea what I was doing, or what was the matter with me, or when I'd go back to London. "Figured I'd run, get some fresh air, keep that stench of death away."

"You want company?" The look on his face told me he knew the answer was no, and yet he still asked. I swallowed against the spontaneous tightness in my throat.

"Sure, but don't you need to be at Buck's?" I had so far managed to avoid all invitations to both Hunter and Harley's places of work—even despite the detailed map to Cream and Sugar Harley provided yesterday on six of her post-it notes stuck together, which also said the first coffee was on her. There was a picture too, a tiny cartoon Harley winking as she held a coffee cup. I smiled when I saw it, properly smiled for the first time in ... I wasn't sure how long. Which was a problem.

I should have listened to my gut when I first arrived and marched my ass out of this apartment as soon as she came barreling into the bathroom in her underwear. I should have recognized her for what she was: dangerous, a threat to the very fabric of my existence. She was too bright, too alive, too fucking magnetic. I already knew that if I spent any amount of time in her company, no matter how minuscule, I would want more. And that was not a good idea. I had so far managed to not look her up on social media, but it felt like it was only a matter of time.

Hunter cleared his throat, and I snapped out of my head—and away from the increasingly frustrating thoughts of Harley.

"Sorry, did you say something?" I squeezed the back of my neck.

"Just that I don't need to be at Buck's until later, so I've got time for a run." He shoved his feet into a pair of trainers.

"Alright then." I led the way to the front door.

My calves and quads were screaming as I collapsed onto Hunter's stoop. Six miles and I was ruined, which was embarrassing. But even as the burn of exertion radiated throughout my body, I could admit that it felt good. Satisfying in a way I had missed.

"Fuck man," Hunter said, hands braced on his knees as he sucked in deep, noisy breaths. "You set a brutal pace."

"You kept up."

"Barely. I thought you'd be all out of shape after sitting on your ass for a week and a half." He hinged back up to standing, hands on his head.

"I am." I stood, wincing as I stretched out my calves.

"This is you out of shape?"

"Out of shape-ish." That was the life of a professional athlete. Even in the off-season, I still worked out most days. I hadn't gone more than two weeks without any sort of training in years, maybe even since college. I enjoyed it on the whole, and it had the added benefit of keeping me out of my head, which I was very much in need of now. For as long as I was in New York, I would make the effort to work out —or at least get out of the apartment from time to time—because I couldn't be a sorry sack of shit forever. Well, I probably could, if I wanted to really marinate in my own self-loathing.

"Remind me not to run with you when you're in-shape."

I smiled, enjoying the rush of endorphins, and the brief amount of time spent in another person's company. I should probably do more of it, both the physical activity and the socialization. It certainly couldn't make anything worse—or maybe that would depend on both the form of physical activity and the company.

The last six months, maybe even a year, had been utter shit. Each new bad decision fueled the fire until the flames licked the clouds. But I could turn it around, right? I just needed to, as Arturo so eloquently put it, get my head out of my ass and back on the pitch. This spiral started when things went wrong with my game, so theoretically all I needed to do was sort out my game and things would start to fall back into place. My life would right itself. This was what I needed. A reminder that I was better when I was working hard, pushing myself to my limits. I needed to refocus. Part of me wondered if I also needed to be back in London to do it, but the mere thought of getting on a plane made me want to heave. I didn't need to be in London; in fact, it was probably better if I wasn't. Sorting my head out would be easier while I was away from everything that had been suffocating me.

"Well, I need to get inside and shower before I head out ..." The sentence dropped away as Hunter climbed the stoop and let us inside. I knew what was coming before he said it. "You should come tonight, kick back, have a couple of drinks."

I followed silently up the three flights of stairs. Part of me was tempted to say yes, to drink until my brain shut off and I could forget everything, pretend I was any other person enjoying a warm June night. But the forgetting and the pretending were part of the reason I was here in the first place. The time for forgetting and pretending was over, it was time to start getting my shit together.

Harley was standing in the middle of the living room—in the smallest pair of shorts I had ever seen—gaping at us when we walked in.

"Holy shit, how did you get him to leave?" she asked.

"I didn't. He was already leaving," Hunter said, like I was not part of the conversation.

"And he agreed to the company?" Her eyes were wide.

"He did." He clapped me on the shoulder before disappearing into his room. The shower started up shortly after.

Harley watched me kick off my shoes and head to the kitchen for a drink. I was sure I could feel the track of those eyes as they roamed my back. I didn't like how aware I was of her, it was unsettling.

"So, you voluntarily left the apartment." Not a question.

"I did."

She pursed her lips. "And you didn't come and see me? Even after I drew you that spectacular map. I'm offended."

"Are you?" A bolt of anxiety shot through me at the thought she might actually be offended, which was ridiculous. What did I care if I offended her?

"No, you'll get there eventually."

"Will I?"

"Yes." She was so confident, there wasn't even the slightest hint of uncertainty.

"What makes you so sure?"

"Do you like coffee?"

I gulped down the rest of my water, how on earth did this woman's brain work? Did she always just say exactly what she was thinking? It must feel good, being that free. "What does my opinion on coffee have to do with anything?"

"Do you like coffee?" She repeated, coming to lean against the counter opposite me. There was a tinge of pink across the top of her cheekbones, not a blush, just color, like she'd been out in the sun. It was all too easy to imagine her, face turned up to the sky, a smile playing around the corners of her full ruby lips.

"Yes." The word was slightly choked as I dragged my attention away from her mouth.

"Then you'll get to Cream and Sugar."

"Your place of employment."

"Correct." She was probably right; my curiosity would eventually get the better of me. But I didn't want to admit that just yet, I'd rather keep this push and pull going a little longer.

"There are plenty of other places to get coffee Harley, I ran past at least twenty between here and DUMBO."

"There are," she conceded. "And you could get a great coffee at every single one. But my coffee is better." Her coffee. Not Cream and Sugar coffee, *her* coffee. And said without a shadow of self-consciousness, or doubt, or anything else. It was just a fact.

I smothered my smile with sheer force of will. "Is that so?"

"Uh-huh ..." Her smile grew as she watched me fight mine. "My coffee is transcendent."

"I didn't realize coffee could be transcendent."

"That's because you haven't tasted mine." She winked and for a beat I was sure she'd said *you haven't tasted me*. But no, coffee. She was talking about coffee. Perfectly innocent. Only Harley didn't make it sound innocent. Harley made coffee sound salacious, and I was once again fighting a losing battle to keep my attention away from her mouth.

I cleared my throat, needing to break the tension that was gathering in the air between us. "I need a shower." I dumped my glass in the sink and ran, her throaty laugh chasing me down the hall.

8

HARLEY

Jake retreated at speed down the hall and darted into the bathroom. Some might say that he was running from me—and I suppose in the literal sense he was—but he was softening, I could tell. He almost smiled just now, it didn't matter how much he tried to stop it, the smile was there, playing at the corners of his lips.

He really didn't stand a chance—we were going to be friends in no time.

I wasn't interested in examining why it was so important that I beat Jake into friendship submission. But I couldn't deny the need. At the very least, I needed to see the man smile. I needed to be the one to make him smile. I'd like to be able to say just the once would be enough, but I already knew that it would be an addicting feeling, seeing his face finally break free of its perma-scowl. Just the thought of it had me grinning as I skipped to the fridge for a drink.

If it wasn't for Chase and her girls' skating night, I would be sorely tempted to stay in tonight and torture Jake with my friendship some more—seeing the pinch between his brows was fast becoming one of my favorite things. A fact that should probably concern me but, once again, I wasn't going to examine the feeling. And I wasn't about to ditch my girls, not even for something as delicious as watching Jake squirm. Besides, I felt pretty confident that I was going to see him tomorrow, certainly by the end of the weekend.

Rock 'N' Roller was a disco dream. Ordinarily it was, for the most part, a standard roller rink, but tonight it was decked out in all things disco—and I was in heaven. Pretty sure I was born in the wrong era; the seventies would have been a trip (both literally and figuratively).

I hadn't even known this place existed before January, when Chase had rediscovered her love for skating, and then insisted that the rest of us needed to join her. I was, without question, the worst in our group. But what I lacked in skill and general coordination I made up for in attitude, enthusiasm, and costume design. It was also stupid fun, even when I was on my butt for half the time.

Chase wolf-whistled as I walked in toting my skates over one shoulder. Jemma waved from beside her, minty green skates already laced and ready to go.

"Ladies," I cooed, coming to a stop in front of them. "How are you both?"

"Ready to make the most of my one Friday night off until November," Jemma said as she pulled me into a hug. I so admired her for how she'd managed to grow her business from one wedding to bonkers busy in a matter of months, but I did not envy the work-life balance that skewed heavily to work. She never complained, but that shit had to get exhausting.

"Figured you'd be spending it with the hot bearded one."

"He's on Pie Guy duty for the night," she said.

Chase nodded in confirmation. "They are The Pie *Guys*. For one night only, according to Nash."

"It won't be one night only," Jemma added.

"Definitely not, the bromance is still strong after all these years." They both grinned. And there was a twinge of something under my ribs. Not jealousy, but a sour kind of sadness. I wasn't going to be that giddy again. The best I could hope for was fond companionship. Most of the time it didn't bother me, but sometimes, if I let myself think about it, it was a little depressing.

I plastered on a smile as Odette and Darcy arrived. I was going to have a fun night with some of my favorite women. Where was the problem? So, what if I wouldn't have *that* love again? The fact I felt it once was a gift, one I certainly didn't take for granted. Just because it was gone now didn't mean I was alone or particularly unhappy. I had amazing friends and—up until almost two weeks ago—an outstanding sex life. I was not going to feel sorry for myself.

"Harley, where do you get these things?" Odette asked, waving a hand at my booty shorts, which had rainbows front and back and white faux fur around the legs for the clouds. They were a particularly good find.

"I have a gift." I shook my butt in her direction. "And look who's talking!" Her impossibly long legs were wrapped in gold fishnets, over which she had a black metallic playsuit. She was a total smoke show.

"Why, thank you." She curtsied.

Darcy looked like she stepped straight out of an episode of Charlie's Angels, in a pair of apple green shorts and cropped white tank, her copper hair hanging in perfectly bouncy waves past her shoulders. Also a smoke show.

With skates on and music blasting it was time to roll.

Chase, unsurprisingly, was the most skilled of our troop;

but she'd been an ice skater as a kid, so I considered that an unfair advantage. Although I had also attempted ice skating as a kid, it was usually the draw of the hot cocoa that got me to the rink, much to my former figure skating mother's dismay.

Jemma and Darcy had taken to our collective hobby with ease, both of them already smooth on their feet after only a few months. I would be jealous if I didn't love watching them all zoom around so much.

Darcy glided past and spun so she was facing me and skating backward. Such a show-off.

"I received an interesting email today," she said with a sly grin I recognized as Trouble with a capital T.

"Oh yes ...?" I wobbled, arms flailing before I bent my knees and regained a tentative balance. When all else failed, get low —that was Chase's sage advice on my first day skating.

"Mm-hm ... another one from the Coffee Champs." Of course, she was choosing to bring this up now.

"This again, really?"

"What again, really?" Odette asked as she hooked an arm through mine, a risky move if she wanted to stay upright.

"Our dearest Harley has been nominated for the best barista in New York."

Chase and Jemma joined the conversation with a chorused, "What?!"

I was going to kill Darcy. I had been very clear that I wasn't interested in the Coffee Champs last year.

"We are not talking about this."

"*Again?* You've been nominated before?" Odette asked, nearly taking us both down. I was tempted to throw myself onto the floor just to escape this conversation. A twisted ankle and bruised butt would definitely be worth the escape. I shook my head right as Darcy said—

"Yup, last year."

"Darcy!"

"Harley!" She fired back, poking her tongue out for good measure. I was sorely tempted to push her over.

"Wait." Chase joined Darcy in her backward skating so she could eyeball me properly. "You got nominated for this last year and then what?"

"She needed to accept the invitation and then there was an in-person competition, but Harley declined to attend."

"What? Why?" Came the outraged squawk from Odette.

I took a steadying breath so as not to bite my friends' heads off. "Because I don't need to prove myself in some competition." As far as I was concerned, the whole thing was just unnecessary. I respected the other people who wanted to be part of it, but I had no interest in participating in the circus myself.

"You've already been nominated three times this year," Darcy said, guiding us to the closest exit. We all stepped off the rink—some more gracefully than others—and made our way to one of the red vinyl booths that lined one wall. I would have preferred to continue skating, at least then I'd have something else to focus on that wasn't this growing sense of discomfort in my chest.

"Three times, Harley, by our customers, who love you."

I slid in beside her and picked up the menu to distract myself even though I always ordered the same thing. "And I love them, too," I assured her. "But I don't feel the need to be a performing monkey to prove I'm good at my job."

"Oh, please! Are you trying to tell me you wouldn't thrive making coffee in front of an audience?"

"I thrive making coffee five days a week. I don't see how that would change depending on the number of people I'm in front of." It was mostly true. I loved making coffee. I loved all of the people I got to see and speak to everyday. I truly loved my job—but it was just a job.

"Liar."

Jemma, Chase, and Odette were all watching us with curiosity and mild confusion. Was it so strange that I didn't want to do this? To put myself out there like that?

"It would be great for business," Darcy said when I remained silent.

"Darcy, we've barely been able to keep up with business for the last seven months."

"It's slowed down now, and it was only out of control because of Jemma and the fact she happened to plan a wedding for someone famous. No offense, Jem."

Jemma shrugged. "None taken, it's totally true. Although the wedding just got people in, they stayed because you're all amazing."

"And this is an opportunity to show more people how amazing we are."

"I'm not stopping you from being part of it, Darce, Cream and Sugar should definitely be in the competition."

"Cafés can't participate without a barista."

"But last year—"

"They changed the rules. No barista, no entry."

"Well, that's bullshit."

"Maybe, but that's the rules," she said. Was she lying just to get me to agree? She was making direct eye contact, which never happened when she was being sneaky.

"I'll think about it, okay?"

"Yes! Okay! Yes, thank you, Harls. You know I wouldn't bug you unless it was super important to me." She made a high-pitched squealing noise as she clapped.

"I'm not saying yes."

"I know, yes, I know, but you're thinking about it, that's

something." I was never going to hear the end of this, she was absolutely not going to let it drop until I said yes. But I just didn't know if I could do that. It felt like putting too much of myself out there, and I had made a promise to myself not to do that again.

"Can we talk about something else now, please?" I asked, making pointed eye contact with everyone at the table.

They all nodded, Darcy most enthusiastically as she rolled her lips together to keep from grinning and ducked behind her menu.

I wanted a drink, a strong one, but alcohol and eight wheels secured to my feet didn't sound like the most intelligent combination. So, instead I ordered my usual large basket of waffle fries and a loaded hot dog.

Conversation flowed as we ate and, to not draw attention to the fact I was feeling all funky, I cracked jokes and smiled and pretended like everything was fine. It wasn't hard to pretend; I was surrounded by friends—by four incredible, intelligent, badass women. It was difficult to be ungrateful about that. Did any of them see through the smiles and the jokes? Did anyone I know see through it? Over the years I had gotten too good at squashing things down and putting on a happy face. It wasn't always a lie—a lot of the time I was happy, but not *always*.

With bellies full of fried food, we made our way back onto the rink as the disco vibes kicked into high gear. I lingered closer to the edge than everyone else, but I was starting to feel a little more sure on my feet, which was nice. I even managed to do a couple of wobbly transitions, to whistles and cheering from the others.

Moving also helped to shake off the last of the funky feels that had set up shop in my chest. Before too long, my smiles weren't strained, and the giggles slipped out as naturally as breathing.

My feet were aching, the same way they did every time I went skating, but even still, when the ladies said they were ready to call it a night, I knew I wasn't going home. Not just yet, and not when I would just be in bed far too aware of the person in the next room. It was a good thing I knew just the place to go.

Marion Snyder, Jemma's former landlord and all-around octogenarian badass, opened the door to her impeccable and cozy home with a frosted martini glass in one hand and a cigar in the other. Her white bob was deliciously blunt and the weak-latte colored silk loungewear she wore hung off her frame like it was made for her. Because it probably was. Fuck, I loved this woman.

"I was starting to wonder if you were going to show," she said, ushering me inside and nudging the door closed with one bare foot. "Love the shorts, by the way."

"Of course you do," I said, shaking my butt in her direction. "I need to get outside."

"You bet you do—we both know how Ronnie felt about you and your cigars inside. Scoot."

She blew a kiss at one of the many black and white photos of her late husband that adorned the walls. "Vodka and glasses in the freezer, olives and lemons on the counter if you want it dirty or with a twist." Fuck. I. Loved. This. Woman.

With a martini glass in hand, I made my way out onto the patio through the French doors off the kitchen and smiled. Six women sat around a low table covered in playing cards and colored chips. Ladies' card night.

"You in?" Olive asked around her cigar, waving a couple of cards at me as she collected the rest.

"I'll sit this one out." I sipped my drink, enjoying the sharp, cold track it made down my throat. As much as I loved my girls, and I really did, there was something about sitting around with a bunch of cigar-smoking eighty-year-olds that just hit different. All this knowledge and wisdom and experience right here, at my disposal.

I was about to take a seat off to the side of the action when Mrs S said, "She's not sitting out."

She shot me a look that emphasized the fact this was not optional and patted the seat next to hers on a narrow bench. "Come on, Harley, we'll float you the first few hands, but you know the buy-in after that."

"Yes, yes, a hundred, I'm aware," I said, and sipped my drink. "Because you ladies do not fuck around."

"What's the point when you might die tomorrow?" Bette said and they all clinked their glasses in agreement.

"The game's blackjack." Maisy winked at me as cards began to sail across the table, everyone tossed a chip into the center, and we were off.

Blackjack had never really been my game, but tonight I was on fire. It may have been the martinis giving me a little extra pep in my step, or maybe it was getting to soak in the brilliance that was these women.

Was it weird that I was already looking forward to Friday nights with my fellow widows where we would drink too many martinis and smoke cigars while playing cards and talking shit? Actually, I shouldn't wait until I was eighty, I needed to institute a card night for my own ladies pronto.

The conversation eventually turned to me and what juicy gossip I could provide the table. I was always expected to provide the table with juicy gossip.

"I am without gossip tonight ladies, I'm so sorry."

"Bullshit!" Dot cackled. Dot needed to be cut off. No more martinis for Dot.

"Bullshit nothing, thank you very much." I did my best to look innocent and highly offended.

"Oh, come on, Harley, you've gotta give us something," Olive whined.

"I have a new roommate." There was zero appreciation for the statement. "*He* is my friend's cousin and a professional soccer player." The addition perked them all up considerably.

"Now this is sounding more promising!" Bette said. "Have you seen him naked yet?"

"Bette! Excuse you." I gasped and took a sip of my martini.

"She's seen him naked." Maisy clinked her glass to Dot's. My potential denial was hampered by the fact that yes, obviously I had seen him naked—and not just last week. But that was ancient history, it didn't count, and I was not opening that can of worms right now.

"He wasn't totally naked."

"What does that mean?" Shirley asked around the stub of her cigar.

"He was in a towel."

"So, he was *mostly* naked."

"And I was pointing a knife at him at the time, so it wasn't the sexy way you're all thinking."

"There was a knife?" Bette looked positively giddy at the prospect. So bloodthirsty, I bet she'd love some of those dark mafia romances Darcy was always talking about.

Mrs S raised a perfect brow. "There's a story there." She wasn't wrong, but the day had caught up to me in a rush.

"One for another night." They all booed as I emptied my glass and stood. "Ladies, it was a pleasure as always."

"You are not leaving us on the cliffhanger of almost naked with a knife involved?!"

I grinned, hinging at the waist in a bow. "Until next time."

. . .

My alarm ripped me out of sleep right as Dream Jake was running a hand up over the curve of my ass, purring in my ear that I was such a good girl, because apparently, I had developed a bit of a praise kink.

I groaned, rolling onto my stomach, wishing I had an extra five minutes to indulge in that fantasy a little longer. I probably wouldn't even need five minutes, considering how worked up I was. But I was not indulging, and not only because I didn't have an extra two minutes, let alone five. I was not indulging because I was not having sex with Jake—not this time. He needed a friend. I would be that friend. As a friend, I was going to help him get out of the apartment and into the world.

With a squeak, I toppled out of bed. I had fifteen minutes to get out of the apartment if I didn't want to be late. It was a good thing I'd dealt with my hair last night—thank you, drunk Harley, for your service.

9

JAKE

Blair was calling.

If I hadn't been dodging her calls for over a week, I would have let it go to voicemail, again. But then I figured I was probably one more voicemail away from her just turning up and giving me a reaming in person, which was not ideal. I'd rather delay that from happening as long as humanly possible. Talking to the woman in person was infinitely more frightening than over the phone—at the very least I could keep my facial expressions to myself.

Even with the decision made, I still hesitated for a second before sliding my finger across the screen.

"Bl—"

"You are one lucky motherfucker, you know that." Maybe I should have let her go to voicemail.

"Hello to you, too," I said, overly cheerful, as I leaned on the balcony railing and watched the sun make its slow ascent. At least her call hadn't woken me; an alarmingly erotic dream—starring one Harley O'Connell—had done that. I needed fresh air as soon as I was conscious

"Oh, no. No, no, no, you don't get to play the Blair-is-over-reacting card today. Not after letting me go to voicemail for a fucking week! What if I had something urgent to discuss with you?"

"Then I would have called you right back." Probably. Our opinions on what constituted urgent often differed.

"A likely story." She snorted over muffled voices and the hairs at the back on my neck stood up.

"Where are you?"

"Heathrow."

My heart thumped hard. "Bullshit."

She said nothing, but my phone vibrated with a text, a photo of Blair shooting me the bird with a departures board behind her. If I hadn't answered this call, she totally would have got on a plane. I shuddered.

"Taking a trip? You really could do with a vacation." My phone vibrated again, another photo—this time a boarding pass to JFK. Was she still going to do it? I really didn't need Blair here, not now. I might have made the decision that I needed to get my shit together, but that didn't mean I knew how to go about it.

"If you send me to voicemail again, I swear to God, Jake, I will come over there and kick your ass in person. Don't think I won't."

"No more voicemail," I agreed, out of sheer self-preservation.

"Good."

"Was there something you needed to discuss?"

"No."

"No?"

"No, this was more of a test. One I was kind of hoping you were going to fail, because it's been too long since I've been to

New York. But, of course, today you decide to answer your phone."

"I don't know whether to say sorry or you're welcome."

"How about '*I'll never send you to voicemail again, Blair, because I would be nowhere without you*'."

"How about '*I'll bring you cookies when I get back*'?"

"That would be appreciated. But do not send me to voicemail again."

"I will not send you to voicemail again."

"Thank you." Her tone was crisp. "Things do seem to be calming down, which is encouraging. The press ate up your apology—it was a good thing I made you film the thing before you took off without a word in the middle of the night—and the fact that no one has eyes on you seems to make everyone more inclined to believe it. Like you're too sad to do anything but sit on your ass and watch superhero movies." She was alarmingly close to the mark.

"Okay, that's good, right?"

"It is." She paused. No more good news then. "Unfortunately, there's still no word from Arturo. I've got a meeting with him Monday about a new contract, so I'll try and sound him out then, but I can't make any promises."

"I get it. Thanks Blair, really." As much as she busted my ass, I wouldn't want anyone else on my side.

"Yes, yes, you're very grateful. What are you not going to do from here on out?"

"Have sex in the back of a cab?"

"That's one, what else?"

"No blowjob selfies."

"That's another, and?"

"And no sending you to voicemail."

"Very good," she said with a smile in her voice and then hung up without another word.

I let my head drop forward, my shoulders slumping with the action. I wasn't even sure what I wanted Arturo to say. Football had been my entire life for so long, I didn't know how to operate without it, didn't know who I was without it. I guess this situation was providing an opportunity to figure that out.

The only time I had really let myself be anything aside from an athlete were those three weeks before I left for Barcelona. I was just any other kid, then. Hanging with friends, fucking around, falling in love, not that I had ever admitted that last part to anyone—let alone the one I'd gone head over heels for. But then I left for Barcelona, football once again consumed my life, and that was that.

What would have happened if I just told her how I felt?

A knock had my head popping up and I turned to the door to find Harley waving with a wide smile on her face, like my thoughts had conjured her.

I waved back, but suspicion rattled along my nerves as her eyes darted to the door handle before she hightailed it down the hall and out of the apartment.

What the hell was she up to now? I pocketed my phone and grabbed the door handle. Nothing happened. The thing didn't budge at all. She had *not* just locked me out. I didn't even have a shirt on, for fuck's sake.

I tried the door again, only to have the same result. She locked me out. Was this some kind of retaliation for the door in the face incident the other day? I would say it until I was blue in the face that I'd been doing her a favor that morning, one she clearly did not appreciate.

What was I supposed to do now? Wait around until she got home from work? Hunter was still out; my guess was he hadn't come home. He was always leaving his balcony door open, according to Harley's post-it notes. Would I get lucky?

Not. Today.

Hunter's door was also locked, and I had a feeling that Harley had done it before she left—just to fuck with me. I dropped onto one of the chairs and ran my hands through my hair. This was a less than ideal situation. I was three floors up and had no interest in scaling the side of a building to get down. I wasn't fucking Spider-Man. The fire escape was on the other side of the building, and the balcony didn't extend past the edge of the living room. So even if one of Harley's windows was open, I wasn't going to be able to just climb in. Even still, I went to the edge of the balcony.

Harley was fucking with me. She had to be.

Her window was open, not a lot, but enough that if I got myself onto the sill, I'd be able to get it the rest of the way open and slip inside her room. The only problem with that plan was the gap between the balcony and the window. The four or so feet looked a hell of a lot bigger when I was standing here, considering crossing it three floors in the air.

Nope, not doing it. I was just going to wait here for Hunter, he would let me in and I would not have to go dangling off the side of a building. I sent him a quick text asking him to call me because a text would not communicate enough right now.

All I had to do was wait.

Harley was chatting away to a redheaded woman with a high ponytail when I walked—okay stormed—into Cream and Sugar. I wanted to hold onto my anger about the fact she locked me out of the apartment, because who the fuck does that? But then she saw me and she smiled. It wasn't just a smile, lit up her entire face and made her eyes particularly sparkly, and my heart stopped. I also momentarily forgot how to speak.

"Good morning! What can I get you there?" she asked,

with that radiant smile that was rearranging my insides. She was the devil, but she was a cute one, I'd give her that.

"You locked me out."

Her head tipped to one side. "Did I?"

"I got inside." Obvious, yes, but it deserved emphasis. Especially after I waited for an hour to hear from Hunter and, when there was nothing, I was forced to do the Spider-Man thing and scale the wall. The whole thing was dicey as fuck.

"The fact you now have a shirt and shoes on does suggest that, yes. Congratulations."

"Congratulations? *Congratulations*. I had to scale a wall. I could have fucking died." Or suffered a career ending injury at the very least, but maybe my career had already suffered a fatal blow? "You are not laughing."

She smothered what was absolutely a laugh with her hand, eyes dancing with delighted amusement. How would it feel to strangle her? How would it feel to kiss her? Whoa, where the fuck did that come from? There would be no kissing. I already knew how it felt to kiss her, and I was not in need of a refresher. She locked me out. That's what I needed to focus on. Not her twinkling eyes, or the round apples of her cheeks as she smiled, or the perfect curve of where her neck met her shoulder. I still remembered how the skin there tasted.

No. Fuck. She locked me out. She. Locked. Me. Out.

"You've gotta be kidding me, right? What were you thinking?"

"I was thinking you needed a little more ... encouragement to get outside. And look at you! Out in the world." Her hands didn't pause their work as she spoke.

"I went out yesterday."

"Two days in a row. Good for you!"

"Harley."

"Jake." My name on her tongue sent a hot bolt of something

I wasn't willing to name down my spine. This was all part of her plan. She locked me out because she knew I'd march my ass down here to confront her about it. And here I was, like a sucker.

"Are you gonna give me your coffee order, or are you gonna make me guess?"

I wanted to get up and leave. To tell her that I was onto her, and I wanted nothing to do with this friendship she was so determined to force on me. We weren't friends. We never had been. I would not be lured in with coffee and then trapped. Not happening. I was going to say it. I didn't want to be her friend. I'd be back in London soon enough, and what good would this friendship do me then? I was going to tell her to shove her coffee and then I was going to leave. Any second now—

"Black coffee. Strong. With a dash of milk." I slid onto the only empty stool at the counter. It was just a coffee.

"Alright then."

"I'll take an egg and bacon bagel, too."

Her smile stretched. "You got it."

"To-go. I'll take both to-go," I said, attempting to regain some control of the situation. I was hungry and in an establishment that served food. It didn't mean anything. No friendship was being accepted.

A steaming have-here cup was placed in front of me a moment later. I wasn't even surprised, but I still leveled Harley with a flat glare. Her face once again lit up in response and my chest went all squirmy and warm.

"Oh, I'm so sorry ... you said to-go, right?"

"I did."

"Because you've got somewhere else more pressing to be?"

"I might."

She nodded, humming away as her hands continued their smooth work behind the coffee machine.

I blew across the top of my mug, the steam curling away to the gleaming chrome coffee machine, before taking a sip. And fuck, as much as I did not want to admit it, Harley could make an outstanding cup of coffee.

"Not sure I'd call it transcendent ..." I said as I sipped again. Which was a complete lie because, fuck, it was really good. Bitter, but not overpoweringly so, with just the slightest hint of sweetness, and surprisingly creamy considering it was mostly water. I refused to give her the satisfaction of admitting as much aloud.

"Those are fighting words, Davenport."

"That right?"

"You dis my coffee, you dis me."

"Not dissing. You just talked a big game, is all." I shrugged as I took another sip and pretended like it wasn't the best goddamn coffee I'd ever tasted.

"I over-hyped? In your opinion?" One arched eyebrow communicated the challenge in her statement, and I had to work hard to keep my smile under wraps. "Two ice lattes and an Americano." She added, delivering a tray to someone waiting at the to-go window.

"I mean ..."

"You can deny it all you want, but you are desperate to slam that thing down and ask me for another."

"Am I?"

"Aren't you?" she said with a knowing smirk. I wanted to wipe it off her face. With my mouth. No. No, I didn't want that. I wanted a coffee and some food and to leave. That was it.

"Egg and bacon bagel," the redhead said as she deposited a plate in front of me.

"Thanks." The word was low and rough. I cleared my throat.

"Darcy, this is Jake. Jake, this is my boss, Darcy," Harley said, and the redhead—Darcy—did a double take.

"So, this is Jake?" Her sharp green eyes did a slow lap of my face and chest.

"Good to meet you, too?"

She turned back to Harley. "Did you bring him in so we'd stop saying he was a figment of your imagination?" Um, what? Since when was I a figment of Harley's imagination? Did this mean she'd been talking about me? I should not care what she'd been saying if she had, and yet I couldn't deny that I was curious.

"I didn't bring him in, I've been here since seven, remember? He came voluntarily."

"You and I have different definitions for voluntary," I said, reminding them both that I was right here.

"Sorry," Darcy said with a warm, if not slightly calculating, smile. "I'm not usually this rude, or weird."

"Yes, you are. Table four." Harley pushed a tray in Darcy's direction.

"Anyway, it's great to meet you. Enjoy your breakfast." And then she was gone with coffees for table four.

As subtly as possible—which was difficult considering we were only a couple of feet apart—I watched Harley work. She was smooth and efficient, constantly smiling and giving every customer her undivided attention while she spoke to them. More than one man faltered in the face of her sunny smile, which walked the line between innocent and devilish. It was mesmerizing. She was mesmerizing. Which was why I should get my breakfast wrapped up and leave—immediately.

I didn't.

"You need another?" Harley asked, clearing my first mug and empty plate.

"Sure."

Another smile. This one was the secret kind that made me desperately want to know what thoughts hid behind it. But I wouldn't let myself ask.

"So, what are the New York Coffee Championships all about?" I asked instead, because I wanted to keep speaking to her, wanted to keep her attention on me. It wasn't a good sign, but I could go back to ignoring her as soon as I walked out.

"The—how the hell do you know about them?" It was a stronger response than I was expecting.

"Flier." I pointed to the piece of paper stuck to the coffee machine in front of me.

For the first time since I arrived, Harley's hands paused, and a truly murderous expression settled on her face. She extended a hand and wiggled her fingers in my direction. I pulled the flier off the coffee machine and slapped it into her waiting palm.

"Darcy ..." she said as her boss arrived back at the counter.

"Mmm?"

"Care to explain this?" Harley shook the paper in the air.

The redhead paled. "You said you'd think about it—"

"Thinking about it does not equal yes."

"I know that. I just figured that you're a reasonable person and, after some consideration, you would come down on the side of *let's do it*."

"When have I ever been a reasonable person?" I coughed to cover my laugh and Harley shot me a sharp look.

"Now is always a great time to start. Come on, Harley, please, *please*. You know I wouldn't ask—"

"Unless it was important to you, yes, I know."

Since first meeting Harley twelve years ago, and seeing her again now, I had become convinced that she was one of the least flappable people in the world. But, apparently, I was wrong. There was color dusting the tops of her ears and along her cheeks. Her hands were curling in and out of fists. She was *pissed*. I'd bet that if she wasn't surrounded by people, she'd have a lot more to say about whatever was happening right now.

Instead, I watched her school her face into a calm smile as she resumed making coffees. "Fine," she said, so flat it sent a chill down my spine.

Darcy squealed as she clapped and pulled Harley into an awkward half hug.

"Thank you! Thank you, thank you, thank you! You will not regret this, I swear."

"It'll be great." Harley nodded, the smile coming nowhere near her eyes. Did her friend not see how uncomfortable she was? Part of me was tempted to butt in, to jump to Harley's aid, but it wasn't my place. Harley was a grown woman, perfectly capable of making her own decisions, and could take care of herself, even with that black storm cloud bobbing above her head.

I paid my bill and left, telling myself I shouldn't care. I almost believed it.

10

HARLEY

By the time Darcy and I locked up Cream and Sugar, my whole face was aching from the fake everything-is-fine-and-I'm-not-in-a-shitty-mood smile that I'd been wearing for most of the day. It was making me sour. I didn't like being sour. Worse was the fact I wasn't sure who I was more annoyed at—Darcy for railroading me, or myself for not anticipating it. There was also the underlying frustration about the fact I should be fine with the Coffee Champs, but, for some inexplicable reason, I was not.

Darcy, to my profound shock, had not mentioned them again—I had taken note that her smile throughout the day was very much genuine though, unlike mine. If I had to guess, I'd say she was avoiding the topic out of fear that I would change my mind. It was a smart move. Not that I would actually change my mind. Now that I was (begrudgingly) committed, I wouldn't back out. The idea might even grow on me—it was doubtful, but stranger things had happened, probably.

Now, here I was, four o'clock, with the whole evening

stretching ahead of me, a number of interesting invitations, and zero interest in anything other than slothing on the couch with a buffet of chicken fingers, popcorn, and peanut M&M's. If I had not remedied my sexless issue during the week, I might have been more motivated to get naked, but I was sated for a couple more days at least.

The problem with this *slothing on the couch with food that would make Murphy shudder* plan was that, even if Jake was in his room, I would be all too aware of him being in my general vicinity. I wanted to be alone, not kind of alone—properly alone.

Maybe I just needed a walk, to clear my head, work off the funk, and then those naked invitations might sound more appealing than chicken fingers. Only time would tell.

Half an hour later, I was no more inclined to see or speak to another human being for the rest of the night. But I had decided to scrub chicken fingers off the menu, thanks to a spontaneous craving for wontons and spicy salted shrimp. I might even get some of the garlic broccoli with almonds—make Murphy slightly less inclined to torture me with burpees next week.

The apartment was quiet when I let myself in, but I knew better than to think Jake was out. Sure enough, as I passed his door on the way to the bathroom, the low hum of recorded voices filtered into the hall. It was too much to hope that he'd spontaneously go out twice in one day.

Once I had mostly rinsed the smell of coffee away—it was never entirely gone—I pulled on a pair of sleep shorts and an old tank and prayed to all the gods that Jake would stay in his room. If I was being honest with myself, seeing him today had me a little flustered, which was unsettling because I didn't do flustered. I did flirty. I did fun. But flustered? It wasn't me. Not that I was going to let myself think about it. No, I was going to eat too much Chinese food and chase it down with some ice cream while I watched a movie before going to bed nice and early, like the responsible adult person I was.

It wasn't my usual plan for a Saturday night, but it was exactly what I needed right now. Starting with those wontons and spicy salted shrimp.

I should have expected that it would be today, when I was least in the mood for it, that the universe would choose to have fun at my expense. As soon as I picked up my phone to dial Panda Prime and order dinner, Jake stepped out of his room in a pair of low hanging shorts—and no shirt. Lord, help me. Was he that comfortable in my presence now that he didn't need a fucking shirt?

"Hello?" I jumped at the sharp voice in my ear.

"Huh?"

"Panda Prime, can I take your order?" Whoever it was on the other end of the line did not sound happy with me. If they weren't the best wontons around, I might have something to say about the fact they didn't have an app for me to order on. But Panda Prime was old school, it was part of their charm.

"Oh! Yes please, one serve of the wontons, one of the spicy salted shrimp, one garlic broccoli." I paused, debating whether or not to ask Jake if there was anything he wanted. He'd probably say no. He'd been a recluse up until this point, I saw no reason why that was going to change. Yes, he'd been at Cream and Sugar today, but that was mostly about me locking him out, which was childish on my part—and delightfully satisfying.

He'd say no to a dinner invitation. I was sure of it, which was the only reason I mouthed, *you want anything*, while pointing at my phone.

"I'm okay," he said, shaking his head and I breathed a tiny sigh of relief, too soon. "Actually, do they have chili beef?"

They did, I already knew this because it was Hunter's

favorite. "I'll also have one chili beef and the vegetarian eggrolls."

An hour later, Jake and I were side by side on the couch, with a spread of food laid on the coffee table in front of us, watching *Princess and the Frog*. He wasn't just pretending to watch, either, he was actually watching, he was laughing in all the right places and asking questions. It was all very natural. Alarmingly so.

"This is one of the most underrated Disney movies," I said around a large mouthful of broccoli.

"So, you've said, at least twice already." He took a bite of eggroll. "These are really good."

"Yes, I know. And there's no need for that tone."

He shook his head. "No tone."

"Did you know this was the last hand drawn animation that Disney produced?"

"I did not know that."

"Plus, the soundtrack is outstanding." I had been trying to keep all chatter movie related, but I was running out of shit to say. My mouth was going to go rogue soon, I could feel it.

Once *Princess and the Frog* finished, Jake announced it was his turn to choose the movie. Because, apparently, we were making it a marathon. I could leave, of course, but I wasn't tired yet. At least that's what I was telling myself.

"Let me guess ..." I started, tapping my fingers against my forehead. "*Percy Jackson*. No! *Star Wars*." I couldn't remember if he was a *Star Wars* fan or not, but I got that vibe.

"Does that tone mean you don't like *Star Wars*? It's a classic, but I don't know if I'm in the mood for it today."

"*Star Wars* is fine, it's just—"

"Fine?" He was predictably appalled. "It's a lot more than *fine*. It's—"

"I don't need a cinema lesson, Jake, just pick a damn movie." Okay, so that was a little sharper than I intended.

"I got it!" He crowed, oblivious to, or unaffected, by my snappiness. "Close your eyes."

"What? Why?"

"Because you need to guess what movie it is by the opening credits. Go on, close 'em. Don't you trust me?"

"No," I said. "I don't think I do." Especially after I locked him out today. That little stunt was asking for retaliation.

"I'm not asking you to trust me with your life, Harley, just a movie choice."

With a sigh, I closed my eyes and waved a hand in front of my face. He didn't say anything, but the remote buttons clicked away. Everything down my left side prickled with awareness. All my other senses were heightened because I couldn't see anything.

"Ready?"

"As I'll ever be."

"Okay. And ... go."

Vague sounds filled the room.

"There's bugs? Is that bug noise? Oh! This sounds dramatic." I leaned forward, like it was going to help me hear better. "What the hell is that?" I tipped my head to one side. "Some creepy music, and yelling, okay ... I got nothing. Wait, did someone say tasers? What's that noise? More talking ... gatekeeper? *What is this?* Oh, something's happening, shit's gone bad...shoot her?! Shoot who? What happened? It's all quiet now. I have no idea what's going on. Can I open my eyes yet?"

"No! No, you need to wait, you'll figure it out."

"Will I, though?" I'd gone into this thinking I'd get it in less than a minute, how hard could it be to guess a movie from the opening scenes? My confidence was swiftly waning. Maybe he was fucking with me, and I wouldn't even know the movie.

"Yes, I swear you will."

"Okay." I went back to listening. "Is that water? And people speaking Spanish ...? Twenty million dollars! Wait, who? Hammond? Seriously Jake, I've got nothing here. I have no idea what this is."

"Keep 'em closed." One large hand covered my eyes, and I sucked in a breath as my heart thumped. Too close. This was way too close. I took hold of his wrist, swallowing hard. My skin was on fire, my stomach had bottomed out, and I was seriously regretting all those wontons. He smelled really good, too, like a perfect mix of both of our body washes—because, yes, of course I had taken a whiff of his, maybe more than once. But it was so damn manly, yet fresh.

I steadied myself and resolutely ignored the warmth gathering between my legs. "Jake—wait, what is this now? Doctors? A movie about doctors? Are they in a hospital?" I was only getting every few words because my concentration was shot to shit thanks to Jake's hand on my face and my body's answering reaction. I knew that hand was attached to an arm, and the arm was attached to a chest, and that chest didn't have a shirt on it. I also remembered all too well what those hands could do to my body, and I had a feeling he'd have become even more skilled since I'd last experienced it. I needed to stop thinking about this.

"*Postmortem contraction of the posterior neck ligaments, velociraptor?*"

"Velociraptor!" I squealed. "It's *Jurassic Park!*" His hand disappeared in a blink and I opened my eyes. He was closer than I'd been expecting, close enough for me to see the golden flecks at the center of his blue irises. Those eyes were flicking between mine, and there was a zing in the air that made me think leaning a little closer was a good idea. But it wasn't—it was a bad idea, so I cleared my throat and leaned away.

"I thought the music would come on sooner," he said, with a sheepish smile as he straightened up, widening the gap between us.

"Me too."

We fell silent, eyes on the screen, but my attention was squarely focused a couple of feet to my left. How could it not be? The hairs along my arms prickled and stood on end, straining in his direction. Every nerve was doing the same, waiting, wanting, now desperate for something to happen after the reminder of how it felt to have his hands on me. But it was not going to happen. He was Hunter's cousin, for one, and even though he never admitted it, I knew Jake had some feelings the first time. Feelings I conveniently ignored as an eighteen-year-old little asshole, because we had fun together and I wanted to continue seeing him naked for as long as humanly possible. I might be a flirt with a diverse portfolio, but I was no longer an eighteen-year-old asshole. *He's no longer a love struck twenty-year-old either.*

I ignored the voice that would have me crawling into his lap in a hot minute if I gave it half a chance.

"So, London, huh?" I said, in a vain attempt to pull my brain out of its lust spiral.

A slight cough and then, "Yep." It was troubling the way that one short syllable, spoken in his gravelly voice, rattled every vertebra on the way down my spine.

"Who do you play for?"

"For Chelsea."

I nodded, like I had any idea about English soccer teams.

"How long have you been there for?" My eyes darted to him and back to the screen. Yes, I needed to focus on the movie, on Jeff Goldblum, he really was a sexy individual. I should stay focused on him and not the equally sexy man beside me.

Jake shuffled, was he coming closer, or moving further away? I glanced at him again and found his eyes on me.

"About six years."

I nodded again, taking a large gulp of water. "How do you like London? I've always wanted to go there." Liam and I talked about it, didn't we? Where we'd go one day. London was on his list, Paris on mine. All those places he'd never see ... that was enough to douse the sexy feelings swirling between my hip bones.

"It's an incredible city and I like my club—"

"But?" I said, pulling myself back into the conversation and away from the memories that were threatening to swallow me.

"But what?" His eyes darted over my face, and I got the impression that he saw far more than I wanted him to.

"It just sounded like there was going to be a but ..." I shrugged, turning back to the TV. Even still, I saw from the corner of my eye the way he ran a hand up through his hair from back to front and back again. The action left everything in delightful disarray.

"I guess I've been feeling homesick recently."

"Well, England is not the only place they play soccer."

"Football." He knocked my knee with a knuckle, bringing my attention back to how close we were. Why did this feel like a betrayal, when none of the others had?

"Football. Well, there are other places where they play your brand of football."

He nodded but didn't say anything else.

We both went back to watching the movie—not that I was

really absorbing any of it. It was difficult to focus on anything when I was so preoccupied with Jake's presence, and then feeling guilty for said preoccupation.

"What about you?" he asked after a few silent minutes.

"What about me?"

"What—what have you—what do you do with yourself? Is it just coffee?"

My eyebrows shot up to my hairline as I rounded on him, ready to rip him to shreds if the uber successful soccer—sorry, *football*—player wanted to talk down to the barista who 'just made coffee'. Fuck that.

"I didn't mean—that came out wrong."

"I should hope so."

"Do you still draw? You were starting art school not long after I left, right?" How the hell did he remember that?

"Right, yes, I started but didn't finish." It was hard to come back from a semester of pretty much zero attendance. As soon as Liam was gone, so was my fire to create, it never came back the same, either. I couldn't remember the last time I'd even wanted to pick up a pencil.

"You didn't like it?"

"It wasn't the place for me." Not without him. At first, nowhere felt right without him.

"That's a shame—not in the way you're thinking," he rushed to add. "Because, from what I remember, you were so talented."

His opinion shouldn't matter to me, and yet the simply spoken statement sent a rush of warm tingles skittering across my skin.

"I figured you made coffee by day and then painted the town at night."

A laugh slipped free at the idea of it. "Literally."

"Literally," he agreed.

"I channel my art in other ways now. Coffee. Clothes."

"You make clothes?"

"No, I just like playing with them. It feels like a less permanent form of art, which suits me."

"Less permanent?"

"It's hard to explain."

"So, I guess that just leaves you more time to dominate the New York coffee scene." He was talking about the Coffee Champs, and I had no interest in discussing them. "As much as I hate to admit it, and despite not having any kind of sample of the competition, I'm pretty sure you'd kill it."

I bounced up onto my knees and punched his shoulder. "I knew it! You were just fucking with me when you said my coffee wasn't transcendent."

"Maybe."

"Definitely," I said with another punch. He caught my wrist and held it, not pulling me closer but stopping me from moving away. My heart stuttered as goosebumps shivered up my arms. This wasn't supposed to happen. We weren't supposed to be all ... zingy.

Blue-green eyes bounced between mine, watching, waiting, a quiet battle playing out behind them. I could see the question; would it be a mistake? I wanted to say yes, kissing him would almost certainly be a mistake, but as my attention darted down to his plush lips it was difficult to think of why.

His hand slipped down to my elbow then reached for my waist, and I moved without conscious thought, my body leading as my mind spun. I shuffled closer, my knees brushing the side of his thigh as his arm snaked all the way around my back and, with very little effort, he dragged me across his lap.

What the hell are we doing?

Our lips hovered so close I wasn't merely breathing air, but him, too. It was heady. Had it been like this the first time? Had the air between us been this charged? Had I wanted to kiss him so badly I could come out of my skin with the need for it? I couldn't remember. At some point I had started to think of my life in two parts: before Liam and after. It was difficult to remember much of the before—he wiped my slate clean, his presence clearing everything that came before.

But this, now, this feeling swirling in my chest and heating my blood, it was bigger than anything.

Jake's grip on my waist tightened, bringing me closer, enough for our noses to bump and, even with the thoughts of Liam trying to edge in, I couldn't take it anymore. I closed the last of the space between. The moment my mouth met his, I came alive.

I wanted to devour but he wouldn't let me, slowing our pace until the kiss was little more than a maddening sip, like he was relearning the shape of my lips.

He made a sound that was half sigh, half groan, and all sex as our tongues met, sending my pulse into overdrive and turning my bones to jelly.

Our chests came flush as the kiss deepened and I slipped my arms over his shoulders, letting my fingers explore his hair. My head swam in the feel of his hungry mouth. He was a good kisser before but, as I expected, his skills had only improved in the last twelve years. I happily let myself be led.

His hands slid down over the curve of my ass squeezing, pressing me against his hard length between us, right as the door slammed open and Hunter came barreling inside.

I launched myself off Jake so quickly I almost toppled onto the floor.

What the fuck was that?

I couldn't decide if I was relieved or wanted to strangle Hunter for ending what was one of the best kisses of my life.

Of. My. Life. Liam's included—which rattled me all the way down to my bone marrow. He was my one. He set me on fire and challenged me and loved me without question and he was everything. My big love.

It's not something you get twice, right?

11

JAKE

Hunter stopped short when he saw Harley and I together on the couch. Not together-together, because she couldn't get off me fast enough when the door opened, but beside one another. I pulled a pillow onto my lap to cover the hard-on currently tenting the front of my shorts.

"What are you doing here?" Hunter asked, glancing between us. I assumed he was talking to Harley, because where the hell else would I be?

"I do live here," she said, her cheeks pink and lips swollen. From me. I did that. How the hell did we go from casually watching kids' movies to *that* kiss?

"Yes, but it's Saturday night. When do you ever stay home on a Saturday night?"

She shrugged. "What are you doing here? Aren't you supposed to be working?" Was the annoyance in her tone about the fact we were interrupted, or was it something else? I didn't let myself look in her direction.

"Forgot my phone. Have you seen it?"

"Nope." She turned her attention back to the television, her eyes avoiding me entirely.

He circled the kitchen island before disappearing into his room. I didn't move, neither did Harley. What was she thinking? Did the kiss feel as explosive to her as it did for me? We were good together before, but that was something else altogether. Raw electricity, sharp and dangerous.

"Harls, can you call it?"

She swiped her phone off the coffee table and dialed. A second later something buzzed under the couch. We looked at each other. A long moment passed before I dropped onto the floor and saw the phone.

"Is it ringing?"

"It's out here!" she called.

He ran out. "Thank God. I thought the fucking thing was dead and I was never going to find it."

"If you would just turn on the find my phone thing, it would be fine." She dropped hers on the coffee table.

"And have you keeping tabs on me? I don't think so," Hunter said, walking backward toward the door.

"Oh, yes, because I have nothing better to do with my time than stalk you."

"Your words. See ya." And he was gone.

I was acutely aware of Harley beside me, frozen, same as I was. I didn't know what to do, what to say. It was clear that we were not going to pick things up after the interruption, but sitting here pretending like nothing happened was going to be next to impossible.

Before I could voice any of the thoughts rolling around in my head Harley shot to her feet. "I'm going to bed," she said and all but ran out of the room.

I understood the urge to flee. I would have done it, too, if my mind wasn't currently an empty pit of *what the fuck?*

I should leave. I should get up, pack my bag and get the fuck out of this apartment. Maybe even New York. I didn't want to head back to London just yet but staying here seemed like a really bad idea right at the moment. But if I left, would Harley think it was about her? I guess it kind of was about her, but more my inability to actually deal with being around her after a kiss that shook me down to my bones.

Okay, so I wouldn't leave. I'd sleep on it. Then tomorrow, if things were still this unbearably awkward, I would say goodbye to Hunter properly before running away—like a man.

I slumped into the couch cushions. What the fuck did I do now, though? Sit up until I passed out, maybe? Because going to bed and getting any actual sleep tonight while I was trying not to think about that kiss was not happening.

It took ten minutes before I was ready to climb the walls. Sleep. I just needed sleep. Once I was asleep, I could stop thinking about the feel of Harley's lips on mine and the taste of her tongue.

The problem was, once I was in my room and the apartment was silent, all I could hear was Harley's pacing. Step-step-step-step-step-pause-step-step-step-step-step-pause. I'd been in her room this morning, so imagining her striding in one direction and then the other was all too easy. This was worse than half watching the rest of *Jurassic Park*. At least then I could pretend she wasn't still here.

A shower, that would do it. I'd take a cold shower and turn my brain off. Except when I got into the bathroom it smelled like her, because of course it did. I still stripped off my shorts and boxer briefs and turned on the shower all the same.

Her scent billowed around me with the steam, laughing at the fact I thought this might provide a reprieve from her. It was quite the opposite.

I didn't know where I hoped that kiss might go. Honestly,

in the moment I hadn't been thinking about anything other than the feel of Harley. The weight of her in my lap. The press of her breasts on my chest. The drag of her fingers through my hair.

Now I was hard again.

Jerking off in the shower wasn't a good idea. Harley's room was right there, and the door didn't have a lock. She could just walk right in. My dick strained harder, heat shooting down my spine. What would she do?

I fought the fantasy for all of three seconds before I squirted a little of her body wash into my hand and wrapped it around my cock.

Harley shuffles into the room, pawing at her face before she sees me and those whiskey-colored eyes go wide before her initial shock fades, bleeding into lust. Two long breaths pass as we watch each other.

"Were you thinking of me?" she asks.

"Yes," I all but purr as she drifts forward to the edge of the shower. The water splashes her toes. I turn to face her, fist slowly pumping. "All I've been doing for two weeks is thinking of you."

Another step forward and I wish I wasn't standing in a bath. I wanted my shower back in London—it was big enough to lay her out on the floor or have her sit on the seat and feast. Stray drops of water lands on her tiny shorts, on her tank, turning the already thin fabric sheer, and my mouth waters at the sight of her nipples, tight and hard.

"Me too." Another step forward, and another. She reaches out a hand and runs it down my chest, nudging me out of the way so she can climb in too. She pulls her tank off as she steps under the water, drops collecting on her eyelashes and sliding in rivers between her breasts. I'm held in place by her hand on my chest as she drops to her knees in front of me. I can't breathe,

can't move, can barely think of anything but the feel of her wet skin on mine.

And then—

I bit down on my fist in an effort to smother the groan. It wasn't terribly effective—not surprising considering I came so hard my knees almost buckled. I took in a few heaving breaths as my heart rate settled. That was intense, and yet nowhere near enough to even take the edge off.

I was in trouble.

The apartment was empty when I dragged my ass out of bed on Sunday and I noted a pang of disappointment. I had no idea what time I'd gone to sleep, but if I had to guess I'd put it somewhere around four, when my brain finally decided to shut the fuck up. At first, it had only been about Harley—because it was useless trying to avoid it—but then it shifted as the rest of my life bled into it, too.

I pulled on a shirt and a pair of shorts, forgoing the shower, and looked at my duffle bag. I'd packed only the necessities. If I was going to stay, I'd need to do a load of laundry or go shopping. Probably both.

Was I going to stay? I didn't actually need to leave New York, just the apartment. Just far enough away so I was out of Harley's orbit. Only, I didn't want to be out of her orbit.

It wasn't just about Harley, though. The run with Hunter had rattled something free, something I'd been trying to smother, and I wanted more of it.

First, though, I needed coffee.

I stepped out onto the sidewalk. There were plenty of coffee shops in Brooklyn, a number of them only a short walk from Hunter and Harley's apartment. I did not need to go to

Cream and Sugar. But, if I was going to get a coffee, I might as well get the best, right? What was the point in going to one of the many spots nearby, when I knew they would come off second best—and that was being optimistic. The debate was embarrassingly short, then I took off down the crowded street and toward the potential awkwardness that awaited me. If things were awkward, then I needed to know, because if it was then I'd leave. Probably. At the very least, my turning up at her place of business might help to clear the air.

Like yesterday, there was a crowd on the sidewalk when I arrived at Cream and Sugar. It was bigger today; people milled around clutching their to-go coffees in one hand and children, dog leads, or cell phones in the other. I skirted around them and made for the door.

I spotted Harley the second I walked in, her curls contained in two wild knots on either side of her head, two sets of large hoops hanging from her ears. Despite the smile she wore, she looked tired. Was it because of our kiss? Had she been up half the night, too, tossing and turning and driving herself mad? Or was it just the end of the week weighing on her?

When she saw me, her smile was more reserved than it had been yesterday, tempered by awkwardness. Or was it? Maybe I was projecting, was that what it was called? I was all awkward, so I assumed she was too. I wasn't just awkward; I was crawling out of my goddamn skin. Was it because I wanted to kiss her again? Did I want to kiss her again? Yes, obviously, I wanted to kiss her again, even knowing it was probably a bad idea.

Leaving twelve years ago had been necessary. It nearly killed me, but it was necessary. Harley was very clear about the fact we were only a fling, no strings, no expectations, and I respected that. It made sense, considering I only had three weeks left in the States and she was starting art school in the fall. It wasn't our time, or maybe a fling was all we were supposed to be? I tried telling myself that as I boarded the plane to Barcelona, but it still felt like my heart was cracking in two.

And nothing had changed, not really, my life was in London and Harley's was here. There was no future for us. That should have been enough to put an end to the constant spiral of thoughts, but it wasn't. My brain kept saying *what if...?*

What if...?

What if...?

"Good morning," the redhead—Darcy—said as she passed me carrying two plates. "You after food or just a coffee? Oh, you're Harley's guy from yesterday, right?"

Harley's guy.

"No, I'm not—I—ah—I was here yesterday, but I'm not—"

"It was Jake, right? There's an open seat at the counter—if you plan on staying, I'd claim it."

"Sure, okay, thank you." *Harley's guy.*

The last available stool was once again directly in front of the coffee machine, and I slid onto it, not sure if I was staying.

Harley peeked at me. "Well, well, back again so soon ... you want the same as yesterday?"

"Yes, yep, same as yesterday, to-go, thank you, please." If I could have slapped myself on the back of the head, I would have. *Harley's guy.* That wasn't me, it never had been.

She nodded. "How's your day so far?"

"Honestly, I pretty much rolled out of bed and came straight here." Was that giving too much away?

Another nod, and I noted that her smile didn't quite make it to her eyes. So, I wasn't the only one who was awkward. I couldn't decide if that was better or worse. I didn't want her to be awkward, too, but there was an element of comfort knowing I wasn't the only one tangled up.

There was no chatter, no teasing, and when my coffee and bagel slid across the counter a couple of minutes later, they were both to-go, just like I asked for. She wanted me to leave. Because we fucked things up last night. Because the friendship I didn't even want was ruined before it even began. That hurt more than it should.

I left.

Hours later, well past the time when Cream and Sugar would have closed, Harley finally walked in the door, and I almost went full overprotective-father and demanded where she'd been. The words, *you could have been dead in a ditch somewhere* actually threatened to come out. I managed to restrain myself, just.

"Hey there, why is your eye twitching?" She slung her bag onto one of the armchairs and went to the kitchen, retrieving a beer from the refrigerator.

I waved off her offer for one of my own. "No, thank you, and my eye is not twitching."

Her lips pursed as she opened her beer. "It kinda is."

"I'm leaving." I'd packed my bag and then paced the apartment for most of the day. It was undoubtedly why my eye was twitching. She didn't need to know I hadn't said anything to Hunter.

A sip and then, "Okay ..."

"You want me to leave."

"Why would I want you to leave?" Her genuine confusion had me second guessing myself, but I plowed ahead all the same.

"Because it was awkward earlier."

"At Cream and Sugar?" Another sip. I was momentarily distracted by the movement of her throat as she swallowed.

I blinked. "Yes. You were less ... you." It was the only way I could think to explain it. Like the Harley had been turned down. It was a little way back up now, which was encouraging.

"I'm not sure how to take that."

"It's a compliment."

"Then that's how I'll take it." Her mischievous smile was back, too, making her eyes twinkle with amusement.

"Are we really not going to talk about it?"

"Talk about what?" She knew exactly what, but she was going to make me say it.

"The kiss."

"Oh *that* ..." She waved a hand, the one not holding the beer. "Honestly, Jake, we don't need to make it a big deal or anything. It's fine. I think we can put the whole thing down to being understandably overcome by the Sam Neill, Laura Dern, Jeff Goldblum throuple, you know? Things got a little heated. Then they cooled off." Things only *cooled off* as she put it because Hunter walked in. What would have happened if he hadn't? I wasn't entirely sure I wanted to follow that particular train of thought, certainly not right now.

"And that's it?"

"Sure, why wouldn't it be? It happened, but we're both grown-ups, there is no need for you to run screaming for JFK. Unless you want to—in which case, I will wish you a warm bon voyage." Was it really that simple? I guess if I didn't want to kiss her again it might be. Did that mean she didn't want to kiss me again?

"I don't want to run screaming for JFK." Or anywhere else.

"Okay, then." She saluted me with her can.

"Okay, then," I echoed, because I wasn't sure what else to say.

"Well, if that's cleared up and we don't have anything else

to discuss at this juncture ... I'm going to shower the coffee from my pores." She curtsied.

"You're still drinking a beer."

"You never have shower beers? Jake, I implore you to start living a little." She patted my chest on the way to the bathroom.

HARLEY

Jake was sitting at the Cream and Sugar counter, on what I now considered his stool.

Over the last week, we had settled into a rhythm of sorts. A rhythm that saw us dancing around one another and the zingy fucking tension that was like an ever-present third person in the room whenever we were together. But we didn't acknowledge it. Not ever. It was the big, fat, sexy elephant we were both resolutely ignoring at all times.

Like today, when he turned up just as our first rush for the day died down, a sheen of sweat coating his forehead and temples and winking at me from the hollow of his throat. Fucking hell, no one should look that attractive after a run, or whatever he'd been doing. He looked like he'd stepped off the pages of *Men's Health*.

Naturally, my brain was now showing me so many other ways I could help him get sweaty—none of which would be happening. Sexy thoughts were officially off the menu, as was any further dwelling on the kiss. I had been doing quite enough of that and it was driving me up the fucking wall. I'd had nowhere near enough sleep thanks to my overactive, imaginative brain and the horny-as-fuck dreams it was creating for me. Most of the time I very much appreciated my imagination—right now, not so much.

Ordinarily, I was the first person to throw caution to the wind and indulge in some naked, sexy fun times. I was of the opinion that anyone who wanted to indulge in sex *should* indulge—as often as possible, and in whatever (consensual) way they pleased. Sex was something to be enjoyed and explored, which I opted to do on the regular. But there was something about Jake that hit different, and I wasn't sure how I felt about that. I wasn't going to erase that feeling, even ignoring it was difficult enough, but I could put a pin in it.

However, he was currently making a mockery of my decision with his stupid, handsome face.

It just didn't make sense, this warm bubbling under my ribs. It wasn't there the first time; we'd had fun, but there weren't any *feelings*—at least not for me. As curious as part of me was, the rest was terrified and guilty of what it meant.

I took a slurp from my now watery iced coffee. I was no longer thinking about any of this, because it was making me mopey, and I wasn't any fun when I was mopey. My customers came here for smiles, not scowls.

"You want another?" I asked Jake. He nodded, his gaze snagging on mine and—despite being in a cafe full of people—it almost felt like we were alone. Like everything and everyone else just faded into the background. Ridiculous, certainly, but a zing of something danced its way down my spine all the same.

Coffee. I was making coffee, not appreciating the man's jawline and how his stubble would feel on my tongue.

I slid said coffee across the counter less than a minute later —I'd been working on my speed for the Coffee Champs—and enjoyed the view of Jake's long fingers as they curled around the cup. I was not thinking about those fingers doing anything else. But I needed to stop looking at him like he was my next meal. I said I was going to be his friend and, yes, we hit a little speedbump with the kiss, but it didn't change the fact that he needed a friend, and I was going to be that friend. Whether he liked it or not. Friends. Just friends.

"Look at you, just a regular New Yorker enjoying his coffee..." I pulled out my phone and lined up a photo. His hair was delightfully disheveled, blue-green eyes smiling even though his mouth wasn't. He took a sip, watching me, and I click-click-clicked. What I really needed was a pencil in my hand instead of a cell phone. My palms warmed at the thought.

"What's your social media handle?" I asked, even though I knew it and had already done a deep dive into his photos. Honestly, most of them were kind of bland—staged shots from his marketing team, probably. Bor-ing.

"Jakedavkicks, why?" So suspicious. I mean, he probably had a right to be—but still.

"Because I'm tagging you." I sharpened the image and brightened it up. Darcy shot me her get-your-butt-back-to-work look, so I grabbed Morgan and set her to work on the line of coffees and took up the vacant stool at the counter. Jake's knees knocked against mine as he turned to face me.

"Tagging me in what exactly?" He sipped his coffee. On this side of the counter, I was close enough to smell him, which was a problem. The fact I couldn't put my finger on what it was exactly was driving me bonkers. It was something earthy and rich, it tickled my nose and made the hairs on the back of my neck stand on end. I wanted to bury my face in his chest and huff him.

He'd asked me a question though, before I got all distracted. What was it? Oh! "A photo ... I'm tagging you in a photo, obviously. You do know how Instagram works, right?"

"Yes, Harley, I am aware of how Instagram works. What? Why are you making that face?"

"I'm not making a face." Not intentionally, anyway. "Your page is just kind of … sterile. I'm guessing you don't really do much with your own social media, huh?" There were plenty of posts, sure, but they weren't anything special.

"The public sees enough of me. I have no interest in showing them anymore."

"So, you're just fine with letting the press control your narrative?"

"Control my narrative?" he said, eyebrows rising in surprised amusement.

"Okay, confession time, I may have done a teeny-tiny bit of googling. But, in my defense, I am a naturally curious person and you locked yourself in our spare room for like a week. Hunter had only given me breadcrumbs of an explanation, so I was merely forced to take matters into my own hands. Anyway, maybe if you took control of your own social media, you could avoid looking like the asshole."

"Harley, I am the asshole." The statement sent a chill across my skin because I could tell he believed it. He really did think he was the asshole here. And look, I could see how he had *behaved* like an asshole. But behavior didn't make a person.

"Are you though, are you really?"

"Yes," he answered without hesitation. "I issued a public apology for my behavior. I issued a private apology to Pierre, and he told me to go fuck myself, as he should. I'm not giving people any more to salivate over. Why would I? Why should I?" He needed a hug. I could tell. If I didn't think I'd get all sorts of ideas by delivering that hug, I'd do it.

"It's your best outlet to show people who you really are."

"They see who I really am." Wow, stubborn much?

"And what's that?" I already knew what he was going to say.

"A football player." Bingo!

"Sure, that's what you *do*, but what else?"

"Nothing else, that's literally all they need to know."

"But you could be showing people the person behind football." I tapped out a quick caption, it pretty much wrote itself: #hotmendrinkingcoffee.

Jake was less than convinced. "Why would I want to give them more ammunition to torture me with?"

"I'm not talking about the press—although, if you posted a little more, you might get ahead of them and take the wind out of their sails when they're trying to break stories. But I'm talking about your fans, the people who have your back no matter what, you know?"

He opened his mouth like he might say something, then closed it again with the tiniest shake of his head. Whatever else was going on there, I wasn't getting to the bottom of it today.

"Just a little food for thought."

Before he could say anything else—like maybe thank me for my genius insights—Cecilia arrived in a cloud of freshly cut grass and *Marc Jacobs Daisy*. The girl really knew how to make an entrance. At least she was on time today.

"Hi! Hi, hi, hi." She threw her bag under the counter, grabbed an apron from the hook and stopped dead as she turned, and her eyes locked on Jake. "Holy shit."

I glanced between them. "Jake, this is Cece. She is working with us over the summer and doesn't usually swear at customers." I shot her a pointed look.

"Cece, this is—"

"Jake Davenport," she said, although it was more of a wheeze than actual words and I watched as Jake curled in on himself. He hadn't expected to be recognized—and he didn't like it one bit. I wanted to lean over and wrap him in a hug but resisted. My fingers inched closer to where his hand was flattened beside his coffee.

"Yes, it is, but right now he's just a customer, and a friend of mine. So be cool."

"Sorry! I'm sorry." Her cheeks were all red. "I just didn't —he's your friend? How have you never mentioned that you're friends with one of the best strikers in the Premier League?"

"I'm just gonna go," he said, and my hand went rogue, reaching out and snagging his.

"No!" Cecilia and I said together. Jake and I both looked at our joined hands.

"No," Cecilia repeated. "Please stay, I'm sorry, I won't stand here and fangirl. I can be cool. I can keep my shit together." I had a feeling she was saying it for her own benefit as much as Jake's.

"Don't feel like you need to leave," I added, dropping his hand, and his shoulders relaxed a fraction as he lowered back onto his stool.

"This is amazing though," she continued, making no move to stop staring and start working.

"Cece," I said, attempting to nudge her into action. "You weren't going to stand here and fangirl, remember?"

"I know, I know." She rounded the counter and slid onto the stool beside Jake—so still not working then. "But oh my god, I needed this today."

"You needed to see Jake Davenport today?"

Her cheeks went even pinker as she glanced at him and then away. "I mean, not him specifically, no offense—"

"None taken," Jake said, a smile starting to twitch at the corner of his lips. He might not want to be recognized, but it was hard to not like Cecilia Hughes.

"I just needed something *good*." She sniffed and I noted that her eyes were ringed in red.

"Why, what's happened?"

"My summer program was canceled." She slumped onto the counter with a sob—because she and I were soul mates in our love of some drama—and Jake shot me an alarmed look.

"The whole program? How can the whole program be canceled?"

"No coach, just like Trent said before he left to fuck half of Europe over the summer."

Another alarmed look from Jake and I smothered a laugh as an idea went *ding-ding-ding* in my head.

"No coach, that does sound bad."

Jake's eyes shot to mine, a sharp warning in them. I ignored it.

"If only there were someone here with nothing to do and the skill to coach soccer."

Cecilia's head shot up and she looked at me like I was being an idiot. "Harley, you don't know anything about soccer."

"Amazingly, Cece, I was not talking about me."

"Then who—" Her attention snapped to Jake, and he froze, so still he might have stopped breathing. "Him?" she said now, looking at me again with her thumb poking in his direction. "Why the hell would Jake Davenport want to come and coach a summer soccer program at Franklin High School?"

"It's difficult to know unless you ask ..."

She turned slowly, his eyes going wider the closer she got to fully facing him. "You wouldn't—you—would you, um, be maybe interested in coaching a summer soccer program for my JV team? No you wouldn't, why the hell would you—Jake Davenport—want to do that? That's ridiculous. Although, the entire team would legitimately shit themselves if you said yes."

"That sounds messy," Jake said, panic tightening the

corners of his eyes.

"Yeah, sorry, you don't—you don't need to say anything. It's fine."

"It's—I'm sorry that you lost your coach, but I—"

"Would have to be a real asshole to say no," I finished for him, and his eyebrows shot so far up his forehead they almost touched his hairline.

Cecilia glanced between us, attempting to understand the silent conversation that was going on. It wasn't that difficult to read; mostly me saying *do it, do it, do it* and Jake saying *Harley, you are the devil and I hate you, no.*

"It's only five hours a day. You'll be done by lunch." I could tell Cece was trying to play this cool, but she looked so darn hopeful.

"For how long?" I asked.

"It starts the Tuesday after the July fourth weekend and runs for six weeks." Her eyes were still bouncing between us like she was watching a tennis match.

"Can I have some time to think about it?"

"Yes, yes, of course! Oh my god!" She leaped off the stool. "Okay, I'm going to get to work now."

"That'd be great—you can start by taking these to table four." I nodded at the loaded tray.

"Sure yes, I can do that." She grinned as she took the tray and continued chanting *ohmygodohmygodohmygod* as she walked away.

I returned my attention to the line of coffees waiting for me as Jake's eyes drilled into my head. Had I just thrown him under the bus? Maybe a little, but this could be exactly what he needed. It was keeping him in touch with the game but on a very different level—where it wasn't actually about him. He could share his knowledge, get a bit of confidence back. That was a good thing.

"What the hell was that?" he whisper-hissed after two solid minutes of silence.

"She needs a soccer coach. You happen to be an outstanding soccer player, from what I've heard … what's the harm in giving it a little thought?"

He made a skeptical noise. "No harm at all. Thank you for playing unwanted matchmaker."

"You're welcome."

"I was being sarcastic."

"So was I." I winked before handing a few cups off to the to-go window.

Jake stewed for another couple of minutes in silence before standing abruptly.

"See you at home!" I called, as he left with a backward wave. Cecilia watched him go with bald longing on her face. He'd be coaching that team in no time.

I stepped out onto the street ahead of Darcy as I continued to scroll and swipe through profile after profile on *MatchMe*. There were four million men in New York. Four million men who were not Jake Davenport. And I was going to find one of them to have sex with tonight. So far, no one was really summoning any kind of tingle in my favorite French-cut lace underwear, but I was determined.

Darcy locked up and dropped her keys into her bag with a heavy sigh. It was enough to pull me out of the black hole.

"You know that if you don't take a day off soon, your head is going to explode," I said. Darcy was what was commonly referred to as a workaholic. I was surrounded by them. Chase, at least, was doing better at taking time off for a little fun. "Burn out, Darce, beware, beware."

"I'm fine. And I'm taking a whole weekend off."

"Oh yeah! The fourth up at Jem and Nash's, right? I totally forgot about that."

"Maybe I shouldn't close us for the whole four days. Maybe two would be enough."

"Do not talk yourself out of a vacation, no matter how small. You are going for the full four days, and you are going to enjoy it."

"Yes, ma'am." She saluted me. "You should see if Jake wants to come along, too."

"No, I shouldn't."

"Why not?"

"Because no, just no."

"Have you had sex with him?"

"No."

"So, what's going on?"

I wanted to be able to tell her that nothing was going on, that I had not had sex with Jake, nor did I plan on having sex with Jake at any point in the future.

"We kissed," I confessed, and she cackled something that sounded like *I knew it*, and maybe *Jemma owes me ten bucks*. I chose to ignore that, because if we were going to talk about it, then we needed to stay on topic. But maybe we didn't need to talk about it. It was just a kiss. We didn't need to talk about a kiss. A kiss was nothing.

"And how was it? Good?"

"*No.*" Lord, help me, good was not the word I'd use. Good was entirely too vanilla a word for that kiss.

"So, it was bad?"

"No." It was the opposite of bad. The complete opposite. As far from bad as you could possibly get.

"I'm confused."

"It was so good I briefly forgot my own name and how to

speak both English and Spanish. I think I could see sounds." Music had color for at least twenty-four hours.

"Wow."

"Yeah." My lips tingled at the memory.

"And?"

"And what?"

"And what's the problem?"

"No problem. Everything is peachy keen."

"Peachy keen—"

"That's right. Peachy keen. So peachy keen, in fact, that I am going on a date."

"*What?*"

"Tonight. I'm going on a date tonight."

She slapped her forehead into her palm.

"What?" I asked.

"For an intelligent woman, you really can be an idiot sometimes."

"Thank you, friend. I love you, too."

"Harley! You cannot think that sleeping with someone else is a good idea when you obviously like Jake."

"That's not—no, no, I don't like him."

"Are you sure about that?"

"Yes, I am."

I ignored her snort in response. Operation *sexual palate cleanser* was happening. Tonight. It was the only way forward.

I said goodbye to Darcy at the corner and we went our separate ways. I could tell she was desperate to say more, to try and talk me into something with Jake, but she didn't get it. She didn't understand that my heart was held together with tape and some sad, brittle glue. It couldn't survive another fall—and that was exactly what Jake would be. A fall. From a great height.

I didn't have the strength to do it again.

· · ·

I managed to get inside and into the bathroom without seeing Jake. I showered quickly and dressed in something cute and semi-slutty, because I wasn't in the mood to flirt too hard. My boobs could do the heavy lifting in that department.

My stomach dropped as I stepped out into the living room to find Jake sitting on the couch, scrolling the Netflix menu. What was he doing? Why wasn't he in his room hiding? Okay, he didn't have to hide, but could he just be not here right now? I fidgeted with the hem of my shirt, feeling exposed.

"You heading out?" he asked.

"Yes, yep, I am." *On a date.* The words lodged themselves in my throat. Admitting that I was going to see someone else, to use them to distract me from my feelings—no. There were no feelings I needed distracting from. I was going on a date because I wanted to, and that was all there was to it.

He didn't move from his spot on the couch, but his eyes made a slow trip up from my feet. "Where're you off to?" Did he suspect that I was going to meet another guy?

"Just out." I pushed my chin up, daring him to push the topic. His gaze darted down to my chest. Of course, he knew what I was doing; my clothing wasn't exactly subtle.

"Would you like some company?"

"N—no need," I squeaked, then cleared my throat. "I'm meeting someone."

"Is that right?" His voice was rough, his eyes burning.

"Yup. I better get going—don't want to keep them waiting." I swiped my bag from the armchair and all but ran out the door. I sagged once in the hall, pleased to be out of his magnetic tractor beam of hotness. This date was exactly what I needed to right the ship and clear Jake out of my head.

13

JAKE

What the actual fuck?

Harley was going on a date.

Granted, she didn't actually say she was going on a date, just that she was *meeting someone*—but in that fucking shirt? It wasn't particularly revealing, and yet I could still see her nipples. That was a fucking date shirt, not a meeting a friend for a drink shirt.

A date! Fucking, fuck.

I thought she was going to come home—and I was not acknowledging just how easily this place had started feeling like home—and I could give her some shit about throwing me in the fucking deep end with the teenager earlier, Ceciliy? No, Cecilia. What the hell had Harley been thinking, suggesting I could be a coach? I didn't want to coach high schoolers. That sounded like an actual nightmare.

Instead of being able to talk it out and tell her she'd lost her mind and was going to have to let Cecilia down easy, she walked out of the bathroom in that gold shirt. It made her skin look like it was lit from the inside. She was glowing, shimmering, a beacon drawing me in, and it took every piece of willpower I possessed to not go to her and tackle her straight into the bedroom. To taste her lips and swallow the sounds she'd make. I thought about those sounds far more than I was willing to admit.

We'd fallen into an easy kind of companionship over the last week—friendship, I was sure she'd call it—one that did not include any mention of our kiss. It was for the best, or I had thought so until three minutes ago when she walked out to go on a date with another man.

But why shouldn't she go on a date with another man? It wasn't like she and I would go on a date, was it?

I stood from the couch and started pacing. What was I supposed to do? Wait for her to get back? That was going to drive me mad, and what if it wasn't until tomorrow morning? I swallowed against the spontaneously rising bile. There was no way I could stay here and wait, not when I already felt like I wanted to punch something.

Unless ... unless I could see what she was up to? Would she be updating her social media? I shouldn't look. I should just leave Harley to her date.

Nope, that wasn't happening.

A notification popped up as soon as I opened the app: @harleywho has tagged a photo of you. Me, drinking coffee, and she had added the hashtag #hotmendrinkingcoffee. It wasn't a bad photo, either. Should I repost it? Maybe. No, that wasn't why I was here; I was here to do some light stalking. That didn't sound good—I just wanted to make sure she was okay. That was all.

I checked her story and there was a timelapse of her making coffee, a photo of her and Cece, but nothing about her date. That was enough, I should stop, I definitely should not scroll.

But I did. Just a little, then a little more, and before I knew it was two years back, then five, then ten.

Who the hell is that?

It was messed up that I was jealous of a guy in a photo from over a decade ago, but it was difficult not to be when Harley looked so fucking happy with him. She was smiling at the camera, and he was looking at her with nothing short of adoration. There were so many photos of them together, and then they just stopped. All of her photos did, actually, there was a gap of over a year. What happened?

Now I really was edging into invasion of privacy territory, and yet I couldn't stop my finger from tapping the guy's profile. Liam Michaels—I really wished I hadn't. Dead, Liam Michaels was *dead.*

I slapped my phone down onto the couch and scrubbed my hand over my face. I did not want to know this. I didn't want this information if she didn't tell me.

Fuck. Now I really needed a distraction.

Hunter picked up on the first ring.

"Hey Jake, what's up?"

"Nothing, why would anything be up, you want to get a drink?"

Not quite an hour later, Hunter and I skipped the lengthy line outside Buck's Brewery and slipped inside the squat red-brick building. The place was wall to wall with bodies and part of me regretted my decision to leave the apartment. But, considering the alternative, being jostled by drunken idiots didn't seem quite so bad.

"You know it's your night off, right?"

He shrugged. "Keeps the staff on their toes. Plus, Harley texted."

"Harley texted wh—" Then I saw her. And her *date*.

Her back was to me as she leaned across the high-top table. What the hell was she thinking with this guy? He looked like a child, with his bullshit white-boy dreadlocks and pristine white polo shirt. She was way too good for him. Admittedly, there was an excellent chance she was also too good for me, but that was beside the point. Had Liam been good enough for her? Fuck, here I was thinking this would provide a distraction.

"You good?" Hunter asked when he realized I'd stopped walking.

I turned away from Harley. "Yep, sure, all good." Had she texted Hunter to tell him she was here? Is that why he suggested Buck's and not somewhere else?

Despite my mood, and general Harley related distraction, I could appreciate the vibe that Hunter and Holden—although I suspected the decor was mostly Hunter, because Holden was more the business brain—had created in the place. It had a mismatched, come as you are feel that helped to set me at ease, even with Harley and her date smiling at each other over in the corner. The interior was industrial, a mix of warm wood and what looked like reclaimed brick, with a scattering of mismatched soft furnishing and tables. None of it should have worked together, and yet it all did.

We joined the back of the queue for drinks and two pint glasses slid across the bar toward us before we'd managed to order, the bartender giving Hunter a two-finger salute and we raised our glasses in thanks.

"So, what the fuck's up with you and the spontaneous need for an alcoholic beverage?" Hunter asked as we stepped off to the side.

"I hope that's not how you speak to all your customers?"

He laughed. "Well, you're not my customer right now, you're the shut-in who's been mooching on my couch."

"I'm not a shut-in," I said with a pout. "And I'm not mooching ... anymore." I'd started buying groceries, mainly so I didn't keep eating take-out and completely destroy my nutrition. Maybe I needed to cook dinner. Cook dinner for Harley. Like a date, but not a date. That was probably a bad idea. Would she tell me about Liam?

"Anyway, what's with the need to leave the apartment after dark? Did you get the text from Harley about back up, too?"

Harley's text to him was about back up? What did that mean? "Back up?"

He nodded in her direction, and I followed his gaze like I didn't know she was there. There was a good chance my look of surprise was more of a grimace. The guy had to know he was batting well above his average with her.

"Why would she need back up with a dweeb like that?" I asked, my tone sharp enough to slice the dreads clean off the guy's head.

"We're all loaded guns."

I turned back to him sipping my beer. "Huh?"

"That's how Harley explained it to me. The first thing you learn when handling a gun is to treat them all like they're loaded, right?"

"Right."

"So that's how she—and most women, I guess—think of men. We're all loaded guns, with the potential to be handsy fuck-heads at best, and murdering rapists at worst. So, sometimes she brings them here so she has back up if she needs it—a precaution."

I glanced back over my shoulder. The guy didn't look like a murdering rapist, but I guess that was the whole point.

"That's fucked." Not the fact that Harley, that women, considered all men loaded guns, but the fact they *needed* to.

"Yes, it is. It's why I've made sure our security are vigilant to call out any bullshit behavior, you fuck up, you're out." He took a large gulp from his beer, and I resisted the urge to turn and look at Harley again.

"So, you're not here to back up Harley, you just decided you wanted a night out with your dearest cousin?"

"Exactly. Figured I'd seen Cream and Sugar and it was time to see your baby, too."

"Awww—and yet, you can't stop watching Harley ..."

I snapped my eyes back to him. "That guy looks like a dipshit."

"A lot of them do."

"What's she doing with him?" I shouldn't care. I should be focusing on my drink and my cousin.

"Right now, having a drink, later maybe riding his face." He shrugged and I spontaneously wanted to punch dreadlocks teeth in. I practically inhaled half my beer. Harley's date activities were none of my business.

I needed to change the subject. I needed to think about something, *anything*, else that was not Harley.

"This place is cool."

"Thanks." He watched me for a long moment. "What's going on with you and Harley?"

"Nothing?" I barked. "Nothing is going on. Why?"

"You look like your head is about to explode at the thought of her in bed with that guy. I agree that she's too good for him, but your reaction seems a little more ... extreme."

"I—no—I just think she should be careful. That's all."

"Uh-huh." He continued to watch me, sipping his beer and not at all convinced by my, admittedly woeful, lying. "You sure I didn't walk in on something last week? That night I came home because I forgot my cell phone ..." So, he did realize something had been going on that night. I wasn't surprised; I'd been so desperate to keep kissing her.

"Nothing is going on," I said, more forcefully this time, and he gave a small nod. Change of subject, I really needed to change the fucking subject.

It was on the tip of my tongue to ask about Liam, instead I said, "She tried to get me to coach a high school football—soccer—team today."

Hunter barked out a laugh. "Harley did?"

"Who else?" I said and relayed the events from Cream and Sugar. It was kind of like some wild fever dream, but still. I wasn't a coach.

"Why not?" Hunter said, rapping on the bar for another drink. Two more glasses materialized shortly after.

"Why not what?"

"Why not do it?" Seriously? Had he lost his goddamn mind?

"Do you really want me to answer that?"

He rolled his eyes. "Okay, princess, but what the hell else are you doing right now?"

"Ouch."

A laugh. "Seriously, though, what's the harm in helping them out? Cecilia sounds like a good kid, from what Harley's said, and if it's the difference between the program running or not—" He shrugged. "You'd be helping the next generation and all that shit, too. That's good karma, right?"

"I do need some good karma."

He bowed his head, attention drawn by one of the bartenders.

Coaching. Coaching was not something I had ever considered—coaching teenagers even less so. But maybe Hunter, and Harley, were right? Maybe this was a way to tip the scales back in my favor. I didn't believe in God or the universe or any of that; but the idea of karma, of some sort of scales that constantly required balance ... somehow, that made sense to me.

It wasn't a sure thing, not by a long shot, but I was willing to give it some actual thought.

The following morning, I got up and left the apartment for a run, making a concerted effort not to listen at Harley's closed door. I didn't know if she came home last night. I didn't know if she was in there with the dreadlock guy, or if she was at his place.

I didn't want to know.

By the time I got back, her door was open, but she was conspicuously missing. Had she been there all night? Had she returned and then left again? The endless loop of questions was going to make me mad today, but there was no getting around it. The only way to get answers was to text her and that was not happening.

Here I was in need of another a distraction.

Hunter bounded into the kitchen like a puppy, snatched the coffee out of my hand and swallowed it in two quick gulps.

"Shit, that's awful," he said, shuddering. "Where's Harley's cold brew?" Before I could answer he was yanking open the refrigerator and pulled out a pint jar with *Harley's cold brew* written on tape on the front. "Here it is." Underneath it said *drink and you die*. I'd seen the jar when I was looking for creamer and decided to leave it be. Hunter clearly put less stock in her threats than I did.

"She's all bark, that one," he said with a grin and guzzled some of the coffee straight from the jar. I had my doubts about Harley being all bark, especially if she caught him drinking straight from the source.

"Man, I needed that." He replaced the lid, put it back in the refrigerator, and grabbed a banana from the bowl on the counter. "Alright, I'm out."

"Where're you going?" My tone screamed *take me with you.*

"To play some ball, you wanna join?"

Yes, obviously I did. Play it cool. I cleared my throat. "Sure."

"You're good on a skateboard, right?" I hadn't ridden one since I first arrived in Barcelona, but it wasn't like I'd gotten less coordinated in the intervening years. It couldn't be that hard.

"I can ride one, if that's what you mean."

"That's all I need to know, let's do it."

Hunter slung a duffel bag across his chest and handed me a neon pink board as he picked up a black one with an orange skull and crossbones on it. I stuffed my feet into a pair of trainers and grabbed my baseball cap as we left.

It was a shaky start, I almost ate it in the first block, but soon enough the muscle memory kicked in and I found a rhythm. It felt good. Better than good, it felt *free.* There were plenty of people milling on the sidewalk, but not a single one was looking my way. They couldn't care less who I was.

Hunter picked up speed and I did my best to keep pace. It had been too long since I'd been out, doing nothing in particular, just hanging out. I missed it. The freedom of being no one, of having people want to be around you for you and not what you can do for them.

The weather didn't hurt, either. I got that New York was miserable for a few months of the year, but right now the sun was high, there was a slight breeze scattering the dropped leaves across the sidewalk, it was warm, and nothing was fucking gray.

London was gray a lot of the time, and it was depressing as fuck after a while. But then I stopped going out for the most part, unless it was to The Bridge to play and train, or the Nelson Arms to drink. I guess the English weather wasn't the only thing that was depressing.

We arrived at a fenced-in basketball court and Hunter waved to four guys already tossing the ball between them.

"Nash, Mack, Murphy, Greyson, this is my cousin Jake—he's staying with me and Harley. Jake, this is Nash, Mack, Murphy—Harley's brother—and Greyson." He pointed at each man in turn, and I nodded at them before shaking each of their hands. Hunter's cousin Jake. Not Jake Davenport, Chelsea striker. Just Jake. If I had to pick a blood relative of hers out of the mix, it would not be the tall, lanky yet muscular ginger who looked in better shape than I was.

"Good to meet you all."

"You too, Jake. With you here, we've got even teams, good news!" Mack said as he smoothed back his head of wild blond curls and slipped on a baseball cap backward.

"You still won't make a single shot," Hunter said, as he stole the ball from Nash—a big guy with a beard and hair secured in a messy knot at the back of his head—and took off down the court.

"You play dirty, Buchanan." Mack went after him. And that, apparently, signaled the start of the game.

Hunter wasn't wrong about Mack; he was an absolutely hopeless shot. He did manage to get one in but was so close to the ring he was almost directly underneath it. The others were better, Murphy and Nash in particular, and Hunter was more of a trash talker than anything else.

I took a gulp of water as Murphy said his goodbyes and jogged off. The guy had barely broken a sweat while the rest of us were breathing hard at the end of our second game. If I stayed in New York a little longer, I might need to talk to him about training.

"So ..." I stretched out my shoulders. "Did you see Harley this morning?" I'd been going for casual but, judging by Hunter's laugh, I missed the mark.

"I fucking knew there was something going on with you two."

"There's nothing going on."

"Then why are you asking if I'd seen her? You wanna know if she spent the night with dreadlocks?"

"No." I snorted.

"You are such a shitty liar."

"I'm not lying."

"Your attempts at playing it cool are not working." He threw the ball at my chest. "She's my best friend."

"And what am I?"

"My cousin—and a fuck-boy."

"Tell me what you really think."

"Am I wrong?" He wasn't, and the truth of it stung more than I'd like to admit, but I was done with all that. He took my silence for confirmation. "Exactly, which means you will not be fucking around with her." *Again.*

Mack snorted as he stretched out his quads.

"What?" Hunter said.

"Nothing." Mack shrugged. "Just that Harley is kind of a fuck-girl—said with respect—and she can probably decide who she is and isn't allowed to fuck around with, don't you think?"

"That's not what I'm saying."

"I know what you're saying," Mack cut in. "*I'm* just saying that she'd probably slap you if she heard you talking about her like that."

"Says the guy who just called her a fuck-girl?"

"Pretty sure she'd appreciate the title."

"I'm looking out for her," Hunter said, his tone defensive.

"Which is admirable, sure. But, if there is one thing I know about Harley, it's that she is more than capable of fighting her own battles—and then some."

I grinned. Not that I was intending on fucking around with Harley—I had a feeling that would do far more damage to me than it would to her—but, as much as I tried to deny it, there *was* something between us and I was curious to see where it would go.

"Having said that," Mack continued, now speaking to me. "You dick around with her, you hurt her, and I'll fuck you up." He snatched the ball from me, and we all watched as it left his hand, sailed in a smooth arc and landed with a rattle of chains. Mic. Drop. Despite the casual delivery of the threat, I was confident he'd have no problems following through on it. With Nash more than happy to back him up, if I had to guess.

"I'm not dicking around, with her or anyone else." I should probably stop talking, otherwise I might confess to the kiss and that would be a mistake. "I saw her on a date last night and didn't see her at the apartment this morning. I was just curious..." Even though it was none of my goddamn business. I adjusted my cap, scratched my head.

"Are we playing another game or what?" Greyson asked, bringing an abrupt end to the conversation.

"You want more punishment?" Hunter fired back with a grin as he jogged to the center of the court.

I glanced to my left as Mack stepped up beside me. "In my experience, Harley is kind of an open book," he said. "If you're curious about anything, maybe just hang out with her, ask questions, listen to the answers." He clapped me on the shoulder and joined the others, the conversation over.

Hunter howled like a manic wolf as he sank the final shot of the game. I didn't remember him being quite this obnoxious when we were younger. He ran a few circles around Greyson.

"You're a fucking show pony, Buchanan," he said, rolling his eyes and shoving Hunter away.

"I'm a fucking show pony who wiped the floor with you, Palmer."

"As much as I would like to see you lose a game to bring that ego down ..." Mack said, "I have actual work to do today."

"Aww, don't be sore because we got the better of you, Mackenzie." Hunter pouted.

"Jesus, not you, too." Mack punched Hunter's shoulder. "And I think having a professional athlete on your team should earn you a handicap."

"He plays soccer, not basketball."

"Still a fucking athlete though, not a chef," Mack said, pointing at Nash, and then at himself, "or a pie maker."

My mouth spontaneously watered, fond memories of diner pies swarming. I hadn't had a slice of decent pie since I left the U.S. at twenty.

"Speaking of pie. I have work to do."

Nash nodded as he swallowed a mouthful of water. "Me too. It was great to meet you, Jake."

"You, too."

"How much longer are you here for?"

"No solid plans at the moment." At least another couple of months if I took up the coaching opportunity.

"Jemma and I are having some people at our place upstate this weekend. You still coming?" he said with a nod at Hunter.

"Sure am."

"You're more than welcome to come, too, if you want."

"Thanks, that sounds good."

"No pressure, the house is pretty much a disaster—aside

from the kitchen, which we've just finished—but it's water-tight and there's a dam to swim in. Alright, I've gotta run." He left and, after a round of goodbyes, the rest of us dispersed also.

A weekend away—surely Harley would be there, too. This could either be a brilliant idea, or a terrible one.

14

HARLEY

I lay perfectly still, listening to Jake move around the apartment. I knew it was him and not Hunter because they sounded different, not that I could quite explain how. When the front door closed, I launched out of bed and straight into the shower. I raced through my morning routine, giving little thought to what clothes I pulled on before I skipped down the stairs and out onto the sidewalk.

I came to a somewhat unfortunate conclusion last night.

I needed to have sex with Jake.

Despite his general hotness and outstanding bone structure, having sex with Jake really was something I had been hoping to avoid. He was Hunter's cousin, for starters, though that didn't stop me last time. Then there was the fact he was in a vulnerable place right now, what with being at the center of a legit sex scandal. As much as I enjoyed no strings sex on the regular—which our situation was literally made for, considering he was going back to London at some point—I wasn't about to take advantage of Jake like that if he wasn't into it. Although, he certainly seemed into it when I was on his lap with my tongue in his mouth. But that could have been a glitch—a Jeff Gold-blum-Laura Dern-Sam Neill induced glitch.

Things would have been so much easier if last night had just gone to plan. Operation sexual palate cleanser was a bust.

Chad, although not terribly bright, was sweet and funny and had managed to keep his eyes on my face and not my nipples. He was also supremely hot. I was able to overlook the bad dreadlocks thanks to the tattoos down his left arm and the lip ring that was giving me *Crowned Prince of the Valbaran Fae Ruhn Danan* kind of ideas. It really was an encouraging start. His bed was almost certainly a mattress on the floor in the brownstone he lived in with twelve other people, but he had large hands and the kind of walk that made me think there was something interesting in his pants.

Things had been looking up.

Then Jake fucking Davenport walked into Buck's and I knew it was the beginning of the end.

I didn't end the date right away, instead I tried to play it cool and stay engaged in the conversation. Chad had so much potential to fuck Jake Davenport right out of my system, and yet it was not to be. I kissed him for a solid thirty minutes, just to be sure but, when all I could think about was how Jake would look with a lip ring, I knew the plan was dead in the water. Apparently, the only way I was going to be able to get Jake out of my system was if he was the one doing the fucking.

Which was a problem. If I could drop onto the sidewalk in a full tantrum, banging my head until I no longer wanted to have sex with my former fling and current houseguest, I would. But New York sidewalks were disgusting; so, instead I opted for stomping across the street to Cream and Sugar. Coming here was probably a mistake—Darcy was going to have a field day about me being here on my day off—but I needed to get out of my apartment.

As expected, Darcy pounced the second I walked through the door. "What are you doing here?" she asked, copper ponytail swinging jauntily as she came to a stop in front of me.

I looked over both shoulders. "Is that how you speak to our customers?"

"You're not a customer. You are an employee, here on your day off. What happened?"

"Nothing happened, can I not be both a customer and an employee?"

"Harley, I love you, but I can count on one hand the number of times you've come in here when I wasn't paying you to."

"There is no food or coffee at home."

"Liar." She was right, my pantry was stocked, and I always kept a jar of cold brew in the fridge. "Spill it."

"Yes, do tell," Jemma added around a mouthful of her jam slathered croissant—we must be out of her signature crumpets —as she patted the stool beside her.

"Don't you have work to do?" I said, giving her a pointed look.

She lifted her chin in the direction of the wall that separated Cream and Sugar from Weston Events. "I'm doing it. Supervising next door."

"This is you supervising construction work?"

"In my defense, Matt and Owen don't actually need any kind of supervision, I'd probably—definitely—be more of a hindrance than a help. I'll be taking them lunch once I'm done here. I'm also kind of planning stuff." She waved a hand over the open notebook beside her plate. "And, technically, it's my day off."

"There is no rest for the celebrity wedding planner."

She laughed. "God, please, do not call me a celebrity wedding planner."

"But you are Jem-Jem," I crooned as I slid onto the stool beside her.

"Shut up and spill the beans."

"There are no beans to spill today. I am 100% bean free."

"Is it about Jake?" Darcy asked as she propped herself on the opposite side of the counter, a knowing smile curling her lips. She ignored my outraged squawk at the question and spoke to Jemma. "He's been here pretty much daily for over a week, and this one has been all ... twitchy."

"I am not twitchy."

"Odette said she's been all agitated too," Jemma added.

"Where is Odette?"

"Don't change the subject," they said in unison.

I rolled my eyes. "There is nothing to tell, ladies, I promise." Nothing aside from an outrageous case of sexual frustration, something I wasn't that well versed in. If I had an issue, I tended to deal with it. Only, right now, I couldn't. Wouldn't—*shouldn't*—deal with it.

They both looked predictably suspicious, but I wasn't talking about it. I had a feeling that once those floodgates opened, shutting them wouldn't be an option. *There is nothing to talk about.*

"So, when's the deadline for the coffee competition thing you insist we be a part of?" Being intentionally vague on the name was fooling no one, but I needed to pretend like it hadn't been sitting in the back of my head like an imposing peak to climb. My own personal Everest, just waiting for me to work up the guts to conquer it.

"Seriously?" Darcy's eyes narrowed into slits.

"Yes, seriously. I need to know, don't I? And can I get a strong iced latte and the BLT bagel with avocado and haloumi?"

"Let the record show that I am onto you, Harley Mariana

O'Connell, you would not be trying to distract me—us—with the Coffee Champs unless there was something going on with the hot soccer player." She paused, letting that sink in. "But, because the deadline is fast approaching and we need to get you ready, I'll allow it."

"How generous of you."

I was no more enthusiastic about the prospect of getting up on stage and making coffee like a performing monkey than I was before. However, I had made the commitment and I wasn't going to back out. I was determined not to get ahead of myself, there were a lot of amazing coffee makers in New York, so making it past the preliminaries was in no way guaranteed. Although, considering I made an outstanding coffee and was—if I did say so myself—a highly entertaining individual, our chances of progressing felt pretty solid. Plus, the mere mention of it had Darcy bouncing around like a kid who was just left unsupervised at a candy buffet; I'd have to be a hard-hearted bitch to want to stomp on that much excitement.

Jemma laughed as Darcy attempted to control herself, but she was still vibrating with excitement. "What is happening right now?"

"Harley has finally agreed to the Coffee Champs!" Darcy squeaked, pointing at the flier that was stuck to Edith, despite the number of times I'd taken it off—it popped back up every time.

"Why?" Jemma asked, eyeing me.

"Why what?"

"Why agree after years of blatant refusal?"

"I was strong armed."

"Untrue! It was entirely your decision." My eyebrows sailed up to my hairline and Darcy choked on a laugh. "Okay, so there might have been some persuasion."

"Less persuasion, more emotional blackmail, but the result is the same."

Darcy smiled, not in the least bit remorseful, as she launched into a very detailed explanation of the Coffee Championships. Despite this, there wasn't actually that much to it. I accepted the nomination on Cream and Sugar's behalf. Then—to get to the main event, which happened in August—we would need to pass a mystery visit as a team.

Naturally, we would blow away any mystery judge who stepped through our doors, because we were the best. I believed it unquestioningly. Soon enough, everyone else would see it, too. Why couldn't all of the rounds just be done that way? I'd happily take the uncertainty of a mystery judge if it meant I didn't have to get up on a stage.

"So, all I need to do is say we're in."

Darcy nodded. "And then we wait."

It sounded easy enough, and yet there was still a nervous bubble in my stomach at the prospect of failing. Failing Darcy. Failing myself. I knew that feeling and I wasn't interested in experiencing it again.

"Harley!" Cecilia screamed from the door, and I nearly fell off my stool as Darcy and Jemma jumped in alarm.

"What? What's wrong? What's happened?" I asked.

"You tell me?!" She grabbed me by the shoulders and shook. "Did he think about it? Is he going to do it?"

"Is who going to do what?" Jemma looked between us.

"Jake!" Cecilia squeaked.

"Harley's Jake?" Darcy said, pointing at me.

"Jake *Davenport*." Cecilia had that teenage *I'm surrounded by idiots* tone.

Jemma blinked. "Is that your Jake?"

My Jake. I liked the sound of that far too much. "He is not *my* Jake. But Hunter's cousin, Jake, is Jake Davenport, yes."

"Oh, shit!" Jemma said, like it was just now occurring to her that she knew who he was. "The striker for Chelsea?"

"Yes!" Another squeal from Cecilia.

"How did I not put that together before now?" Jemma shook her head.

"I have no idea," I admitted. Of all the people I thought would recognize Jake, it was Jemma, being English and all, but then I figured maybe she wasn't a big soccer fan.

"Can we focus, please?" Cecilia waved her arms around. "Did he think about it?"

"Cecilia needs a coach for her soccer intensive and I may have suggested that Jake could help," I said, filling in the gaps for Jemma.

"And?!"

"And I didn't see him this morning, so I don't know if it's a yes or a no. Sorry, Cece."

She deflated. "I'll just get to work."

"You don't need to make that sound so bad, you know," Darcy said, and Cecilia tried to smile but it was uncharacteristically flat. I felt bad for not having an answer for her. Maybe I should have stayed home last night and talked the coaching thing through with him. I knew his knee-jerk response was no, but it could be really good for him, and he'd be helping out one of my favorite people, who currently looked like there was a bag of dead puppies at her feet.

He'd probably be at home right now. I could go and get an answer for her. But, despite telling Jemma and Darcy I was not twitchy, that was exactly how I was feeling. Twitchy and fucking unsettled. Which meant that I was not going home, not just yet.

Instead, I spent most of the day sitting in the park across the street from Cream and Sugar, reading a book. I couldn't remember the last time I'd done it, just let myself do nothing much of anything and it was so good. Why didn't I make more time to just read? Especially books that were as gloriously smutty as this one, Darcy was really onto something.

I paused with my key in the front door. I'd been avoiding coming home for a good portion of the day, but it was time to stop dragging my feet and face the hot man currently sleeping in the guestroom. Jake was my friend. My hot man friend who I very much wanted to have sex with, but probably shouldn't. I couldn't help what my vagina wanted.

With a slow breath, I pushed open the door and was met with the most incredible smell. Rosemary, garlic, and some kind of roasting meat had me salivating as I drifted through the apartment like a cartoon character on sweet smelling fumes.

"Honey, I'm home ..." I said as I slid into the kitchen and stopped short when I found Jake standing over the stove with my pinkest, frilliest apron adorning his chest. *Oh my*. I wasn't the greatest cook, but when I took a turn around the kitchen, I liked to look the part. Jake, however, looked better in my apron than I ever had—it was unsettlingly hot. Why the hell did I think it would be Hunter in here cooking?

Jake turned, a beer in one hand and a disarming smile on his face. Something decidedly gooey—and not just sexy— happened in my chest. Shit.

"Hey, hi, you're cooking."

"I am, I figured that would be okay ... there's another pint of double chocolate Belgian fudge in the freezer for you, too."

I whistled. "Ice cream and a home cooked meal—are you trying to seduce me, Mr Davenport?" Oh lord, why did I just say that? I was tempted to slap a hand over my mouth, but the damage was done.

His eyes went wide. "No—what? I—no. I'm not—there is no seduction here, I was—I'm cooking. Just cooking."

"Just cooking?" I needed to shut my mouth, right now, before I said anything else that got me in trouble. "Well, it smells amazing."

"Thank you. It's not quite done yet."

"Means I've got time for a shower?" I didn't need a shower but, if it got me out of this room, I'd have one. Preferably cold.

"You certainly do."

I scurried down the hall, trying to get myself under control. Jake was cooking—something I found extremely attractive on a man. Liam had been a great cook, even when the average diet of a nineteen-year-old was ramen noodles and cheap beer. He still ate ramen noodles, but they were the best goddamn ramen noodles I'd ever tasted.

Slamming the bathroom door behind me, I went to the mirror. My cheeks were all pink, my eyes were wide, and there was a distinct, bubbly feeling going on in my chest. It was freaking me the fuck out. I wasn't used to this feeling, and there was a part of me that whispered it was a betrayal. To Liam. To what we had. No one had come close to making me feel this way since him. And I definitely didn't feel this way with Jake the first time. So, what the hell was going on now?

Did I even want to know?

Did I want to dig into this feeling with a man who didn't have a life in the same city as me? In the same *country* as me? Jake was going back to London. I was staying in New York. There was no future for us now, just like there hadn't been a future for us twelve years ago. So why the hell was I getting all... tangled about it? It was frustrating.

I turned away from the mirror. I just needed to shove all of this deep, deep down and be cool. Put on the happy Harley mask. I could do that.

STELLA'S AUTHOR

15

JAKE

I wasn't trying to seduce Harley. Not intentionally, anyway. But if cooking her dinner meant we'd get to eat together, which might appear somewhat date-ish, then I wasn't complaining either.

"He's finally made himself comfortable," Hunter crooned as he walked into the kitchen. He grabbed a drink from the refrigerator and leaned against the counter beside me, gazing into the pot I was stirring. "Dude, that smells fucking amazing."

"And you smell like pussy." It wasn't strictly true, he smelled like sex—but potayto-potahto. I didn't need to ask what he'd been doing since we parted ways at the basketball court earlier.

"I bet I do," he said. "Willow. Former gymnast, current yoga instructor, I have never seen a body move like hers."

"It's Will-a," Harley said. "Not Willow."

"Right, yes, Willa. Do not judge me, Harls. You sleep with more people than I do." A spike of something hot and angry hit me square in the chest.

"And yet I still manage to remember their names." Harley brushed it off with a serene smile.

Hunter turned his attention back to me. "I didn't know you could cook."

I shrugged because, honestly, neither did I. My attempts at cooking in the past weren't bad, they just weren't that great either. But then, not much cooking was required when you had a nutritionist planning ninety percent of your meals and eating out for the rest.

"Guess I was in the mood to try something new."

"Our little boy is growing up ..." Harley said. She tried to pinch my cheek, but I swatted her away. "How is Willa?"

"Fine."

"Sounded a lot better than fine a minute ago. *I have never seen a body move like hers* ... that's what you said."

"You are a creepy eavesdropper, you know that?"

"I am no such thing. You talk too loudly. Anyway, why only fine? Inquiring minds want to know." She pulled two bottles of wine from the fridge, one white, one rosé. "Which one?" She asked me.

"The rosé."

"All day." The bottle of white was put back and she grabbed two glasses, hesitating on a third. "Are you staying or going, Mr Things-with-Willa-are-fine?"

"Going. And there's really nothing to tell about Willa—like I said, things are fine. I don't think we'll see each other again."

Harley bumped the refrigerator closed with her hip and watched Hunter for a long moment. "You like someone else," she said.

He frowned. "What?"

She abandoned the wine bottle. "You like someone! Who is it?!"

"Have I missed something?" I asked, looking between the two of them.

"Harley likes to think she's psychic."

"My level of psychic ability notwithstanding ... you're into someone and you're deflecting."

"You're psychic?" Honestly, I wasn't even surprised. If anyone I knew was going to be psychic—or think they were—it was Harley.

"I don't like to put a label on it, but I have a strong intuitive sense, and I trust it implicitly."

"And your intuitive sense is telling you Hunter is into someone?"

"That's correct." We both turned to him. "Who is she?" Harley added.

"I'm showering," he said without looking at her, then escaped down the hall.

Harley watched him go, eyes narrowed, and started mumbling to herself as she went back to her task and poured two glasses of rosé. "He'll crack soon enough," she said, handing me a glass.

"How do you know? You might be wrong."

"Unlikely." It was difficult to fault her confidence. "Cheers." Our glasses clinked.

Harley started to clear the table—of what looked like mostly her things—before setting it for dinner. Dinner for two. I'd be lying if I said I hadn't thought about eating dinner with her when I started cooking, but it wasn't the only motivator. I'd also wanted something to do with my hands and to occupy my mind—it was more effective than I anticipated. Now, though, as I watched Harley swaying around the kitchen collecting plates and cutlery, humming along to fifties jazz I put on earlier, I was forced to admit that perhaps I'd made a mistake.

Because this all felt very domestic, very natural, if I was

being honest. I wanted to lean into it, into this feeling of what could have been. I didn't let myself think of it often, or at all, really, but right now it was difficult to stop the thoughts as they rolled in.

What would have happened if I'd told Harley how I felt all those years ago? For all I knew, she'd felt the same and, like me, was too scared to put herself out there.

What if …? What if …? What if …?

I watched from the corner of my eye as she shimmied to the refrigerator and collected ingredients for a salad. Could I let myself just be here, without questioning it, without reading anything into it, without letting my heart get involved, again? It was hard to say, but I was willing to try.

I could give myself—give us—this one night.

We settled at the table with my lamb and Harley's salad, and she grinned at me, like this was the most normal thing in the world. Maybe for her it was, maybe for her there weren't any thoughts of what if this, or what if that. Whatever the case, I couldn't deny how much I enjoyed being the one she smiled at like that.

I waited with some trepidation as she sliced off a piece of lamb and the fork made its way to her mouth. It had been a risky choice, and difficult to find, but after being introduced to lamb in London it quickly became one of my favorite meats.

"This is so good!" she said around a mouthful; relief and pride bloomed in my chest. I was glad I went to three butchers to find it.

"Thank you."

"Seriously, you can cook, Jake." What I could do was follow instructions, but I accepted the compliment with a nod all the same.

Harley wasn't wrong; the lamb was excellent. Part of me was surprised I'd actually managed to pull it off. After a few silent minutes of eating, I felt her watching me and glanced up from my plate.

"So ..." Harley said.

"So ..." I echoed.

"Did you give any thought to the coaching thing?"

My fork paused halfway to my mouth as my stomach flipped. Because, yes, I had been thinking about it and I hadn't come up with a single solid reason why I should say no. Rather than admit that, I shoved the forkful of meat and salad into my mouth and chewed. Harley grinned like she knew exactly what I was doing.

"I've never coached before," I said eventually.

She sipped her wine and shrugged. "There's a first time for everything."

"I'd be a shit coach."

"How do you know if you've never tried?"

"Just a feeling."

"Could be a bullshit feeling, though. What else are you going to do?" And I guess that was the million-dollar question. Not just while I was in New York, but if I returned to London—whoa, *if*? If I returned to London? That wasn't an *if* it was a *when*, right? Returning to London wasn't a question. Or it hadn't been anyway.

"All I'm saying is, you've got an image problem right now, and if you want to shed that asshole tag then maybe helping out a group of high schoolers in their time of need isn't such a bad idea. Could make for some wholesome content, too."

"It's all about that content, huh?"

She poked her tongue out. "Not all—the wholesome content is a happy side effect."

"And if I am bad at it? Coaching."

"Then you're bad at it. But, for the record, I don't see how you could be bad at it. Also, it's only for a few weeks."

"Six is longer than a few. And it's a long time to be doing something you're no good at."

"Ah, but maybe you get better at it the more you do it—and if it's with a bunch of girls like Cece, it'll be fun. She is one of my all-time favorites."

"She certainly seemed like a character."

Harley nodded. "It also has the added bonus of keeping you in touch with the sport that has always been a huge part of your life," she said, eyes darting to me and then back to her plate. "An indefinite suspension sounds rough."

We hadn't talked about why I was here, but I wasn't surprised that Harley had done some digging. I'd done my own digging, too. "You been looking me up?"

"I am a naturally curious person."

"Along with being psychic."

"That's right. It must be hard, losing something that you love, something that's such an integral part of you."

"It's not just a part of me, it is me." It was both frightening and depressing all at once. If I was nothing without football, if it was the only thing that made me *me*, what the fuck was I supposed to do without it? Who was I without it? I'd never let myself think about what came after playing. I'd never considered myself patient enough to coach. I guess this was an opportunity to find out.

Harley didn't acknowledge the statement, but I could practically see her wheels turning. "And they gave you no indication of when you could go back and play?"

I shrugged, recalling the conversation with Art. *Get your shit together, Davenport.* It wasn't exactly a timeline.

"When I have removed my head from my ass—at the very earliest."

She chuckled, eyes roaming my face. "Well, from where I'm sitting you look like you're doing okay in that department."

"Thank you."

"You're welcome."

I took a long gulp from my wine, feeling uncomfortably exposed as we watched one another. We might still be talking about the shitshow that was my career, but the air between us had shifted, had turned warm and alive.

Was she thinking about the kiss? Or further back ... all those nights wrapped up in one another. Had she missed me in those first few months, like I'd missed her? Like a part of herself was lost? That feeling had eased—eventually—but now I was here and, looking at her, it was clear that it never truly went away. I just got better at ignoring it, finding the right distractions. Would it be like that again this time? Getting on the plane back to London with a hole in my chest? As much as I had tried to tell myself otherwise, I had fallen in love with her twelve years ago. Would I again? Had I ever really stopped?

Whatever the case, I'd walked away and forgotten about her once, I could do it again.

Not right now, though. Right now, I could stay here and talk to her a little longer.

"Anyway, that's enough about me and the mess I've made of my life. What about you?"

Harley blinked. "What about me?"

"Well, my career is pretty much over, but you've got an opportunity to take yours to the next level ..."

"My job is just fine as it is." Job, not career. I didn't miss the distinction.

My pause was loaded, and I was pretty sure she wanted to throw a cherry tomato at my head.

"Why don't you want to do those Coffee Championships?"

"I'm doing them." So defensive.

"You are," I conceded. "But you don't want to—how come?"

She chewed on the question along with her salad. She

didn't want to talk about it, that much was clear, but I was pretty sure she was still going to. All I had to do was wait her out.

"I just—I guess I don't see the point."

"I would have thought the point was proving you make the best coffee in New York?" I said, daring her to disagree.

"I don't need to prove that I make the best coffee in New York. My customers already know it, that's what matters to me. Darcy makes out like we're all hard up for business, but we were out of control busy after Dallas and Duke's wedding."

My fork paused halfway to my mouth. "Should I know who those people are?"

"Duke Prince, the actor?" The name tickled a memory somewhere in the back of my brain, but Harley was still talking. "Anyway, it was out of control busy and now we've made it to this nice busy-but-still-chill spot, and she wants more. And I get that more customers equals more money, but there's a limit, you know? Or there should be. Or maybe I'm just being naive, and I'd think differently if it was my business. But it's not my business, obviously. And I don't want it to be my business. Who needs that stress, right? I—I don't know. Sorry, I didn't mean to unload all that on you."

"All good, I'm the one who asked."

"That's true," she said with a small smile. "Maybe it's my own fault."

"Sorry, you lost me, what's your own fault?"

"My skill with coffee." When I didn't answer right away, she added, "To be part of the Coffee Champs you need to be nominated."

"And you've been nominated?"

"A few times."

I was failing to see the problem. "That's good, isn't it?"

"Yes. And no. I don't know."

"You lost me, again."

She blew out a breath. "It's this big opportunity, right, which—is it just a big opportunity to fail?"

"Harley—"

"And I know that's ridiculous," she rushed. "I know it is. And I want to support Darcy. But I, just ... it's a lot."

"But if things are already going well, if you have nothing to prove, what have you got to lose?"

I could see the question rolling around in her head. She was quiet for so long I figured she was done talking.

"What if I'm not good enough?" The words were so low I almost missed them. And they were like a knife right to the chest. She didn't think she was good enough? I wanted to flip this table and tell her that she was enough. More than enough. She was exactly as much as she needed to be. Not a bit more. Not a bit less. She was Harley and she was fucking perfect.

But I didn't say any of it. Every word was lodged in my throat.

Harley shook out her shoulders, refusing to look at me. "It's a lot of pressure, you know? And it ..." The sentence trailed off.

"Harley—"

"It's fine," she said, swallowing heavily. What was she so scared of? Did she not see what everyone else did? That she was this incredible ray of fucking light that literally every single person couldn't help but gravitate toward? How could I tell her that without sending her running? She already looked like she was a second away from bolting.

I just needed her to stay.

"I'll do the coaching," I said, desperate for anything that would stop her from getting up right now. Her head bounced up but I didn't give her a chance to say anything just yet. "I'll do the coaching, on one condition ..."

Her eyes narrowed. "And what's that?"

"That you hear me when I say you're enough, Harley. You're enough now, right now, just as you are. You're enough if you win the Coffee Championships, if you lose, if you decide not to compete at all. You don't need to change or be anything other than yourself. Y–you're perfect."

Harley watched me, her face uncharacteristically blank before a smile took over her face and my heart beat so hard I was sure she'd be able to see it.

"So, will I be doing the coaching?" I asked, because the silence was threatening to choke me.

She nibbled her lip. "You certainly will."

Harley was singing in the kitchen when I got back from my run the following morning. It had been a long one—further than I'd run in years, probably—but discovering new streets and corners of Brooklyn made me keep going well past the point of comfort. My legs were deadweights, and my lungs were burning, but I felt good. And I was grateful for the distraction after last night, I could still see the look on Harley's face when she asked in that tiny voice—*what if I'm not good enough?*

Then I told her she was perfect.

That showed more of my soft underbelly than I would have liked.

The singing and dancing suggested that vulnerable Harley was no longer at the wheel this morning.

"I bet you're one of those people who looks really effortless when they run, aren't you? Like you're in a Nike commercial, or something." She was in a pair of those tiny sleep shorts and a tank that didn't quite meet them. That slice of skin between the two was going to drive me mad. Friends, wasn't it? We were friends. I couldn't say I'd ever wanted to taste a friend's pussy before, though, so that was new.

I kicked off my shoes and went directly to the refrigerator, guzzling down half a bottle of water to bring back some moisture to my throat and douse the heat now rolling under my skin —heat that had nothing to do with my run. "Good morning to you, too." I tossed my sweat-soaked cap onto the counter, my shirt followed.

"Aren't you making yourself at home, shirtless in the kitchen?"

I thoroughly enjoyed the way her eyes roamed over my chest, appreciative and hungry. "That a problem?"

"Not for me," she said with a wink. Yep, flirty Harley was definitely in charge of proceedings right now. Good to know. "You want coffee?"

"Sure."

She pulled a jar from the refrigerator; it was like the one Hunter drank directly from yesterday, only there were no death threats scrawled across the front. "Hunter likes to think that he's being all sneaky and rebellious by drinking the one that literally says *do not drink me*." Dark curls bounced as she shook her head. "He's so predictable." She lined up two glasses, threw some ice in each, and topped it with the coffee. "Creamer?"

"A little." I took a sip; it was really fucking good. "Is the other one the same?"

"Depends on my mood. Sometimes I mix up instant to punish him." A grin. I knew she wasn't all bark. The noise she made as she took a sip made my balls tighten.

I cleared my throat and found a spot on the counter that required my undivided attention. These were all very unfriendly thoughts. It wasn't my fault, though—I knew how that sound tasted as it vibrated against my tongue.

Would it be so bad for me to taste it again?

16

HARLEY

Jake's chest was glistening with sweat. Not a lot of it, not *too* much, just the right amount. Now, all I needed to do was stop staring at it and make my brain focus on breakfast.

After last night I decided to make us breakfast as a thank you. Both for Jake cooking me dinner, and the rest.

So, I was making French toast. It couldn't be too hard, could it? It was just bread soaked in eggs.

Jake was all casual and hot as he watched me get myself set up. Bowl. Eggs. Bread. Spices. Sugar. I flicked on the oven for the bacon—a trick I learned from Darcy, who was the reigning Queen of breakfast.

"Cream or milk?"

"What have you got?"

I narrowed my eyes. "Do you always answer a question with a question?"

His smile was lopsided and unexpectedly loaded. What was I doing, again? Flirty Jake was making it difficult to concentrate.

French toast. I was making French toast.

"So, what's your secret ingredient?" he asked, moving half a step toward me.

"Secret ingredient?"

"For your French toast."

I snorted and cracked the eggs into my bowl, before adding a glug of cream and a dash of vanilla. Was there an actual ratio for these things? Possibly. Probably. Could I look up a recipe? Yes, but where was the fun in that? I retrieved a whisk from the drawer. "You will be the first to know, just as soon as I figure it out."

His coffee paused in midair as his jaw went momentarily slack. "You've never made this before, have you?"

Did I tell him that I'd attempted it while drunk and nearly set the kitchen on fire? Maybe not. "I've eaten it, that counts. French toast is bread and egg. It cannot be that difficult."

"Famous last words."

"Please turn down your enthusiasm ... it's distracting." I poked my tongue out and returned my attention to the bowl.

"So, the secret ingredient is unqualified confidence?" Jake said, peering over my shoulder. It smelled good so far, a good sign.

"I take offense to the *unqualified*," I said with a pointed look. "But, in my experience, confidence is the secret ingredient to most things."

He dipped his head. I took it as an agreement, even if he didn't mean it that way.

Soon enough, we each had a plate loaded with French toast, bacon and strawberries, all drizzled in maple syrup.

"Good enough to eat," I said as we sat.

"That remains to be seen."

I sliced off a corner of French toast and shoved it into my mouth. It was sweet and cinnamony and altogether delicious.

Take that Jake Davenport. So much for unqualified confidence. I was a goddamn natural!

Jake took a bite of his and gagged. I threw a strawberry at him.

"It's good," he conceded.

"I know."

This was what I needed. A return to semi-normality after what turned into an unexpectedly intimate dinner. Was cooking meals for one another going to become a habit while he was still in New York? I couldn't say I hated it, if the answer was yes. Maybe it could become a friendly challenge?

Hunter and I, despite living together for years, had pretty much always had opposite schedules. He was in bed when I was leaving in the morning and by the time, I got home he was often gone. We were ships passing in the night. Which honestly suited both of us just fine, because it meant that we always had enough space. I'd been told people needed space from me—I was, apparently, a lot. Too loud. Too wild. Too happy (like it was a bad thing, but also these people didn't know me at all). Too this. Too that. Too *everything*.

Once upon a time, it might have bothered me, but it didn't anymore. All the toos were just me. And if that bothered someone, they were more than welcome to go and find less. Liam had never made me feel like I was too much. Neither had Jake, come to think of it. Perfect. That's what he said last night. I couldn't quite wrap my mind around that.

I glanced across the table and found him watching me, an unreadable expression covering the blue-green oceans of his eyes. What would have happened if I didn't meet Liam? Would Jake and I have stayed in touch?

"So ..." he started, pushing a strawberry through the maple syrup lake that was left on his plate. "What are you up to today?"

"You angling for an invite?"

"Nevermind."

"Now that you mention it ... I do have something I need to deal with."

"What's that?"

"I have a hole in my heart."

He opened his mouth, closed it again, delightfully shocked. "Shit, Harley, that sounds serious. Were you—were you born with it?"

I nodded, holding onto my smile as best I could. "I don't know. But it is a hole that can only be filled by genuine 70s bell bottoms and a crochet halter top."

The look on his face morphed from concern to flat and unimpressed in point-two of a second. "Ah, so this is less a medical concern than a fashion one." He popped the last piece of strawberry into his mouth, and I tried to ignore the way his tongue darted out to catch the stray drop of maple syrup on his lower lip. He would taste absolutely delicious right now.

I cleared my throat. "Let's not trivialize it."

"Heaven forbid."

"Do you thrift?" I asked.

"Is thrift a verb?"

"Are you an ass?"

He laughed, loud and long, with his hands in his hair. My fingers twitched. If I had a pencil, I would have captured every angle on paper. With only a fork in one hand and a knife in the other, I was forced to settle for memorizing them instead. Part of me hated that he was even hotter now than he had been at twenty. There wasn't much softness about him, even then, he was all lines and angles—it was part of the reason I'd loved to draw him so much—but he'd grown into them now, they were longer, sharper, perfect.

"I can't say that I do thrift, no," he said, and I blinked to clear the lusty haze that had settled across my eyes. Right, we were talking about thrifting.

"Everyone should. Actually ... if everyone did then I wouldn't find nearly as many gems as I do. So, maybe just some people—more people—fuck fast fashion, is what I'm saying, you know?"

"And the 70s is your decade of choice?"

"I don't limit myself to just one decade, when there are so many to revel in. I go where the vibe takes me." It was my basic life philosophy.

"And, today, the vibe is taking you to the 70s?"

"Yes, it is." I tapped my phone, turning up the 70s gold playlist which, until this point, had been whispering through the apartment. "Where is it going to take you?"

"The vibe?"

"Yeah, where's it taking you?"

"I guess we'll have to wait and see."

"I guess we will."

I stuffed my feet into an old pair of Vans and waited by the door for Jake. One of the many things I'd noticed about him since he first arrived: he took long showers. Really. Long. Showers. I managed to braid my hair and discard three outfits before the water finally shut off. I tried not to think of what he was doing in there, but it was useless thanks to my overactive imagination. I had an all too vivid visual of him standing under the spray, water running over his broad chest and down.

Down.

Down.

Down.

I nibbled my lip, letting my mind wander. Would he jerk off in there? Considering I'd been letting my fingers wander most days, I had a feeling that the answer was yes. Would he start slow? One hand drifting down over his abs, through the soap suds streaking his torso, to grab his already hard cock. What I wouldn't give to watch that show ... maybe join him. It was fine in the fantasy.

"Harley!"

I jumped. "Yes! What?"

Jake was standing in front of me looking highly amused. His t-shirt made his eyes look ridiculously blue. "You were zoned way out. What were you thinking about?"

"Me? Nothing. Crochet."

"Crochet?"

"Yep. Are you ready? I thought you changed your mind."

"I have a routine."

"Is that what you call it?" Nope, I was not going to allude to him jerking off in my shower. That was a truly terrible idea. "Let's roll," I said, because I needed to get us the hell out of the apartment immediately.

I took a slow breath as soon as we were out on the street, letting the fresh air settle my jangling nerves. It was a mistake to think about him in the shower—I would not be making it again. Lesson. Learned.

It was one of those days that made me love New York even more than usual. Sunny, but not too warm, the slightest breeze, and everyone was happy. It was difficult to be anything else when the weather was like this. It made me want to plan more trips out of the city. More hikes. More beach days. More exploring. This would be the summer of adventure.

Jake and I walked side by side through the late morning crowds that were milling on the sidewalk. I stepped around a mom with a toddler stopping every two seconds to point out something or other. What must life be like when you were that new to the world? When you were seeing everything for the first time? Look at that flower, that rock, that leaf. There was nowhere you needed to be. You were just experiencing life, being amazed by it at every turn. Imagine seeing the sun for the first time! A vibrant blue sky. Even rain would be magic.

"What's that smile for?" Jake asked, nudging my arm with his elbow.

"Just thinking about what it would be like if you were seeing things for the first time."

"What things?"

"Everything. Imagine waking up one morning and looking out the window and just seeing it all, the birds, the trees, the people."

"That would be pretty unreal."

"Totally unreal. I'd love to know what babies are thinking." At his quizzical look I added, "Because they're literally seeing everything for the first time, learning how the world works. Bananas, right?"

"Bananas," he echoed with a smile.

"We're here."

Modern Thrift was one of my favorite stores in Brooklyn because not only did it always have an outstanding selection, but the staff were amazing and set aside pieces they knew I'd like—that was customer service.

I led the way inside and immediately spotted Claudia behind the counter. She waved from her perch on a yellow, vintage diner stool, her red hair was cropped close on the side, but her curls ran rampant everywhere else. She was dressed in a powder blue boiler suit with Hank stitched over her left breast and Boss Bitch over the right.

"Thank god you're here. This skirt came in yesterday and it was literally screaming your name. I set it aside, but then I caught Sandy trying to abscond with it at closing yesterday."

"Bitch."

"When you see it, you'll understand."

"Don't leave me in suspense."

Claudia jumped off her stool and skipped down the aisle toward the fitting room and staff area.

"So," I started sweeping my arm in a wide arc. "Welcome to Modern Thrift. Over here you will find mens, this side is womens. Fitting rooms are up the back. What size pants do you wear?"

He frowned. "Why do you need to know that?"

"Because we're going to choose outfits for one another, duh."

"Are we now?"

"You bet. Fifteen, twenty minutes perusal time and then we rendezvous at the fitting rooms for a fashion show. What do you think?"

"I think I'm going to regret coming here with you."

"That's the spirit. Let's synchronize our watches!"

"I don't have a watch."

"Neither do I, but I've always wanted to say that."

Jake shook his head and laughed. "Are there any parameters to what we can choose?"

I considered the question, tapping my cheek. "No parameters, per se. But we're making a few stops today ... so I think we also choose one mystery item at each store and then, when we get home later, we each have to wear whatever the other person chose out for one drink tonight."

"I am not agreeing to that."

"Why not!?"

"Because I have no idea what you'll pick. Or, rather, I do know what you'll pick and that is infinitely more concerning."

"Come on, Davenport, live a little."

17

JAKE

Come on Davenport, live a little.

The look on Harley's face was full of friendly challenge. As much as I did not trust her as far as I could throw her—maybe even half that when it came to her choosing clothing for me—I had never been one to back down from a challenge. It was one of my issues.

I crossed my arms over my chest, and she grinned, already sure I was about to say yes. Of course, I was going to say yes, but I pretended to think on the idea a little longer.

"Fine, you're on," I said eventually, and she *whooped*, doing a shimmy of excitement.

"See you in twenty minutes!" And with that she bounded off into the men's section. To select clothing. For me.

Lord, help me. What the hell did I just agree to?

Rather than let myself think too much on what Harley was choosing—the most ridiculous items in the place, if I had to guess—I turned my attention to what I could find for her. One of the more frustrating things about this assignment was, even if I chose something either hideously ugly, or highly embarrassing, Harley would wear whatever it was with the unflappable confidence of a runway model.

Actually, I'd known a few runway models and I was pretty sure Harley had more confidence than they did. She was so comfortable in her own skin, so unapologetically herself in all ways. It was enviable, really.

Or it would be, if I wasn't up against her in this thrift store challenge. I should have asked more questions ... like did we have any chances to veto items? Because if she came at me with chaps, I was not putting those bad boys on. No fucking way.

Three racks later and nothing was jumping out aside from a crochet sweater vest that was orange, brown, and white with tiny yellow flowers all over it. It practically screamed Harley, so naturally I needed to pick it up.

I moved onto a new rack and then I saw them, buried among a bunch of jeans. After a brief check to make sure Harley wasn't watching I pulled them free. They looked like yoga pants, only with a frill on each hip, and silver paw prints on both knees. And they were metallic pink. I had no idea if they'd actually fit her but there was no way I could leave them here.

Mystery item number one: found.

The twenty minutes went by in a whirlwind and before I knew it I was approaching the fitting rooms and a grinning Harley, swinging back and forth on her heels. What on earth did she have hidden behind her back?

"So ... how did you go?" she asked, eyes running over the items I was holding. I made sure the metallic pants were well out of sight.

"Just fine, and you?" From what I could see, there were no chaps. A good sign. There was, however, a bright purple shirt covered in pineapples wearing sunglasses—and it looked at least two sizes too small.

"The pineapples really spoke to me," she said as she saw me looking at it.

"Oh, yeah? What exactly did they say?"

"They whispered your name. Over and over. Jake. Jake. Jake. Jake." She stepped closer each time she said my name until we were nearly toe to toe.

"I bet they did," I croaked. "What else have you got?"

"I'll show you mine if you show me yours." She wagged her eyebrows, and I couldn't stop my answering smile. It would be a lot easier to keep my shit together if she wasn't so fucking cute.

"Okay, how do we do this?"

She tossed her pile of clothing into one of the two fitting rooms. "You go in here. I'll be right next door. Now, hand over your goodies."

"You sound like a pervy uncle at Christmas."

She cackled with laughter. "Oh boy, your family holidays sound like a treat."

I tossed her the things I found and stepped into my fitting room.

"You found me bell bottoms!" she squealed from the other side of the curtain.

"I couldn't leave you with that hole in your heart, now, could I?" I'd also found what looked like a crochet halter top but was going to keep that a secret just a little longer.

"You're a good one, Jake, don't let anyone tell you otherwise."

I ignored the warmth that spread through me in response. It was time to see what she found.

There were three full outfits. Along with the pineapple shirt, there was also a black turtleneck sweater with a wolf pack howling at the moon on the front—was she serious?—and a red cowboy shirt with white fringing across the chest. And, for the pants, a pair of bell bottom blue jeans—looked like we'd be matching—some shorts so tiny I wasn't sure they would cover my ass, and red pants that also had fringing—to go with the shirt, obviously.

Oh boy.

What to try on first? Nothing, preferably. I would like to throw open the curtain and march straight out onto the street. But I wouldn't, because then Harley would be disappointed, and I already knew I didn't want to disappoint her. I was a sucker now, just like the first time.

"Pineapples first!" she called.

"And do you have a vision of what they'd best go with?" I asked, pulling my shirt over my head and toeing off my shoes.

"I can see them with the shorts or the bell bottoms." There was a pause, and I could imagine her shimmying out of her dress. The curtain between us fluttered. "No, the shorts, definitely the shorts."

I held up the offending item. They were neon green and teeny-tiny. "Harley, these shorts are not going to fit."

"Oh, they'll fit," she said and then started cackling hysterically. Did I miss something? She hadn't even seen me in them, and she was already laughing—it did not bode well. But I wasn't going to back down now; I had my honor to maintain. My dignity, however, was about to go out the window with smiling pineapples wearing sunglasses. Who the hell would have purchased this shirt? And why?

The pineapple shirt didn't go past my belly button, and I could only do up two buttons. But I got the thing on, so I marked that as a success. The shorts, however, were so tight you could make out the veins on my fucking dick.

"Get out here, Davenport."

I glanced down at myself. "Do I have to?"

"Yes, you have to! Get out here!"

I popped my head out of the curtains, keeping my body

obscured. Harley was standing there, in sunshine yellow crochet booty shorts and the crochet sweater vest. Those things would have looked ridiculous on anyone else. But not on her. She was fucking adorable.

I, on the other hand, could have been an extra on a low-rent 80s porn set.

"Seriously, Harley, I'm not—I can't—"

"Just get out here!" She reached through the flimsy curtain, took hold of the front of my shirt and yanked me forward. "Oh, my god! The pineapples are perfect!"

"Are they?"

"Yes!" She took a step back to take my outfit in properly. "I told you they'd fit." Her eyes made a swift trip down before they bounced back up to my face, heat simmering behind them.

"Okay, next!"

I was unceremoniously shoved back into the small, curtained cubicle.

The cowboy ensemble was worse than the neon green shorts. Red, apparently, was not my color.

"Yee-ha!" Harley hollered as I stepped out then smothered a laugh with her hand. "That is terrible."

"Thank you, so much."

"What about me?" She lifted the corners of her purple skirt and curtsied. Once again, she looked incredible. The shirt was a lighter shade of purple than the skirt and the sleeves were so wide you could fit a watermelon in each one. Was there nothing she couldn't pull off?

"You look ..."

"Like a lavender fairy, yes, I know. This one—not your best work, I'll be honest. That first one, though, I'll be wearing that tomorrow. Ready for the final one?"

"As I'll ever be."

She skipped back into her fitting room with a flourish,

flicking the curtain closed behind her. I stepped back into mine, happily tearing the shirt off. I was already itchy, and it was about to get worse because next up was the howling wolf turtleneck. That thing was pure polyester.

And it was awful. Made worse by the skintight bell bottoms.

"You've out done yourself," I said.

Harley did a happy dance, this time unable to smother her laugh. "The wolves—"

"Are ridiculous," I finished for her.

"Are *amazing*."

"I have questions: one, who makes something like this thinking it will sell. Two, what kind of person buys it?"

"Both valid questions."

"I thought so." I adjusted myself, trying to give my dick some relief from the suffocating denim.

Harley's bell bottoms were miles too long, but aside from that fit her surprisingly well. And matched with a Mr Happy shirt she was a 70s dream girl. *My* dream girl.

We visited two more thrift stores. At each one we indulged in a fashion show of the best and worst things we could find; and, of course, we continued to collect our mystery items, which would be revealed later on. I was exceedingly pleased with mine.

"I'm starving," Harley said, looping her arm through mine as we left the third and final thrift store. "Let's eat."

"Sounds good."

I was towed to a hole in the wall Korean spot that smelled so good my mouth started watering the second we walked in the door. Harley shoved our bags under the narrow table and we sat. She didn't even bother to look at a menu, just waved over a waitress and rattled off an order.

"So, come on, admit it—you had fun."

I chewed the inside of my cheek to keep from smiling too soon. "It was okay."

"Okay! Just okay?!" She slapped the table. "You were enjoying yourself, I saw it! Look!" Her phone was turned in my direction and on the screen was a photo of me. I was smiling, wide and genuine, my thumbs stretching out the striped suspenders I had on. I told Harley I didn't need them—because when the fuck was I going to wear a pair of suspenders—but I was pretty sure she bought them for me, anyway.

"Alright, you got me, I had fun."

"I knew it!" She snapped a photo as another waitress delivered some water to the table along with a couple of bottles of something else.

"What's this?" The label was in Korean but there were strawberries. The other had what looked like plums.

'Delicious, that's what it is." She uncapped both, tapped the neck of hers against mine. "Cheers."

"Cheers." It was sweet—so sweet it set my teeth on edge—but she was right, it was delicious.

We sat in silence for a few minutes sipping our too sweet drinks and watching one another. I wanted to know what she was thinking. What secrets hid behind those whiskey eyes?

"I am going into work tomorrow, and you know that Cecilia is going to ask ..."

"About the coaching."

"Ding-ding. So, what's it gonna be?"

I took another sip to delay answering. "I still think I'm going to suck as a coach." Mostly. Maybe.

"But ..."

"But ..." God, was I really going to say yes? "I can't think of a reason to say no."

Harley squealed, drawing the attention of half the restaurant. "You have to be the one to tell her. She will die. Die!"

"Am I going to regret this?"

"No, absolutely not. In fact, I think it's going to be an enriching experience for you."

"Enriching, huh?"

"That's right. I think you're going to grow as a person and maybe even break out in some kind of heartfelt musical number before the six weeks are over." She looked far too amused by this suggestion.

"I hate you," I said, but it lacked heat.

She smiled. "No, you don't."

There would be no musical numbers, heartfelt or otherwise, but I'd be lying if I said part of me wasn't looking forward to the challenge. I'd worked with some incredible coaches over the years and learned from every one of them. What kind of coach would I be? Could I help these girls? Teach them something? As much as I didn't want to admit it to Harley, after some thought last night, this did feel like the right decision for me right now. It was a six weeks. I could give these girls a six weeks.

After that, who knew? But, for the next month and a half, I was going to be a coach. Assuming they still wanted me.

"I'm excited for you."

"Thank you, I think."

Her smile was particularly twinkly. "So, what else is there to Jake Davenport?"

"What else what?"

"What else aside from soccer—football, whatever."

"Nothing." And there it was, the depressing truth. All I'd ever wanted, all I'd ever needed, was football.

I'd never regretted the decision to drop out of college. I might have passed my classes, but I wasn't exactly passionate about a business degree. And then I was playing football professionally and nothing else mattered.

Harley laughed. "Come on, there has to be something else. No one is just one thing. We're all tapestries, made up of the people and things we love."

"Really?"

"Yes, really." She leaned forward. "So, come on, what else is in your tapestry?"

The arrival of our food gave me an excuse not to answer. Far too many plates for the space were squeezed onto our table. One was a vibrant mix of greens; broccoli, beans, and snow peas. Another was sizzling meat with more vegetables. Then there was blushing pink shrimp, a small bowl filled with bean shoots, and, finally, rice sprinkled with fried shallots.

It all smelled incredible. Garlic, ginger, and lemon grass dominated the fragrance but there were other things too, notes of chili and herbs. My mouth watered.

"This looks amazing." I glanced across the table at Harley as a piece of broccoli disappeared into her mouth. She hummed, bouncing in her chair in what I assumed was a happy dance.

"I fucking love this place," she said after she swallowed, spearing a piece of meat. "Don't think I won't try and eat all this alone."

That wasn't happening. I followed her lead and dove in. As soon as the first piece of food—a green bean—was in my mouth, I understood her happy dance and willingness to eat everything alone. It was outstanding.

I ate well past the point of feeling full because, holy shit, I just couldn't stop. Everything was so good, even the plain rice tasted better than any rice I'd ever eaten. What the hell did they do to it?

The conversation didn't come back around to Harley's

tapestry theory, instead she talked about anything and every-thing else. Cream and Sugar—her home away from home. Her brother, Murphy—a pain in her ass but she loved him anyway. Hunter's brewery—the next big thing, if she had anything to do with it. Roller-skating—which she was terrible at but was deter-mined to improve. I was getting a front row seat to the Harley show.

She threw her napkin down on the table and slumped in her chair. "Okay, I need to stop, or you will literally have to roll me home."

"There's nothing left."

"Well, it's a good thing I need to stop then, isn't it?" She winked as she stood and stretched her hands over her head. "Seriously, though, I need to walk. Let's move."

My phone rang as we stepped out onto the sidewalk. Blair.

"Who is Harley?" she asked before I'd even had a chance to say hello. I glanced around, the feeling of being watched crawling up the back of my neck. How did she even know about Harley?

"A friend," I said, my eyes finding the woman in question as she bounced along beside me, our bags of thrifted clothing swinging from each hand.

"Jake, I have known you for almost a decade. During that time, you've had a handful of actual friends, and at no point have any of them been female. Who is she, really?"

"She's Harley, and she's a friend."

Harley grinned at me. "Look at you, making us friend offi-cial." She punched my shoulder. "I knew I'd wear you down eventually."

I gave her a shove. "How did you—" I started before Blair cut me off.

"You should know by now that I know everything. I am omnipresent. Also, she's been posting photos of you on social media, I get the notifications when she tags you. That jumper with the wolf pack on it was really something." Harley did *not* post a photo of me in that. Who was I kidding? Of course, she did. I guess I should have been grateful it wasn't one in the shorts. Although, thanks to the blowjob selfie, the world had already seen my dick.

"You look happy," Blair said.

I suppose I was happy. Being around Harley, though sometimes frustrating, was surprisingly easy. Natural, even. It wasn't just Harley either. "I'm—"

"Happy," she repeated. "Maybe it's time for you to show a little more of yourself, Jake."

"Blair, we've talked about this."

"I know. I know we have, but things are calming down here and maybe, if we show the people that you're not a reclusive asshole, things will get even better. Show them you can be normal, fun, happy."

I didn't want to admit that Harley had basically said the same thing. Because the thought of putting more of myself out into the world still fucking scared me. I was picked apart enough in the media as it was, did I really want to give them more of me? Not only more, but parts that were private? Parts that I wanted to protect and hold close? What if I posted a photo of Harley and that put a target on her back, too? I didn't want to be responsible for that.

"Just think about it, okay?" Blair said, her voice softer now.

"Fine, yes, I'll think about it. Was that all?"

"No, actually, I had an interesting call yesterday."

"Oh-kay..."

"From Tomas Posey."

"As in Man City Tomas Posey?" That was unexpected.

"The very same."

Why was she drawing this out? Was she trying to kill me with anticipation? "And are you going to tell me what he said?"

"He wanted to see if you were interested in discussing coaching opportunities."

I stuttered a step, my eyes darting to Harley. "Coaching?"

"Mm-hm, he did preface the offer by saying your playing days were probably over and you'd be lucky for them to take you because they're not scared of a little press. The jackass. It's still interesting, though."

"What did you tell him?"

"That I'd speak to you, but coaching wasn't currently on your radar." Not until the last couple of days, anyway. I wanted to tell Blair about the high school coaching but that was going to be a larger conversation, one I'd rather not have with Harley skipping along beside me. I squeezed the back of my neck, feeling tension coiling there. Coaching at Man City. It piqued my interest more than I expected it to.

"Indeed." She paused. "But I did tell him you were on vacation, so there's no need to rush an answer. We can discuss it properly when you get home."

Home. She meant London, obviously, but London wasn't home. I wasn't sure it ever had been, not even after six years. That was another thing I wasn't about to get into right now.

"Thanks, Blair."

"Just doing my job. Well done keeping your dick in your pants, by the way." The smile in her voice was bright.

I laughed. "Just doing *my* job."

"Keep it up." And she was gone. I pocketed my phone and tugged on the peak of my ball cap.

"I need ice cream," Harley said, breaking through my introspection.

I glanced sideways at her. "I thought you were so full I was going to have to roll you home?" In only two short weeks,

Harley and Hunter's apartment had come closer to feeling like home than London ever had. That should probably concern me, but I'd ignore it for the moment.

She hooked her arm through mine. Home. "My savory stomach is full. My sweet stomach is wide open."

"You know you don't actually have two stomachs, right?"

"I think of it more of a division, half savory, half sweet. Or maybe it's a stomach goblin, who sits there directing food."

"You're odd."

"So I'm told—doesn't change the fact I need a triple scoop on a waffle cone though."

18

HARLEY

I was of the belief that ice cream had the power to fix anything.

Most things.

Some things.

The very occasional thing.

But, in the event a cold scoop of creamy sweetness couldn't literally fix a problem, it was a solid and delicious distraction.

Jake and I stepped up to the counter of Sweet Scoops and I peered through the rounded glass at the rows of frozen distraction—I mean perfection. What was I in the mood for? Mint choc-chip? Strawberries and cream? Orange creamsicle? Classic vanilla?

I peaked sideways at Jake, what kind of ice cream would he choose? Was it the same every time, or did his flavor choice depend on his mood?

When the blue-haired college student got to us I panic-ordered hazelnut, strawberry and cookies 'n' cream. Jake went with mint choc-chip, vanilla and mango. I had a feeling he panic-ordered also. Why else would you ever put mango with mint choc-chip?

"There were too many choices," he said, looking at his cone as we stepped back out onto the street.

"I usually order the same thing every time, but today I wanted to mix things up. I think the hazelnut was a mistake."

"Hazelnut is a solid choice," he assured me. "I don't know why I went with mango."

I laughed. "I knew that was a panic-decision!"

"It really was."

I took a tentative lick of hazelnut, which was delicious. It was hard to go too far wrong at Scoops. But now the decision making was over, my brain was able to focus on other things.

Blair.

Who the hell was Blair?

It was an irritatingly unisex name. But I prided myself on knowing people and the way Jake said it told me, in this case, it belonged to a woman, no question. A woman he was familiar with, cared for, trusted. There was warmth and teasing in his tone. Which shouldn't bother me, because Jake's relationship with mystery-woman Blair was absolutely none of my business. And yet, I couldn't deny the sharp spike of jealousy under my ribs. Especially when he called me his friend.

She's Harley, and she's a friend.

Why did mystery-woman Blair care who I was to Jake? Who was *she* to Jake? Not a sister, I knew he was an only child. Maybe another cousin? Not on Hunter's side, I knew pretty much the entire Buchanan family tree. She could just be a concerned friend, or perhaps the hot piece that kept his bed warm in London. Whatever the case, it wasn't any of my business. It didn't change the fact that he considered me a friend— just a friend—even after the brain melting kiss. The brain melting kiss that I still wasn't thinking about.

Friends.

That's what I wanted, wasn't it? To be Jake's friend. To

make Jake my friend. I'd done it. I'd succeeded. We were friends. So, why did I want to squash my ice cream right in his face and stomp off in a huffy huff? It was just because we'd had a good day together. The thrift shopping was highly successful, and Jake had been a good sport. He literally tried on every ridiculous item of clothing I picked for him, even the neon green shorts that I was pretty sure were supposed to be in the women's section. He put them on. He put them on and left the fitting room. He even submitted to me buying him the pineapple shirt, which made me stupid happy.

And he found some outstanding items himself. The crochet shorts and sweater vest combo were so good I'd worn them out of the last store.

That was the only reason I was feeling gooey—the pineapple shirt and a pair of crochet shorts. I was a simple girl at heart.

We wandered back in the direction of home, and I very much wished I hadn't said we needed to go out for a drink together later. More time around Jake was not what I needed right now—better to just let us both off the hook with our mystery items and retreat to our own rooms. Seeing him in the waistcoat I picked out for him was going to mean more temptation than I was capable of resisting right at the moment, so I would do the responsible thing and put myself on lockdown. In my room. *Alone.*

"I don't know why I let you talk me into that ice cream," Jake said as he crunched down the last bit of his waffle cone with a groan.

"You didn't have to eat the whole thing."

"Yes, I did." It was true. Not finishing a Sweet Scoops cone was an impossible task—it just kept calling to you until it was gone.

"Come on, then, my food coma is also calling."

The three flights of stairs up to my apartment had never felt quite as long as they did with Jake's presence at my back, raising the hairs at the nape of my neck and down my arms. I was just so *aware* of him whenever he was in the general vicinity. My body hummed like a tuning fork, like it was trying to match his frequency. It was a foreign feeling; as many people as I connected with on a physical level, and there were plenty, it was never like this.

Had it been this way before and I had somehow forgotten? It was difficult to imagine forgetting this, though. This was the kind of feeling that was branded onto your skin and your bones, the kind of feeling that once found you'd chase it down to the ends of the earth.

I let us inside and breezed past the kitchen, bee-lining for the solace of my bedroom, but I stopped to watch Jake collapse sideways onto the couch and then roll onto his back.

"I hope none of your mystery items are skintight, because I am sporting an ice cream baby right now," he said, rubbing his stomach, which still looked perfectly defined from where I was standing.

"Oh, please, that is not a food baby"—I dropped my bags onto the floor to properly cradle my rounded stomach—"*this* is a food baby." I rubbed it fondly and Jake laughed.

"What are you going to name it?"

"Hazelnut."

"Mine's Mango."

I laughed. "To remind us of the dangers of panic-ordering."

"Exactly."

I flopped into the armchair. "Who's Blair?" I hadn't meant to ask, but my curiosity got the better of me and I wasn't going to be able to focus on anything else until I knew.

Jake rolled his head to the side so he could look at me, a

smirk playing at the corners of his mouth. "Do I detect a hint of jealousy?"

"You do not," I scoffed. "Friends are not jealous of other friend's happiness. I was merely curious about her."

"How do you know it's a *her*?"

"Educated guess."

"That right?"

"Uh-huh." I shrugged and let my attention drift past Jake to the balcony so I wouldn't bore a hole in his head with my overly eager eyes. I shouldn't have asked. I should have kept my mouth shut and just let the mystery eat me alive from the inside out.

After a torturously long pause, Jake said, "Blair is my manager." My eyes snapped back to his and held. The intensity in his look sent a thrill down my spine.

His manager. Blair was his manager. It really was embarrassing how relieved I was, especially considering Jake was only my friend. He wasn't *mine* in any way that mattered. Nor did I want him to be.

"And is she a good manager?" I asked, because I needed to say something and *thank god* didn't seem like the right reaction, even though that was what I wanted to say. I also managed to squash the urge to do a small, seated happy dance.

"She is excellent at what she does, yes." The admiration in his tone made me smile.

"How long have you worked together?"

"Since the start of my career, pretty much—and hers. Most people told me I was mad when I said I was going with a manager who had no clients and no track record. I think most of them didn't like the fact she's a woman in a heavily male dominated industry. But I trusted her right away, unlike so many of the slimy assholes I'd met up to that point. It wasn't even a question for me —yes, she was untested, but she was also fearless and tenacious.

She drives me fucking crazy ninety percent of the time, but there's no one else I'd rather have in my corner." He paused. "She saw the photos you posted, that's why she called. To check in—and laugh at me for the wolf pack sweater. So, thank you for that."

"You're welcome." And she wanted to know who I was. To make sure I wasn't dragging him into another scandal, if I had to guess.

He lifted his cap and scratched his head, leaving a trail of hair spiked where the rest was flat. "She actually said the same thing as you."

"I like her already. But I say so much, so you'll have to narrow it down."

"About taking more ownership of my social media, showing the real me."

"She's right, you should listen to her."

"You mean you." A throw pillow came sailing at my head. I caught it.

"Well, if you take that particular piece of advice, you get to listen to both of us at the same time. It's a two-fer."

"Please remind me to never introduce the two of you."

"Maybe I'll introduce myself, slide into her DMs."

He shook his head but was still smiling. And now I knew that I needed to meet Blair. I wasn't kidding about sliding into her DMs.

"Okay, I think Mango has gone down enough. I'm ready for your mystery finds." He sat up.

Right, we were still doing that. And then going for a drink—at my insistence. It was probably still a bad idea when all those gooey feelings were persisting.

"That's okay—we don't—"

"You are not backing out, this was your idea."

"I know it was, you're not imaginative enough to come up

with it, and I'm not backing out of anything." I launched the throw pillow he'd tossed at me.

He cocked an eyebrow. "Sounds an awful lot like you are."

I straightened my back. "I am not."

"How about I give you a little something to get us started?"

"What kind of little something?"

"Think of it as a bonus find."

A bonus find? My curiosity was officially piqued. He reached for the bag at his feet, a flash of neon purpley-pink peeking out as he pulled it onto his lap. I leaned over the arm of my chair, eager to get a look at the goods. This was only going to cause me more problems, I could feel it.

"Are you ready?"

I leaned over a little further. "Yes! Give it to me, already!'

His smile was heady. Danger, Harley, that smile was danger.

"It's not much," he said, rummaging in his bag.

"Just hand it over, Jake!" I snatched the crumpled ball of fabric from his hands and flattened it on my thighs as I dropped back onto my butt. My eyes immediately welled up. It was a crochet halter top.

"I wasn't entirely sure what a halter top is ... but that's gotta be close, right?"

I sniffed, willing the emotion to subside so I could speak. A crochet halter top. He'd found me a white, crochet halter top. He listened. Not only did he listen, but he thought about me when he didn't have to. And that small gesture had my heart beating overtime.

"It's—is it wrong?"

I cleared my throat. "No, not wrong. It's perfect, actually, thank you."

"You're welcome—you want to see the rest?"

"You have set the bar exceptionally high, so yes, I definitely want to see the rest." Although going for a drink was now looking like an even worse idea than it was before.

"One thing at a time or all at once?"

I pursed my lips as I considered. "All at once. You first."

"Get ready to be blown away."

I nodded, keen to lighten this *feelings* mood that had struck me. "Hit me."

He stood, now towering over me in my puffy armchair. "First, I found these ..." A pair of what looked like yoga pants came out of the bag. Only they were metallic pink and had frills. Holy shit, they were incredible.

I rolled my lips together to keep from full-on grinning as he handed them over. There were silver paw prints on the knees.

"Oh my god," I squeaked, holding them up to examine them in all their glory. But I wasn't given too long to marvel at them because he was pulling something else out of the bag. Purple and blue tie-dye. It was a shirt, which he handed over with stone-faced reverence. It only had one sleeve that flared out from the elbow and a bedazzled neckline. Holy shit, number two.

Finally, he presented me with a pair of pristine magenta Ugg boots, also with bedazzling, this time in the shape of a cat's head. I couldn't keep it together, I descended into an uncontrollable fit of giggles.

I needed to see it all together, immediately. But first it was my turn to show off a little and continue to lighten this mood.

"Wow," I said, wiping the tears from the corners of my eyes.

"I did good."

"You really did."

"Good luck beating all of that."

"Oh, I think you'll find my items are very competitive," I crooned, swiping my bag off the floor. He paled, just a fraction.

"Do your worst, O'Connell."

"Just remember you said that."

I started him off easy with the cobalt blue bowler hat, which he took and immediately put on his head. I wanted to be pissed that he didn't look as ridiculous as I'd hoped, but it was difficult when he looked hot—and smug because he thought that was as bad as it was going to get.

Next up, a pair of jeans that were a classic eighties cut. Narrow at the waist and ankle, wide in the hips and with pleats down the front. I was confident they were going to be at least four or so inches too short, which would only enhance the overall look.

Then there was the crowning glory of the ensemble.

"No," Jake said on an exhale as I pulled the waistcoat from my bag.

"Oh, yes."

"What is that?"

"A waistcoat."

"You have got to be kidding me."

"A deal is a deal, Davenport. Do your worst, that's what you just said, isn't it?"

"That thing is made for a child." There was a reasonably good chance he was right, but he still needed to wear it. And I was going to get a photo—for Blair, naturally.

It was a shade or two lighter than his hat, with bright gold buttons, some gold brocade at the edges, and—my personal favorite thing—white fringing across the chest. Like the shirt he tried on at Modern Thrift, but so much better.

"Harley, you've lost your mind, I cannot wear that." He was edging away like it was radioactive.

"Now who's trying to back out?" I said, wiggling it as I followed.

"Nuh-uh, can't do it, won't do it." He shook his head, tripping over a shoe in his haste to escape me and the fashion crime I held in my hands.

"We made a deal, Jake."

"I'll wear anything else. I'll wear the pineapples." It was hitting below the belt bringing up my favorite item of the day.

"Ah, but that wasn't the deal. My shirt is bedazzled."

"And you'll look incredible in it, like you did in everything else you put on today." He said it so casually, like it was just a fact. My ears went warm. He was still talking, though. "But I can't wear that. I'll flip you for it. Heads I wear the pineapples, tails I wear … that."

I barked out a laugh. "And have you hustle me with your lucky coin? Not happening." He faltered, clearly not expecting me to remember his double-headed coin. I wasn't falling for that again.

"Fine, what about ro-sham-bo."

"Are you serious?"

"Deadly. I cannot wear that."

I considered it. "Best of three?"

"Best of three," he agreed.

"Alright, you're on." I slapped my right fist against my left palm. He did the same.

We lifted our hands in sync once. "Ro." Twice. "Sham." A third time. "Bo."

He watched, brow bent in concentration as my hand went flat. Paper. He had scissors. Was it childish to make him think he had a chance of winning? Yes, but that didn't stop me doing it.

"One more and that abomination is staying home," he said.

I rolled my eyes; I was really going to enjoy watching him sit at Rudi Blue in the waistcoat. "Yeah, yeah, let's just get on with it. shall we?"

We lined up again.

Ro. Sham. Bo.

"Ha!" He crowed, only to realize that my hand was once again paper, beating his rock. So predictable.

"She's all tied up." I bounced my eyebrows, as he attempted to cover his panicked look.

Ro. Sham. Bo.

I wiggled my scissor fingers at him. "You're going to look great, trust me." I said with a smile and patted his shoulder on the way to my bedroom. "Let's be ready to roll in thirty. Do you want the first shower?"

"You cheated." Jake said as he stormed into my room after me and stood close, too close.

I did my best to put space between us, but it wasn't terribly successful. His hot guy smell was all up my nose, mixed with a little thrift store mothball. "Excuse me?"

He moved with me. "You cheated."

I snorted. "You lost a game of chance, and it must be because I cheated? I know that you're competitive and all, Jake, but that's just sad." I dropped my new pieces onto the disaster zone that was my bed.

"Just admit it." He stepped closer, close enough that I could once again feel the warmth of him. I glanced sideways and up. Had his eyes always been that color? If I wasn't staring at him in the flesh, I'd assume they were fake. They weren't just green, or blue, or gray, they were this mottled combination of the three that changed depending which way you looked at him. Right now they were a dark aquamarine, like some tropical, storm covered ocean.

"I admit nothing." Last time I checked, being naturally gifted was not considered cheating.

"I want a rematch."

"Really?"

"Yes, really. I am not wearing the waistcoat."

"And what do I get if I win?" I asked, crossing my arms over my chest.

"Me, in the waistcoat," he said.

I snorted, shook my head. "I'm pretty sure I already have you in the waistcoat. What *else* do I get? You have to make it worth my while." Oh, wow, that sounded a lot more suggestive than I intended. Jake obviously thought so, too, because his attention dipped to my mouth. I felt that look all the way down to my toes. I swayed just a little closer despite knowing it was a bad idea.

He cleared his throat mirroring my move forward. We were so close. All I'd need to do was push up onto my toes and I'd be kissing him. Just like that.

His voice was rough when he asked, "What do you want?"

My heart thumped, heat simmering just below my skin. "I'll have to think about it." I didn't need to think about it. There was nothing I should want from Jake Davenport and yet I couldn't get my mouth to say the words.

He nodded, pupils swallowing those chameleon irises. "So, we have a deal. One more, I get the pineapple shirt and you get ..." The hunger on his face as he looked at my mouth nearly undid me.

"Something to be determined," I said—it was embarrassingly breathy.

"Not sure I like it." The words were almost a purr. "But I feel good, I think I've got you figured out."

I fought a smile. "Is that right?"

"Oh yeah, let's dance."

"You're a dork."

Ro. Sham. Bo.

"Fuck!"

I swallowed my laugh. I could have let him win, sure, but I didn't want to.

"I don't know how you're doing it," he said, still so close.

"You don't need to know how, just that I am, and that you are wearing the waistcoat. Now, if you're not going to take the first shower, I will."

What was I doing? I could let him off the hook right now. I could tell him that I was only fucking with him, and we didn't have to go anywhere in these ridiculous clothes. It would be the smart thing to do, to put an end to this day here and now and not encourage whatever the fuck was happening. There was a lot of crackly tension and eyes looking at mouths. That shit was dangerous, and I should stay the hell away from it.

But I'd never been very good at staying away from things I knew I should. So, I didn't say anything else, just stepped around the wall of man in front of me and marched across the hall with Jake's eyes on my back.

I had a feeling I was setting myself up for trouble.

19

JAKE

Harley was skipping down the street, her purple Ugg boots scuffing every couple of steps. She looked ridiculous, and completely adorable. But I wanted to punch myself right in the face because, unlike her, I looked like a fucking idiot.

The jeans were too short by a few inches and the waistcoat, as expected, was absurd. The fact that a blue bowler hat was the most normal part of the whole ensemble was really saying something.

"We should take a selfie."

"No, we shouldn't." I tugged at the gold brocade hem of the waistcoat.

"But I told Blair I'd send her one."

I stopped short and gaped at her. "You what?"

She grinned. "Blair, your manager. I told her I'd send a pic."

"Yes, I know which Blair you're referring to, thank you." I shouldn't have been surprised that she really did slide into Blair's DMs. "But why are you sending her a pic?"

"Because we're friends now," she said with a shrug. "She's great."

Yes, she was, and the thought of Blair and Harley meeting in real life was enough to terrify me and bring a smile to my face all at once.

"I'm not taking a selfie."

"But you look so good ..." she teased, nudging me with her elbow. "My feet are scorching, by the way. Who thinks Ugg boots are a good idea in summer? You couldn't have chosen a pair of flip flops?"

"And ruin the integrity of the outfit? Absolutely not. Also, I don't think you can complain when I am wearing this." I tugged at the waistcoat again. Harley had used a hair elastic to keep the thing closed because, as I had expected, the buttons came nowhere close to doing up on their own.

"Just one little selfie ... please, Jake?" She pouted and batted her eyelashes, and I did my best not to smile.

"Fine, fine. *One*."

"Yes!" It was more a squeal than a word as she dragged me to a nearby bench.

One little selfie turned into an impromptu fifteen-minute shoot, which I refused to admit I enjoyed. Even with a bunch of onlookers, some of whom joined in. One photo had Harley being held up by me and two other guys who'd been walking past. It was all completely bonkers, which kind of felt like Harley's standard setting. Except for earlier, when I gave her the crochet top and I thought for sure she was going to cry. I'd been tempted to snatch the thing off her and burn it to stop whatever was happening. But I got the impression that it was a happy kind of sad, which made me curious as hell, if I was being honest. Was it about Liam? Did it stir up memories she'd rather forget? It nearly killed me not to ask.

When we made it to Rudi Blue, a bar that looked more like

an abandoned warehouse except for the line halfway down the block, I almost turned and ran. Walking down the street in this clown get-up was one thing—going into a bar was quite another. But it was too late to back out now.

She led the way inside and through the gathered crowd, which was surprisingly large considering it was a Wednesday. Only a few of them looked at us like we might be mad, but any surprise at the clothing faded when they realized one of the two people was Harley. This was absolutely her M.O.

She said hello to no less than ten people between the door and the bar.

"You come here often, then?"

A sultry smile curled her mouth. "Is that a come on?"

I laughed. "More of an observation."

"I know the owners and some of the people here are regulars at Cream and Sugar, too. I'm not an alcoholic."

"I wasn't suggesting you're an alcoholic, Harley. What's that?" I asked, nodding to what looked like a box jutting into the room from one wall. There was a window cut into the side with a narrow counter that numerous people were leaning on.

"The Pie Guy must be in."

I had no idea what that meant.

"That he is," a woman behind the bar said. She was dressed in black from head to toe, her dark hair swept up into a high ponytail, and she was looking at me like she could will me to burst into flames if she wanted. I swallowed.

"Chase, this is Jake, Hunter's cousin who's staying with us. Jake, this is Chase, one of the owners of this fine establishment." Harley leaned over the bar and smacked a kiss to the woman's cheek before she was shoved away with a laugh.

"Good to meet you." I extended a hand, which she shook with surprising strength.

"You too. What the fuck are you both wearing?"

"We played thrift roulette."

"There was a name for it?" I said.

Harley nodded with a wide smile and did a small turn so Chase could appreciate a three-sixty view of her outfit. My eyes darted to her ass without permission, I was positive Chase noticed.

"It was her idea." I threw a thumb at Harley.

"Of course, it was." Chase snorted. "What can I get you?"

Like she had at lunch, Harley didn't bother asking what I wanted, just went ahead and ordered. And I was once again alarmed at how incredibly sexy it was. She just radiated confidence at all times.

Two drinks later, one her choice and the other mine, I was finally put out of my misery when Harley announced we could leave. We said goodbye to Chase and Mack, who it turned out was The Pie Guy working away in the Rudi Blue kitchen.

I tore off the waistcoat the second Harley and I were outside—surely walking shirtless was better than gold brocade and white fringing?—but after the first wolf whistle I grudgingly pulled the abomination back on.

Harley was uncharacteristically quiet on the trip home. It was unnerving. As we walked in the front door—with me finally peeling off the waistcoat for good—I was about to ask what she was thinking when she spun and pinned me to the spot with a fiery look.

"I think I'm ready to call in that 'something else' from earlier."

I faltered. "Really? I figured you'd leave me squirming a little longer."

"I considered doing that." She watched me through her lashes and my pulse pounded in my throat.

"But ...?"

"But, well—" A look of uncertainty passed across her face,

and she fidgeted, before marching into the living room. Was she nervous? Since when did Harley ever get nervous? "I have a proposition."

"That sounds ominous." I dropped onto the couch as she paced in front of me.

"Nothing ominous, at least I don't think it's ominous. I'm just going to spit it out, okay?"

"Okay ...?"

"I think we need to have sex." Of all the things I thought she might say, that was not it. Friends. Weren't we supposed to be friends? She'd been more than happy to brush off the kiss, but now we needed to have sex?

"Ah—excuse me—you—you think we should—"

"Have sex, yes. You and me. I cannot be the only one being driven to distraction by the tension here." She waved a hand between us.

Thank fucking god this thing wasn't one sided. I rubbed my hands on my thighs to stop from reaching for her. "You're definitely not."

"Okay, see, so we just need to get past it, right? One time to get it out of our systems, no strings attached, just two adults getting naked and making each other come."

"That—you want to cash in your ro-sham-bo winnings for sex?"

She stopped pacing, scrunching up her nose. "Well, when you say it like that it sounds skeezy."

"Harley, I don't know. I mean, we've had sex before." A lot. We had sex *a lot* before. Did I want to do it again? Yes, obviously. But that didn't mean this was a good idea.

"Yes, that's—that is true."

"And it was more than once." A lot, lot more.

"Also, true. But that was twelve years ago, and a bunch has changed, happened, whatever, since then. So, I'm sure that this time around once will be enough. Just to scratch the itch." She gave a small shimmy as she said it.

I was already confident that one time would never be enough when it came to Harley. But that didn't mean even once was a good idea. It was the opposite. It was mad. "Once?"

"Just once. And then we can, you know, get on with our lives."

Get on with our lives. That sounded great and so easy. After months of uncertainty there was part of me that was starting to think I might know what I wanted to do with life. And it wasn't playing. But this was not the time to be thinking about it when Harley was standing here saying that we should have sex.

"This is a bad idea," I said, because one of us needed to.

"Possibly," she agreed with a nod.

"Probably." But who was I kidding? There was no way I was going to say no to her. "But—"

"We should do it anyway ... right?"

I let the pause stretch just a little. "Right."

She flicked her Ugg boots off and they went sailing into the kitchen as she wagged her eyebrows at me. I laughed, but it dried up as she dropped into my lap.

"This—we're doing it now, right now?"

"Did you have another time in mind?"

"No, I—what about Hunter?"

"He's out for the night, sent a text while we were at Rudi." Right, well, that was good, I guess. No risk of being interrupted.

"I think I need a drink," I said, swallowing with an audible gulp. There was no need to be nervous, we'd done this before, and I very much wanted to do it again. But I thought I'd have a little time to prepare.

She adjusted her position until her thighs were either side of mine and I became acutely aware of the fact I was shirtless. I also didn't know where to put my hands. Hers landed on my shoulders, warm and soft and sending heat rolling down my spine.

"I am choosing not to be offended by the fact you need to be drunk to have sex with me."

"I do not need to be drunk to have sex with you." I barely even needed to be conscious, if the dreams I'd been having since our kiss were anything to go by. I took hold of her hips and squeezed, relishing in the feel of her before migrating up to settle at the valley of her waist.

"So, we're doing this." Her voice shook ever so slightly as her fingers walked down the front of my shoulders. I was amazed that you couldn't see my heart pounding out the front of my fucking chest.

"It certainly looks that way." My voice was rough as I looked at her mouth. Those rosy fucking lips that I'd been thinking about since our last kiss.

"Are you sure? We don't have to if—"

"Harley, yes, I'm sure. Are you?"

She nodded. "Ye—" I didn't wait for her to finish before I took her face in my hands and kissed her. After a beat of surprise, her lips softened as she sighed, and I felt that relief deep in my gut. She swallowed my groan eagerly, pressing her hips down and rolling them. I nearly blacked out and we'd only just started kissing. One time, just to get it out of our systems. She was delusional. I was sure that Harley O'Connell wouldn't leave my system until I was dead and buried. Maybe not even then.

Our kiss broke as I pulled her shirt up and over her head, ripping it in the process. I tossed it over my shoulder and cupped her breasts.

She gasped. "Jake! That was my new favorite shirt."

"I'll buy you another one." I felt her smile as our mouths

came back together, hot and greedy. "I need the rest of these clothes off."

She nodded. "Bed. Naked." Her fingers sank into my hair and took hold of the short strands, tugging just enough to make my cock twitch beneath her. I stood and Harley wrapped her legs around me, strong thighs squeezing until I didn't even need to be holding her up.

We bumped our way down the short hall. "Yours or mine?" I asked, palming her perfect ass.

"Don't care," she panted as her thighs squeezed, pressing the warmth of her pussy into my stomach. "Just get naked."

"Yes ma'am." I kicked my door open because it was two steps closer and stumbled inside as Harley sucked at the junction of my neck and shoulder. Holy fuck. "More." She did it again and I pressed her back against the door as it thudded into the wall behind us.

"You like that?" Her lips trailed up to my ear and she sucked the lobe into her mouth, teeth grazing over my skin. My cock strained, desperate to get near that mouth, those lips, that tongue.

She landed on the bed with a bounce and immediately reached for me, pulling me forward by the belt loops of my ridiculous jeans. She made short work of the button and fly before tugging them off with enthusiasm.

"I have been thinking about getting you naked for over a week," she confessed before planting a kiss just above my belly button, looking up at me with hungry eyes.

"Fuck, Harley." I groaned, and she smiled against my skin, her hums vibrating across her lips. She was going to kill me.

Her fingers teased along the edge of the waistband of my boxers, but if I let her near my cock right now this whole thing was going to be over embarrassingly fast. So, instead, I knocked her hands away and dropped to my knees, leaving us face to face.

"Hi," I said, sliding my hands over her hips, bringing her to the edge of the bed. One time, we only had one time and I really didn't want to rush things.

But I still needed her naked, right now.

"H—i!" She yelped as I flipped her onto her back, and I tugged on the waist of her skintight pants. I should have found something looser, easier to remove. She wiggled and I watched with rapt attention as every inch of new skin was revealed. I'd seen it all before, of course, but it was different now. She was incredible. My eyes trailed along the lines of her waist and hips, then moved to her breasts, full and round, tipped with stiff peaks that strained against her pink, lace bra. She was a fantasy come to life. She was *my* fantasy come to life.

The purple metallic pants flew over my shoulder and then Harley was reaching for me, dragging me up and over her, letting as little space come between our bodies as possible. I tried to master the will to slow us down, even a little, but the brake lines had been cut and we were barreling full tilt toward naked. I couldn't say I was mad about it, not when she was laid out beneath me, so eager and fucking beautiful.

Her nipples pressed against my chest, but I needed the lace out of the way so I could feel all her skin on mine. I rolled us over, bringing Harley on top and trailing my hands up her back to flick the clasp. The straps went slack, and I peeled them down her arms as she sat up, curls bouncing. I went with her, almost groaning at the view of her uncovered breasts. She was fucking perfect.

I rolled us back over, her curls forming a dark halo on the sheets as I leaned over her. I ghosted my lips across her skin, grazing her nipples, and she shuddered, whispering my name. But I had gained some control. I took my time, exploring and relearning her body with hands, lips, and tongue until she was writhing and begging and wet. Not that I had dipped beneath her underwear just yet, but they were dark, soaked with her need.

"Jake, as much as I appreciate your dedication here, you are killing me," she mumbled, hips rocking as she clawed at the bed covers.

"You want more?" I asked, nibbling her left hip bone.

"Yes. God, *yes*." The desperation in her tone had me smiling. I curled my fingers into the sides of her underwear, she lifted her ass off the bed and then she was bare, and I took a second to just look at her, because, fuck, she was perfect.

I trailed my hands up her legs, my lips following, kissing up from one ankle, past her knee, along her thigh. She squirmed, whimpered.

And then I was there, breathing her in, before I licked. One long tortuous lick and her hips shot off the bed. I pinned her down with my hands, my mouth, and lost myself in her.

"Oh, shit! Yes, yes, yes." She made a garbled sound as her hands fisted in my hair. I followed the movements of her hips and relished the small cries that dropped from her lips. I could do this all night and still want more. I could devour her whole and it wouldn't be enough. I would never have enough. But it was just this once, this was all I had. So, I would draw as much pleasure out of her as I could. I wouldn't stop until she was a woman-shaped puddle of satisfaction.

20

HARLEY

I was staring at the ceiling, waiting for my breathing to even out, Jake's shoulder brushing mine.

Jake and I just had sex.

Jake and I just had *outstanding* sex.

It wasn't like all the sex twelve years ago was bad, far from it, but it certainly had never been like *that*. Whatever just happened, it was something else entirely. Was it a one-time outstanding fluke? Had all that pent up need resulted in the singularly most unbelievable sex *of my life?* That was probably it.

It definitely could not be that good again.

"Wow," I said, though it went nowhere near communicating everything that was going on in my body, my head, my heart. The fact there was anything going on in the heart region was somewhat concerning. There was an alarming amount of *feeling* happening around that particular organ. All warm and soft and thumping to the beat of fu-ture-plans. Oh no, no, no. No future plans here, heart. None whatsoever.

I turned my attention to my still shaking legs—the muscles

had gone into full spasm. If I never walked again, it would absolutely be worth it.

"Wow is right." Jake rolled onto his side, propping one hand under his cheek. I did the same. He looked fucking adorable. Which was not a thought I should be having when we were not going to have sex again. *Mine. Mine. Mine.* My heart said. No. One and done. That's what I said. That's what we agreed to. My stomach was doing a weird bubbling thing. Was that butterflies? Did I have butterflies right now? After we just had sex? That was new.

I cleared my throat. "So ..."

"So ..." he echoed with a lopsided smirk.

"One time."

"That is what we said, yes." His eyes skittered over my face.

I pursed my lips. "And if it was, say, one—"

"Night?" he finished for me, and I couldn't help the grin that split my face.

"Yes, one night. That could work, too?"

"Could mean we're just being thorough."

I really liked the way this man's mind worked. "Right, yes, and it is important to be thorough."

"It is." He edged closer—God, he was gorgeous. Why did I let him leave the first time? A wave of guilt rushed up at the thought. Jake staying meant no Liam, and I wouldn't wish him away for anything.

"Where'd you go?" Jake asked as one hand slipped over my hip, his fingers drawing circles.

"Nowhere."

He watched me, seeing more than I'd like. "We don't have to do anything else. Once. We can leave it at once if that's what you want." It wasn't a question. If I wanted to stop right now, he would.

I didn't want to stop.

"No. I—more, I want more."

"Harley, it's okay."

"Jake, stop talking and kiss me."

He didn't, not right away, anyway. Instead, he slid one leg between my thighs and pressed up with just the right amount of pressure to scatter my thoughts. His cock, already hard again, nudged my stomach. Good god. There was something to be said for the stamina of a professional athlete.

"One night," he said against my lips in a seductive whisper before he finally kissed me. His tongue swept into my mouth, gentle yet claiming.

One night. This was fine. Like we said, we were just being thorough. Tomorrow morning, we would wake up purged of all lust because we were thorough and did not just stop at one go 'round. We owed it to ourselves to make sure it wasn't a fluke. It was the responsible thing to do—and I was nothing if not responsible.

I hooked my leg over Jake's hip, marveling at the way our bodies fit together, seamless and smooth. It had never quite been that way before, not even with Liam. But I wasn't letting my mind stray that way again, not when I had a gorgeous, naked man right here, about to make me come again with little more than some well-placed pressure.

He licked a path along my neck, and I arched into it, gripping his shoulders as I rode his leg. So close. I was so close.

"Let me feel you, Harley," Jake whispered as one hand slipped down between us, two fingers sinking deep. His groan was low and quite possibly the sexiest sound I'd ever heard.

"Yes, Jake." My breath was already shallow, my heart thumping hard. His thumb swept in circles across my clit. "More."

He complied, his fingers pumping and curling to hit the spot that had stars dancing at the edges of my vision. *Ohmy-*

godohmygodohmygod. I ground myself down onto his hand and pulled his face to mine in a needy kiss. I wanted to tell him yes, that it was so good, that I was going to come, but the words were gone, replaced with little more than moans and whimpers.

My orgasm exploded and Jake groaned into my mouth as I tightened around his fingers.

"Condom," I mumbled against his mouth once I had regained the ability of speech, and pushed one shoulder until he was on his back. I straddled him and, as much as I wanted to sink onto his perfect cock immediately, I was not going to be that girl. It was safe sex or no sex. Every time.

He fumbled on the nightstand for the pile of condoms that we were now going to work our way through. I snatched the foil packet from him and tore it open with my teeth.

"Fucking hell, are you trying to kill me?" he groaned and I teased along his length, not letting it slip inside but getting it good and slippery.

"Not just yet ..." I sat back and admired his cock again. It really was something. Long and thick.

"Harley, *please.*" I liked the sound of him begging—if I wasn't so impatient to get him inside me, I'd draw this out a little longer. But I was too greedy to wait. I smoothed the condom down his cock, lined it up and sank low. We both groaned because, fucking hell, it felt incredible. Better than the first time, better than any time, every time.

I rolled my hips, testing, as his hands moved up and down my thighs.

"Fuck. So good. Ride me, Harley, use me."

I moaned, finding a rhythm that was already making my legs shake. I anchored my hands on his thighs, letting my head drop backward.

"*Fuck.*" He palmed my breasts and squeezed, tweaking my left nipple. "So fucking perfect." His hands dropped to my hips, one thumb once again finding my clit as he started to thrust up.

"Yes," I gasped, losing my rhythm as another orgasm crashed over me. He hooked one arm under my leg and flipped us, pushing that leg over his shoulder and sinking so deep it practically sent me cross-eyed as I cried out his name.

"Harley, fuck," he grunted, with my short nails digging into his wide shoulders.

"Keep going," I panted, feeling my orgasm go on and on as he drove into me and hit that spot over and over and over and over. Was it possible to black out from too much pleasure? Was that a thing? It wasn't something I'd needed to consider before, but right now I felt perilously close to some kind of edge I hadn't known existed.

"One more."

"The last one hasn't even finished yet," I wailed.

He made a garbled noise, but he kept going, hips pumping as he dropped his mouth down to mine and kissed me hard, our tongues clashing and teeth clicking in desperation for one another. I wanted to stay here forever. In this moment of impossible pleasure.

Jake came with a groan, one hand squeezing my ass and the other by my head before he collapsed on top of me breathing hard. His weight was glorious, pinning me to the bed. I was already sad about waking up tomorrow.

"Fuck," he mumbled into the crook of my neck. "I think I nearly passed out."

I laughed, pleased I wasn't the only one who felt like the sex was transcending time and space.

With the condom taken care of, he returned to bed and immediately pulled me into his chest. I didn't stop him. We only had one night, after all, so there was no point fighting the attraction. I was going to be a zombie at work tomorrow, but I didn't care, not when he was kissing me again. Deep and slow, dragging me under.

We were pressed together from mouths to hips, legs tangled, and it didn't feel like enough. I wanted more, wanted to get closer. Our kiss turned more heated and desperate as his hand wandered down along my side to my ass and squeezed. I moaned into his mouth.

He rolled me onto my back, his hands everywhere, and started to kiss a line down my throat. He continued down, licking, nipping, sucking, until he passed my belly button.

"Already?" I panted, letting my fingers thread into his hair.

He peeked up at me with a devilish smile. "I need to make the most of our one night."

"Well, don't let me stop y–*oh my god*," I finished on a cry as he dropped his head, took my clit in his mouth, and sucked.

I threw my arm out blindly, slapping my phone to silence the wailing alarm. At some point during the sex marathon, Jake and I had migrated to my room—after the shower, maybe? I peeled my eyes open and stretched, feeling the delightfully satisfying ache in numerous muscles, from my shoulders all the way down to my calves.

We had been *very* thorough. But that was the light of a new day slicing through my blinds, which meant the itch scratching was done. It would not be happening again. Nor did it need to, because of all the aforementioned thoroughness. The itch was out of our systems, well and truly dealt with, and we could go back to being friendly, platonic roommates until he, sooner or later, got back on a plane to London.

Of course, the sheer caliber of the sex did pose a slight problem. The first time had not been a fluke. In fact, every time after only got better. Like off the fucking charts good. It was somewhat unsettling. But not something I was going to dwell on, because it wasn't happening again.

"Morning," Jake said, his voice so sinfully gravely it had heat pooling low in my stomach.

"Good morning." I tipped my head to face him. His hair was a riot—not as bad as mine, I was sure, considering he'd really enjoyed having his hands in my curls—but it was sticking up every which way like he'd been good and used, which I suppose he had.

It would be all too easy to roll all the way over and onto his chest, slide my hand down, and take hold of his cock that I already knew would be hard. I squeezed my thighs together and swallowed. Yes, it would be all too easy to follow that thought all the way to its conclusion. Again, and again and again.

One night, Harley. One. Night.

If I didn't have to be at work, I would be sorely tempted to blow off that one night rule. Rules were made to be broken, after all, and willpower had never been one of my core strengths.

What was it about him that made me want to linger, when so often all I wanted to do was escape as soon as humanly possible? It was just the orgasms—that had to be it. He had delivered an impressive number of them, and I was still in the come down phase.

Only, I had a feeling it wasn't just about the orgasms, because right now I would be just as happy to sit and have breakfast with him, even if he was wearing a shirt, even if we were in public when there was no chance of him eating me for dessert. What the hell was happening to me? No strings. This was supposed to be a no-strings-one-time-turned-one-night-sex-fest that I would walk away from.

Space, that was what I needed now. Some time and space—

and a shower to wash our sex smell off my skin, even though I would much rather bathe in it than scrub it away.

I rolled out of bed, away from Jake—and his sleepy sex hair and intoxicating smell—and ignored the low groan that followed as I stood. That sound threatened to render me unconscious, but I managed to stay upright. Was there anything about him that was unattractive? There would be, there always was. I just couldn't see it right now, in the post-orgasm haze.

One foot in front of the other.

"I need a shower," I said. Not that I needed to explain myself, but an awkwardness I was unaccustomed to slid across the back of my neck. Did he feel it, too, or was it just me? I stumbled a step, my legs taking a second to adjust to being upright. When I was sure my muscles were not going to let me down, I beelined for the bathroom.

Once safely ensconced, I took a second to look at myself in the mirror and smothered a moan with my hand. There was a hickey on the top of my left boob, another on my opposite hip bone and a third just above my belly button. I prodded each mark, nibbling my lip as I remembered Jake putting them there. I could see the ghost of his hands on my thighs, where he'd peeled them open to feast on me. I gripped the vanity to keep myself upright.

One night. That was supposed to be enough. To bleed the lust from my veins and replace it with mild indifference. If anything, it had done the opposite. I wanted to march back into my room and keep him there for the rest of the day. The rest of the week. The rest of time. What. The. Fuck. I didn't do this. I had great sex and I moved on. *Wham. Bam. Thank you, sir. We had fun. I'm out.* That. Was. Me.

Not with Jake, though. Why did it feel like there might be strings where I had said there should be none?

I wrenched the faucets on and waited for the bathroom to fill with steam, ready to rid myself of his smell in the hopes that it would purge him from everywhere else, too. One night of outstanding sex and it was time to get on with my life. Just like I said.

The shower was too hot, but I stepped in anyway. His body wash was right there next to mine and, for a second, I seriously considered using it. Then I gave myself a mental slap and squirted a healthy dollop of my own lavender one onto my glove and scrubbed.

I stepped out of the shower, once adequately scrubbed, and cursed myself for not bringing clothes in here with me. Would he still be in my bed, all sexy and naked and lusty?

He wasn't in my bed. I ignored the spike of disappointment at finding my room empty and started rummaging for something to wear. I decided on a pair of cut-offs and a Fleetwood Mac tee, then attempted to tame my hair into some space buns before heading out to the kitchen.

Jake was there, standing at the counter in a pair of athletic shorts and no shirt. Heat sizzled across my skin, and I pressed my lips together. He turned at my *good morning*, which didn't sound like actual words but more of a garbled collection of syllables. Apparently, being in his presence was turning not only my bones to mush, but my brain too. Cool. Coolcoolcool.

His eyes swept up from my feet in a slow track until they made it to my face. My entire body was on fire.

"Hey, you okay? I made coffee." He was so casual, like his blood hadn't turned to lava just because I was in the room.

"Me? Okay? Yes, better than okay. I'm great, perfect!" My smile was walking a fine line between normal and manic. "So glad we had all of the sex last night because I was right, it's totally out of my system. No tension here this morning. I feel great. *Great.*" I needed to stop talking. I stuffed my hands into the back pockets of my shorts to keep them from waving around. "How about you? Better, right? It's better. Great, even." Why was I saying *great* so much? "Did you say coffee? I'd love some coffee." *Shut up, Harley. Shut up. Shut up. Shut up.*

He watched me rattle on with an understandably bemused look on his face. I took a slow breath in an effort to settle my galloping pulse as I crossed the living room.

"Thanks." I accepted the glass of cold brew stained with just the right amount of milk.

"I was paying attention," he said as he saw me analyzing before I took a sip. I really needed to get to work.

"To me?"

"To your coffee."

"Ah, yes, coffee." I took another sip and openly studied his chest.

"To you, too."

My eyes jumped to his and I felt like giggling, which was ridiculous. I took another gulp of coffee, wishing it was stronger. Although stronger coffee probably wasn't what I needed when I was already feeling so jittery.

Jake and I stood on either side of the island, watching one another. What was he thinking? He looked cool as a fucking cucumber. Why was he cool as a fucking cucumber. Or perhaps the better question was why was I *not* cool as a cucumber? I couldn't be further from cool cucumber status. I was about to climb on the counter and throw myself at him.

That was my cue to leave—or, technically, the fact I was already going to be ten minutes late was.

"Well, thank you for the coffee. I wish I could stay." No. No, I did not wish that. Yes, I did. Gah! I needed to go. Right now. "Um ... anyway, I'm already going to be late. So, I should get going."

"I guess I'll see you later, then."

"Not if I see you first," I said and then let out the pitchiest, squawking laugh. Where the hell did that come from? It was like a dying hyena.

"Okay," he said with a smile that told me he saw through my absurd attempts at chill.

I dumped my coffee into a to-go mug, swiped my bag from its hook and hightailed it outside and into the fresh air in the hopes it would clear my head.

It. Did. Not.

There wasn't much that was going to help clear my head at this point. Although a few days away from Jake's sexy tractor beam would definitely help.

I was willing to admit that I had made a miscalculation about the whole *one night with Jake would be enough to burn the lust out of my system* thing. In theory it sounded good, like it had the potential to work. And I guess if the sex had been fine, I would have been able to walk away with a spring in my step and get on with my life as advertised.

Maybe this was more of a fake it 'til you make it kind of scenario. All I needed to do was pretend I didn't want to have sex with Jake again.

I laughed and it drew looks from a couple of early morning runners. There was no way I was going to be able to convince myself I didn't want to have sex with Jake again. I absolutely did. The escape to Jemma and Nash's place this weekend could not have come at a better time.

21

JAKE

I went back to bed after Harley left for work. I'd been tempted to crawl back into *her* bed, but I settled for my own, which was easy enough seeing as the sheets still smelled like her. It took all of two minutes before I was asleep again. Not surprising, after spending most of the night awake.

What a night. What a *fucking* night.

When I woke up alone at nine, I could almost convince myself that I'd dreamed the whole thing—not that anything in my imagination could have been that good. Then, I rolled over and buried my face in the pillow she'd slept on (albeit briefly) and I knew that it was real—and so much better than I remembered us being together. So much better than it had been with anyone else. Harley and I fit. We *worked*.

It wasn't just physical, either. It was more. She was branded on my skin, on my tongue, on my cock. On my fucking soul, if I was being brutally honest.

She wanted last night to be singular. I respected her opinion, while also respectfully disagreeing with it. Because why the actual fuck would I not want to repeat last night as frequently as humanly possible before I had to go back to London?

But what if I wasn't going back to London? What then? What would that mean for us? It wasn't something I could talk about, when Harley was so determined to keep some distance between us.

I stepped out of the shower, dried off, and dressed. Would I go straight to Cream and Sugar, or would I wait? Waiting was probably the smart thing to do. I knew from my regular visits that Cecilia wouldn't be in until around eleven for her shift, and she was the one I really needed to see. It couldn't hurt to eat something first, though, before I was potentially assaulted by a teenager. She was going to hug me when I told her, I was sure of it.

The other thing I needed to do, aside from submitting to being a high school soccer coach for a month and a half, was figure out how I was getting to Nash and Jemma's place upstate. Hunter was going, I could easily ride with him. But then, I could see Harley in a cherry-red convertible, her curls blowing in the wind as we cruised on the highway. The thought was enough to have me smiling at nothing as I stood in the middle of the living room.

Time to get myself some breakfast, and the best coffee in Brooklyn.

I dialed Blair as I stepped out onto the sidewalk.

"What's wrong?" she answered.

"Hello to you, too."

"Jake." How she managed to imbue so much violence into a single syllable always amazed me.

"There's nothing wrong. I just wanted to talk to you."

"About? Is it the Man City thing?"

"Yes and no."

"What the hell does that mean?"

"I don't want you to freak out."

"That is not an encouraging start to this conversation."

"I'm doing a coaching program for some high school students. Here in Brooklyn."

"Have you signed anything?"

"No, no, nothing signed. But I might today." *Okay, here goes nothing.* "I've been thinking about stuff—"

"Stuff? You've been thinking about *stuff*?"

"I'm not sure if I want to come back to London, Blair." I blew out a breath and braced.

The silence that followed was heavy.

"That's a lot to drop on a girl, Jake."

"I know, I'm sorry, I wanted to say something yesterday, but I didn't—I still don't—"

"Jake, hey, it's okay. Am I surprised, yes. And no, honestly. Looks like I have some research to do. Don't sign anything binding without me looking at it." She hung up. Well, that went better than I expected. And the relief at telling her was palpable.

I might not know what my future looked like just yet, but that was a step in the right direction.

I stopped across the street from Cream and Sugar and watched Harley chat to customers at the to-go window. It had only been a few hours since I'd seen her last but, even still, I stared with my jaw slightly slack because I would never get tired of looking at her.

What would she think about me staying? Was I staying? There was a big difference between not going back to London and staying in Brooklyn. There were a lot of other places I could go, right? Maybe I could travel, and actually see places outside of hotels and football pitches. That sounded good. Even better if I was with a certain curly-haired woman.

Harley disappeared from the window, and I jogged across the street before slipping through the door. There was no hiding once I was inside. Her eyes landed on me immediately and went wide. Did she think I wouldn't come in today? Like I was at all capable of staying away from her. I was already an addict—maybe I had been from that first moment I saw her twelve years ago.

Her attention snapped back to the coffee machine as I slid onto a stool. The blonde woman beside me glanced my way, her sharp blue eyes narrowing a fraction before she looked at Harley and sipped what looked like strong, black tea in a pregnant silence.

"Jake, hi." Darcy appeared from the kitchen with three plates balanced on her arms. "You after breakfast, or just coffee?"

"Breakfast," I said, and Darcy nodded.

"I'm sure Harley's got you covered." She winked as she turned to deliver meals to their recipients.

"Jake?" The blonde was smiling. I glanced at Harley, who was looking everywhere but at me, the tops of her cheek bones were pink.

I turned to the blonde. "Yes ..."

Blue eyes twinkled. She was pretty. "I'm Jemma, a friend of Harley's. She's apparently forgotten her manners this morning." She held out a hand and nodded in Harley's direction. Her accent gave me a small twang of London nostalgia. Had I been rash in talking to Blair? "And Nash told me you're coming up to the farm this weeke—"

"He's what now?!" Harley squawked as something clattered behind the coffee machine. "Wh—how did you—why are you coming to the farm?"

It took a beat to smother my smile so that I was able to answer with a straight face. "Because Nash invited me." And the look on Harley's face was making me so very glad I accepted the invitation. She gaped like a dying fish for a solid five seconds.

"What is wrong with you?" Jemma asked, looking highly amused by Harley's reaction.

"Ah, nothing. Nothing is wrong with me. I'm just wondering why this is the first I am hearing of all this." She waved a hand at me, and I covered my laugh with a cough.

"Is it a problem, me joining everyone at Jemma and Nash's farm?"

Harley pursed her lips. I wanted to suck them. "No. It is not a problem."

"Glad to hear it." I turned back to Jemma. "It's great to meet you, Jemma."

"You too, Jake. I've heard so much about you."

"Is that right?" I would happily shave off my left eyebrow to learn what Harley had been saying about me. Her blush had spread down her neck.

"And this is Odette." Jemma leaned back, revealing a woman beside her with bubblegum-pink hair, striking gray eyes, and a button nose.

"Good to finally meet you, Jake," Odette said, shooting Harley a wide grin. A silent conversation passed between the two of them.

"And you," I said.

Before any more pleasantries could be exchanged, Cecilia arrived and planted herself next to me. "If it's a no, I need to know up front or there is no way I'm going to be able to focus. I mean, my focus is probably going to be non-existent, anyway, because we're in the same room, but it will be worse if you don't put me out of my misery." She blew out a breath, ponytail swinging as she bounced on her toes. "Okay, let me have it."

"Well, now I'm thinking I might need to reconsider if my presence is going to be that much of a distraction ..."

She grabbed my arm, nails digging in. "Please don't be fucking with me. Are you seriously saying yes?"

"But if I'll be too much of a distraction—"

"No! Holy shit!" She squealed and hugged me while also jumping up and down. "Sorry, it's probably not super appropriate to be hugging my NEW COACH! Sorry, again, I shouldn't be yelling in your face but ohmygodohmygodohmygodholyshit!" Half the place was watching us, which usually would have given me anxiety about being recognized but it didn't, not this time. The only anxiety that was swirling in my gut right now was about whether or not I could actually help these kids.

"The program starts on Tuesday, yes?"

She was nodding before I'd even finished the sentence. "Yes, yep, Tuesday, that's right."

"Okay great. Is there any way I can swing past the school and check out the facilities before then?"

"Yes, of course, we can go now!"

"You're working."

"Yes, that's true, I'm working. I'm working."

"But after that?" I suggested and Cecilia started nodding again.

"Jesus, just go now," Darcy said as she stepped behind the counter. Cecilia and I both looked at her. "I am not going to stand in the way of whatever is happening right now. If you have somewhere else you need to be Cece, I grant you leave."

Cecilia's squeal was so high pitched I was amazed half the glasses didn't shatter. "Thank you, Darcy! Thankyouthankyouthankyou!"

"Yeah, yeah, just get outta here." She glanced at me and my still full coffee. "Actually, he hasn't eaten yet. Clear a few tables and when Jake is done you can go."

Another squeal and Cecilia darted behind the counter, dropped her bag, grabbed an apron and got to work. And I prayed that I had not just made a mistake.

"You're such a good boss lady, Darce," Harley said with a fond smile.

Darcy blushed. "I know. Now get back to work."

"Rude," Harley scoffed. "I've been working this whole time."

"No, you haven't, you've been staring."

"At who?"

"Seriously?" Darcy raised an eyebrow and Harley, who had been poised to argue some more, snapped her mouth shut. "Now, what food can I get you to go with that coffee?" Darcy asked me.

"I'll get the egg and bacon bagel with haloumi."

"You got it." She disappeared into the kitchen.

"On that note it's probably time for us to do some actual work, too," Jemma said as she and Odette stood. "It was great to meet you, Jake."

"You too."

"And we'll see you tomorrow. Harley's got the address and everything, and I think she and Darce were going to get the train I think so you can head up with them." She smiled as Harley tried to incinerate her with her eyes.

"Sounds good, thanks, Jemma."

They left and, for a second, it felt like Harley and I were alone in this tension filled bubble. Her eyes were locked on mine, and I could see that she wanted to say something, but she didn't, just rolled her lips together to forcibly keep the words in. I wanted to drag each word out one by one, preferably with my tongue.

"You're coming to the farm," she said eventually.

"Yep, you sure that's okay?"

"Yes, of course, why wouldn't it be? We're going to have a great time."

Yes, we were.

Not quite an hour later, my bagel and two coffees were sitting heavy in my gut as I approached Franklin High School. It was an imposing building, four stories high and stretching for an entire block. Was this really a good idea? What the hell was I even going to teach these kids? Did I need to make up lesson plans or something? That sounded like something teachers did. Was I a teacher now? No, I was a coach, that was different, but some planning was probably still required, right? Otherwise, I was just going to turn up on Tuesday and what? Make it up? Honestly, it was a strong enough strategy when trying to plan made me feel like a shitty substitute teacher.

Cecilia had been talking almost nonstop on the walk over, and I tried to listen, but I'd only caught every third or so word as I started second guessing this decision. But we were here, now, so there was no backing out.

"So, this is it. We train a block over."

I nodded, rubbing my spontaneously sweating palms on my shorts. I was an adult, there was no reason for me to be feeling this fucking nervous. It was football. I could do football. Football was literally my thing. And if all I did for the next six weeks was get some kids more excited about football, then I would consider that a win.

The facilities weren't as bad as I was expecting, but they were still a long way from what I was used to. Not surprising, considering what I was used to was the top of the sport. I could work with it, though, and that was the main thing.

Cecilia was quiet for the first time since we left Cream and Sugar as she watched me take everything in. She was nibbling her lip.

"Is it—is it enough? You're not going to change your mind, are you?"

I glanced at her. "You could be playing in a gravel ditch, and I wouldn't change my mind, not now."

"Oh, thank god!" She said, clapping both hands over her face. "Okay, good, great, so what—I mean is there anything you need?"

"Do I need to speak to anyone? Confirm that I'm coming on board? Do I need to sign something?" And did I need some kind of license to work with minors?

"Mr Reynolds is head of PE, we can see if he's around."

"That'd be great."

Cecilia led me inside, through the empty locker rooms to an equally empty office.

"It's not locked, so he must be around here somewhere," she said.

"What do you need, Cecilia?" The question arrived before the man did and then he was in the doorway. Classic gym teacher. Polo shirt, shorts, whistle around his neck, and a floppy ball cap on his head.

"Mr Reyolds, hi, this is Jake Davenport, he's the one I was telling you about. He's going to run the soccer program."

He gave her a strange look, then glanced at me and extended a hand. "Good to meet you, Jake, thank you for coming on board. It means a lot to the girls."

"I'm looking forward to getting started," I said as we shook.

"Everything you need should be in the storage rooms—

Cecilia can show you where they are. Otherwise, I assume you've got a program to take them through?"

I had nothing, but he didn't need to know that. "I do."

"Good to hear. I'll see you on Tuesday." And that was it. Nothing to sign, no background check to make sure I wasn't a sociopath. Although maybe I shouldn't be encouraging background checks. It was like he already thought I was on board.

"Did you tell him that I'd do it?" I asked Cecilia as we made it back out onto the street.

"Maybe ..." She smiled.

"That could have gone bad."

"Could have but didn't." There was no remorse in her tone —it reminded me of Harley. "I was pretty sure Harley would be able to talk you around." In all honesty, she didn't have to do too much in the talking me around department. It was my fear of fucking it all up that I needed to get over.

Now though, fear was the last thing on my mind. Instead, I could feel a familiar, if recently lost, buzz under my skin— excitement, nervousness, and anticipation colliding. This could be good. This could be exactly what I needed.

22

HARLEY

After a few hours of stewing over the fact that Jake was coming to the farm, I was mostly over it. Was I happy that what should have been a few days of Jake-free time would now be Jake-full time? No, no I wasn't, but I was trying to accept it because it wasn't going to change. Also, he deserved a fun farm weekend away as much as the next person, maybe even more considering the last few months he'd had.

It was time to turn the frown upside down. From what Jemma had said about the farm, it was a big place and avoiding him there would surely be easier than avoiding him in the confines of my three-bedroom apartment, where we shared both a wall and a bathroom. If I squinted at it just right, I could almost convince myself that this was a good thing. That it would provide exposure to Jake—for desensitization purposes—while also allowing me to get some much-needed space. The more I repeated it to myself, the more likely I was to believe it.

Everything was going to be just fine.

. . .

Darcy had decided that Fridays were now training days. Today it was all about speed.

As such the counter was lined with customers, all of whom were watching me with fierce, unwavering attention. I got it, if I was waiting for my coffee, I'd be the same. But it wasn't just about their coffees.

I bounced on my toes, stretching my neck and shaking out my shoulders.

"Just do it!" I ordered Darcy.

She grinned, thumb poised to strike the timer she held. "Who's ready for another speed round?!"

The small crowd whooped and hollered and whistled as I punched the air in front of me. Rocky, eat your goddamn heart out. I was the hero today.

"Three." She paused, looking around, because she was intent on driving me mad, apparently. "Two." Another pause. Yep, she was torturing me. "One. Go!"

I launched into action, not letting my brain get in the way of what my body knew how to do. I could be blindfolded and still make these orders, no question. The cheering around me faded into a hum as I kept my focus squarely on the line of coffees in front of me.

Americano.

Flat white.

Latte.

Latte.

Americano.

Double espresso.

On and on they went until I slapped the service bell as the last cup hit the counter and Darcy stopped the timer. Each customer came to collect their coffee, but no one dispersed, everyone was keen to hear the result. I pressed my hands flat together and touched them to my lips, sending a small prayer up to the coffee gods, anticipation fizzing in my stomach.

She looked down at her stopwatch, her lips a flat line to keep from giving anything away, then scanned what felt like every face in the crowd before coming to me.

"How did it feel?" she asked, still infuriatingly unreadable.

"It felt good. I felt good. Please put me out of my misery!"

"She's beaten her record folks!" Everyone erupted and started chanting my name. I bowed and curtsied—maybe this wouldn't be so bad after all? I couldn't deny the buzz of energy zipping along my skin. Or was it just because I was in my comfort zone that this was making me all warm and fuzzy?

"Now everyone can get out, because we're closing in half an hour." They thought she was joking, and usually she would be, because she'd never shove someone out before they were done. But this weekend was her first vacation in over a year. So today, she was not fucking around. "Out. Out. Out. Everything in the cabinet is half price."

We cleaned up in record time, both of us riding high on today's successful training. It was starting to feel like we could actually do quite well in the champs, which was both exhilarating and terrifying all at once.

Darcy pulled the door closed with a flourish and then kissed it. "Is it bad that I'm already dreading—no, dreading is too strong a word—but I'm already not looking forward to coming back on Tuesday?"

I threw an arm around her shoulders. "Darce, you are entitled to a vacation, and one that's longer than a few days. But we need to talk about your bag."

"My bag? What's wrong with my bag?" She glanced down at the small duffle in her hand.

"Nothing's wrong with it, it's just tiny. There are no roller skates in that thing."

"No, there are not. Does Jemma even have a place to roller skate up there?"

"I don't know, but if she does, I'd like to be prepared." I gestured to my rolling suitcase.

"Uh-huh … well, I plan on being in a bathing suit and not much else for the next three days. So a larger bag was not necessary." It was a fair point. Maybe I didn't need to pack the travel size badminton rackets? But if I didn't, then who would? If someone wanted to start a badminton tournament, I had them covered.

A revving engine drew our attention and we both watched as a sleek, cherry-red convertible pulled up across the street. I wasn't a huge car person but even I could admit it was beautiful. Just like the man who was stepping out of it.

Jake looked movie-star-on-his-day-off good. I had to work hard to keep my tongue in my mouth. Holy. Fucking. Hell. He was in a pair of cut off jean shorts that hit a good three inches above his knees—and dear god did the man have just ridiculously attractive legs—and a simple white tee with the sleeves rolled up, just a little. He was James Dean, and he was trying to kill me. Although the fact he was standing on the sidewalk barefoot would mean he'd probably need a tetanus shot.

What the hell was he doing here?

"You know you're gonna catch something standing around barefoot, right?" Darcy said as she started to cross the street. I attempted to stop her with the power of my mind, but it didn't work. We were supposed to be catching the train. We were not getting in that car. It probably didn't even have a backseat. He smiled, and even with the sunglasses perched on his nose I could feel the track of his eyes as they slid up my legs. I focused on putting one foot in front of the other as I followed Darcy across the street.

"What are you doing here?"

"Thought you two might like a ride?"

"Yes please," Darcy said at the same time I said, "We're fine catching the train."

She shot me a have-you-lost-your-mind look. I responded with one that said I-am-not-getting-in-that-car-I-need-some-space-from-the-hot-soccer-playing-house-guest-who-I-very-much-want-to-have-sex-with-again-and-I-need-you-to-support-me. Something clearly got lost in translation, because the traitor merely rolled her eyes and tossed her duffle bag in the backseat —because it did have one, of course.

"I was quite looking forward to the train ride." I pouted.

"Is that right?" he said, his smile telling me he absolutely knew I was lying. It wasn't that I had anything against trains, I'd been catching the subway my entire life, but I got bored and restless on longer trips. Even still, I would take that restlessness over watching Jake drive this car.

"I wanna drive," I said, crossing my arms.

"Absolutely not."

"It's a three-and-a-half-hour trip, you can spare me at least thirty to forty minutes of that."

"Do you even have a license?"

"If I say yes, can I drive?"

"Only if it's true."

"Of course, I've got a license."

"You're not driving."

"Give me one good reason why I can't drive. I am a *great* driver." I stomped my foot for emphasis and shot Darcy a look when she snorted. I excelled at our speed training today, you'd think the least she could do was back me up now.

"Please, you probably drive like a teenager hopped up on sugar and Red Bull who has just watched every *Fast and Furious* film back-to-back."

I wanted to argue, but it was actually a pretty accurate

depiction of my driving skill level and enthusiasm—and it suited this particular car perfectly. "I'll be good."

"No, you won't."

"No, I won't, but look at this thing!" I waved at it. "It's begging to be driven like a *Fast and Furious* extra is behind the wheel." There was another snort from Darcy as she climbed into the back seat, then stretched out. Vacation mode: activated.

"Harley, no," Jake said, without even the slightest hint of him wavering.

"Would you rather me drive now, in the confines of Brooklyn, or out on the highway?"

"Neither," he said, not missing a beat. "Get in."

"You're no fun."

His smile turned wolfish. "I am, actually. I'm *lots* of fun ..." he said, his voice a low, gravelly whisper. My knees wobbled ever so slightly but I managed to pull myself together and not trip too far down the lust spiral his words conjured.

"I'll buy all the road trip snacks." It was a tempting offer, and he knew it, but not one I was quite ready to accept.

"For both of us?" I asked.

"Yep."

"I don't want any sn—"

"Whatever we want?" I cut Darcy off before she finished that sentence because who didn't want road trip snacks?

"Whatever you want," he confirmed.

"Okay, deal."

The traffic heading out of the city was horrendous and I amused myself by surreptitiously ogling Jake's legs. His shorts had ridden up and he was showing a serious amount of thigh.

His left flexed every time he had to shift gears. Those were athlete legs, and I was mesmerized.

We finally made it onto the highway, only for me to see a roadside diner.

"Pull over!" I waved madly.

"Can we put a little more distance between us and the city before we stop for snacks? You know the drive isn't actually that long, right?" He had on his best dad voice and a picture of him holding a wild-haired child popped into my head. What the—no, no thank you! Where the hell did *that* come from?

"Are you reneging on your deal to buy all the snacks?"

"No, I am not reneging. I am merely saying that we do not have to get them here."

"But I want them here ... *please*." I looked up at him, batting my eyelashes for a little extra pep and he heaved a sigh that said *yes, we'll pull over but I am not happy about it.*

I had the door open before the car had come to a complete stop because I was following my nose, and the neon sign that promised nachos. Oh, yes, mama wanted some nachos.

"You are not eating nachos from this place," Jake said as I doused the chips in queso. He looked so disgusted I laughed.

"What are you getting?" I asked.

"Nothing, I'm not hungry."

"What about Darcy?" Miss 'I don't want any snacks'.

"She requested Salt and Vinegar Pringles and Skittles."

I knew she'd get something. "Solid choices."

"Which can be eaten in the car."

"As can these."

"You are not eating truck stop nachos in that car."

"I think you'll find this is more of a diner than a truck stop."

He pointed out the window to a large truck. Okay, so he might have me on a technicality there. "I don't actually care what you call it. They are not coming in the car."

I accepted defeat and took a seat at one of the outdoor picnic tables under a large blue and white striped umbrella.

Darcy came to collect her Pringles and Skittles and then returned to the car with an annoyingly knowing look.

I bit into a chip laden with queso and guacamole. They were surprisingly good, considering where we were. I licked the rogue drips off my thumb and hummed in satisfaction. Jake bit one of the sour straps he impulse purchased when we got to the counter. Such a panic buyer.

"You want some?" I held up a chip and looked at him over the top of my sunglasses.

"No thanks."

"Oh, come on ..." I lifted a chip that was drowning in gooey cheese. "You know you want a little bite."

He looked at me, then the chip, then back at me. "I really don't."

Was the issue nachos generally, or just nachos purchased from a truck stop? It had to be the latter, because who in their right mind had a problem with nachos generally? Nachos were an ideal food. He needed to have a bite. It was now my mission to get Jake Davenport to eat my truck stop nachos. I shuffled up onto my knees and leaned my elbows on the table. He tried to be subtle about his peek down the front of my shirt, but I still caught it.

"Why won't you have a little bite?" I asked, pushing my lower lip out into a pout.

"I don't want one."

"Of course, you do ..." I crawled halfway over the table.

"You're not going to drop this, are you?"

"Nope," I said with a grin.

He took the chip. "Fine, but it's your funeral. Nachos now. Naked later."

I gaped, dropping back onto my side of the table. Nachos

now did not mean naked later. There would be no naked later. He shoved the chip into his mouth and licked his fingers clean. Nachos had never been so sexy.

I cleared my throat. "It's good, right?"

"Better than I expected," he conceded but still waved away the offer of more. Leaving me to eat almost the entire tray.

The rest of the trip was spent fighting over music choices. Darcy fell asleep in the back shortly after we left the diner, so it was essentially me and Jake alone in the confines of a very sexy car, our thighs separated by little more than inches.

We made another stop because I needed to pee and I was also in need of something sweet after the nachos—Reece's Pieces, to be precise. Jake tried to tell me he wasn't getting anything else but bought a bag of gummy bears and sour worms. How had I not noticed that the man had a serious sweet tooth?

"What's the address?" he asked as we passed through a picturesque town. It looked like a postcard with the wide, tree-lined streets, quaint shop fronts, and locals chatting along the sidewalk. I wanted to move here immediately and set up a cafe. Ooh, no, a bookshop! Or a florist! Maybe all three. And then I'd be in on all the local gossip and help solve the little grievances in town because I would hear everyone's side. I would be a vital member of this community.

"Harley?" Jake pulled me out of the fantasy.

"Hmm?"

"The address, what is the address?"

"Oh!" I glanced down at my phone. "We need to go through town, then ... it looks like the driveway is on Flat Rock Road."

"Which one is that?"

"You'll know when we get there."

"And how's that?"

"Because I'll tell you," I said. "You may not trust me behind the wheel, but my sense of direction is second to none."

We cruised through town, and I managed to direct us to Bell-Meadow Farm with only one u-turn. A total success, by all accounts. Jake, though, seemed to think it might have been better if we didn't drive fifteen minutes out of our way. I ignored him.

We passed under a rusted metal arch and up the drive through a tunnel of enormous oaks that flanked the way to what was obviously the main house. I wasn't sure what I had been expecting. Jemma had shown us a few photos of the place she and Nash bought a few months ago. It was a two story, sprawling farmhouse that once upon a time would have been glorious. It still had a ways to go before it was returned to its former glory, but I could totally see that it was going to be incredible. I could not wait to see it when they'd finished.

Jemma came barreling out the front door, waving and squealing, and crushed me and Darcy into a hug.

"Finally! I was about to send out a search party."

"We're not even late."

"The navigator had some issues," Jake said with a smirk that I wanted to kiss off his face. No, no, I didn't because there would be no kissing.

Jemma released me and Darcy, shoving us aside. Charming.

"Jake, so good to see you again, I'm glad you could make it." She beamed, pulling him into a hug, which he looked hilariously awkward in.

I poked out my tongue at him. "It was a fifteen minute detour."

He straightened as Jemma let him go. "It was fifteen minutes in *one* direction. That's a half hour round trip."

"Tomayto-tomahto." I returned my focus to Jemma as Jake grabbed our bags from the trunk.

"Harley what the hell is in here?" he asked, testing my bag's weight.

I wrestled it away from him. "The *essentials*. Jem, this place is so cool!"

"You haven't even seen any of it yet."

"I've seen enough." And the sheer size of it meant that staying away from Jake was going to be just fine.

"Come on, I'll show you to your rooms and we'll get you all drinks." Yes, drinks were most certainly required.

23

JAKE

Despite saying that she wasn't going to give a tour yet, Jemma spoke constantly as she ushered Darcy, Harley, and myself inside the large, rundown farmhouse. I was sure that at some point it had been beautiful and that it would be again one day soon. But, right now, the place was rough. Holes in the walls, some in the floors. We probably should have signed a waiver before we crossed the threshold.

Darcy was shown to a room on the first floor—off the pristine and fully functioning kitchen, which appeared to be the only thing in the entire home that was finished. Not surprising when I recalled Nash was a chef—and then we climbed the stairs, which creaked and groaned a disturbing amount.

"We've had it checked out, it's structurally sound," Jemma said over her shoulder, picking up on my increasing panic about the ceiling falling down on our heads.

"Good to know."

"But some of the rooms aren't exactly habitable just yet, so not everyone is sleeping in the house. Nash and I are out in the small house, Chase and Mack have a camper."

I nodded, but I was having trouble focusing. To keep my mind off the house collapsing I had let my eyes drift to Harley, who was skipping just ahead of me. There was a hole near one of the back pockets on her jean shorts and, with every other step, I was given the tiniest glimpse of the red lace underwear she had on. I needed a cold shower immediately.

"Okay ... I've got you guys here. I hope that's okay." Jemma pointed to two doors.

I nodded and shrugged, like of course this was absolutely not an issue. Harley smiled and did the same, but her jaw still twitched.

"There's a Jack and Jill bathroom between the rooms so just remember to knock!" Jemma giggled like the prospect of us walking in on one another was hilarious. Harley was staring daggers at her.

"Noted," she said. "And where is your sex-machine of a boyfriend?"

Jemma snorted. "He's around somewhere, maybe down at the dam with Chase and Mack? Please do not let him hear you calling him a sex-machine."

"Why? Is being called a sex-machine offensive?" The question was for Jemma but had somehow been directed at me. I gaped, unsure of how to answer. Harley's eyes skated down my chest, and lower, before coming back to my face. There was a pink stain painting the tops of her cheeks. The air around us grew heavy and charged. She blinked, breaking the moment.

Jemma was shaking her head. "Anyway, it's not fancy, but it'll be comfortable. Get settled and come down when you're ready." She gave our arms a squeeze and turned to leave.

"No!" Harley yelled and Jemma stuttered a step.

"No, what?"

"No need to get settled." Harley opened the closest door

and shoved her bag inside. "Let's head downstairs and get that drink."

Jemma glanced at me, but Harley was already dragging her down the stairs by her elbow.

"He's fine, he's fine," Harley said. "He probably needs some space after being stuck in a car with me and Darce. Let's go."

I watched them leave, attention once again zeroing in on that minuscule glimpse of red lace.

Was Harley right? Should I be tired of her company after that drive? She was clearly tired of me. I wasn't, though, and I was starting to think that I wouldn't get tired of her. In fact, sitting beside her had been a new kind of torture, one I welcomed because I was turning into some sort of masochist, apparently. I pushed open the door to the room she had not claimed, needing to give myself something else to focus on.

As Jemma had said, it wasn't fancy, but there were no holes in the floor, ceiling, or walls, and the bed looked like it had fresh linen, so I was not going to complain. I dropped my bag on the floor and flopped onto the white comforter with a huff.

Part of me understood why Harley was so adamant that our one night be just that, one night. But, if we enjoyed one another's company—which I was quite sure we did at this point—and were both on the same page as to the expectations of the situation, I didn't really see the problem in that one night becoming two or three or four.

There was no way she had managed to get anything out of her system. I knew it because I hadn't, either. I wanted her just as much, if not more, than I did before. So why continue to fight this pull that felt as natural as breathing?

Because *feelings* didn't heed expectations, no matter how explicitly you laid them out. Feelings did whatever the fuck they wanted, whenever the fuck they wanted, something I knew all too well. So, Harley was just protecting herself, being smarter than me, who was happy to drown in her and forget that the outside world existed.

She'd made her decision and, if I was thinking logically, I could appreciate that it was probably the right one—even if I didn't like it.

I shoved off the bed and poked my head into the bathroom. Like the bedroom, it was clean and intact, if a little outdated. The counter and tiles were faded lime green set off with a seventies brown, an odd combination. I was nearly going to have to fold myself in half to get in the shower, but I'd make do.

I stepped outside onto what I assumed was destined to be a large patio area, feeling like a complete interloper. It hadn't occurred to me when I accepted this invitation that I'd be spending a weekend with a bunch of people I didn't actually know that well.

I had met most of them only once, Darcy a handful of times, Hunter didn't arrive until tomorrow, and Harley, who was my main connection to any of these people at the moment, was avoiding me.

What was I doing here?

Despite the awkwardness crawling across my skin, I could appreciate the scenery. Rolling green pastures, broken by a large dam currently twinkling in the rich, late afternoon sunlight. But what did I think I was doing here? Making friends? It wasn't exactly a skill of mine. And once your face was splashed everywhere, it was easy to be suspicious of people's motives. Being invited here, even if it was just because I knew Harley and Hunter, it felt nice because I knew it had nothing to do with how I could kick a ball.

The loneliness I'd felt when I arrived in New York bled

into my mind. A loneliness I'd all but forgotten about while sitting at the Cream and Sugar counter or on runs with Hunter.

Jemma appeared beside me with two large glasses, one of which I accepted before she hooked an arm through mine.

"Cheers," she said, tapping our glasses together, a small amount of the liquid sloshing over the side.

"Cheers." I sipped, citrus and salt exploding across my tongue.

"Good, right?"

Another sip. "Very."

She seemed to be waiting for something, not that I was sure what it could be. Maybe I should have stayed upstairs a little longer.

"So, how do you all know each other?" I asked when she hadn't filled the increasingly expectant silence.

Her eyes flicked up to my face, before she answered. "I was the chef at Cream and Sugar for a few years. I only left last December." Another chef. The completed kitchen made perfect sense.

"Oh, yeah? Why'd you leave?"

"Darcy fired me."

I choked on my margarita.

"It was for my own good," she assured me. "I was using it as an excuse not to pursue my event planning business full time. She shoved me out of the nest and took away the excuse. Then I hired Odette—who you met yesterday, she's coming up tomorrow with Hunter—and off we went." She sipped her drink. "Nash, Chase and Mack all went to high school together."

She watched Nash, her gaze warm.

"And you and Nash ...?"

"We planned his sister's wedding together last year. It was in *People*!"

"Magazine?"

"Yes! I sent at least ten copies to my mom." She giggled.

"And then you two ..." What, got together? That sounded lame. I took another gulp of margarita.

"After some bumps," she said with a smile. "But what's life without some bumps?"

"Indeed." We clinked glasses again.

"Speaking of ... you and Harley?"

I once again choked on my drink. "Me and Harley what?"

She raised an eyebrow in that way women did, speaking volumes without saying a word, and I tried not to look like I was squirming as I chugged down half of my margarita. There wasn't anything to say about me and Harley. We'd had our fun, but it was over now. A tune started to play in my head, and I almost choked for the third time. Not love, *definitely* not love.

"You okay there?" she asked with a tilted smile.

"Fine," I spluttered.

"So, there is something going on." It was no longer a question.

"Going on? No. Nothing is going on. I'm staying with her and Hunter. That's it."

"You just choked on your drink for no reason, then?"

"Wrong pipe."

"Uh-huh." There was a pause as she watched me. "She deserves to be happy."

I nodded, because what the hell could I say to that? Of course, she deserved to be happy. Everyone deserved to be happy, didn't they?

"You do too, for the record," she added.

"Ah, thank you." And there was that awkwardness again.

"You're welcome." She smiled, eyes going unfocused for a beat. That was definitely not her first margarita. I steered the conversation away from sticky topics like Harley and her happiness, and toward the dilapidated farmhouse behind us. After a beat of hesitation, she accepted the new direction and talked me through all the changes she and Nash were planning. It all sounded incredible. Would I get to see it? I knew Blair would be able to work some magic to get me out of my contract ... but I still wasn't sure how Harley would react to me wanting to stay in New York.

Later that night, I found Harley standing in the hall—one of the halls—looking this way and that, mumbling to herself. The same woman who said she had a sense of direction that was *second to none* was lost in a house. I smothered my smile as she scratched her head and then set off in the wrong direction.

I followed until she stopped again and mumbled a little more.

"You don't know where you're going, do you?" I asked and her back went ramrod straight before she spun on her heel to face me with what might have been a superior, haughty-type look, had she not stumbled and caught herself on the wall. I tried not to laugh, but those margaritas were strong.

"I know where I'm going. I was just giving myself a little tour."

"At twelve-thirty?"

"Is there a better time? No one else is around. I can really get my snoop on." To illustrate her point, she opened the door to her left, revealing an empty cupboard.

"So much to see."

"Oh, shut up."

Before she could storm off in a huff, which I was pretty confident she was about to do, I kicked the door closed, took her by the waist and turned us around.

She let out a squawk, one hand landing on my chest. "How do you know where you're going?"

"Because I have an actual sense of direction," I said as she peeled herself off me.

"And I don't?" she snapped, tripping over her own feet as I walked her backward.

"After your display of navigation skills today … the jury is out," I teased and booped her on the nose. Fucking margaritas.

She swatted me away. "Are you following me?"

"Are you avoiding me?"

"I asked you first."

"I was going to bed."

"Oh! A likely story! If you were going to bed and knew where you were going, you wouldn't have found me wandering the halls now, would you?" She arched an eyebrow. "So why are you following me? Trying to get me naked with all of my friends downstairs?"

"I am not trying to get you naked, Harley." The statement would have been more believable if my eyes didn't skim down her body as I said it. I was so desperate to get her naked again I could barely see straight. Or maybe that was the margaritas, too?

"But you were following me?"

"No, I wasn't. But you have definitely been avoiding me."

"Absurd," she said with a snort.

"Really?"

"Yes, really." She turned and stomped off ahead. I caught up with her in two steps.

"You still don't know where you're going," I said, choosing to let the fact that she'd been avoiding me since we got out of the car go. For the moment.

"I'm tired," she said with a sniff.

"Me too, come on." I offered my hand and this time she

didn't bat it away. Instead, she took it and let me lead her to our rooms. My skin pressed against hers was a blissful relief after her averted glances all night. It shouldn't hurt so much to have her push me away.

Before I could get too carried away with holding hands, like a fucking middle grader (a drunken middle grader), we arrived at our rooms. Thank fucking god.

"Here we are," I said, still holding her hand. I looked down at our twined fingers and didn't want to let go. It was too nice, but I wasn't going to draw attention to that right at the moment. Instead, I cleared my throat and regrettably dropped her hand.

"Thank you for getting me to my room. However, I still refuse to admit I was lost." She was trying hard not to smile.

"Of course not. You don't even need a tour from Jemma tomorrow."

"Definitely not." Curls bounced as she shook her head.

We stood staring at one another, the air between us zinging. I could close the space so easily. Just lean in and we could be kissing. I really wanted to be kissing her right now.

Instead, I took a step back toward my door. "Well, I guess I'll see you tomorrow."

"You will."

"Good night, Harley."

She didn't move, just watched me take another step away from her. "Good night, Jake."

24

HARLEY

I stood in the hallway—leaning heavily against the wall—for at least a minute, staring at the space where Jake had been. I'd been trying to drink away my worries, or rather my sexual frustration, since we got here, but it hadn't really worked. I knew that what I should be doing was going into my room, downing at least one large glass of water and going the fuck to bed. But I was so keyed up, the chances of me falling asleep in the next hour—or two—were slim to none.

Bed, Harley, it is time. For. Bed.

In my haste to get as far away from Jake as quickly as possible earlier, I hadn't actually given my room a second glance. On first inspection, it kind of looked like something out of a horror movie. The wallpaper was peeling, the floorboards were rough, but the bed was made up with a white textured comforter and there were at least four pillows. I wanted to crawl into that cocoon of cozy and go to sleep immediately. But first teeth, because I'd rather my tongue was not plastered to my mouth first thing tomorrow morning,

I pulled open the door to the bathroom and immediately

remembered that it wasn't *my* bathroom but *our* bathroom. Jake was standing across the room, also frozen in the doorway. All those margaritas seemed to have had the opposite effect to what I hoped. He looked ridiculously good. Like *eat him for breakfast* good. Or a midnight snack, as the case may be. Would it be so bad if our one night wasn't just one night? I nibbled my lip, imagining the feel of his fingers curling around my hips. *Yes.* No! Yes—I mean, yes, it would be so bad. A bad, bad idea to turn the one night into more.

"You didn't knock," he said with a slanted smile that went straight to my nipples.

"Neither did you."

We moved into the bathroom with slow steps, each approaching the other with trepidation.

I dropped my toiletries bag onto the counter and rifled for my toothbrush and toothpaste—and discovered I had forgotten the toothpaste. Shitty, shit, shit.

"Missing something?" he asked, watching me in the cracked mirror.

I pushed my chin up. "Could I please borrow your toothpaste?"

He squirted a small blob onto his brush before handing the tube to me. I was careful not to let our fingers touch as I took it.

We brushed our teeth side by side, eyeing one another in the mirror. I wasn't sure I'd ever been so turned on while brushing my teeth. It wasn't sexy, or it hadn't been until right now. But then, I was pretty sure that Jake could make anything look sexy. He spat his mouthful into the sink and kept going. No one should look that good with toothpaste foam dribbling down their chin. He spat again, rinsed again. I did the same. So mundane and yet I was ready to throw myself at him.

Bed. Must go to bed. Alone.

"Well, good night, again."

"Night, Harley."

It took approximately three and a half days for me to get to sleep. Leaving me feeling like a sleep-deprived zombie when I woke up. I was used to running on less than the recommended eight hours, but this was reaching Harley-will-be-speaking-in-tongues territory.

The tossing and turning and the increased Jake-related fixation couldn't be about the shared bathroom. We had been sharing a bathroom for *weeks*. It was by no means a new situation and should not have caused my sleep to be as atrocious as it was last night.

Granted, at home, we had not actually been in the bathroom together unless we were naked. Maybe that was the problem? I now associated Jake and bathrooms with sex, rather than mundane things like brushing one's teeth and flossing.

A recalibration was required.

I threw off the covers and marched to the bathroom door, pressing an ear against it. There was nothing, no hint of movement, not in the bathroom, or the bedroom beyond. Even still, I knocked, loud.

Only when ten long seconds passed with no word from behind the door did I slide it open. The opposite door—Jake's door—was closed, which was a relief and also just a little disappointing.

The water pressure was surprisingly good, and I stepped into the old tub. All I had to do was not get naked with Jake while we were here, which would be easy because all the sexual tension had left the building.

I groaned, shoving my head under the water. The sexual tension had not, in fact, left the building. The sexual tension had settled in and invited friends. But that did not mean we needed to have sex again.

"Who the fuck am I kidding?" I said to the shower curtain as I swatted it away from my legs. Me and self-restraint were not friends. I was, I had always been, a throw caution to the wind kind of girl. Sex was sex, and I never had trouble walking away, no matter how good it was. But could I really do that now? When there already seemed to be feelings creeping in at the corners?

I wrenched the water off and stepped onto the fuzzy pink mat, wrapping a towel tight around my boobs. If I wanted to have sex with Jake again, then it could only happen if I kept my feelings in check and maintained the no strings rule. The same rule that I'd never had a problem maintaining before.

That was not completely out of the realms of possibility, was it?

I pulled on some cut-offs and a tank, wrestled my hair into a pair of messy knots and went in search of the only thing that was going to make me feel more human.

The kitchen was empty, and I took a moment to appreciate just what Jemma and Nash had done. It was a dream, a Joanna Gaines, straight off the pages of some fancy magazine dream. Rustic and warm, but still modern. The island was seven or eight feet long, black stools running the length of one side. The counters were all gray speckled concrete, the cabinets distressed white with black hardware. There was no other way to put it except that I was *in love.*

And then there was the coffee machine. Gleaming chrome, three groups. Her name was ... Lydia, and she was my new best friend.

"Good morning, beautiful ..." I whispered, edging toward her, fingers itching to run along her curves.

"You talking to me?" Nash asked and I jumped so high I swear I nearly hit the roof.

"Jesus Christ!" I planted a hand against my chest, sure that my heart could have broken a rib.

"Why so jumpy, Harls?" He smiled, eyes lighting up and crinkling at the sides.

"I am not jumpy, I just wasn't expecting you to come creeping up on me like a goddamn cat burglar." It defied logic that a guy as big as Nash could be so light on his feet.

"How about I get you a coffee to make up for it?"

I blocked him as he went to get past me and closer to Lydia. "And have you deny me the chance to work with Lydia? I don't think so." That was mostly it, I couldn't say the rest.

"Lydia?" His biceps twitched as he scraped his hair up into a messy bun. That action should not have been as hot as it was, but he had really nice arms. In truth, Nash had really nice everything. Jemma was one lucky lady. I was so happy that she found her happily ever after. She deserved it, and then some.

I gestured to the coffee machine; Nash looked confused but didn't question it. Nice arms, and smart.

"What's wrong, you don't trust me to make you a coffee?" he asked.

"No! No, that's not it." I shook my head vigorously; it was too much.

"You don't!" He laughed.

I considered denying it, but there didn't seem to be much point. "It's just that I am *particular*."

"Who's particular about what?" Jemma asked as she wandered into the kitchen. She went straight for Nash, stepping under one arm and reaching up wordlessly for a kiss. My chest pinched.

"I was just telling your boyfriend that I am more than capable of making myself a coffee, that's all."

"What she means is that she doesn't trust me to make her a coffee." He was half right; I didn't trust anyone to make me coffee.

"I'm sure you make a perfectly good coffee," I assured him, and Jemma snorted out a laugh while Nash gaped at me.

"Them's fightin' words, Harley. You think you make a better coffee than I do?" He was so offended.

I pursed my lips. I really didn't want to offend the guy in his own kitchen but also, yes, I probably did make a better coffee than he did. "I mean ... it is my job."

"Sounds to me like we need ourselves a coffee challenge," he said, and I did my best to smother my smile.

I stepped up to him. "You're on."

"Oh, god." Jemma groaned.

He crossed his arms over his wide chest. "Now?"

"And have your girlfriend be the judge? No offense, Jem."

"None taken, I want nothing to do with this." She filled the kettle and set it on one of the six burners on the stove. Even if she wanted a coffee, she wasn't going to get in the way of this. "At least wait until Hunter and O arrive."

"Yes, good. When Hunter and Odette get here, it's on."

"You really think you're gonna beat me in my own kitchen, short stuff?"

"I don't need to resort to trash talk, Nashville."

He smiled. "Am I allowed to cook in my own kitchen?"

I swept an arm out. "Be my guest."

"You hungry?"

"Starving."

Breakfast came together quickly, Nash and Jemma working in perfect unison. Watching the two of them was like witnessing some kind of synchronized swimming. Except with fewer nose peg things and coordinated outfits.

They were magic together.

I shuffled on my stool cradling an iced coffee—Lydia was a dream, as expected—convincing myself that I was only happy for them and not at all jealous. The sticky sensation in the pit of my stomach said otherwise, but I ignored it.

The three of us ate, with Jemma explaining the vision she had for Bell-Meadow. It sounded incredible, and I could not wait to see all those pictures in her head be brought to life. I'd always known she was destined for more than the Cream and Sugar kitchen. As much as I'd loved working with her, I was glad she'd found this new path, where she was meant to be.

It was close to ten by the time I was suitably stuffed full of breakfast tacos, and it was still just the three of us at the kitchen island large enough to be a sacrificial altar. Everyone else was choosing to have a little lie-in, apparently. Not that I blamed them, I'd love it if I could stay in bed past seven, but my body clock didn't really let me, no matter what time I went to sleep. The fact I didn't get up until eight this morning had been a small miracle.

With washing up taken care of, I excused myself, needing some space from the love birds and the uncomfortable feeling under my ribs.

Of course, I should have expected that the minute I decided I needed a little space, Jake would appear. And, of course, he was glistening after a morning workout or whatever the hell he'd been doing.

"Morning," he said, falling in step beside me as we climbed the stairs. I should have gone to explore the yard—or literally anywhere else.

"Good morning. How did you sleep?" I asked, resorting to small talk because my brain was malfunctioning with all his skin on show.

"I always sleep like shit the first night somewhere new."

My eyes bounced up to his face. "Me too." The fact that I

wanted to crawl into his bed rather than thrashing around in mine didn't help things, either. Heat sizzled down my spine as our gazes held and anything else I might have said dried up on my tongue. Just once more, would that really be so bad?

I opened my door, marching inside as he did the same and then there we were, just like last night, on opposite sides of the bathroom. Fucking hell. If Nash had not put quite so much garlic in those breakfast tacos I would walk out. But I really wanted to freshen my breath up. So, I did. With Jake standing there watching me.

I brushed my teeth with more force than was strictly necessary, but it helped to distract me. Okay, that was a lie. There was no distracting from the path of his eyes, like a warm touch down the side of my face and neck. Why was he just standing there, leaning against the doorframe? My gaze flicked to him in the mirror and away just as quickly as he caught me.

Stay strong Harley, do not succumb to the hot man tractor beam!

"What do you want from me?" I demanded as I dropped my toothbrush into my bag.

"Nothing, Harley, I don't want anything from you."

"Then why are you hanging around all the time!"

"All the time? I'm just waiting to shower. I haven't seen you all morning." God, why did he have to be right?

"Yes, fine, but you've been—"

"I've been what?"

"In my head, Jake! You've been in my head! *Constantly.*"

His eyes turned smokey as he stepped further into the room. "Is that right?"

I swallowed, my throat spontaneously dry, heart thudding. "Yes."

Another step closer, then another, and our toes were

brushing as he backed me up against the counter. "What have I been doing in your head?"

Oh no, I was not going there. "I think you know."

"I don't think I do ..."

"What do you want me to say, Jake?"

He didn't say anything, just kept watching me, stripping me bare.

"What? You want me to say that maybe I like you, is that what you want to hear? Well, fine, I like you, okay, are you happy now? How about I've not been able to stop thinking about you? Even before we had sex again. Because that's true, too. Congratulations! I think we should probably just keep having sex! Why not, right?"

"Why not?" he said, and I gaped.

"*Why not?*" Why not? Was he serious? I was already teetering dangerously close to head over fucking heels, and he wanted to know why we shouldn't keep having sex?

"Yeah, why not? I'm going to coach Cecilia's team, but I've made no commitments beyond that. It could be like before ..."

I narrowed my eyes. "What exactly are you suggesting?"

"I'm not suggesting anything, you're the one who said we should keep having sex." He was right, I did say that. But I wasn't serious. We could not continue to have sex for another six weeks if I wanted to keep my head, not to mention my heart, which was getting more and more involved with each passing second. Not good. My heart didn't get involved in these things. My heart stayed locked away, safely unattached.

"It's not a good idea," I said. And I meant it. I was pretty sure, almost positive, I meant it.

"Then why say it?"

"Because I don't think clearly when I'm around you! I say outlandish things like we should keep having sex, even though we agreed it would just be one night and then we'd move on. That was the deal."

"That *was* the deal, yes, but ..." His eyes dropped to my mouth.

I licked my lips. "But?"

"But maybe ..."

I was swaying toward him, smothering the last of the space between us. Could I really do this? Could I really keep my head and my heart in check? Firmly unattached. That was the only way this could happen. "No strings. Until you leave. Because you're leaving."

He swallowed, a slight shadow passing briefly over his eyes before he nodded. "Right."

This was a terrible idea.

25

JAKE

Harley and I stood there watching one another for a long minute. My fingers twitched with the need to reach out and grab her. It wouldn't take much, the space between us was minuscule at best. I really wanted to kiss her.

What would she think if she knew I didn't want to leave, didn't want to go back to London? Would that make her pause? I could tell her, should tell her, but the fear of her rejection kept the words in my throat. Six weeks. I had six weeks to try and change her mind. To make her see that maybe we could be more than we were before.

She nudged me backward, grabbed the back of my neck and jumped. Had I not been half-expecting it, the move would have broken my nose. Her legs locked around my waist, bringing our faces together as I gripped her thighs. I didn't want to let go. Ever.

"Right now?" I asked. I thought I'd be able to get a shower in first, at least. Apparently, that was lower on Harley's priority list.

"Just a quick one."

"I'm not sure I can be quick with you."

"Make an effort," she said and kissed me hard, tongue diving past my lips and sweeping into my mouth. I groaned, my mind emptying save for her. The taste and smell of her, the sounds she made and how she felt in my hands.

Finally. The word was a hum along my bones, a warmth in my blood. I didn't like the idea of being quick. But I'd make up for it tomorrow, and the day after, and the day after.

I stumbled against the bathroom counter, dropping her onto the green Laminex. She froze in my arms, lips, hands, even her breath stopped.

"What—"

"Shhh," she hissed, flattening her hand against my mouth. I licked her palm, and she shot me a stern look even as her legs squeezed my waist. "I thought I heard—"

There was a knock. "Harley!"

"Hunter," she said, her head dropping onto my shoulder.

"Harley?" Was he in her room?

"I don't think we should tell him about ... this," I whispered. The confession had guilt sliding through my gut.

"Agreed," Harley said. She went to untangle her legs, but I held her in place.

"I guess you'll just have to be quiet."

"I'm not very good at thaaaaat." Her hips rolled against my stomach as I sucked her neck.

"Make an effort."

Her answering laugh was little more than a puff of air, ruffling my hair.

"See? You can be quiet when you want to." I let my hands trail up her ribs, toying with her tank.

"Harls, you in here?" We both froze again.

"In the bathroom," she said, and her eyes went wide.

"What are you doing?" I whispered, hands flattening on the counter either side of her thighs.

"Maybe I can get him to leave."

"Being quiet would have got him to leave!" I really did not want to have to stop what we were doing. Not now. Not when it felt like it had taken so long to get here.

"Well hurry up, it's time to go swimming," Hunter said.

"Sounds good, I just need a minute." To my great relief, she remained where she was. But I had no intention of being *that* quick.

"No sweat, I'll wait."

"He'll wait?!" I said.

"No. No don't wait. The truck-stop nachos did a number on me."

"How many times have we said not to eat that shit?" he said with a laugh, because of course she'd make a habit of eating the things.

"I know, I know, but the heart wants what the heart wants. Now, can you get out?"

"Fine, I'll see you downstairs."

We stayed there listening for a couple of long moments before Harley was once again attacking my mouth.

"Naked," I said, pulling down the neck of her tank so I could get at her breasts. Then I had one of her stiff-peaked nipples in my mouth, sucking, tongue swirling, and she arched, her breath leaving her in a hiss.

"Quiet."

"That was qui—"

I bit her, not hard, but enough that she'd feel it later. She didn't make a sound, but her hands went to my hair and pulled.

"Good girl," I said, and she whimpered. "I knew you could be quiet."

"I—"

I bit her again. She pulled my hair again.

"Not a sound. Just in case."

She tugged on my hair bringing our mouths back together and kissed me with a fierceness that had my knees close to buckling. I had no fucking idea how I was going to convince her we should be doing this a lot longer than six weeks, but it wasn't something I was going to let myself think of right now. Not when I had this woman against me, burning and eager and so fucking sexy.

As much as I wanted to lay her out on a bed, we probably couldn't risk that now, so the bathroom counter would have to do.

I flicked the button on her shorts as her hand disappeared into mine and a hoarse groan rolled up my throat. But Harley was still mostly clothed, which really needed to change. She wiggled out of her shorts with my help and once they were off, I knocked her hand away. Any protest she might have made died as I placed a finger to my lips.

"I don't want to bite your pussy, Harley, but I will." Okay, maybe I did want to bite her, just a little.

She gaped, then ripped her shirt over her head and spread her legs wide.

She was *perfect*.

"No noise."

She nodded as she licked her lips and I dropped to my knees in front of her. Hooded eyes watched me, her breath coming in short pants.

I wanted to drag it out, to torture her until she was silently begging, but I was impatient and also mindful of the fact we could be interrupted at any moment. I slid a finger through her wetness, groaning as I parted her until I could take her clit between my lips and suck. The fact I could not just stay here for the rest of the day was a travesty.

Her fingers were once again in my hair, twisting and pulling as her hips rolled. It took no time to feel her oncoming orgasm and I edged her closer, slipping a finger inside, quickly following it with a second and she pressed down against my hand, greedy and wanting.

"Fuck Harley, look at you." If I didn't have a job to do right now, I'd sit here and just stare at her. She was mountains, and valleys, and smooth, soft plains. I wanted to learn each and every part of her, study her with my hands, my lips, my tongue.

She watched me down the length of her body, lips parted on a silent cry as I curled my fingers upwards, sucking her clit into my mouth. Her juices coated my chin, as I lapped at her, drawing her closer and closer. And then she was there, fists in my hair, squeezing until my scalp burned, holding me tight to her pussy as her hips rocked and she rode out her orgasm.

When she stilled, I gave her one last lick before regrettably stepping back. If it were up to me, I really would be there all day, all night.

Harley, however, had other plans. She pushed off the mirror where she had slumped backward, a condom already pinned between her teeth, and pulled me to her by the front of my shorts.

Her lips were at my ear as she rolled the condom down my cock and I focused on not passing out from sheer sensory overload.

"Fuck me so hard I see stars."

"Happy to oblige." My hands drifted up her legs, taking her thighs and spreading them wide as I drove into her in one long slide that had us both gasping for air.

I paused for a beat, her thighs in my hands, her hands braced on the counter. I watched her, giving her one last chance to change her mind. Her answer was an arching back, pushing me deeper still. Fucking bliss.

With slow, measured strokes I withdrew and filled her over and over until we were panting and sweat soaked.

Frustrated with the rhythm, Harley locked her legs tight around my waist, heels digging into my ass and pulled our mouths together. *More*, she said without words, and I was helpless to obey.

Our lips broke apart and I trailed a hand down her chest, pinching one nipple then the other before sweeping down to her clit. She bit her lip, arching into me, and the warm, squeezing pulse around my cock told me why.

I could make her come all day and it wouldn't be enough. I would still want to wring more pleasure from her. Again. And again. And again.

"You like that?"

"Don't stop," she panted.

Rather than obey this time, I stepped back and pulled her off the counter, spinning her to face the mirror as I smoothed a hand along her spine, pushing her torso down.

Her eyes found mine in the mirror as I pushed inside. I would never get tired of that feeling. That warm, slick grip of her that threatened to undo me on the spot.

Harley flattened both hands against the mirror, ass grinding against me. I watched the reflection of her breasts bouncing as I tangled my fingers into her hair, bringing her back far enough that I could reach her mouth. She reached back, digging short nails into my thighs.

"Jake." It was a desperate whisper, a plea. The answering kiss was messy, a clash of hungry lips and tongues, and then my release was rocketing through me, and I came so hard I almost took us both down onto the floor.

I collapsed on top of her, groaning into her neck as my breathing evened out. I was really glad we were going to keep doing that, even if we did have to keep it a secret.

Harley perched her chin in her hands and looked at me in the mirror.

"Well, that was something," she said, wiggling just a little as I slid out of her with a gasp.

"It was," I agreed, my heart still thundering in my ears as I caught my breath. I wished we could just stay where we were, but it was only a matter of time before Hunter came looking for her—or me—again.

"Not terribly quick, though."

"I am not apologizing for that."

Her laugh was low. "I didn't say you needed to."

I didn't want to move, but I knew we couldn't stay here. I gave her butt a squeeze before taking care of the condom and was disappointed to see her slipping her shorts back on.

"I should really shower."

"I should really leave you to that."

"I'd really rather you didn't." I caught her around the waist and pulled her into my chest.

"I'd rather I didn't, too, however"—she glanced across the room—"that shower is not made for two people and Hunter is waiting."

"Valid points," I said, "but we are doing this again, right?"

Her lips pursed, considering—or smothering her smirk. "Yes Jake, we will be doing this again."

"And again."

"And again."

She reached up, her hands at my neck, and kissed me. It was slow and sweet, not the frenzy we'd just been together.

When my cock was starting to nudge against her stomach Harley pulled away.

"Okay, I'm leaving you to it," she said and slapped my bare ass before skipping out of the bathroom. A voice in my head said that Harley was probably right, and this was a bad idea, a recipe for heartbreak, but I wasn't interested in listening to that voice right at the moment. Instead, I turned on the ancient shower and prepared myself to contort under the spray.

Half an hour later, after what was one of the more awkward showers of my life, I no longer smelled like sweat and pussy and I was dressed. I had not, however, managed to wipe the goofy grin off my face. I knew I needed to; there was no way Harley and I would be able to keep this thing to ourselves if I was walking around smiling like a goofball and talking down a hard-on ninety-three percent of the time. But knowing it and getting my face to comply were two very different things. It was going to be a constant struggle for the next six weeks.

Six weeks.

I didn't want to think too far ahead, but it was difficult to keep my brain from straying down that path. Six weeks and Harley might still choose to walk away.

Stop thinking about it.

I swiped my baseball cap from the dresser and left the room.

Darcy, Jemma, and Odette were all in the kitchen, and the conversation came to an abrupt end as soon as I walked in. Not suspicious at all.

Jemma jumped off her stool, fluttering around the kitchen island. "Jake! Good morning! How did you sleep? Can I get you anything?"

"Way to be chill, Jem, I bet he has no idea we were talking about him now," Darcy said, smirking as she cradled a large, steaming mug.

Odette laughed and Jemma shot them both dagger eyes.

"Glad to hear I'm providing entertainment, then ..."

"Oh, you have no idea," Darcy said with a wide grin.

I chose to ignore that. "I'll take an Americano, please."

"Yes, great."

"You've got quite the place here, I took a run around the grounds this morning. It's a lot bigger than it looks."

"It is, and most of it is still rough, but the house is the priority. Once that's done, we'll tackle the rest."

"Makes sense." I nodded, sliding onto a stool. I could feel both Darcy and Odette watching me, but neither said anything. Had Harley said something? No, keeping it from Hunter would be more difficult if she was telling these three. But there was a weight of knowing in their gazes. Could they read it on my face? I'd attempted to get the I-just-fucked-Harley-on-the-bathroom-counter look under control, but maybe I wasn't as successful as I'd hoped.

Jemma handed over my coffee along with two crumpets. "You can't get a decent crumpet here."

"I'd never even heard of them until I got to London."

"And then?"

"And then I ate them every day for a couple of weeks until my nutritionist told me I was destroying all her hard work." I wasted no time slathering the two in front of me with butter and honey.

"Jemma makes the best crumpets you'll ever taste," Darcy said.

"Is that so?"

"She has a low to non-existent bar." Jemma's cheeks were slightly pink. "But she's probably still right."

I bit into one of the crumpets and only just resisted the urge to groan. They were really fucking good. "She's right." I confirmed, as a pang of something like homesickness hit me in the chest. London might not be home, but part of me did still miss it, just a little. Especially when I thought about taking Harley there one day.

26

HARLEY

The dam was fucking cold.

As soon as I took a running leap off the short dock, I remembered why I generally avoided bodies of water that were not the ocean or a pool. Quite aside from the murky water that could be concealing all manner of creatures, everything was *squishy*.

It didn't matter how forcefully I told myself it was just mud, just wet dirt, and definitely *not* a big deal, the feel of it squelching between my toes gave me the heebie-jeebies. As a result, I'd spent half an hour alternating between treading water and floating on my back before deciding I could just sit on the dock and get some sun instead.

Hunter, on the other hand, was having the time of his life and—I noted with both interest and amusement—had barely stopped talking about Odette. There was most definitely a crush forming there. Not surprising, because Odette was a total boss and a babe and had quickly become a good friend, but she wasn't the kind of girl Hunter usually went for. He tended to gravitate to those with a little less substance.

I was grateful for his Odette distraction, because it meant he hadn't yet noticed the bite mark peeking out from my bikini top. Jake had caught me seriously off guard with that. And it was *good*. I pressed my legs together as a wave of heat rolled over me. Why on earth did I think that I would be able to keep this to myself—for three days, and six weeks after that. Surrounded by my friends, one of whom could read me like a fucking book—this was the problem with knowing someone as long as I'd known Hunter. He knew my lying face, my sneaky face, all the faces. This was going to be close to impossible. Unless ... maybe we just needed to not have sex again until we got back home. Yes, we'd still be contending with Hunter, but he was one person. One person who was out of the apartment at least sixty percent of the time.

My eyes followed a wispy cloud as it streaked across the sky. This wasn't just about the sex though, was it? I told Jake I *liked* him. I hadn't meant to. I hadn't meant to say anything at all. But out it came anyway. *I like you.* And I did like him, which was what concerned me most about the whole situation.

"What's with the face?" Hunter asked as he popped up onto the dock and sprayed water all over me.

"What face?" I shielded my eyes as I looked up at him.

"You were scowling at that cloud. It's one cloud, Harls, I'm sure it won't impact your sun for too long." So maybe he didn't know *all* my faces.

"You're impacting my sun." I shoved his leg. "And I was not scowling at the cloud."

"What were you scowling at, then?"

I pushed up onto my elbows. "I wasn't scowling!"

He watched me for a beat, and I resisted the urge to cross my arms over the bite mark. Would he believe I walked into a door, chest first? I snorted out a laugh as I tried to imagine how that would work.

"And now she's laughing at nothing," he said, more drops of water spraying from his hair as he ran a hand through it.

"Sorry."

"For what?" He dropped down beside me, feet dangling over the edge of the dock. "Harley, I have known you long enough to not think anything you do is weird. Or, at least I don't question it, anyway."

I laughed again.

"Is that a bite mark?"

I didn't glance down at it because that felt like an admission. "Whaaaat, *no*."

It was his turn to let out a snort laugh. "Do I even want to know?"

"I don't know, do you?"

There was a pause before he said, "No, I do not." Thank God.

We both went quiet, eyes out over the water. I didn't like silences with most people. I always tried to fill them with noise, with chatter, scared of what they might expose otherwise. It had never been that way with Hunter.

Once upon a time we tried to date. For two disastrously awkward weeks in freshman year of high school we held hands in the halls and made out under the bleachers, trying to be what everyone else thought we were. But we weren't a couple, we never had been. We were just Hunter and Harley. Since our two weeks of temporary insanity (that we no longer mentioned) we had been happily platonic BFFs—he hated it when I called him my BFF, so naturally I did it at every possible opportunity.

I glanced over at him now. Maybe I could talk to him about everything that was going on in my head, in my heart. He was one of the only people who really knew me before and after Liam, who had seen me claw my way out of the dark, alive, but changed. What would he say about this thing between me and Jake? Good idea? Bad idea? Something in between?

"We need floaties," he said, before I could voice any of the things clamoring for attention in my overactive brain. It was probably better that way. There wasn't anything to talk about, right? Jake was leaving. I was staying in New York. We'd both get on with our lives. Just like that. Just like before. What else was there to say?

"Uh, what?"

"For the dam. We need floaties."

"Hunter, you're thirty years old."

He laughed. "Not those kinds of floaties! I mean like the ones you can ride on, like a unicorn, or a flamingo, or a shark."

"I love that your first example was a unicorn." I jumped to my feet. "Yes, Hunter! Why the hell did I not think of this?" A rideable flotation device would mean that I could enjoy the dam without having to stand in disgusting, squelching mud. Hunter was a genius. "We need to get into town."

If I did not find a large, ideally rainbow, unicorn to spend the next couple of days floating around on, I would consider this weekend a grand failure.

We raced into the house, past everyone else, as they lounged on the stretch of grass off the kitchen on a collection of large cushions and blankets.

"I'm driving," Hunter said as we shoved each other through the door, on the way back out.

"No way," I fired back then marched back out and over to Jake. "Where are your keys?" I asked, interrupting his conversation with Mack.

He glanced up at me, eyes darting to my chest and the mark he left there. His ears went a little pink. "Ah ... why?"

I tried to stop my smile from spreading too far. "Because Hunter and I need to go into town."

"Hunter has a car."

A minor detail. "He does, but he's been driving all morning. He needs a break."

"So, you can drive his car."

"I could do that, yes, but I'd rather dri—"

"Nope. No, you are not driving my rental." A predictable response.

"Jake, come on, the town is so close, you probably ran further than that this morning, right?" He didn't comment. "We'll be twenty minutes, max. *Please?*"

He pressed his lips together. Was he trying not to smile? Or was he seriously considering it?

"Pretty please?" I added for good measure. He wanted to say no, I could see that much, but as the other conversations around us broke off and eyes turned in our direction, I could also see that he wanted to avoid a scene. One I was sure he knew I'd happily make.

His eyes darted to Mack then back to me before he relented with a grunted, "Fine." And I beamed in victory as he told me where they were.

"Thank you," I said, dropping in a curtsy before I took off for the house.

Hunter was already in his car when I came running out the front door, waving the keys to one gorgeous automobile.

"I was wondering whose car that was," Hunter said.

"Jake's rental for the weekend." I wagged my eyebrows.

"Did you steal his keys?"

I gaped, flattening a hand to my chest. "I did not steal his keys. I asked, and he said yes."

"Under duress."

"Shut up and get in."

He opened his mouth, poised to say something else, but stopped, mouth snapping shut again. Was it about Jake? About me and Jake? That need to talk to him, to tell him about all these feelings swarming in my chest rose up again, but I squashed it. The feelings were temporary, just like this thing with Jake. Once he left, I would be able to resume my business as usual, casual sex routine with whoever looked good in the moment.

"You all good?" Hunter asked, dropping into the passenger seat, his eyes on me.

"Sure, of course." I ignored the twist in my stomach and turned the key, smiling as the car roared to life. Hunter returned the smile, not commenting on the fact mine didn't quite reach my eyes.

My mood improved remarkably over the next hour thanks to one unicorn flotation device. Although it was not rainbow, it did have a gold horn and neon pink hooves and mane, so I was one happy Harley.

There were a couple of moments during the whirlwind shopping spree that I was again tempted to unload my emotional turmoil on Hunter. I managed to resist each time, even with him looking at me like he knew something was up. It was starting to turn into a game of chicken, and I wasn't sure which one of us was going to crack first. It was usually Hunter, so I was bracing myself for the inevitable: *okay Harley, spill it, what's going on with you?*

I would naturally deny that anything was going on with me and try to steer the conversation in a different direction only to have him steer it right back.

He glanced sideways at me as we strolled down the charming Main Street past quaint storefronts painted in washed white that was perfectly weathered, flower boxes over-flowing with color, townsfolk chatting and laughing. It was the backdrop of every Hallmark movie and it was all done up for the fourth with more flags and red, white, and blue than I had ever seen in one place.

Hunter's eyes were still burning a hole in the side of my head, but I was determined to act natural, so I resolutely ignored him and took an overly large slurp from my iced tea. Thankfully, before he could ask his inevitable question—and I was forced to lie in response—I spotted a thrift store just down the block.

Thank you, Universe.

"Oh my god, yes!" I grabbed his hand and towed him forward.

"I am not playing your thrift store roulette," he said as we stepped over the threshold.

"No roulette today. But I do think we should try and find one item for everyone to take back."

He nodded. "We can do that. Clothing?"

"Whatever speaks to you."

"I don't know what that means."

"You will. Okay, you take the ladies, including myself. And I'll take the gentlemen, including you."

He looked hesitant for less than a second before acceptance settled on his handsome face. "Fine."

"Alright! Let's do this."

The next thirty minutes were spent in thrift heaven. It wasn't a big store, but every square inch was crammed with stuff. There was no rhyme or reason to the layout, women's coats were next to children's shoes, men's jeans and trousers were next to kitchen utensils. It was brilliant. The racks were so high there were small step ladders scattered around, all of which had a sticker on the top telling customers to use at their own risk.

I was more than happy to take that challenge, because I

could see a collection of vintage Polaroid cameras sitting pretty on a shelf just out of reach—and they were calling Jake's name.

When he was here all those years ago, I barely saw Jake without a camera in his hand, he was constantly taking photos —of me, of Hunter, of wherever we were. The two of us spent hours together while Hunter was at work, me sketching— mostly him—as he click-click-clicked away. Now, though, I hadn't seen him take a single picture. And I was thinking that needed to change.

Once I was up, it was clear that some of the cameras had seen better days. A couple of the lenses were cracked, another was missing its buttons. Not ideal. There was one that looked like it was in perfect working order, but my eye was drawn to another tucked into the back. It was an old SLR, not a Polaroid, silver top and bottom with a strip of leather around the middle that was a dusty kind of seafoam green—it was fucking perfect. It wasn't too much bigger than my hand and it was bundled with some film. Success.

Hunter was already waiting at the small counter as I made it there with my armful of treasures.

"How'd you go?" I asked and he gestured to the collection already on the counter. I grinned at the lime green, sequined top hat that sat on top of his pile. "I love it."

"Wait 'til you see what I got for you."

"The hat isn't for me?"

"Nope," he said with a smirk, looking adorably pleased with himself. His attention swept up to my head and the pristine cowboy hat that sat atop it. "Please tell me that is for me."

"Sorry, I got this"—I flicked the brim—"for Nash."

"Nash? Harley, come on, I have dreamed of being a cowboy since we were seven."

"I know, that's why it's for you, ya numbskull."

"Seriously?"

"Yes, seriously." I bowed my head, offering him the hat. He snatched it off and put it on. He looked like an idiot. A really happy idiot. "It suits you."

"Yeah?"

"Yeah."

"Well then, I guess you can have yours too." He reached under the pile on the counter and withdrew a large-ish flat tin. My heart stopped. To anyone else, they would look like a plain old tin of colored pencils. But not to me.

"Hunter ..."

"They're the same ones, right?" I nodded, my throat thick. "I wasn't sure if you still had them."

"I don't." I'd burned them during a particularly low moment when I wanted to wipe everything away.

"Well, now you do. And I know they're not the same, because Liam didn't give them to you, but you just seemed like maybe you could use them."

I breathed steadily through my nose to keep from crying. "Thank you."

"You're welcome." He pulled me into a hug. "I love you, Harls, you deserve to be happy."

The back of my neck prickled, but before I could tell him I thought maybe I might be happy, he kept talking.

"Okay, now for your other thing."

"Other thing? Hunter, it was one item per person."

"And you got two, so sue me," he said. I didn't bother adding that I wasn't the only one with two gifts.

"Are those—"

"Chaps. Yes." He held the brown leather item proudly. They were ridiculous. I loved them.

I rolled my lips together, holding in the laugh. "You got me chaps."

"I did. I thought ..." The sentence trailed off as he watched me for a beat and I got the feeling he was debating what to say. Odd. "I just thought you'd like them."

"I do. With our powers combined, we are one whole cowboy."

"I'm pretty sure that cowboys wear more than hats and chaps, but sure."

"Not the sexy ones."

"Touché."

Ten minutes later we were waved off with all of our finds and a large bag of hard candies, which Hunter had open before we were even in the car, because he was a child.

"You want one?"

"Obviously." I glanced into the bag. "Purple." He dropped two into my waiting palm because he was the best.

We drove back to the farm in easy silence. A couple of times I thought Hunter might ask the question, but he didn't. And maybe he wasn't going to ask anything, and I was just being paranoid. I'd gotten so in my head about everything between me and Jake that I expected everyone else to be tuned into it as well, but that didn't mean they actually were.

Jake was in the hall outside our rooms when I got back, and my heart jumped a little at the sight of him.

"Were you waiting for m—" My sentence was cut off as, with nothing more than a heated look, he tackled me into my room.

"Hi—" I tried again, only to be silenced with another kiss that I happily returned. It started rough and hungry as he kicked the door shut and I dropped my bag on the floor, but it slowed as it deepened, drawing me under, threatening to undo me at the seams. Jake's hands held my face like I was precious as his tongue tangled with mine. Hadn't I decided earlier that we shouldn't do this again while we were here, surrounded by so many eyes and ears?

Any protest about the current proceedings died a quick death as Jake sucked on my bottom lip, letting out a low groan as he did. It was difficult to think anything was a bad idea when he was making sounds like that.

By the time he pulled away, just enough to press his forehead against mine, we were both breathing hard. My lips tingled.

"Hi," I said; the one syllable wobbled.

"I've been waiting to do that since you came running up asking for the keys. That was not twenty minutes."

A giggle bubbled up my throat. What would it be like to come home to this every day? Getting used to that kind of welcome would not be a hardship. "I got distracted."

He smiled, still holding my face, thumbs sliding across my cheeks. "Of course, you did." His eyes darted down to the floor and the bag which had emptied half its contents on the floor as I dropped it. A roll of film was by his bare foot.

A wave of heat rolled through me that had nothing to do with the fact that Jake was still holding my face after kissing the living daylights out of me. No, this heat was sticky and a little uncomfortable because that one little roll of film showed too much, exposing more of my heart than I was used to. I'd been thinking of him. I had scoured every rack in that thrift store, desperate to find just the right thing.

Now, he knew it.

He squatted down, strong quads straining against his shorts, to collect the bag and I took the opportunity to put some space between us hoping it would be enough to help slow my raging heart. This was all supposed to be casual, no strings and no feelings involved, but right now there were feelings and they felt like they were getting bigger by the second. It was too much. I shouldn't have bought the camera. I should have left it on the damn shelf.

Jake pulled me onto the bed with him and onto his lap, putting an end to my attempt at keeping some space between us. Then he opened the bag. The pineapple shaped sunglasses sat on top.

"For me?" he inquired, picking them up.

"To go with your shirt."

He slid them on. "And how do they look?"

My heart pinched. Goddamn it, he was beautiful. "Not as ridiculous as they should."

"I find that hard to believe."

"We got something for everyone," I said, just in case he thought the entire bag was for him. It could be. I would have bought him everything and laid it at his feet like a cat trying to please its owner.

He nodded as he settled the pineapples on top of his head, nestling them into his untamed hair, and glanced down at the roll of film in his hand.

I could lie. I could tell him it was for Hunter, for Mack, for Nash. But what would be the point?

"So, I might have got you two things ..."

There was something alarmingly intimate about this moment.

It shouldn't feel quite so exposing. I had a pair of pineapple shaped sunglasses on my head, for one, and a bag full of things for other people in my hands. But the look on Harley's face was raw and slightly terrified. She felt it too.

"What's the other thing?" I asked, voice rough, raw like that look on her face. Harley took the bag and dug through it until she found what she was looking for.

My heart leaped into my throat as I saw the Olympus logo on the side of the box. "Y–you got me a—"

"Camera, yeah. It came with a few rolls of film too, which was a good thing because I wasn't sure where I was going to find them in town." She handed over the box; it was a little banged up and discolored but it didn't matter. She was thinking of me. The same way I was thinking of her.

I took the box from her, opening the lid with shaking fingers, and worked hard to keep my shit under control.

"It's—is it okay?" she asked, trying to move off me. I stopped her, setting the box aside and shifting her on my lap until she was straddling me. Her hands came to rest on my shoulders. "It's fine, you know, if you don't like it. I don't even know if it will work—"

I cut her off with a kiss. I didn't give a shit if the thing worked or not. I didn't give a shit if it took the worst fucking photographs anyone had ever seen. She got it for me. She remembered.

Harley's arms slid over my shoulders as we melted into one another, bodies pressed together from collar bone to hip, each dip in one of us made for a rise in the other. Mine. It was a whispered plea in my head. Mine. I wanted to keep her. I wanted her to keep me. I couldn't say it aloud, not yet. Instead, I told her with my hands, my lips, my tongue. *Yours, always.*

The kiss slowed, then stopped altogether, and Harley leaned back, her fingers pressed to her lips.

"We should get downstairs. I—I have other gifts to deliver."

Don't leave. I love you. The words rang through my head, clearing out every other thought. But I couldn't say them. Wouldn't say them. Because they scared the fucking shit out of me. Instead, I just nodded, certain my brain would betray me the second I opened my mouth to speak.

She slipped off my lap and stood, straightening her shorts, her tank, her hair, putting herself back together. Did she feel it too? This undertow, sucking the sand out from under our feet, leaving us with nothing to stand on, and no choice but to let go. Was it just me?

Her smile was small, shy, as she picked up the bag. No, it wasn't just me. She felt it, too.

I spent the rest of the day doing my best to not just openly stare at Harley.

Harley distributing thrift store gifts (mine was the best).

Harley in a mismatched bikini; the bottoms were high waisted and pink with cherries all over them, the top was two sunshine yellow and white striped triangles.

Harley riding an inflatable unicorn.

Harley racing on said unicorn against Hunter on a slice of pizza.

Harley on the grass, gloating about her win over Hunter.

It didn't matter what I did, who I was talking to, my eyes found her, wherever she was, whatever she was doing. She was the magnet that always drew me north.

Harley.

Harley.

Harley.

I would have felt worse about all the staring and potentially making her uncomfortable if it was entirely one sided. But it wasn't. In those miraculous moments when I wasn't watching her, I could feel her eyes on me.

Despite all the mutual staring going on, at no point did we ever make eye contact. It was like we'd come to the same conclusion that, if our eyes met, then we'd be found out—or everything around us would spontaneously combust. Either way.

All I wanted to do was throw her over my shoulder, take her upstairs to bed, and worship at her altar into the small hours of the morning and beyond. Although that would mean putting an end to the Odette and Harley show that was currently underway. The two of them were standing on a pile of lumber that had been deemed their stage and singing along to a Lizzo song at the top of their lungs.

Odette was pretty good. Harley, on the other hand, could not hold a tune to save herself. But what she lacked in ability she more than made up for in enthusiasm. And I was still staring.

Harley caught my eye, and my heart thumped against my ribs as heat raged through me. I needed her. I needed her now. But I was forced to wait.

I could get used to waking up like this. One of Harley's arms was thrown across my torso, a bare leg over my thigh, and she was using my right pec as a pillow. My arm was wrapped around her, tucking her warm, soft body close.

There was a constellation of freckles on her shoulder. I traced them with a finger, enjoying the feel of her skin and the fact she was sprawled halfway across my chest.

I edged back slightly to watch her, eyelids fluttering in sleep, dark eyelashes fanned across her pink cheeks. She looked peaceful, innocent, vulnerable, so different from the waking version that barely stopped and had a smile for everyone she met.

What would she do when she woke up? Would it be like the last time we woke up together, when she tried to get as far away from me as possible, as quickly as she could? I hoped not, obviously, and after yesterday I thought not. We could just carry on what we started last night.

She stirred, nuzzling into my chest with a small groan, and I held myself perfectly still, so I didn't startle her. It didn't work. She bolted upright and looked down at me, her hair flat on one side and a wild nest on the other where I'd been dragging my fingers through it.

"Good morning," I said after twenty seconds of her just staring at me. Maybe I'd been wrong yesterday—the staring was kinda creepy. I should probably keep it to a minimum from now on.

"Hi." Her voice was all sleep sexy.

"Hi."

"Good morning."

"Good morning," I repeated, and she nibbled her lip to keep from smiling, but the corners of her mouth tipped up all the same. "You look surprised to see me."

She shook her head. "Not surprised, just ..."

"Just?"

"I don't know ... just wondering if this is real, I guess." She pinched my side and I yelped.

"You know that, traditionally, you pinch yourself to figure out if you're asleep, right?"

The smile she'd been trying to control took over her face. "But where's the fun in that?" And then she was tickling me, and I was wheezing as I begged for her to stop. When she finally relented and I was able to breathe normally again, she was sitting on top of me, thighs spread wide over mine.

Our eyes locked, heat sizzling in her whiskey swirls as my hands slid up from her knees. Yes, I could definitely get used to waking up like this.

Harley hinged forward, eyes dropping to my mouth as her fingers walked up my chest, nails scraping just a little.

"Good morning," she whispered. "I hope you're not precious about morning breath."

I grabbed the back of her head, pulling her the rest of the way down. "Definitely not."

A knock rattled the door and Harley nearly toppled off the bed, in her haste to get away from me, like we were a couple of busted kids. Another knock and she slapped a hand over her mouth, smothering a giggle.

"Harley! Wake your ass up, girl, the coffee challenge is on," Jemma yelled from the hall.

"The wh—" I started, but stopped as Harley jumped off the bed and ran for the door. Naked. She ran for the door, naked.

"You don't have any clothes on," I said, as loud as I dared.

How closely would Jemma be listening? I could imagine her with one ear pressed to the door. Oh shit ... did we remember to close my door last night? I genuinely couldn't remember. But if not, then we were unintentionally advertising the fact I was in her room. We were really bad at the whole keeping this shit a secret thing.

"Harley, *clothes*," I hissed.

"Oh!" she said as she slowed but didn't stop, because of course she wasn't putting anything on. She waved a hand behind her, and I slid off the bed and onto the floor, lying on the uneven hardwoods. If I got a splinter in my ass, she was going to get the thing out with her teeth. The prospect of that was more interesting than I expected.

The door creaked as it opened. "Woah, no, you can't come in, Jem-Jem. I'm naked."

"Why didn't you put something on?" Jemma asked with a laugh, and I tucked my feet in, just in case she got a peek inside the room.

"Because I thought you were going to bang my door down. Now what is this about the coffee challenge?" What the hell were they talking about?

"Everyone's up and they want coffee."

"Well, I would hate to deprive them of a superior product."

"Save your trash talk for the kitchen. And bring Jake down, too." I sucked in a breath. Jemma knew—that wasn't good. I had a feeling that if one person here knew, they all would.

Harley coughed. "Wh—why would I know where Jake is?"

"He's sleeping next door to you and I'm not waking him up."

Harley snorted. "But it was fine to wake me up?"

"Yes, but that's you, my dear friend. I'm not waking up Jake Davenport, Chelsea's highest goal scorer of all time."

"Or just, you know, *Jake*."

"Uh-huh, just wake him up and bring him downstairs."

The door closed but I didn't move, then Harley and her curls were poking over the side of the mattress, and she was grinning down at me.

"Cool hiding place."

"It's not like you gave me enough time to get to the bathroom," I said, standing up. Her eyes moved over my body in an appreciative sweep.

"I really wish I had the time to take advantage of all of this..." She shuffled forward.

"But you have coffee to make."

"I do." A heavy sigh followed. "I already feel kinda bad for Nash."

"You've not beaten him yet."

She laughed and patted me on the chest. "Okay, I need to shower so I don't smell like sex while I'm making coffee."

Before she could protest, I swept her over my shoulder and carried her to the bathroom.

The rest of the group was already gathered in the kitchen around the large farmhouse table when Harley and I made it downstairs, and every pair of eyes turned in our direction as we entered.

"Took you both long enough," Jemma said.

"He's a heavy sleeper." Harley shrugged.

"And here I was thinking you were going chicken." Nash grinned at Harley.

She snorted. "In your dreams, Nashville. Prepare to have your ass kicked."

With that, it was on.

"Alright!" Jemma whistled and I winced. "The rules are simple. To make sure that this little ... competition is completely impartial, everyone will be blindfolded. You will be given two espresso shots, one from Harley, the other from Nash. You will cast your vote for either one or two. I am exempt, because I'll be delivering the coffees to each of our panel." This was surprisingly well thought out.

I took a seat between Hunter and Odette as the blindfolds were circulated and we each tied them on. Would we be getting food along with our coffee? I could really do with a couple more of those crumpets from yesterday morning.

Over the next half hour or so, we drank four espresso shots each. Between each shot we were given a palate cleanser of sourdough toast slathered with butter, which was incredible. Chefs really knew how to eat.

I surprised myself by knowing which shots were Harley's in both rounds. As much as I generally considered coffee, coffee, there was something about hers that I preferred. Not that I could put my finger on what it was, exactly.

By the time we were done, my heart was beating a little too fast thanks to four espresso shots in reasonably quick succession. I tugged off my blindfold and found a plate of golden crumpets in front of me. Jemma winked from the other side of the wide kitchen island as she tallied the votes.

It had been a while since I'd been this relaxed around a group of people I didn't really know. I was sure that part of me didn't think I'd get it again, not with my profile. My friends were all teammates or teammates girlfriends who I'd never be trusted around again—for good reason.

My bite of crumpet soured at the thought of London and that life I'd left behind. There was nothing to miss, was there? An industrial chic apartment I had no hand in decorating. A rigorous, consuming training and game schedule. No friends. Nico might call himself a friend, but I'd barely heard from him after the first week I was here. And I hadn't exactly tried to contact him. He was a good guy, but we weren't friends.

These people that filled the kitchen, they were all friends. My chest pinched. When I left London—*ran from* London—it felt like I was leaving everything behind. Now that I was here, I could see that wasn't true, not by a long shot. I wondered how Blair's research was going—what could my life look like here?

Jemma whistled once again, bringing all of our attention to her. "Okay everyone, the votes have been counted by me, your impartial judge." She curtsied. "And we have a winner."

Harley was bouncing on her toes beside Nash, who was trying to look cool, but it was clear he was just as invested as she was. He scratched his cheek and fidgeted with the knot on top of his head.

Jemma took a breath as she looked over Nash and Harley. "The winner of the inaugural Bell-Meadow Farm coffee challenge is ..." We all drummed the table and Jemma grinned. "Har—"

Harley was squealing before Jemma had even finished saying her name, then she was jumping up and down and fist pumping. A modest winner, naturally. To his credit, Nash took the defeat well, shaking Harley's hand and bestowing a crown on her. Where the hell did the crown come from?

"Harley O'Connell, the Coffee Queen," he said, solemnly.

Her eyes found mine across the room, just for a fraction of a second, but it was enough to set me on fire.

28

HARLEY

I curtsied and bowed my way through the lengthy (and well deserved) applause, adjusting my crown as it listed to the left. I had no idea where said crown had come from, but I appreciated the extra touch. And *Harley O'Connell: Coffee Queen* had a real ring to it.

After being overly confident about my chances of winning since Nash and I laid down the gauntlet yesterday, as soon as I'd stepped into the kitchen this morning—even with the post-orgasm high, thanks to Jake going down on me in the shower, technically half in-half out of the shower—a barrage of self-doubt rose up and threatened to choke me.

It wasn't about making the coffee, I knew I was good at that, it was more the idea of putting myself out to be judged that had a sticky feeling coating my insides. And these were my friends, how the hell was I going to cope when it was a bunch of strangers comparing me to other supremely talented coffee professionals?

I pulled myself up before I went into full downward spiral mode and started second guessing every life choice I'd ever made. Instead, I glanced over at what was probably bad life choice number 789: one Jake Davenport. Only, he didn't actually feel like a bad life choice, not right at the moment.

"Well, I don't know about anyone else, but I need a swim," Hunter said once the applause had died down. "I have got energy to spare thanks to all that caffeine." He stood and rubbed his chest. "Anyone else?"

"A swim isn't gonna do it. I need to run some laps or something." Mack jumped up and bounced on his feet.

Jemma looked over at Jake, a smile twitching at the corners of her lips. "Why not a friendly game of football—*real* football," she added before anyone got the wrong idea about which game she was suggesting. Everyone else turned in Jake's direction, too.

He opened his mouth, closed it again. Part of me said I should try and save him, but another part really wanted to see him play, wanted to see the way he moved, even though it was probably going to make me want to tackle him where he stood. I wanted to do that right now, anyway, so it couldn't really get worse.

"I'm on Jake's team!" Darcy jumped up from her chair and rounded the table to stand behind him.

"Me too!" Odette followed suit.

"And he's my cousin, so obviously I'm on his team," Hunter said with a shit eating grin as he clapped Jake on the shoulder. I was pretty sure that being the person who was currently having sex with him trumped blood relative, but I kept my mouth shut.

"Fine." Mack stretched out his shoulders. "But you only get four."

"We only need four," Hunter shot back, and stood.

"Looks like we've got ourselves a game then," Mack said, already looking alarmingly determined. Jake was still sitting mute at the head of the table.

"You okay there?" I asked as I joined the line of people filing outside.

He snapped out of his daze and stood. "Of course, fine."

"Uh-huh ... well, you could always sit it out, act as ref or something so one team doesn't have too much of an advantage."

His smile was soft, it made my bones go all squishy. *Lock that shit down, Harley.* Feelings were supposed to be off the menu—Jake and I were a casual, very much temporary situation. No room for complicated and unwanted feelings there. Because they were definitely unwanted, without question. Who the hell would want this confusing ache in their chest? Not. Fucking. Me.

"Actually, you could probably do with the workout."

He laughed as his eyebrows sailed up to his hairline. "You think this is going to be a workout for me?"

I shrugged. "I mean, I didn't want to say you'd let yourself go or anything..."

"I know what you're doing."

"I'm not doing anything." I lifted my nose into the air and went to step outside but Jake caught me around the waist and spun us both into the butler's pantry. He was kissing me before I knew what was happening.

His tongue licked along my bottom lip and my arms went around his neck, pulling him closer even as my brain screamed that this was a bad idea. They were all waiting for us, for him. We needed to get outside. But then he was lifting me onto the counter, strong hands gripping my thighs, and that voice got quieter and quieter until it was pretty much gone. The only sound left was our shallow, panted breaths against one another's lips.

Until Hunter and Mack's trash-talking found my ears. Then other snippets of conversation.

"We need a goal." Jemma.

"Where'd Jake and Harley go?" Hunter.

"I'll check inside." Darcy.

Shit.

I shoved Jake away and pressed a hand to my chest in the hopes it would slow my heart the hell down. It didn't. We needed to get outside. Right now. First, though, I needed to get myself under control. I couldn't look at Jake, let alone say anything, so I just turned and left, running for the closest bathroom.

"Jake! Har-ley!" Darcy called through the house. There was silence for a beat and then muffled conversation told me she'd found Jake. I stayed where I was, hiding in the barely functional powder room.

I got that we had done a lot of kissing over the last little while but, Jesus, every kiss just got better with heat and excitement and this intense need for more burning under my skin. It made even the connection I had with Liam seem pale. Or was it too long ago? Had the memory of the intensity faded over the intervening years? Somehow, I doubted it. It couldn't have been like this because if it was, how the hell did I survive losing it?

I ignored the next question as it slid into my head.

How will you survive it this time?

By the time I made it outside, there was a loose game already in motion. It was mostly Jemma yelling *offside* and Mack and Hunter continuing to trash talk like a couple of kids.

"There you are," Jemma said as she spotted me stepping onto the stretch of grass off the kitchen. "I thought we'd lost you."

"Never, just needed a bathroom break."

She watched me a little too close for my liking as she

nodded. I pushed my smile wider, and she narrowed her eyes. Fuck.

"Let's get out there!" Too much, that was too much. "Are they going to wipe the floor with us?" I asked, walking toward the rest of the group.

Jemma fell in step beside me. "Wipe the grass, technically, but yes, probably." She paused. "Is everything okay?"

"Sure, why wouldn't it be?"

"No reason, just thought I sensed ... something."

"I can assure you there is nothing to *sense* but thanks for your concern."

She nodded in response, but I was certain she didn't believe me.

The game that followed could only be described as a trouncing, even with five on four and Jake stuck in goal for a period. Insisting he move into the goalkeeper position was a rookie mistake on Mack's part. Once there, Jake didn't let the ball get anywhere near the goal. Darcy, on the other hand, was so winded we scored three goals when she was the keeper. Not that it was enough to beat them. Eventually everyone stopped keeping score, because there was literally no point.

"I'd like to say we lost because Jake was doing his best, you know?" Mack said as he sprawled out on the grass once the annihilation was over. "But you could tell he wasn't even trying." He threw an arm over his face.

"Did you really expect him to exert himself against a bunch of food industry professionals?" Jemma asked, her cheeks were all red.

"No," he pouted. "But it would have been nice if he looked even a little bit winded. And Hunter will lord this over me until the end of time."

"Milton, are you being a shitty loser?" Chase said, flopping down beside him. "If you're feeling emasculated—"

"Emasculated?! Excuse you, Chastity, but I am not feeling emasculated, nor am I being a shitty loser." He pinched her side, and she slapped him away.

"You are sulking because you were beaten at soccer—by a professional soccer player."

He sat up. "I am not sulking."

"Whatever you need to tell yourself," she said, trying to shove him away as he tackled her.

Everyone peeled off once they had recovered—both emotionally and physically. Mack and Nash retreated to the kitchen to start on our dinner feast, Darcy and Odette found the sunniest spot on the lawn to while away the day, Jemma and Chase went into town.

And that left me, Jake, and Hunter.

I very intentionally did not look at Jake. But I couldn't really look at Hunter, either. How the hell was I supposed to get Jake upstairs and naked with my oldest friend standing here with us? Even if we did manage to disappear, Hunter would probably come and find us anyway.

Maybe I needed that swim he suggested earlier to cool off. It wasn't my fault, though—not after watching Jake run around looking all effortlessly athletic and hot, hot, hot. He even took his shirt off at one point, not that he needed to, because, as Mack pointed out, he wasn't in the least bit out of breath, or sweaty. Well, maybe a tiny bit sweaty, that hot amount that made his broad chest look like it was sparkling.

Jake cleared his throat and my attention snapped away from his twinkling torso. So much for not looking at him. He was smirking, eyes all smoldery and sexy and, holy hell, I needed to get him upstairs immediately. Before I could open my mouth and start digging myself into an awkward hole, Hunter announced he was going to hang with Odette and Darcy. I wanted to question the blossoming friendship with

Odette, because there was definitely something going on there, but I had other priorities right at that moment.

I watched Hunter bound down to the spot where Darcy and Odette were chatting on the grass, feeling Jake's attention on the side of my face.

"I need something from my room," I said, unnecessarily loud as I turned on my heel and headed for the house.

We crashed into my room, already kissing, hands busy with what little clothing was left between us. Jake kicked the door closed and I dragged him to the bed by his boxers. His hands came to my cheeks as my legs met the mattress and then we were kissing again. Kissing and falling and it felt alarmingly accurate for both my head, and my heart.

Falling.

Falling.

Falling.

But it was still temporary, so it was okay. He was still leaving, which was going to royally suck, but it was the right thing, for both of us.

I snapped back into my body as Jake's fingers slipped under the waistband of my shorts, gentle and teasing. I wiggled the worn denim down, giving him unobstructed access, and I felt him smile into our kiss. Those talented fingers explored my body, as his mouth slipped off mine and trailed down my jaw and neck, over my collar bones. When had he taken my shirt off? He licked and sucked, grazing my skin with his teeth. I arched, letting out a hissed moan as his tongue dragged across one nipple.

"More." I barely recognized my voice, low and desperate. Jake was happy to comply. Two fingers pressed inside as he sucked my nipple into his mouth, and I almost came on the spot.

My breathing turned shallow and erratic, my hips rocking in an attempt to up the pressure. Jake was teasing, holding me just shy of tipping over into oblivion.

"Jake, please."

He smiled; it was the devil behind those blue-green eyes as they locked with mine. "I think I like it when you beg." He eased off the pressure with his hand, while dragging his tongue around my nipple in lazy circles. I whimpered, squirmed.

"You want more?"

I watched as he sucked my nipple between his lips, tongue swirling, but his fingers were moving so slowly I wanted to scream. "You know I—oh god—you know I do."

He hummed, it vibrated against my skin, all the way down to my bones. "You want to come for me?"

"*Yes.*" It was more breath than word as he once again sucked hard on my nipple and swept his thumb over my clit. "More. There."

He stopped, the bastard. "More, there ...?"

"*Please.* Please Jake, please make me com—"

His fingers went deep, the heel of his hand pressing on my clit and I choked on a cry. Close. So close. Another lick to my nipple.

"Fuck I could watch you come all day, Harley."

I gripped his wrist. Close. So close.

"Jake, *yes.* I—"

"That's it."

His fingers curled inside me, and I shattered. Jake's mouth met mine, swallowing my garbled cries as I continued to ride out my orgasm on his hand. I ignored the thought that whispered, *I could do this with him forever.*

When I had recovered some of my wits, I nudged Jake onto his back, and he shoved his shorts off as I swiped a condom off the floor. I straddled him and he kneaded my thighs, eyes burning.

"You going to make me beg now?" he asked.

It was tempting. "Maybe."

A devilish smirk curled the corners of his lips as I wrapped a hand around his thick, perfect cock and a hissed breath escaped through his teeth. Yes, making him beg did sound like a very good idea. I pumped slowly, enjoying the view of his abs tensing, as I put the condom between his pecs. God he was fucking beautiful, long, lean muscle wrapped in smooth, tan skin, a map of angle and shadow. I could watch him for hours, days, memorizing every line.

I swiped a thumb through the moisture collecting at the head of his cock and he sucked in a sharp breath. My hand was still moving slow, and he wanted me to go faster, I could see it, but he didn't say anything, didn't beg. Just stayed perfectly still, lips pressed together. A little more temptation was required.

I leaned down, brushing my mouth over his and he groaned. The sound had me smiling. What would it take to get the man to beg? My curls teased his chest as I kissed my way down his torso until I was at his cock. I licked from base to head and his hands fisted in the rumpled sheets, but still remained silent. Impressive.

Sucking his wide head into my mouth I shifted to straddle one leg and rocked my hips to relieve some of the building pressure. Who would have thought getting Jake to beg would get me so hot? Actually, it wasn't that surprising—Jake was naked in front of me, that was guaranteed to get me hot.

"Oh god, fuck me, Harley," he said, though it was more of a groan.

I release his cock with a wet pop. He went to pull me up to him, but I shook my head. "Uh-uh-uh. Fuck me, Harley ...?"

He choked on a breath as I gave his cock a strong squeeze. "*Please*. Please, Harley. I need you."

"Good boy," I purred, grabbing the condom, which had slipped onto the bed beside him, and ripping it open with my teeth.

"Now, fuck, Harley, please, now." It was alarming how much I liked hearing him beg for it. The power was heady and, if I wasn't just as desperate as he was, I would have listened to him say *please, please, please* a little longer. As it was, I rolled the condom on and dropped onto his cock with a low moan. There really was nothing like that feeling of intrusion.

"*Fuck*," he groaned, thrusting up to match my pace. "Harley."

My hands landed on his chest, breasts swaying as we continued our rhythm. It was so good. We were so good.

"Jake."

"I want to draw this out but I'm so fucking close already."

"Me too, me too. Harder." I panted.

"Yes." He held my hips, hard enough to bruise, and I bit my lip to keep from screaming loud enough to draw a crowd.

We rolled to one side, mouths crashing together. Jake hooked my leg over his arm, pressing deeper and I sucked on his tongue. Yes. Yes. Yes.

"Coming," I muttered.

"Yes. So close."

"Bite me."

He didn't need to be told twice, just dropped his head to the crook of my neck and sunk his teeth into my skin. I came immediately. Jake followed quickly after, groaning against the same spot he'd bitten.

We both relaxed into the mattress, breathing hard. Jake let go of my leg and I draped it over his hip, not ready to peel myself away just yet. He didn't seem inclined to, either, as he wrapped a hand around my back and pulled me closer.

He wanted to say something, I could see it, poised on the tip of his tongue, but the moment stretched, and he stayed silent. Just when I was about to ask what was on his mind, he kissed me fiercely and my brain emptied of everything but the feel of his tongue on mine.

29

JAKE

What the hell was that scratching? It was difficult to put my finger on it while still half asleep but, considering the condition of this house—

I sat up, expecting to find a family of rats plotting my demise at the foot of the bed. Instead, there was Harley, curled in the armchair in the corner, naked save for a notebook on her knees. She was drawing. Was she drawing me? As I slept? That was creepy—or it would be, if she didn't look quite so rumpled and fucking beautiful. As it was, my stomach clenched to the point of nausea.

Because I was fucked.

Sleeping next to this woman for the last two nights had made me want more of it. It made me want every night, every morning.

I couldn't decide if I was disappointed or relieved to be heading back to Brooklyn today. Would our sleepovers continue once we were back in her apartment—*their* apartment? Or would she have her way with me and then kick me out? As much as I didn't relish the idea of sleeping in my own bed for the next six weeks, I wasn't about to complain, because some Harley was better than no Harley at all.

"What are you doing over there?" I asked.

"Drawing you," she said without looking up.

"Like one of your French girls?"

She cackled from her seat. "Exactly, but I've taken some liberties because the sheet is covering the good bits." Her eyes darted to me, eyebrows wiggling. I pulled the sheet tighter around my hips and she laughed again.

"You should come back to bed ..."

"Oh, should I?"

"Definitely."

"What do I get if I come back to bed? You gonna bite me again?" Who knew she had such a thing about biting?

"Were you a big fan of Twilight or something?"

Another laugh, this one had her head falling back. I could see the mark from where I'd bitten her yesterday.

"Well, you really got that sexy vamp spot yesterday." She set aside the notebook and stood and, for a second, my brain went entirely quiet. There was only Harley as she sauntered to the bed, hips swaying, breasts bobbing. Fucking perfection.

"How many girls have you bitten?" she asked as she slid across my lap and wrapped her arms around my neck. God, I could get used to this. This *ease*. It hadn't been like that with anyone else, only her.

My arms curled around her back as I considered her question and ignored the ones rolling around in my own head. In my experience, women didn't want to know what you'd done with other women. But, at this point, it shouldn't have come as a surprise that Harley was different. She rocked her hips, once again scrambling what little attention I had.

A question, there was a question, I was sure of it, but my

brain had redirected all attention to all the places where my skin was touching hers, to that maddening rhythm.

The look on her smiling face was expectant. There had been a question, but if she kept moving like that there was no way I was going to be able to remember it.

She knew it, too, but was apparently feeling generous because she repeated the question. "How many girls have you bitten?"

Right, that was it. "None," I said and nearly choked on a breath as she pressed down a little hard. "How many people have bitten you?"

She considered it for a beat. "None, actually." Her head dropped to one side. "I've never felt like I wanted it. But yesterday ..." A shimmy. "It was hot."

Yes. It. Was.

I tightened my arms, pulling her body flush against mine. I really wanted to stay here, in this dilapidated farmhouse bubble. It was so easy to pretend that nothing else existed outside of this place. That it was just us, just me and Harley—and a large group of her friends. But even they were easy enough to forget about when we were in this room, and Harley didn't have a shirt on.

"You gonna kiss me or what, Davenport?" she asked, our noses brushing. "Or are you waiting on me?" She didn't wait for me to answer, just pressed her lips to mine and sighed.

How can I keep this, keep her?

Her fingers slid into my hair, short nails dragging over my scalp, and I groaned. Everything she did threatened to undo me, and it should scare the shit out of me, but for whatever reason it didn't.

Was I ready now, when I hadn't been before? I'd thought I was ready back then, but there was so much working against us. What about now? Were things really so different? Even if they weren't, I knew I would let myself drown happily. No need for air when I had her lips, her skin, her laugh.

Harley's hips rocked, but I had no intention of rushing things this morning. I wanted to take my time, touch every inch of her skin, watch her unravel the same way I was. I trailed kisses along her jaw, down her throat, tipping her head up. She arched, fingers once again in my hair, twisting, tightening, a silent plea for more. I smiled against her collarbone, against the mark I left there.

I made it to her left nipple, and she moaned, pressing herself down on me. I could feel her heat through the cotton that separated us and I wanted more of it. I wanted to feel that heat on my tongue, on my cock. But I still wasn't going to rush getting there.

Starting with the valley between her breasts and then onto her right nipple, I dragged my lips over every square inch of her skin, mapping each dip and curve. Her body was a work of art, one I would happily study every day for the rest of my life.

Harley's stomach was growling so loud I was amazed no one had come to investigate. It was a good thing they hadn't, though, considering until two minutes ago we'd both been naked, and I had Harley bent over the back of the armchair. I would happily have kept her naked for the rest of the day, but we couldn't put off the search for food and coffee any longer.

Just as we were about to step into the hall, my cell phone rang. It had been a blissfully quiet few days, so I shouldn't be surprised that Blair was calling. I knew it was her even without looking.

"I'll meet you downstairs," I said, pressing a kiss to Harley's hair. She grabbed my face and kissed me greedily, fingers tunneling into my hair and one leg hooking over my hip. Maybe

I could just let it go to voicemail this time. But, before I could decline the call and drag Harley back into her room, she pulled away.

"See you down there."

Timing separate kitchen entrances was probably for the best, anyway, especially when we were trying to maintain some level of secrecy. Although, considering the number of eyes in this house, it seemed unlikely that at least one person wasn't onto us. We just needed to delay that inevitable reveal for as long as possible—until I was sure that Harley wouldn't end it then and there.

My cell phone fell silent, but Blair and I had been working together long enough for me to know that if I didn't get back to her in the next minute or two, she'd just keep calling. Persistence; she'd call it one of her strengths.

"That was a good recall speed, Jake, well done," she answered.

"I live to please you," I deadpanned.

"As you should. How are you?" Her tone sounded a little weird, but I chose to ignore it.

"I'm great actually. Enjoyed some time in the countryside—but I'm sure you knew that because you've been stalking my social media—heading back to Brooklyn today. How about you? Has the shitstorm finally died down?" I surprised myself by not being particularly invested in the answer. Of course, I wanted things to have calmed down, but more for Blair's sake than my own. Being so far removed from the whole thing had been a luxury.

A pause. "As a matter of fact, yes, it has. Mostly." The *mostly* wasn't terribly encouraging, but I got the feeling she wasn't done.

"But ...?"

Another pause. "No *but*, more of an *and*." It was difficult to know if it was a good *and* or a bad *and*.

"Okay, and ...?" I prompted when she didn't say anything else. The back of my neck was starting to prickle.

She sucked in a breath. "I have two potential offers."

"Offers? Already?"

"Yes, already, because I am incredible at my job."

"And because I'm your favorite client."

"Considering the hours I've been pulling for you, no, you are no longer top dog. Anyway, one I've already mentioned, Tomas Posey is still interested in having you at Man City on the coaching team. But, if you're not done playing, Liverpool is interested. *Very* interested."

My heart hammered—Man City and Liverpool. They were both great clubs. They were also both in England. Not London, but still England. Was that what I wanted? Swapping one fish-bowl for another?

"Jake?"

"Yes, sorry, here, I'm here. I just—I'm processing?" I didn't intend for it to come out like a question, but it still did. And, honestly, I wasn't sure how much processing was actually happening because the initial reaction to both offers was: no.

"The Liverpool offer is substantial."

"How substantial?"

"You'd be the highest paid player in the league."

I didn't quite know what to say to that. It wasn't like I needed the money, but it did make me think twice about saying no. Blair was uncharacteristically quiet.

"You think I should take it?"

"It's not about me. You need to do what's best for you, and you know that I'll support you."

"Even if you think I'm being an idiot."

"Even then. You could reduce your idiot status by giving it

some actual thought rather than saying no immediately. It's an opportunity to continue playing at the peak of the sport, Jake. And look, I know Arturo hasn't technically said your days are numbered at Chelsea—"

"The writing is on the wall."

"Exactly." She was right. Of course, she was right. I guess I needed to figure out if I was ready to let go of playing altogether. Liverpool was giving me the chance to end my career on my own terms, rather than under the cloud of a suspension. That, more than the money, had me chewing over the possibility of going back.

"When do they need answers by?"

"I don't have anything in writing, but if you're serious I can get contracts in the next few days. You've got more room to move with Man City. Liverpool would want you on deck as soon as possible, before the start of next season."

"That soon?

"You settle in well and you might be captain this time next year." She knew exactly the right buttons to push. I'd been gutted when Art took the captaincy off me. The chance to redeem myself added another level of temptation.

"What about the program I've agreed to coach here?"

"Necessary collateral damage. This is your career, Jake, it takes precedence over a bunch of teenagers. Do you need me to write you a script to let them down easy?"

"No, you don't need to do that."

"Fine, if you think you can handle it, that's great, but if you do change your mind let me know. Otherwise, I can have you booked on a fli—"

"Blair, I can't cancel."

There was a beat of impatient silence. "Why not?"

"Because—because I don't want to." I sounded like a stubborn kid. I cleared my throat and squared my shoulders, hoping my resolve would translate down the line. "I've made a commitment. I intend on keeping it." Was this a mistake? A nail in the coffin for one or both of these offers?

"I don't know if Liverpool will agree to you missing that much—pretty much all—of pre-season."

I paced the room, squeezing the back of my neck. "And so that's it?"

"No, Jake, that is not it. You can change your mind and choose your career over a group of children who you're unlikely to see again."

"Blair—"

"Stop before you say anything else that makes me want to slap you." She paused. "I get that you were hoping I'd have something over there, but I've not heard back from any of the contacts I spoke to. I'm not ruling anything out, but I also have no idea how long it will take. On the other hand, either one of the offers we have right now keeps you in the EPL and that's a good thing. Promise me you will give it some actual thought, please, and not throw it away."

"I will give it some actual thought."

"Good. In the meantime, I will see if Liverpool are open to you starting later. Leave it with me." She'd hung up before I could say thank you.

I was going to miss this kitchen.

There wasn't anything wrong with my kitchen at home; it was a decent size and perfectly functional—but it wasn't fancy. Jemma and Nash's kitchen, *this kitchen*, was big, and bright, and really fucking fancy, and, dammit, I'd never considered myself a fancy kitchen person but, apparently, I'd been converted. I wanted to rub myself all over the speckled concrete countertops, lie on the almost thirteen feet island, and just stare at the vaulted ceiling with its dark timber beams. I wanted to perch myself on a stool while drinking a dirty martini and have someone feed me—Jake would make an excellent shirtless waiter, come to think of it.

Instead, I was forced to sit alone with my coffee and sourdough toast covered with a healthy smear of raspberry jam. It wasn't pretty, or fancy, or served to me by a shirtless man, but it was something.

Unfortunately, the silence and alone time meant my brain was getting louder than I'd like it, obsessing over the soft slowness of this morning with Jake. The last couple of days had been filled with frenzied, needy, dirty sex, and it was a dream. This morning, though, he wasn't frenzied, or needy, or dirty; he was deliberate and tender, and it had left me exposed.

Frenzied, needy, dirty sex was my preference because you could hide in it. You could get swept away with all of those tactile sensations and you were given no time to think, only do. I'd not had any other kind of sex since Liam, and I was perfectly happy that way. I enjoyed the rush of being pulled out of my head and into my body. I guess you could call it a form of mindfulness and meditation for me.

This morning had not been that. It was still amazing, but my brain was far too engaged on what it all meant when it shouldn't mean anything at all—aside from mutually assured shower orgasms, one of my personal favorite kinds. Instead, there was this simmering undercurrent of emotion that made me want to cry and scream and run for the fucking hills all at once.

It scared the living shit out of me.

"Okay, I've got another one!" Odette said, materializing from literal thin air in the middle of the kitchen. She was looking all wholesome and fresh faced in a short, floral dress. The sun had more freckles popping up across the bridge of her nose and had left her hair more pastel pink than bubblegum. It suited her.

I glanced around the otherwise empty room to make sure she was talking to me. "Huh?"

"Avengers edition," she continued, like I hadn't spoken. "Chris Hemsworth. Mark Ruffalo. Paul Rudd. Fuck. Marry. Kill. Whatcha gonna do?" She grinned; she enjoyed this game way too much. We'd been playing it on and off all weekend whenever she came up with a new trio.

This was exactly the kind of distraction I needed right now. "Are they themselves or their characters?"

"Does it matter?"

"It might," I said, spinning my coffee cup in a slow circle.

"Okay, round one: as character. Round two: as themselves."

"Alright." I sat up straight and shook out my shoulders, ready to give this my full attention. No more thinking about Jake and his tender love making. Oh God, was that what happened this morning? Was it love making? My stomach pulled itself into some kind of contorting yoga pose. We made love. We were not supposed to be making love. I was not thinking about this right now. I had other things to consider.

"I'd fuck Thor. I'd marry Hulk and ... no, wait, I can't kill Paul Rudd in character or not, the man is a national treasure. I'm fucking Ant Man, I'm marrying the Hulk, and I'm killing Thor." I took a large gulp of coffee. I was going to need a second one, pronto.

Odette's eyebrows shot up to her hairline. "How are you going to kill Thor?"

"Uhhh ... with my husband the Hulk."

"Thor can literally conjure lightning, the Hulk can't kill him. Have you not seen *Ragnorok*?"

"You did not specify how I needed to execute my choices. Maybe I impale him with one of his own lightning bolts or something." I drained my cup.

"Once again, he can conjure and channel lightning, he is the God of Thunder. I seriously doubt that his own lightning bolt would kill him." I waved off her concern. "Anyway ..." She shook her head. "You're marrying the Hulk?"

I nodded; it seemed like such an obvious choice to me. "I'm marrying the split personality. It's like the best of both worlds. I get the super smart, sensitive Bruce Banner who can fix my Wi-Fi and would cook me breakfast and all that jazz, and I get intense, angry sex with the Hulk. It's literally the ideal scenario."

"I think you might be insane, but it's probably why we're friends. So, round two: as themselves?"

"I'd marry Paul Rudd, because he's hilarious and would make me laugh for the rest of our happy lives together. Fuck Ruffalo, and I still kill the hot Australian. Sorry Hemsworth." I jumped off my stool. "You want a coffee?"

A nod. "But wait, you aren't going to at least fuck the hottest one in the bunch in either scenario?" She sounded genuinely concerned for my mental well-being.

"There are many forms of hotness, O. You put him up against heavy weights—both literal and figurative. Stick him in there with Captain America or Spider-Man and the answer might change. Actually ... I'm not sure it would. Well, Tom Holland is cute as all hell and I would happily eat him alive, but Peter Parker is in high school, right? I can't fuck a high schooler." I shuddered.

She nodded, lips pushed into a thoughtful pout. "I guess I'm just surprised considering *he* looks kinda like him."

"You lost me, he who, looks like who?"

"The guy you're currently having sex with kinda looks like Hemsworth. And, before you try and play it dumb by saying something like *which guy that I'm having sex with because I have such an extensive roster ...*" She raised an accusing eyebrow, and I snapped my mouth shut, because that was exactly what I was about to do. "It's Jake. I'm talking about Jake."

The jaunty tilt to her smirk told me she was confident about the statement, but could she be bluffing? Trying to trick information out of me? Jake and I had been pretty low key, I'd barely looked at him when everyone else was around for fear of giving us away. Yet here we were.

"One: Jake doesn't look like Hemsworth," I said, then kept

talking before Odette could interrupt. "And two: I am not having sex with him."

"One: he doesn't look exactly like Hemsworth, it's more of a vibe. And two: it's cute that you think I'll believe you when you say it's not happening."

There was only one thing for it. Deny. Deny. Deny.

"I'm not sure where you've got this idea from, but I can assure you, it's not happening. You know men and women are capable of being friends and not having sex with one another. Me and Hunt—"

"I heard you guys yesterday," she cut in with a supremely smug look on her face. "I also closed his bedroom door this morning because the two of you obviously forgot to. His bed didn't look like it had been slept in—at all ..." Shit, that was hard to get around.

My shoulders sagged and I handed over her coffee. "Who else have you told?"

She shrugged one ink covered shoulder and took a sip. "No one, and nor do I plan on telling anyone when you're so obviously cagey about the whole thing."

"I am not cagey, there's just nothing to tell." I did not appreciate her patronizing smile.

"Cagey AF." She booped me on the nose as she said it. I swatted her away. "Which either means the sex is bad and you're trying to shut it down. Or it's really fucking good and, for some reason, that's a problem."

"It's not bad," I said.

"Duh, of course it's not, it could not possibly be bad when the air is practically sizzling between the two of you whenever you are even vaguely close to one another. But why is that a problem?"

"It's not up for discussion." Because I barely understood

how I was feeling and attempting to put all this confusion into words would be a laughable mess.

"Is it because he's going back to London?"

"Not. Up. For. Discussion."

"It's because he's going back to London," she said, ignoring the whole *not up for discussion* thing.

"That is actually the best thing about the whole situation." As soon as he was gone, I'd be able to return to my regularly scheduled programming; having emotionless sex with whoever happened to turn me on the most.

"Him leaving is a good thing?"

"Yup."

"I don't—"

"Okay, your turn—fuck-marry-kill, same three." Odette went to argue but I cut her off. "Actually, no, because I cannot have you trying to kill my fictional husband. You have Chris Hemsworth, Chris Ev—no, no, no, that would be too easy. Chris Hemsworth, Brie Larson, and Elizabeth Olsen."

"No!" she gasped. I knew she wouldn't be a Captain America fan.

"You started it."

After a long moment of consideration and a resigned sigh, she said, "Fuck. I have to kill Hemsworth."

By the time Jake and I were tossing our bags into the trunk of his rented convertible, I had managed to talk myself down from the ledge I'd been teetering on earlier. It was a good thing, too, because Darcy had decided to get a ride back to the city with Hunter, leaving me alone with Jake in the sexiest car to ever exist. I was still confused about its effect on me when I was not the least bit interested in cars. If we managed to get home without me trying to rip off Jake's shorts and give him an illegal, in-motion blow job, it would be a small miracle.

Jemma, Nash, and Odette waved from the lopsided porch as we started down the mile-long drive and I did my best not to openly stare at Jake's crotch—or the rest of him. Because, yes, I might have gotten over this morning's *did we make love* freak-out, but that did not change the fact that he was still the hottest guy I'd ever seen in my fucking life, currently driving the hottest car I'd ever seen in my fucking life—and I constantly wanted to get him naked and explore his skin with my tongue.

Right now, he had a real classic Hollywood thing going on. Plain white tee, classic black Ray-Bans sat on his nose, and his hair was an unruly, wavy mess thanks to the wind.

Another James Dean moment that I was very much here for. If he turned to me and winked, there was an excellent chance I would spontaneously orgasm.

The only thing working against the whole look (and my chances of a spontaneous orgasm) was the flat line of his usually plush lips. There was also an occasional twitch in his jaw, but that was surprisingly attractive. Something was on his mind. It had been since he walked into the kitchen mid-Bridgerton edition of Fuck-Marry-Kill. I had to assume it was the phone call, probably from Blair. I wanted to ask, I was dying to ask, but I wouldn't because part of talking myself off the ledge was keeping the *feelings* in this situation to a minimum. He wasn't talking. I wasn't asking. We were at a stalemate, one he potentially wasn't even aware of.

I just needed to get us talking about something else, something neutral, but my conversation skills, the ones I used on a daily basis at work, had decided to abandon me. The timing really couldn't have been worse.

We cruised through town; it was still buzzing with the long weekend crowds. The local pool was close to bursting, full of screaming kids and strung-out parents thanks to the ninety-five degree weather.

"Do you remember that death trap of a pool that you and Hunter took me to?"

My answering laugh was more of a howl at the memory. "They've closed that place down." I could still remember the look on Jake's face as we stood outside the fence. Horror. Pure horror.

"No shit. It was a health hazard."

"In their defense, they really did need to use that much chlorine because of the sheer amount of semen that was probably in the water." My laugh turned into uncontrollable giggles as he shuddered.

"I still can't believe you actually made me swim there."

"I didn't *make* you. I merely said that I was swimming and then you almost cracked your head open jumping in." I wheezed. The diving board had snapped in half as soon as he'd stepped on it, and the lifeguards—always more interested in fucking in the changerooms than they were at making sure no one was drowning—were nowhere to be seen.

"I could have died!" He laughed, head thrown back, all hints of tension gone, replaced by straight, white teeth, and crinkles at the corners of his eyes. God, he was perfect. That smile made my chest feel decidedly gooey and I gave myself an internal slap. *Feelings are off the menu!* No gooiness.

I was starting to think that the whole *no feelings* rule was seriously unrealistic. But it was simple enough to pretend my insides weren't back-flipping.

"But you didn't, you drama queen. And did we have to compete with anyone for space?"

"No," he conceded.

"No. Every other pool in the area was always jam-packed. That one wasn't."

"For good reason!"

"It was fun, though, you have to admit that."

"It was a miracle you weren't arrested for stealing the keys."

"Please, if they didn't care about the place during the day, they definitely weren't going to at night. You loved the night swimming."

A loaded pause stretched between us.

Jake cleared his throat. "Pretty sure it wasn't just the swimming," he said eventually, and even with his sunglasses firmly in place the heat of his look had a hot bolt of lust rocketing down my spine.

I did not need to remember all the things we did that *weren't* swimming, but it was difficult to stop my mind from straying now he'd brought it up. Keeping things a secret from most people meant we couldn't fool around at my place, or his, because he was staying with Hunter. So, we needed to get creative. I had not, up until that point, really been interested in outdoor sex. But with Jake, well, if outdoor sex was an Olympic sport, we would have won gold at least twelve times over.

"No, maybe it wasn't just the swimming." I cleared my throat. "So, how are you feeling about tomorrow? Nervous? Excited? Ready to dominate?"

He graciously accepted the change in conversation. "I'm not really sure what to expect, to be honest. It could be a fucking disaster."

"It won't be a fucking disaster."

"What about you?"

"What about me?"

"What's happening with the Coffee Championships? Your win over Nash must have given you a confidence boost?"

"Yes and no. It did feel good to beat him," I admitted, "Nash is a talented chef, but he's not a barista." I'd been shocked how much of a rush I had with that win, and yes it had given me a taste of competition, but it also gave me a peek of the anxiety that came along with it too.

"You'll do great, Harley."

"Thanks, I hope I do. But I think I need to separate myself from the result, you know? Winning or losing won't change my day to day, and I need to remember that."

"Good point."

"It would be amazing to win, but I'm sure that would come with its own set of challenges, too. If we won that probably opens doors to the state competition, and then national titles."

"There's a National Coffee Championship?"

"Yep, I've watched it a couple of times. The people competing are incredible. I need to create a signature drink if we make it to the next round."

"How do you come up with that?"

"No idea, I told Chase I might need some coaching in the beverage creation department."

Jake's hand covered my knee and squeezed. "You'll do great," he said with an encouraging smile, and I once again ignored that gooey feeling in the vicinity of my heart.

31

JAKE

I slapped my cell phone as my alarm went off. I'd been awake for a good half hour already, staring at the ceiling and listening to the street noise. But I couldn't get out of bed.

What the fuck had I been thinking when I accepted this coaching job? No, it wasn't a *job*, I wasn't even getting paid, an assignment, then? Coaching role? The technical title wasn't actually important, not compared to how hilariously under-qualified I currently felt. I was not a coach. I had never considered becoming a coach—granted I'd never really considered anything after playing. This entire thing was, unquestionably, a mistake.

When I voiced this very valid concern yesterday, Harley told me that I was the best person for the job—role, assignment, whatever—and then proceeded to drag me into the bathroom with her. The conversation came to a pretty abrupt end after that.

I thoroughly appreciated the distraction her nakedness provided, but it didn't help me now. Nor did Blair's radio silence. It wasn't like I expected her to get back to me immediately, but the longer she went without making contact, the more frayed my nerves became.

As much as I was second guessing the decision to coach a bunch of high schoolers, I didn't want to let them down either. What the hell was I going to do if Liverpool wanted me back now? As soon as possible? That was probably part of my stress this morning, the fear of potentially having to crush them under my cleats.

Assuming I agreed to go to Liverpool.

Even with Harley's numerous distractions, the decision had still been there sitting at the front of my mind. The more I thought about it, the more I could see why it made sense. Yes, Liverpool was still in England, but it wasn't London. It might be different. But being the highest paid player in the league also came with its own drawbacks—namely, attention and pressure.

I was no closer to knowing what to do. I'd been tempted to ask Harley her thoughts, but I didn't do it, too scared that she'd tell me to go without hesitation. I wasn't brave enough to deal with that rejection.

Once showered, I threw on a shirt and a pair of shorts, caught a glimpse of myself in the mirror, and then changed.

"Harley," I whisper-hissed into the hall as I opened my bedroom door. I wasn't sure what I wanted from her—just her, I guess. Sleeping in separate rooms to maintain secrecy sucked.

Her head poked out, curls a wild halo. "What's up?" she asked, and maybe waking her was a mistake, because now I just wanted to kiss her and forget about the day ahead. Was she naked? I tried to see around the edge of the door.

"Nope," she said with a devilish smile.

"I didn't say anything."

"Your face did."

"What did my face say?"

"Let's get naked and stay in bed all day."

"My face has a point." I stepped up to her door. She wasn't naked but in sheer, pink underwear, which was somehow even sexier.

"A very valid one," she agreed. "But you have places to be. Is this what you're wearing?"

I glanced down. After changing three times, I'd ended up back in the first thing I put on.

"Yes. Why, what's wrong with it?"

"Nothing."

"Then why ask?" Maybe I needed to go more professional? Teenagers could be assholes at the best of times, I didn't want to start off by looking like a fucking loser. My panic was enough to draw my attention away from the fact I could see her nipples through the flimsy triangles covering her breasts.

"Jake, take a breath, I'm fucking with you. Today is going to be great."

"There's a reason no one ever puts me with the new guys. I'm terrible with the new guys."

"I'm sure you're not terrible with the new guys, and you won't be terrible today."

I shook my head, ready to argue some more, but she cut me off.

"Another breath please." I obeyed. "Okay. Everything is going to be great, and I know this because Cece basically swallowed her tongue the first time she saw you. The rest of them will be the same. You are a professional soccer player, Jake, you have more knowledge and experience than any of those kids could dream of having."

"That's true, but there's a difference between having that knowledge and knowing how to pass it on."

She crossed her arms as she leaned on the door frame. "Sure, but you're not trying to tell them everything you know today and then that's it. You have six whole weeks. This is day one, start small." She was right. I needed to get an idea of where they all were skills-wise before we got into any proper training, anyway.

Day one. Start small.

"Better?"

"Better," I said with a nod. "Thank you."

"You're welcome." Her eyes darted in the direction of the living room then back to me. "That pep talk was quicker than I was expecting, maybe we do have some extra time." She bounced her eyebrows, and I barked out a laugh.

Harley took this as a green light, grabbing me by the neck and dragging my face down to hers as she backed into her room.

I sank into her kiss, arms curling around her back to pull her closer. I was wearing too many clothes, I wanted to feel her nipples scrape against my chest as I buried myself deep. It could only help with the nerves, right?

Her lips broke from mine, eyes shimmering with heat. "Tell me what you want me to do ... *Coach*?" That last purred word had my balls tightening. This was probably not a great idea when I was about to be surrounded by a bunch of teenagers calling me Coach, but I wasn't going to stop, not when she was looking at me like that.

"Get on your knees."

She smiled pushing me back to against the door before dropping down in front of me. "And now?" she asked, fingers toying with the edge of my shirt.

I flicked the strap on her left shoulder. "This. Off." I almost fell to my knees along with her as she slowly slid the straps down both arms then unhooked the clasp and let the fabric fall away. Fucking hell. "Squeeze them."

Her teeth grazed over her bottom lip as she did it and my cock strained against the front of my shorts. I pulled it out, maneuvering my shorts down just enough. Harley's eyes were there immediately, tongue darting out and wet her lips.

"Lick it." She did. One long stroke from base to tip, and I thought my knees would buckle. "Again." Jesus Christ I was in danger of passing out, her tongue felt so good. "Now suck."

"Yes, Coach," she said, lips grazing my head before she sucked it into her mouth with a greedy noise. I groaned. She spat into one palm and her hand took up what couldn't fit in her eager mouth.

Her eyes swept up to mine and held as I ran a finger along the line of her stretched lips.

"Touch your clit," I ordered. She moaned as she made contact.

"How wet are you?"

She released me with a pop. "So wet."

I tapped her cheek then took hold of her hair and said, "Keep going. I want to see you come while you're sucking my cock."

Her smile was devilish as she returned to licking and sucking. She pulled back, tongue swirling, then plunged forward. Over and over. All the while, her fingers circled. Whimpered moans vibrated through me as she continued to move.

She stopped sucking but continued to pump my cock with her hand. "Where do you want to come? Mouth or tits?" If I didn't love her already, that question did it.

"Tits."

"Yes, Coach." She sucked me back into her mouth.

"Fuck, Harley." I was going to come. "Are you close?"

She nodded, moaning.

"Harder." I tightened my fingers in her hair and she moaned again, as her hips rocked against her hand. Heat rolled down my spine.

"Coming."

Harley's hand kept moving as her mouth slid off me and I came with a low groan, painting her skin.

"Oh god," she said, chest heaving, and she shuddered as her orgasm followed a second later. I pulled her hand up to my mouth, sucking her fingers clean while she swayed on her knees.

We were silent for a long moment, just watching one another.

"You made a mess," she said eventually, running a finger through my cum dripping down her chest and circling it around her nipple. It was the hottest thing I'd ever seen. "I'm probably going to get off to that at least twice more today."

"You cannot tell me that when I am about to go and deal with a bunch of teenagers."

She grinned. "I'd say I'm sorry, but I'm not."

I pulled her up to stand and kissed her, careful not to get my mess all over the front of my shirt.

"I should probably get going." Leaving this room was easier said than done.

She nodded. "And I should probably shower."

"I'd like to be the one to clean you up."

"Another time," she said with a wink. "Now, go on, Coach, I will not be responsible for you being late on your first day."

Cecilia was waiting on the street as I approached Franklin High School, her face split into a wide smile as she saw me and the nerves that I'd been managing to keep at bay came roaring back.

Day one. Start small.

"Morning, Coach," she said and, yep, that was going to take some compartmentalizing.

"Morning, Cecilia."

"Cece is fine, everyone calls me Cece."

"Cece it is, then."

Her smile went a little shy before she cleared her throat. "Thank you, again, for agreeing to do this. I know you've probably got way better things to be doing with your time."

"This is the only thing I need to be doing with my time right now," I said, positive Blair would disagree, but there was still no word from her so helping a bunch of kids seemed like a good idea to me.

"Are you ready to get started?"

"As I'll ever be."

I followed Cecilia out to the sports fields she'd shown me last week where, today, a group of girls was waiting. All conversation died as soon as they saw us. Well, as soon as they saw me, probably. Despite being the adult, the coach, in this situation, seeing the kids I was supposed to be in charge of for the next six weeks had the nerves rattling through me with even more force.

Start small.

Cecilia walked a couple of steps ahead of me as we approached the group and they all turned and openly stared, some slack jawed, others audibly gulping. After weeks of not being recognized when I walked down the street, this reaction felt almost novel. It was also a stark reminder of what was waiting for me in London—or Liverpool—if I decided to go back. I pushed the thought aside, even as I checked my phone. Still nothing from Blair.

"Okay," Cecilia said, drawing everyone's attention—including mine—to her. "Everyone, this is Jake. Jake, this is everyone." She waved an arm in the direction of the group. There were about fifteen of them, maybe twenty, all dressed in what looked like the school's athletics uniform. Forest green and white, with a bird on the front.

Start small.

"Morning everyone, as Cece said, I'm Jake and as you probably already know, I am the striker for Chelsea. But, for the next six weeks, I'm going to be your coach." I paused, letting myself settle. "I've been playing football basically since I could walk. I played in junior leagues, JV, varsity, and D1 before I was picked up by Barcelona." My audience's eyes were wide. "I've played professionally for over a decade." It felt strange, laying out my career like that. "Despite all that, I still feel underqualified to be standing up here in front of all of you." That got a ripple of laughter, and a little of the tension in my shoulders eased. "I've never coached, but I do know a lot about football—so I'll do my best, if you agree to do the same. Sound good?" They all nodded. "You can all call me Jake or Coach, or whatever you're comfortable with. Just not Davenport, because I'll think I'm about to be benched." Another laugh. Maybe this wouldn't be so bad.

I rubbed my hands together, ready to dive in. "We're going to take it easy today, some warmups, a couple of drills and an easy game so I can get an idea of where you're all at before we get stuck into the big stuff." The group nodded. "Alright, let's start with two laps and we'll go from there." I said and clapped twice.

"Yes, Coach," the team chorused before taking off around the pitch.

Over the course of the next few hours, I discovered that I wasn't a completely useless coach. It was embarrassing how relieved I was.

It helped that the girls were all engaged and eager to learn, but I also found myself eager to teach, too. To make them better, both individually and as a team. Who the hell was I?

There was a wide spread of skill levels, with a few naturals, and others who obviously loved the game but needed some extra work to bring them up. And I wanted to get them there. I wanted to push them to be better. I might have been playing my entire life, but it didn't mean I didn't have to work for it. In my experience, it was the ones who needed to work for it that made the best players, the hungriest players. I could see a couple of them in the team and I was already excited to watch them improve.

Cecilia was one of the more skilled players, but she was also distracted. At one point she and another girl, Shannon, or maybe Shelley—getting all the names straight was going to be the hardest thing about the next six weeks—almost got into a brawl during the game despite being on the same team. I'd have to get to the bottom of that at some point, because I knew how tension on a team could fester.

As the temperature climbed toward a hundred degrees, it was clear we needed to wrap up early so I didn't have my team passing out from heat stroke. They were all sweaty and grateful when I called an end to the session and headed to the locker room with a collective *thanks, Coach*.

I liked being called Coach more than I wanted to admit— and not just when Harley was on her knees.

I cleared away the equipment with a forgotten warmth in my chest. Harley was right, I'd missed the game. Not the pressure, and the press, and the competition, but the game itself. And, being surrounded by a group of young people who loved it just as much as I did, it was nothing short of a fucking revelation. Could I hold onto this feeling if I went to Liverpool?

The sun was high and hot when I locked up and I found Cecilia waiting for me on the street.

"Hey, everything okay?" I asked.

She jumped, stuffing her phone into her pocket. "Yes, yeah, today was great. I just wanted to say thank you, again."

"Cece, you don't need to keep thanking me."

"That's the last time then," she said with a smile, scuffing the toe of her trainer on the sidewalk.

"So, you wanna talk about what happened with you and …"

"Shelley," she finished for me.

"Shelley, yeah. Look, you don't need to like everyone on your team, but you need to get along and respect them. If there's bad blood, for whatever reason, you're better off clearing the air and moving on before it taints the whole team."

She nodded, head bowed. "You know this from experience." It wasn't exactly a question.

"Yes, I do. I'm guessing you've seen everything that happened?" Another nod. "Kinda hard not to, right? I fucked up. Got in my own head about a lot of bullshit and got benched as a result. I wouldn't recommend it as a strategy."

"It was pretty dumb," she said and I laughed, because she wasn't wrong.

"Yes, it was. I'm glad to be able to provide an example of what not to do."

She smiled. "Thanks, Coach. I'll see you tomorrow?"

"You will."

She smiled. "Bye, Coach."

"Bye, Cece." I waved, my mind already spinning with ideas.

I was halfway home when my phone chimed with a text from Blair, my stomach bottomed out.

Liverpool want you here the week after next, no exceptions, no wiggle room.

Well fuck.

Mack was at the Cream and Sugar counter looking like he stepped out of some kind of pastry porn, thanks to the towering pile of pies he was carrying.

It must be Thursday.

"Mackenzie, all this for me? You shouldn't have." I grinned as he rolled his eyes. He loved it when I called him Mackenzie.

"Harley, it's a pleasure as always." He started to unbox a few of the pies onto their stands. My mouth watered as I spotted a lattice topped cherry number. I didn't think it could get better than his Thanksgiving offerings—the chocolate espresso was my personal favorite—but he just kept raising the bar.

"The pleasure is all mine. You got time to hang out?"

"Just enough for a coffee and a cinnamon roll. I'm not double parked today," he added with a proud puff of his chest.

"I can see that," I said, lifting my chin at the truck parked at the curb, pale butter yellow and with The Pie Guy logo printed across the side. I had seriously talented friends.

"So, how's Jake doing?" he asked, and I almost swallowed my tongue.

"Why are you asking me? Why would I know?" The response basically announced with zero subtlety that I'd been having outstanding and particularly athletic sex with Jake for over a week. I'd like to think there was a time when I'd been chill about it, but I was pretty sure I had zero chill where Jake was concerned. It was a problem.

Mack's eyes narrowed, no doubt reading the sexy subtext of my outburst. "Because he's living with you."

"Obviously." I laughed, trying to play the awkwardness off. It didn't work. "He's good, great. A natural born coach, by all accounts."

"Good to hear. And you? How are you?" His lips twitched into a knowing smirk.

"Also great. Your coffee." I slid the cup across the counter, along with the largest, gooiest cinnamon roll in the hopes it would encourage him to stop talking about Jake.

"Thank you."

"You're welcome." I needed to get him to stop looking at me like he knew my deepest, darkest secrets. "How's business?"

"It's going surprisingly well."

"Surprising to you, maybe, Mackenzie. I had no doubt you were destined for pie success." The only surprising thing, as far as I was concerned, was it not happening sooner. He ran a hand through his unruly blond curls, cheeks going slightly pink. Talented and humble. What a combo.

"I guess I should thank you for that, too, huh? Your post at Christmas kinda put me on the map." He ripped off a large chunk of his cinnamon roll and shoved it unceremoniously into his mouth.

I shook my head. "No, sir, you put yourself on the map, I

merely pointed at you and a few people noticed. Are you anywhere near sick of making pies yet?"

"No, thank god," he said around half a mouthful of cinnamon goo. "That'd be awkward, right?"

"It would," I agreed as a scream came from the kitchen and we both froze. It sounded like someone had been murdered back there. Every customer looked at the kitchen doors, then at me, then back at the kitchen doors. I loved Darcy like a sister, but I didn't want to go in there if I was going to find some knife wielding serial killer. I preferred keeping all my blood on the inside of my body, thank you very much.

Before I was forced to go and investigate the potentially life ending scream, Darcy exploded out of the doors.

"Holy shit!" she wailed, waving her phone in the air. "Holyshitholyshitholyshit."

"Darce, holy shit what? Who died?" I was increasingly concerned for her mental well-being.

"We got in—through, whatever." At my blank stare, she added, "The next round of the Coffee Champs! Harley, *we're in!*"

"HOLY SHIT!" I squealed, then slapped a hand over my mouth. It didn't matter how confident I'd been about our chances, actually hearing we got through was a trip.

"I know!"

Mack was looking between the two of us with a bemused smile. "I have no idea what's happening right now, but it sounds good," he said.

"It's huge!" Darcy said, taking him by the shoulders and giving him a shake. "Like, huger than Dallas!"

"Seriously?" he asked with a laugh. I understood the skepticism, Rudi Blue was still the place to be since Dallas and Duke's wedding of the year last November.

"Harley is going to be crowned the best barista in New

York!" Everyone cheered and anxious heat rushed up the back of my neck.

"Oh-kay, Darcy, just—yes, we nailed the mystery shopper, which is amazing, but we'll be up against some big competition." I'd made the mistake of searching previous winners and the intimidation factor was very real. These were people who had turned coffee into their personality, their entire life. I wasn't sure how to compete with that.

She *pfft*-ed at me. "But Harley will smash that competition, right everyone?" Another resounding cheer, which I of course appreciated, but also found mildly terrifying.

Astounding competition aside, did I even want to be crowned the best barista in New York? There was a lot of expectation that went along with that, wasn't there? And, honestly, I didn't know if I was ready for it. I liked things casual, chill, with as little pressure as possible. The best barista in New York crown was pretty much the opposite of that.

My heart beat an unsteady rhythm against my ribs, and I rolled out my shoulders in an effort to defuse the tension coiling there. The further we got in this process, the more there was to lose. This was why I didn't let myself get invested in things anymore—relationships, jobs, art, it was all transient, temporary. The fact I had been making coffee at Cream and Sugar for over four years did fly in the face of that, but still. I could pick up and leave whenever I wanted, start fresh somewhere new if the mood struck.

Darcy continued to tell Mack, and anyone else who'd listen, that we were about to be New York coffee royalty, as I stood there and sank into the quicksand of my own head.

. . .

It took a while, but I eventually managed to shake off my mood thanks to steadfastly ignoring Darcy and her Coffee Champs enthusiasm. The three slices of cherry pie also helped.

I knew I hadn't actually made a mistake in agreeing to the Coffee Champs, but I guess part of me had been expecting us not to advance. Now that we were, the whole thing felt a lot more real than it did before. I should read up on the next round but I'd rather bury my head under a pillow (or maybe Jake) until I was forced to surface.

The universe was clearly supporting the *use Jake to hide from the world* strategy, because as I stepped out onto the sidewalk at the end of the day there he was across the street. He was focused on his phone, so I took a second to just drink in the sight of him.

Was he getting hotter, or was it just me? No, it couldn't just be me. Even not knowing what the man could do with his tongue—and that was really something—anyone in the street would have to agree that, objectively, he was double-take hot. In the minute I stood there, a couple of teenagers nearly tripped over their own feet as they attempted to stare and walk at the same time. I could only imagine all the gawking that was going on during his coaching sessions. Although, maybe after a week the girls would have become somewhat desensitized.

Unlike me.

If there was an opposite to desensitization, I had that. *Resensitization?*

Jake glanced up from his phone, a smile stretching across his gorgeous face and both my heart and my stomach twisted and flipped—and one four letter word sprang up in my head. I sucked in a breath, more alarmed at the fact that word didn't scare me as much as it should. It wasn't a betrayal yet, not when Jake was still leaving. I would still keep my promise to Liam, to myself.

But, for the moment, for these weeks Jake and I had left, maybe I could also let myself sink into this thing we had. The only reason I could allow it was knowing that it was temporary, knowing that our time together had an expiration date.

"Hey there," he said as I approached, his smile turning ever so slightly devious. I liked that smile more than I wanted to admit.

"Hey yourself. You only just coming from Franklin?"

He nodded, pushing off the pole he'd been leaning on. What was it a about a man leaning—on literally anything—that was so fucking sexy?

"I was running through a few extra things with the defense group."

"Oh yeah? That sounds promising."

"The improvement from all of them, even after one week, is kind of blowing me away."

"Must be something about their coach," I said and nudged his elbow with mine.

He ducked his head, his smile going shy and, fuck, all I wanted for the next four and a bit weeks was to make this man smile, any smile, every smile. I needed to start committing each one of them to memory.

I led the way in the direction of home, but Jake snagged my elbow and gave it a tug.

"I thought we could take a walk, unless you're in a hurry to get home?"

I was usually in a hurry to get him naked, but I guess it could wait. "We can walk." I fell in step beside him, our fingers brushing with each swing of our arms. Not holding hands, just incidental touching. It was making my skin all sizzly.

"I'm in the mood for ice cream." His confession put a little extra pep in my step.

"Well, it's a good thing for you that I'm *always* in the mood for ice cream."

We walked in comfortable, companionable silence for a couple of blocks, and I shook off the thoughts that we could do this all the time if he didn't go back to London. Ice cream on summer afternoons. Hot cocoa when the temperature started to drop. But those thoughts didn't care about broken promises and soul mates.

"We're through to the next round of the Coffee Champs," I said to distract myself from the riot of thoughts rolling around in my head.

He stopped dead. "Seriously? Harley, that's incredible." He picked me up and spun me around. "I am not at all surprised, obviously, because of course you got through. This makes it celebratory ice cream then. Why was this not the first thing you said?" It was a fair question.

"Maybe I was distracted by your legs." He glanced down and, before he could pretend he was confused about why I'd be distracted by his legs, I continued, "you have an athlete's legs, Jake, let's not pretend you don't know that. It's a miracle you can get a bunch of teenage girls to focus with those things in their face all day." We started walking again.

"Uh-huh ... and is this just about my legs or the fact you're freaking out?"

"I'm not freaking out," I said with an unladylike snort. "I'm processing."

"You're freaking out," he nudged me sideways and grabbed my hand.

I shoved him back with my shoulder. "I'm not—"

"Yes, you are." It was irritating how he seemed to *know* me. On the inside.

"Maybe a little," I admitted. "But it's fine. I mean, I'm fine. Darcy is really excited."

"I bet she is."

"I am too, kind of. Or I will be, you know, once I've—"

"Processed," he said.

"Exactly."

He nodded but didn't push the conversation any further, which I was grateful for. Because I was processing. I may not get to Darcy's level of enthusiasm—mainly due to performance related nerves—but I would be excited. I believed it.

The apartment was empty when we arrived home from our Sweet Scoops pilgrimage. I had almost resisted the third scoop, but how was a person supposed to say no to brown sugar and sesame? I certainly couldn't. And it was a dream with my other selections—cereal milk and summer strawberry.

At some point, I was sure I'd grow up and learn to order an appropriate amount of ice cream for one person. Until then, I would continue to knowingly purchase too much and eat well past the point of discomfort, like an overgrown child. At least Jake did the same, although he, too, learned from our last ice cream outing and went with three fruit flavors—green apple, lemon, and peach. Of course, he still said that my cereal milk was the flavor of the day, because it was outstanding.

I was halfway to the bathroom when Jake grabbed me and pinned me to the wall.

"Hi," I managed before he was kissing me like I was a lifeline, his tongue pushing into my mouth as he lifted me onto his waist, pressing me harder into the wall.

"I've been waiting to do that since you walked out of Cream and Sugar," he said against my lips, and I smiled because it felt good to be on the same page as someone after all this time. I liked it.

"Well, maybe next time don't wait so long."

"Next time I won't," he agreed, in a low growly-type voice that did things to my insides. He didn't kiss me again though, just watched me for a long moment. "I've got something that I need to talk to you about, actually."

"If it's how soon can we get naked, I'd say the answer is *immediately*." I wiggled my hips and he groaned.

"That wasn't it, but it's good to know." He stepped back from the wall, putting me on my feet as he did, and a foreboding type shiver ran across my skin.

"What's up? Is everything okay?" I asked.

"Yes, I guess, I just—I've been doing a lot of thinking this last week."

"Oh-kay ..." My spidey senses were tingling, and not in a good way. I couldn't decide if I wanted him to announce he was staying or going. Both options made me feel slightly ill, for different reasons. I tucked my hands into my pockets then took them out again.

"Blair—"

"How is Blair?" I asked, because I couldn't take this stretching tension.

"She's good, great." He started pacing. "She got me an offer from Liverpool, to play for Liverpool. I figured that I wouldn't get another chance to play in the EPL. And it—it's *substantial*."

"That—" I swallowed hard. He was leaving. That was the plan, wasn't it? That had always been the plan. But maybe part of me had been secretly hoping that the plan would change, and that he might stay without me having to ask him to do it. Did that make me an idiot? Maybe. Probably. It didn't change the wobbly feeling in my chest at the thought of him actually leaving though. "That sounds like good news."

"It is," he said, but it didn't sound like he believed it. "It's a really good opportunity—for redemption, I guess. New team, fresh start, and all that." He squeezed the back of his neck.

I remained perfectly still. This was always coming. He was always leaving. So why the hell did I want to kick and scream and rage? "When do you have to be back?"

He blew out a breath as our eyes met. "They want me back next week for pre-season training."

Next week. No, no, no. We were supposed to have another month, more. Not a week. My nose burned with impending tears, but I was not going to cry. Maybe this was a good thing— less time meant it should be easier to get on with my life, right? I could go back to random hook ups with relative strangers. Only, right now, that sounded completely repulsive.

Get it together, Harley, you cannot stand in the way of this.

"So soon! But like you said, it's a great opportunity. And it's what you wanted, right?"

"I'm not going."

The relief was swift and almost had my knees buckling, quickly followed by tightening nerves. I was still torn, still terrified of him staying and what that would mean, of whether I could let myself be happy like that again.

"What do you mean you're not going? You mean you're not going *next week?* Which I get, you've committed to Cece and the rest of the team. But you can't turn down that kind of an opportunity, Jake. It's your career, your future."

He ran a hand through his hair. "I either go next week, or not at all."

I couldn't let him do this. Couldn't let him throw this opportunity away for a future with me that didn't exist, that shouldn't exist. "So, you negotiate. It's a month, basically, and then you're back, for good. A month is nothing in the grand scheme of things, right? I'm sure Blair could talk them around. This isn't a big deal."

"You think I should go? You want me to go?" He wanted me to say no, wanted me to tell him to stay, but I couldn't say it.

The words lodged themselves in my throat. It didn't matter if I wanted him to stay, not when it meant he was throwing away his career.

"It's a really good opportunity. Y—you should take it." The words were bitter, but I forced them out. I couldn't let him stay for me.

33

JAKE

This was not going how I hoped it would. But, at the same time, I wasn't exactly surprised. It was why I'd not mentioned it until now, right? Because this was what I expected Harley to say. She didn't want to fight, and it broke my fucking heart.

Had I been an idiot thinking it would be possible to convince her we were good together? She had to know it, too, but it didn't matter if she wasn't willing to fight for us.

I might be an idiot, but I couldn't just walk away. Not from her. Not again.

"Harley, I get that this is not what we talked about. And I thought I'd have more time to—" What? Convince her?

"Jake, I'm sorry if I gave you the impression that we could be more than we are, but this thing, we're temporary. Just like we were the first time."

Temporary.

The word clanged through my head. Rattled down my spine. Set my teeth on edge.

Temporary.

No. No, we fucking weren't, or we didn't need to be. All

328

she needed to do was believe it, too. I had a feeling she knew it, knew what we could be, she just needed to admit it, accept it. Not that I had any idea how to go about trying to make that happen, especially not when I could see the hard defiance settling on her face.

So much had changed for me in the weeks since I'd arrived in Brooklyn, even before, if I was being honest with myself. It wasn't just about Harley—although she was a very tempting reason to stay—it was the freedom I'd found here, the kind of freedom I thought I'd lost after everything exploded in London. I felt like I could breathe for the first time in too long, and I didn't want to give that up.

It was part of the reason I'd decided against Liverpool, as tempting as the offer was.

The other part of it was the coaching. It was the last thing I ever expected to say yes to, let alone enjoy, and, yet, here I was, invested in every single one of those girls and their successes. I was a coach, and not a bad one either. I wanted to watch the team, my team, grow and improve. I already knew that I wouldn't leave before the six weeks were up, it didn't matter how much money Liverpool threw at me.

Harley was still standing there, waiting for me to say something. I had nothing, or too much, and no idea how to say any of it to make her change her mind.

I took a breath, terrified of putting all my shit out there only for her to reject it, reject me. But I needed to do it. I needed to do what I didn't the first time. "And if we weren't temporary?"

Her eyes shuttered further, and she shook her head, slowly, almost sad. "But we are." There was no emotion in the statement, no feeling. It was just a fact. *Temporary.*

"You don't want me to stay?"

"No." She barely let me finish the question before the word

was out there. "It's not about what I want or don't want, Jake, it's just about what *is*."

That sounded final, heartbreakingly so, but it didn't have to be, did it? I could stay this time, like I couldn't before. We could still do this, except with more permanence. Would that be so bad?

"I've been doing a lot of thinking and I want to stay. I want to stay and—"

"Jake, please." She backed down the hall, fear tightening her face, her shoulders.

"Harley, stop, can't we talk about this?"

Another firm shake of her head. "There's nothing to talk about. I'm sorry." She turned and left, the front door slamming shut behind her, and I stood there wondering what the fuck just happened. Because of all the ways I had anticipated that conversation might go, her running away wasn't one of them. Or maybe it was, and I was still in denial.

What the hell was I going to do now?

The answer was pace—and mutter to myself.

Liam. This had to be, at least partially, about Liam. But I didn't want to run after her and bring up her dead college boyfriend. As much as I wanted to go charging into the streets to find her and figure everything out, I stayed where I was. Firstly, because I had no idea where she'd be and, secondly, she left because she needed space and time. I didn't want to take either of those things away from her.

So, that left me pacing. I could always go to Buck's, but that would mean talking to Hunter about the thing I wasn't supposed to be talking to Hunter about—even though he was probably the only other person that could fill me in on whatever I was missing.

I would have continued to stew in silence if my cell phone didn't start ringing. Blair. Of course, she was calling me now.

She could probably sense my inner turmoil all the way from London, and she knew it was time to pounce.

"Apartment number," she barked before I managed to say hello.

"Pet rock," I fired back.

"Pet rock? What the hell are you talking about?"

"I thought yelling random words was our new form of greeting. Did I mess it up? Was it a word association thing? Let me try ag—"

"What is your apartment number?"

"You mean street number? My place in London isn't an apartment, Blair, are you okay?"

"Jake. What is the number of the apartment you are currently staying in?"

Why the hell did she want to know that? "You mailing me something?"

"Fine. If you're going to be difficult." She hung up and I stared at my cell phone. That was weirder than usual. I'd give her a couple of minutes and then call back, just to make sure everything was alright.

Before I could dial, the buzzer went, and a shiver shot down my spine. No. It couldn't be—she couldn't be here. It was probably Harley—she must have forgotten her keys in her rush to get the fuck away from me.

I braced before pressing the button. "Hello?"

"I knew I'd find you eventually," Blair's voice crackled through the speaker. Fuck. "Let me in."

"No." I jumped away from the buzzer. What the hell was she doing here? And how did she know where Hunter's apartment was? I wouldn't put it past her to wander the streets knocking on doors, but it was too much of a time waste. And Blair was all about efficiency.

The buzzer went again and didn't stop. Fuck. I needed to

let her in, or she was going to stand there all day ringing the goddamn buzzer.

Fuck. Fuck. Fuck.

Just as I was about to reluctantly buzz her in, the noise stopped, and I jumped away from the button. She couldn't be watching, but it really did feel like she was fucking with me. I knew better than to think she'd given up, but I took a moment to enjoy the silence all the same.

"Hello? Blair, you still there?" I waited for an irate response, but none came. It was worse than if she'd been there yelling. Un-fucking-settling.

I would just call and figure out where she'd gone and what she was doing in Brooklyn. I might even apologize for not letting her in.

The door opened and Hunter walked in.

"What are you do—" I started but he wasn't alone. "Blair."

"Jake," she said in a deceptively cheery tone.

I looked back to Hunter. "What are you doing back?"

"It was slow, so I gave myself the night off. Boss perks and all." He glanced at Blair. "You gonna introduce us or ..."

I pinched the bridge of my nose, wishing I could just shove her back out the door and avoid all introductions. Instead, I said, "Hunter, this is Blair, my manager. Blair, this is my cousin, Hunter."

A slow smile curled Blair's lips as she accepted Hunter's outstretched hand. "It's a pleasure."

"Yes, it is," he said in his best smooth-bartender voice. "You in New York long?"

"That depends on him ..." She nodded in my direction as she released Hunter's hand.

He glanced at me, head tipping to one side. The move reminded me of Harley, and I had to resist the urge to rub my chest in an effort to relieve the ache.

"What's wrong with you?" he asked.

"Nothing. Nothing's wrong with me." I did not appreciate Blair's arched eyebrow, which silently, yet strongly, disagreed with the statement.

Hunter was still watching me. "You look weird." He narrowed his eyes. "Is Harley home?"

"No."

"Did you two break up?"

"Break up?!" I scoffed. "How could we break up when—"

"Jake, please stop, you are a terrible liar. I know, I've known the whole time." Before I could ask him how he knew, he continued, "She's my best friend, you're my cousin, and I live here, too. 'Nuff said?"

I nodded. "Sorry, I do want to talk about Harley but ..." I turned to Blair, who had made herself comfortable at the kitchen island and was staring at Hunter's butt. "What are you doing here?"

"Great to see you, too, Jake."

"Seriously, Blair, how are you here?"

"I tracked your cell phone, obviously."

"How—you what? That is an invasion of privacy—wait, does this mean you knew where I was this whole time?"

"Of course, I did."

"Then why did you bother asking?"

She gave me an irritatingly pitying look. "Because I wanted to give you the chance to tell the truth, which you did, so well done. As to what I'm doing here, our deadline for Liverpool is fast approaching and you've been a little too quiet. Are you accepting Liverpool's offer, or not?"

"Not."

"Man City?"

"Also not."

She nodded, not happy but accepting of my decision.

"That's why you and Harley broke up," Hunter said with a knowing nod.

"Y—yes, it is, kind of, we—this thing between us—we figured it had an expiration date. Or she did—I didn't want it to. But how, exactly, did you know that?"

Blair didn't give him a chance to answer. "Is this just about Harley?"

"No, Blair, it's not just about Harley. I've—the coaching has gone really well—"

"So, Man City—"

I shook my head. "I thought I wanted the chance to play again, to redeem myself and show the press and the rest of them that I wasn't washed up and my career wasn't over and basically tell them to go fuck themselves, you know? But, being here, being so far removed from all that scrutiny, I realized that none of those opinions mattered. I'm happy here, Blair, in a way I haven't been in a long time?"

"Are you asking me or telling me?"

"Telling—I'm telling you." I sucked in a breath. "I'm also in love with Harley. and I already left her once and I don't want to do that again." Fuck, there, I'd said it. The decision wasn't just about her, but to say she had no bearing on it would be a big fucking lie.

"You love her?" Hunter asked, eyebrows high.

"I do." Jesus, why did it feel like I was asking her dad for permission, or something equally archaic and stupid? Even still, I wanted him to be okay with it.

"Fucking finally," he said with a laugh. "I'm pretty sure she loves you, too."

"I'm not so sure about that."

"Before you two have a heart to heart," Blair interrupted, coming to stand in front of me. "You're right, no one else's opinion matters. Not even mine, incredible I know." She gave me an uncharacteristically soft smile. "I'm glad you're happy, Jake, I guess I've got some more work to do."

"Yes, but not now, take a few days—enjoy New York."

She smiled. "If you insist."

"I do."

"Well, it looks like I'm going to find myself a hotel. I'll speak to you in a few days."

Hunter and I watched her leave; as soon as the door clicked shut, my attention went straight back to him.

"How can you be so sure she loves me too?"

"Okay, look, I hoped she would have put all her shit on the table by now, but seeing as that hasn't happened, there's some stuff—I don't love that I'm telling you this and not her, but it'll help you to understand her."

"Okay ..."

"A couple of months after Harley started art school, she met Liam," he said and my stomach rolled, the old photos of them flashing through my head. "From literally the day they met they went everywhere together, totally inseparable. I wanted to hate the guy—I felt like he was taking her away from me—but she was so happy. He treated her well, accepted her unconditionally, wasn't a dick-bag or an obnoxious prick like a lot of the people at their school. The relationship wasn't perfect, but show me one that is, you know? They were good together for almost two years."

"What happened?" I felt guilty for already knowing more than I should when Hunter was wringing his hands and couldn't look me in the eye, but I didn't interrupt. I wanted to know the whole story.

"He died." Even knowing they were coming, the words still sucked all the air out of the room. "Skating to her place one night, he got hit by a car. The driver took off and he was just left there to bleed out."

"Fucking hell." Someone so young, gone, for no good reason, not that there was ever a good reason.

"It ruined her," Hunter went on, "she didn't leave the house for weeks. Barely made it to the funeral. For a while she tried to go to school, but eventually dropped out. She wasn't the same Harley—she was gone, lost in her grief. It was like that for ... I don't even know how long. Little by little, she started to come back, but she was never quite the same." He finally looked at me. "Not until you came back."

"Me?"

He nodded. "These last few weeks, she's been like the old Harley. Not everyone sees it, because she's always the first one to dance on a table or do body shots or some other crazy shit like that, but underneath it she's sad. She doesn't think I see it, either, but I do, I always have. Since you got here, though, that sadness in her—it's different, muted."

I didn't know what to say to any of this. My heart broke for Harley having to go through that loss. If I could take away her pain, I would, without question. I couldn't pretend to understand what was going on in her head, but the fact her first instinct was to run made more sense knowing what she'd lost.

"She's been with plenty of people since Liam, but none of them got under her skin like you have. Just like you did the first time."

"The first time?"

He snorted out a laugh. "Yes, I knew about it then, too. But that's not what's important right now. What's important right now is what you're going to do, now you've got a little more of the Harley puzzle. She wants you too, Jake, you've just gotta help her get out of her own way. How are you going to do that?"

I had no idea how I was going to do that.

34

HARLEY

I needed two things:

    1. a lethally strong martini

    2. someone to punch, hard

In the interests of safety, for both me and the sorry individual getting pummeled, the punching needed to happen before the drinking—I wasn't a complete monster. Which was why I had turned up on Murphy's doorstep an hour ago and insisted he let me punch him.

Unsurprisingly, he was not immediately thrilled at the prospect and suggested the punching bag as an alternative. That was obviously not going to cut it on the grounds it would not satisfy my need to punch a *person*. I wasn't usually so prone to violence but, right now, it needed to happen, because the alternative was to fall into a heap and cry for the next month because I was fucking things up and I didn't know what to do.

Rather than think about that I was going to punch my brother.

After substantial negotiations I agreed to wear gloves and

for Murphy to have what looked like a mattress strapped to his chest. It wasn't ideal, but it was protecting both of us and I still got to punch him—so that was a win.

Time moved in a weird blur of too fast and too slow, and I didn't stop until my shoulders were burning and I was a sweating mess. I did feel calmer than I had when I ran out of my apartment and away from Jake and all his expectations. The look on his face, all broken and disappointed, was burned into the back of my eyelids.

"So, you wanna talk about it?" Murphy asked as he helped me pull off my gloves. We'd spent the better part of the last hour in silence—except for his random grunts when I landed a particularly good punch, and notes on my form; keep your guard up, straighten that wrist, blah, blah, blah—as I worked out my frustrations on his well-protected torso.

"Talk about what?" I said, stretching out my shoulders and neck. I would not be discussing my non-relationship status with my brother.

He barked out a laugh. "Whatever has you channeling Rocky, or is this your new standard setting?"

"Can't a girl just be in the mood to punch something with no explanation?" Was that so difficult to believe?

"You wanted to punch some*one*, you were very clear on that, and, no, with you Harley there is always an explanation." The fact he was right made me want to punch him again. It was a shame I'd taken the gloves off.

"Well, if there is an explanation, it is not one you are going to hear," I said, folding forward into a hamstring stretch.

"Is it about Hunter's cousin?"

I popped back up. How did he even know about Jake? "No it is *not*." I was going to punch him again, safety precautions be damned. I went after him with a fist raised and he ran.

"I was just asking!"

"Well don't!" I growled.

"Okay, fuck, okay. Not asking, not prying." He raised his hands in surrender and I lowered my fist. "You want a shower?"

My shoulders sagged. "Yes, please, and some clothes that don't smell like sweaty coffee." It would have been nice to flee my apartment with a change of clothes.

"You got it," he said with a nod and led the way inside.

Once showered and dressed in clean, if ill-fitting, clothing, I was beginning to feel less like I was about to dive headfirst into a downward spiral, which was a relief considering how out of control I'd felt before.

It wasn't even Jake's confession that had me teetering so close to the edge, it was the fact I hadn't seen it coming. I thought we were on the same page, the same *temporary* page. Yes, there was mutual attraction, but it wasn't supposed to be going anywhere; we were supposed to still be going our separate ways.

Or was I lying to myself? Had I seen it coming and just chose to ignore it and pretend like I hadn't already lost my heart?

Fucking hell. I'd been so careful over the years, enjoying all the physical fun without the heart complications.

And then came Jake.

I'd like to be able to say it was just our history that had me all up in my feelings, but it wasn't. It was him. I'd gone and fallen in love with him. Like an idiot.

Unfortunately, that didn't change the fact that I had promised my heart to Liam. I promised him *forever*. I didn't get to change my mind just because he was gone, that wasn't how forever worked. Forever was forever.

I groaned, pressing the heels of my hands against my eyes. Jake looked back at me.

It was time for that martini.

. . .

Mrs S answered the door in a pale sage ensemble, the silk once again hanging off her narrow frame in a way that screamed personalized tailoring. One day, I was going to sneak a peek in the woman's closet.

"To what do I owe the pleasure?" she asked, ushering me inside and nudging the door closed.

"I need a drink."

Her eyes ran over me in a swift appraisal. "Looks like you need a lot more than that, darling, but a drink is a good place to start."

We walked through the living room where the usual group of ladies were gathered. No cards this time, though.

"Ladies," I said with what I hoped was a smile; it was hard to tell, given my mood. "What am I interrupting?"

"Not interrupting. Never interrupting," Dot *tsked* with a you-should-know-better look. "It's book club night." And yet, there was not a single book between them.

"But whatever's brought you here is probably much more interesting." Maisy leaned forward in anticipation. They were all like a dog with a bone.

"Oh for god's sake, let the girl get a drink first." Mrs S steered me into the kitchen and started making a very large martini. Bless her.

When we returned to the living room, the conversation stopped abruptly, and all eyes turned to me—the main event. But I wasn't going to just spill my guts straight away. I needed to ... honestly, I didn't know what I needed aside from another drink, and I hadn't even started the first one. I took a large gulp, the alcohol making a warm track down my throat and into my belly. I would very much like to wipe this day from my memory altogether. How many martinis would that take?

The conversation started up again and flowed around me as I sat guzzling my drink. I could feel the anticipation of every other person in the room, desperately waiting for me to open my mouth. I wasn't sure I was ready, which was apparently irrelevant.

I braced as I felt Mrs S draw a breath beside me. I tried not to look at her, but it was no good.

"So," she said against her glass as she took a sip. "What's got you all... whatever this is?" Her hand waved in a vague circle at me. I didn't blame her. Walking around in my brother's old sweats wasn't exactly normal for me.

I considered the question and, for a second, the idea of lying almost seemed like a good one. I could tell her and the rest of the group I was perfectly fine, that there was absolutely nothing wrong, and I was just here for a good martini. But what would be the point of that? These women were a veritable brains trust. I'd be an idiot to not tap into that. And, I guess, I wouldn't have come here if I wasn't prepared to dish. You didn't come to Mrs S if you were planning on keeping your mouth shut.

"It's a man," Shirley said before I could say anything.

"The hot, almost-naked roommate!" Dot added with unrestrained glee and an adorable little clap.

"There was a knife, wasn't there?" Maisy asked. And, yep, I forgot I'd told them that.

"Yes, it is about the hot, almost-naked roommate," I confirmed, and they hummed in that way old women did, like they'd known the answer all along.

"So, what's he done?" Mrs S asked, toying with her glass.

I tucked a rogue curl behind my ear. "Maybe he hasn't done anything."

"Then what have *you* done?"

I took a slurping sip of my drink as I considered how best to explain the tidal wave of emotion that had drowned me this afternoon. It hadn't exactly receded.

"I don't know if I could say there is anything specific that either of us have done." That was a lie. He had done something. He had decided he was staying, thereby reneging on our *temporary* deal. I blew out a breath. I just needed to tell them, didn't I, just get it all out.

So, I did. I proceeded to give them a probably too detailed account of the entire Harley and Jake story. And, over the course of recounting the events—both from now and twelve years ago—it became clear to me for the first time that I had quite liked him back then. More than I had ever admitted to myself.

When I was done, I slumped into my chair and let my head drop back.

"So, you were happy to use the boy for his body, then he was supposed to go back to Lisbon—"

"London, Maisy," Dot snapped, cutting Maisy off. "For God's sake, turn your ears up."

"Actually, it was Liverpool," Shirley cut in.

"Well, whatever, Lisbon, London, Liverpool. He was leaving and now he's not?" That about summed it up.

"Doesn't look like it." I plucked up my drink for another sip but found my glass empty. Boo. Mrs S wasted no time in offering me a fresh one. She was an angel, truly.

"So, you get to keep seeing the boy naked, what's the problem with that?" Maisy hiccupped as she wagged her eyebrows at me. Maisy was a horndog.

"The problem with that, you old hussy, is that she obviously likes the boy," Olive said, and several heads nodded along with her, including mine, because she was right, I did like the boy. It happened without my permission, and it threatened to break all my long-held promises, but I liked the boy—*loved* the boy even—and I didn't know what to do about it.

Mrs S shifted on our shared couch and set down her glass. "You can't keep hiding from it, Harley."

"Hiding from what? Who says I'm hiding from anything?" I asked, hiding behind my drink.

"Me, I do. You are fierce and wild and wonderful and everything a young woman should be, but you can't keep hiding from love, honey." Her steel gray eyes pinned me in place, I squirmed under the weight of them and sipped my drink.

"I—I promised him forever," I whispered.

Those eyes flashed with heavy sadness. "I know you did, and I wish you could have had that with him." She smoothed my hair back. "What happened to Liam was a senseless tragedy—"

"It was my fault though, if it wasn't for me asking him for Taco Bell at midnight, like a fucking idiot, he wouldn't have even been there. He—" I choked on the words. *He might still be alive.* But he wasn't. He was gone and it was my fault, and the last thing I could do for him was keep my promise.

"Harley." She squeezed my shoulders. "I need you to hear me, his death was not your fault. I understand why you feel responsible. You don't think I felt responsible for Ronny? You don't think all of us have felt responsible at one point or another? But you can't hold onto that.

"It was not your fault, it was the son of a bitch who hit him and kept on driving. Liam's death is not on you. It was an accident, it shouldn't have happened. And someone your age should not have had to deal with it. But you really think Liam would have wanted you to keep blaming yourself? Keep yourself closed off for the rest of your life? Because I don't—he would have wanted you to be happy, Harley. *Really* happy. It's time to take that patched-up heart of yours and open it up to the possibility of love again."

My lip wobbled. "I don't know if I can."

"I know you can." She gestured to the other women gathered around us. "*We* know you can. You're too young to keep it locked away. There is more love out there than you could possibly imagine, and you deserve it—stop pretending you don't just because you've had it once already."

Dot covered my hand with hers, and the others all looked at me with wise, sympathetic eyes. They had all experienced loss, their loves leaving them alone in the world. But there had been so much *life* before that.

"It's not fair," Olive said, sensing the direction of my thoughts. "It never is."

"But none of us get to choose the hand we're dealt," Bernadette added. "We just have to make the best of the cards we're given."

Tears slipped down my cheeks in hot tracks. I couldn't do it. I didn't know how to do it. Not again.

I wanted them to be right, I wanted to believe that I could love Jake and we could have something good and real. But what if, *what if Jake* ... it was the part I hadn't let myself think. What if something happened to him, too? How would I do that again? I guess I needed to believe that future Harley could handle it.

My eyes moved over the women surrounding me. They couldn't have known what they would have to face. The loss, the heartbreak, the pain. If they could all get through it, then maybe I needed to give myself a little more credit too. And, if I needed help, I knew just where to come.

I blew out a shaky breath and finished my drink in two icy cold yet searing gulps.

"That's a woman with a plan," Shirley said with a grin.

"Let's not get ahead of ourselves, there is no plan," I countered with a soggy laugh. "But I do have a little more courage than I did before." And that was something. "Thank you, ladies."

They all smiled, warmth and pride radiating from their wise, wrinkled faces and, for the first time in a long time, my shoulders felt a little lighter. My breath grew deeper with the relief of it. He'd want me to be happy. Jake made me happy. Could it really be that simple?

Mrs S stood with me. "Now, you go home, you strip that boy naked—"

"And send photos!" Dot cut off Mrs S and the room descended into a fit of cackled giggles. Old women were total pervs and I loved it.

"On that note, I will bid you all adieu."

"Don't do anything we wouldn't do!" Shirley hollered as I bowed.

Mrs S caught my hand as we made it to the front door.

"Thanks, again," I said. It was lame and not enough, but it was all I had.

"You don't know what's going to happen, it might hurt, but you can't be scared of the hurt, because it means there was love. And that will always be worth it, you hear me?"

"I hear you." I sniffed.

"Good."

"You're my hero."

"I know." She let go of my hand and tapped my cheek. "Do send pics though."

I smiled. "Actually, there's some pretty outstanding ones online already."

I stepped out onto the street, energy sizzling under my skin. What now?

Was this one of those moments where a grand romantic gesture was necessary? Was this that kind of moment? I probably shouldn't have had those two martinis, because they were seriously impairing my grand romantic gesture game. But it was okay. Maybe I didn't need the full gesture, I just needed to go home and tell him the truth—and hope like hell we could still have something real.

35

JAKE

It had been hours since Harley left, and I was no closer to figuring out what the hell I was supposed to do. I had discarded: call her ruthlessly until she answered—too stalker-ish; and make a missing person report—too extreme. I actually wasn't sure you could even make a missing person's report until said person had been missing for a day or something. So, that plan was dead in the water from the start.

If I sat here staring at the door and willing her to come through it much longer, I was going to tear my hair out.

Hunter had been no help. After the big *what are you going to do* moment, he admitted as we ate Chinese take-out that it would be better to let Harley cool off. All she needed was some time and then she'd be back, he was sure of it. Initially, I believed him.

Now, too long later, I wasn't so sure.

I could tell he was trying to be chill, and I appreciated his efforts, but if he asked again about a beer, I was going to slap him. I knew I'd feel bad about it afterwards, because he was just being supportive, but that would not stop it from happening.

"You want a beer, maybe something to eat?" he asked, ignoring the remnants of our Chinese take-out spread across the coffee table.

I stood up. "Actually, I think I need a walk." No, a run. I needed a run.

"Sounds good, I'll come with you." He went to stand up.

"No," I barked and regretted it as he fell back on his butt. "Sorry." I scrubbed a hand over my face. "You don't need to do that. I just want to get some air, clear my head, you know?"

He nodded. "She'll be back, Jake, she will."

"I know, I just—the waiting is making me feel like I'm losing it." I didn't wait for his response, if there was one. I went directly to my room and changed into some running gear.

It took a couple of miles before my brain no longer felt like it was a kicked hornet's nest. The longer my feet slapped against the sidewalk in a steady rhythm, the clearer my mind became. Not entirely, of course, but it was enough, for the moment.

I'd left my cell phone at the apartment. It seemed like a good idea at the time, but now I was beginning to wonder if she'd come back to find I was gone. What if—no, stop. I needed to get out. I needed the run. As it was, if she'd walked in, I would have launched myself at her and never let go, maybe cried at her feet a little. I needed to chill the fuck out.

I wasn't sure if it had come to me slowly, or in one sledge-hammer moment of clarity, but it had literally always been Harley. Since that first day on Hunter's porch, my whole world had rearranged itself to make her the center. I'd ignored it back then, or tried to, anyway, telling myself that my career needed to come first. It was my time, after all. But she'd been there in the back of my head. Every other woman was compared to her, whether I realized it or not, and none of them were the same. How could they be? There was only one Harley. And she was the one, my one. Some part of me had always known it, but I was just too scared, or too stupid, to see it.

I wasn't scared or stupid anymore.

That wasn't entirely true, I was still scared out of my fucking mind, if I was being honest. Now, though, it was about whether she wanted me too.

When I had pushed myself well past the limit of comfort and was teetering on the edge of vomiting—I deeply regretted the chili pork—it was time to head back. And after a couple of blissful, empty-minded minutes the questions came roaring back,

Did she love me too? Would she be there? Or would I be left to wonder about her well-being, and her feelings, until tomorrow?

One question was answered when I rounded the corner onto Harley and Hunter's street. Because there she was. Pacing the sidewalk in front of her building, mumbling to herself, from what I could tell.

What was she waiting for? Me, please be waiting for me.

I slowed as an aggressive contingent of butterflies started wrestling practice in my stomach. Maybe I should turn and run, because if I didn't ask her how she felt I could pretend she loved me, too. I could pretend it just wasn't our time. I'd said that to myself when I left twelve years ago. Told myself that she felt the same, that we weren't meant to be.

No. That wasn't happening, I wouldn't let myself wonder again. Not when I was planning on staying whether she wanted me here or not. What if she didn't—nope, no speculating.

Just fucking talk to her.

I took one step closer, then another, and she stopped her

pacing and turned in my direction. The handful of hours we'd been apart might have been months for how relieved I was to see her standing there. Even in the oversized sweats she was wearing. Whose clothes were they?

Talk. I needed to talk.

Unfortunately, everything I had planned to say—I'd made up a whole speech during my run—made a swift exit from my brain. There was nothing save for *I love you. I'm sorry. I love you. I'm sorry.* She wasn't saying anything, either, just watching me with the same intensity I was watching her. Did she worry I was a figment of her imagination, too? Was she too scared to blink, just in case I disappeared?

We closed the distance in measured steps, neither speaking, only watching. It might have been the longest she'd gone without speaking when she was awake.

"Jake," she said at the same moment I said, "Harley."

"You go first," I added.

"No, you, you can go first."

"I'm sor—"

"Actually, wait, I do want to go first."

I rolled my lips together and gestured for her to continue.

She swallowed and let out a wobbly laugh. There were faint rings of red around her eyes. Had I put them there?

"I don't actually know where to start," she confessed.

"The beginning is usually a good place."

"But where is the beginning?" She blew out a breath. "The first time I saw you, at the ripe old age of eleven, I told myself that you'd be my husband one day." I nearly crumbled to the ground and cried in sheer relief, but she wasn't finished. "The next day I heard you tell Hunter I was lame because I liked S Club 7." Her lips twitched into a smile at the memory. "I was heartbroken. But I still practiced writing Harley Davenport for at least a month."

"Did you nail it?"

"I had that thing down to a fine art." She paused, eyes roaming over my face. "Then, seven years later, you turned up on Hunter's porch."

"And I told myself I was going to marry you one day." I continued as she gawked, "I think my world rearranged itself that day. Obviously, I did not recall the previous meeting and calling you lame. In my defense, I was a punk-ass teenager at the time."

"All relationships have their trials," she said with a smile and a shrug, then blew out a heavy breath. "I don't think I realized it until you left just how much I actually liked you. And there were days when I seriously considered getting on a plane and surprising you in a trench coat." We both laughed, but hers was heavy. Her eyes were shining with tears. She was thinking about Liam, the love she lost.

"I know about Liam. Hunter—"

"He told you?"

"A little. Harley, I'm so sorry."

She nodded. "I'm sorry I didn't, couldn't tell you myself. Part of me wanted to, but I don't let myself think of him if I can help it." A pause. "I lost everything when I lost him. I was supposed to have him forever. We'd talked about marriage and kids and traveling, the house we were going to buy—I was going to paint the door a different color every month, and he would hate it because he was more of a purist artist, and I was a 'slap it all together and see what you get' kind of girl. But then it was gone, it was all gone in one fucking second. He could have lived if that driver had just stopped, but they didn't, they left him there to die alone in the gutter." The tears streamed down her face and my heart cracked open to see her hurt.

"I didn't just mourn him, I mourned our future, too. That future that had been so real I could touch it, smell it—it all died along with him. I couldn't fathom wanting it with anyone else." She wiped her cheeks. "For a long time, I wasn't sure how to put myself back together. Some days, just putting one foot in front of the other feels like more than I'm capable of. I got really good at hiding, at smiling to cover it all up. I stopped talking about him, because talking about him made the pain so much worse. Talking about him made me remember what I'd had and what I'd lost, and it made me so angry.

"Then you appeared in my bathroom and I—I don't know what happened. I started to remember who I was before. I remembered that there was a time I was happy, and it wasn't because of Liam. I think ... you might have saved me, Jake."

And now I was crying along with her.

"But being with you, I didn't know how to do that and not break my promises to him. Even just being as happy as I've been these last few weeks felt like a betrayal. I figured that if we were temporary, if there were no strings, if it didn't mean anything, and you were leaving, then I could have my happy cake and eat it too. Once you were gone, I'd—"

"Be sad again?"

She nodded, fresh tears pouring down her cheeks. "But I don't want to be sad again." I couldn't take the distance any longer, so I closed it, folding her into my chest. Her fingers curled into the front of my shirt as she cried with sobs that shook her whole body. I kissed her hair, over and over, rubbed circles on her back. I just wanted to take this pain away.

Her head popped up. "I want this to mean something, Jake, I want all the strings. I want them, you know, attached." She let out a tear-soaked laugh. "My strings. Your strings. Attached to each other. I don't want temporary. I'm sorry I ran out before, I just—I needed a minute."

"You can have as many minutes as you need."

"But we're—you're still staying?"

"I'm staying. I don't know what happens after this soccer program is done, but what I do know is that, whatever happens, I want to be with you—however that looks. I was prepared to stay whether you wanted me to or not. I just hoped that you'd want me to."

"I do, I really do want you to. I—" she faltered. "I love you, Jake."

My breath left me in a relieved whoosh, and I brushed a kiss across her mouth because I had no words. Even if I did, none of them were enough for what I wanted to say to this woman. She thought I saved her, but really, I knew she'd saved me—from myself, from a downward spiral, from everything.

"I love you," I whispered against her lips. It wasn't enough, would never be enough. "IloveyouIloveyouIloveyou."

"I love you, too."

I cradled her face, pressing kiss after kiss to her lips, her cheeks, her nose, her chin, her forehead. Her laugh, free and relieved, loosened something in my chest. I thought I'd chased her away. But she was here, saying she loved me back.

We stood there laughing and kissing and mumbling *I love yous* until Harley's stomach rumbled, and she announced she needed ice cream, again. And, because I would happily give her whatever she wanted for the rest of our natural lives, I just took her hand and led the way.

36

HARLEY

Hunter shuffled into the kitchen and mumbled something that sounded an awful lot like *oh for fuck's sake*. He should be grateful—five minutes earlier and he would have found Jake bending me over the kitchen island. For good luck, obviously, because today was the day. Today I was standing up in front of a legit crowd and making coffee against other talented baristas. If I wasn't so excited, and now sated thanks to aforementioned bending over, I'd be really fucking nervous. I guess it was a good thing I had such an incredible boyfriend.

A month later and it still sounded weird. Fucking amazing, but still weird.

"I think I preferred it when you two were trying to keep this whole thing a secret. At least that way I wasn't confronted by all this canoodling in my kitchen first thing in the morning." He rubbed a hand over his face.

"One: this is *our* kitchen. And two: *canoodling?*" I peeled myself off Jake's naked chest but waited until Hunter was watching before I slapped him on the butt.

"Charming," Hunter deadpanned. "And if this is not canoodling then what else would you call it?"

"A few minutes ago I would have called it fu—"

"Lalalalala!" he yelled, fingers plugged in his ears. "Please, for the love of god, I do not want to know what my best friend and my cousin do when I'm not here—and I especially don't want to know about it if it occurred in the kitchen. Just no. This is where we prepare and eat food, Harley."

I grinned as I threw a strawberry at him. "Prude."

He caught the projectile and shoved it in his mouth. "I don't see how not wanting to know about your bare ass on the kitchen counter is me being a prude."

"How do you know it was my ass?" I wiggled my eyebrows.

He leveled me with a flat look. "Seriously?"

"I'm kidding, I'm kidding. Sheesh, someone is a little touchy today. Everything okay? Why are you even up this early?"

He shrugged but didn't answer. "Despite not wanting to hear about your bare anything on the kitchen counter, I am really happy for you two. I guess I did the right thing after all." His offense had morphed into smugness.

"Right thing? What are you talking about?"

"Well, if it wasn't for me inviting Jake to stay here then all of this ..." He waved a hand at us as he grabbed a glass and filled it with water. "Wouldn't have happened, would it? So, you're welcome."

"Hold on. You—no, you didn't plan all this."

"Of course, I didn't *plan* it, how could I when I didn't know Jake was coming? But, when he turned up, it was an opportunity to help you both."

"You meddler! You, the man who constantly tells me not to meddle. You did not know we were going to end up *here*." I humped Jake's leg as a visual aid.

"I didn't know for sure, but I hoped. And look, I was right."

"So, you knew the entire time?!"

"Yes, Harley, I knew the entire time," Hunter said with a roll of his eyes. "I've known you since we were seven and you are one of the least subtle people I've ever met. There is no secret you can keep from me."

"Untrue! I can keep a secret."

Both Hunter and Jake laughed, which was incredibly rude. As much as I wanted to slap my friend for meddling, I couldn't actually be too mad, because it was absolutely something I'd do. I also got to see Jake naked every single day as a result, and that was very much worth Hunter's intervention.

"I'm going to bed." Hunter shuffled back the way he came, clutching his glass. "The thing starts at two, right?"

"Sure does."

He saluted as he left.

"Oh, I am totally setting him up," I whispered as his door clicked shut.

"No, you're not," Jake said with a kiss to the top of my head.

"It's happening. He meddled. That is a green light for me to meddle."

"I don't think that's true."

"It really is." I slapped his butt again. I could slap the man's butt all day long. "Okay, I gotta go. Coffee calls."

He grabbed my face, thumbs sweeping across my cheekbones as his fingers slid into my curls. The touch sent familiar shivers across my skin. Our lips met, slow this time after the frenzy earlier. He kissed me deeply, tracing the shape of my mouth with his. My hands went around his waist, and I sunk into it—the fact I was going to be late was the very last thing I cared about as our tongues teased one another.

Mine. This man was mine, and I was his.

I'd come so close to throwing this away, these kisses, this

love. But Mrs S was right, Liam wouldn't have wanted me to be alone and sad. And loving Jake now didn't mean I loved Liam any less then. It meant I got a double shot.

"Okay," I said, reluctantly pulling away. "I really do need to go."

"One more minute," he muttered against my lips.

"Jake, I'm gonna be late."

He growled, lifting me onto the counter. I leaned back, trying to keep my mouth away from his. He started attacking my neck instead.

"We can pick this up later."

He kissed me hard. "You bet we will."

I jumped off the counter and gave him one last kiss. "I'll see you there?"

"I'll be there at midday." He slapped me on the butt as I skipped out the door.

Darcy looked like she was on her third double espresso when I floated into Cream and Sugar. We had talked about not opening today but she needed the distraction before this afternoon.

"As happy as I am for you," she started, "this euphoria kind of makes me want to punch you in the boob."

I reflexively covered the girls for fear she'd follow through on the threat.

"I wouldn't actually do it."

"Is this just about my euphoria or have you had too much coffee this morning?"

"I didn't sleep at all last night because I was so nervous. Getting out of bed required more caffeine than usual."

"Okay, no more coffee for you. Water and food." She could do with a little euphoria too, and perhaps I was the person to help bring it to her? I didn't see her with Hunter, which meant I had two set up projects.

"Why are you looking at me like that?" she asked as she placed a large tray of muffins on the counter.

"I'm not—what? I'm not looking at you like anything."

"You're looking at me like I'm about to be part of a scheme."

"There is no scheme!"

Her snorted *uh-huh* suggested she didn't believe me.

"Go and eat."

"I don't think I can." She covered her mouth with one hand.

"Darce, this whole thing was your idea and you're not even the one who has to play performing monkey today."

"You're going to be so fucking amazing," she said, and I smiled at the fact she could still pump me up while feeling like she was going to vomit. What a boss. What a friend.

"Thank you, now go eat." I shooed her away and took over filling the pastry cabinet with today's muffins.

At some point between opening and closing up for the day, Darcy's nervous stomach had transferred to me. I thought I'd been managing pretty well, right up until Jake appeared on the sidewalk. For a second, everything went into slow-mo, the world became blurred and all I could see was him. *At Last* started playing in my head.

I blinked and everything went back to regular speed and the nerves doubled down—because if Jake was here, it was time to go. Then he smiled at me, and it didn't matter if I made the best coffee of my life today or the worst because, whatever happened, I had him.

"You ladies ready?" he asked, leaning just in the doorway.

"Yes," Darcy and I said together. I didn't feel ready, not really, but I'd get there. Fake it 'til you make it was my current mantra. *I am a coffee champion.*

Jake caught me around the waist as I stepped outside and I buried my face in his chest, breathing him in to settle some of my more stubborn nerves.

"You're going to kill it, Harley," he said against my hair. "And, if for whatever reason, you do not walk away as the coffee champion of New York, well, I will do my best to make you forget about it."

I tipped my head back to look at him, "And how do you plan on doing that?"

"You'll just have to wait and see ..."

"Such a tease." I slapped his chest.

"Okay, that's enough of all of that," Darcy said, swatting at us.

I took Jake's hand and held it up. "Is this okay?"

"Yes, that's fine." She narrowed her eyes at me as I smiled.

I am a coffee champion. "Let's go do this thing."

I left Darcy and Jake at the door of the Pavilion; they both wished me luck and Jake gave my hand a reassuring squeeze. *I am a coffee champion.*

"Even if you can't see me, I'll be there, thinking of all the ways I'm going to make you come tonight." He paused, holding my gaze. "How are you feeling now?"

"Like I'm not going to be able to focus on making coffee."

"Then my work here is done. Knock 'em dead." He kissed my forehead and followed Darcy inside. *I am a coffee champion.*

As soon as I stepped on stage with the rest of the competitors—whose names I had mostly forgotten the second we were introduced backstage—my brain emptied of pretty much everything, even Jake and his promises for later. I was the poster girl for hyperfocus.

Coffee. Coffee. Coffee.

Each round had three events, speed, accuracy, and latte art —all underpinned by taste—and one competitor was eliminated at the end of each until there were only three of us left. The fact I had made it to the final three made me think I really did have a shot at taking out the whole thing.

The final round had an extra event—the signature coffee. By the time we were done, I was so wired I could have powered half of Manhattan.

I hadn't let myself look at the audience, for fear seeing Jake would distract me, but once we were done my eyes sought him out. I found him easily—and then I saw the rest of them. A couple of rows from the front, Jake stood in the middle of his entire team, Cecilia standing proudly on his right, and they were holding a banner that said *Harley is our coffee champion*.

I caught Jake's eye and waved. He grinned, nodding at the banner like I might not have seen it. *Yes, I see it.* I loved that man so much it scared me sometimes.

"Alright, everyone, we have seen some incredible talent here this afternoon, haven't we?" Kelsey, the emcee, said to raucous applause. She was right, the competition had been unbelievable, and I honestly had no idea if I'd done enough to win. For the first time since Darcy had mentioned the Coffee Champs, I really wanted to win.

"Before we get to the winner, I'd like to thank all of today's competitors. The caliber this year has really been something and we can't wait to see you all back next year. Like in our previous rounds, the scores from each event have been tallied and we have a winner. But first, our runners up." She paused and waved an envelope at the crowd.

"The second runner up ... Marco Hernandez from Coffee Time in Harlem." Everyone clapped as Marco accepted his group handle trophy. When he returned to stand with me and the other finalist, Kelsey continued, "Our first runner up … Harley O'Connell from Cream and Sugar in Greenpoint!"

Jake and the team yelled and jumped and screamed and made general nuisances of themselves as I stepped up to Kelsey and accepted my group handle trophy with a wide smile and bowed for the cheering crowd.

"And that, of course, means our winner is Nina Cho from Hot Press Coffee in Chelsea." The crowd roared again but I was pretty sure my cheer had been louder—not that it was a competition.

My cheeks were hurting from all the smiling.

The *Harley is our coffee champion* banner was currently hung across the Rudi Blue bar, Chase had made a cocktail in my honor and there was more pie and ice cream than I had seen in one place, maybe ever. It was, in short, the perfect party.

Made all the more perfect because Jake was by my side. I hadn't felt this kind of bone-deep contentment in so long, I'd convinced myself it didn't exist, that maybe I'd imagined it the first time. But it did exist—and here I was, warm and cozy and glowing and so fucking happy I could literally burst.

"Do we need to start planning for next year's domination?" Jake asked, one hand sliding back and forth across my back before it slipped under the edge of my shirt.

I took a sip of my Harley cocktail and leaned into him. "I don't think so."

"Why's that?"

"Because it would be unfair for me to have that on top of all of this." I smiled up at him. "And, besides, you still owe me a little something, remember?"

"Oh, I remember, and there is nothing little about it." He swallowed my laugh as he kissed me so hard my head spun.

I didn't like to think of fate, or destiny, or any other plan from the universe, because I hated the idea that Liam was meant to be gone for Jake and I to be together now. But maybe we would have found our way here no matter what else happened, no matter what decisions or mistakes we made. Because, right now, I couldn't imagine wanting to be anywhere else in the world.

"Of all the bathrooms, you just had to walk into mine," I said as our kiss broke.

"And I count myself lucky every day."

"I love you, Jake Davenport."

"I love you, too, Harley O'Connell—you and all your strings."

EPILOGUE
JAKE

The front door was blue.

The front door had not been blue when I was here two weeks ago, but it was really fucking blue now—with the exception of a small white heart between the number and peephole. Something I had come to terms with over the last year, life with Harley would never be boring.

I dug my keys out of my pocket, *Eye of the Tiger* accompanied by off-key singing came muffled through our very blue door. She'd made no mention of painting the door when she was in Montreal last week, or in any of our FaceTime calls since she got back home. But I guess we'd been pretty distracted.

The door swung open just as I was about to unlock it.

"Jake!" Harley squealed, jumping at me so quickly I stumbled back into the opposite wall as I caught her. "You're. Home. You're. Home. You're. Home." Each word was punctuated with a kiss. "I thought you were meeting me there?"

"You're not the only one who can plan surprises." I glanced at the door.

She grinned. "It looks good right?!"

"Not as good as you do." Fucking hell, I'd missed her. As much as I was enjoying coaching at Montreal, every goodbye was a little harder than the last. Yes, we were on the same coast, which was why I accepted the offer from Montreal instead of LA, but it wasn't enough. I didn't just want to be on the same coast. I wanted to be in the same city, in the same apartment, waking up in the same bed every morning.

I'd been willing to wait for it, because I told myself that Harley and I had all the time in the world. Then I stepped off the plane an hour ago and as soon as I turned my phone on Blair was calling with *the news*. It shouldn't be a surprise that she'd come through, after so many years working together I knew better than to doubt her. She'd really outdone herself this time though.

Head coach. Head coach *and* in New York. Part of me was still wondering if I'd imagined the whole phone call.

Harley was covering my face in kisses. "You couldn't have got here like a half hour ago?" she said, bouncing her eyebrows. "Give us more time?"

"I was supposed to be here two hours ago." I dropped my lips to her neck as I moved in the general direction of our doorway. "How much time do we have?"

She tugged me up by my hair just as we crossed the threshold. "We have zero time."

"Zero? Are you sure?"

"Technically negative two or three minutes." She unwound her legs and I set her down but didn't let go, not yet.

"But I missed you," I said, like this might somehow freeze time. A guy could hope.

"I missed you, too. I always do." She tapped my chest, looking vulnerable for a beat before she squashed it. "But I really do need to go, or Darcy will kill me."

I reluctantly let her go and went back for my bag that had

been dropped when she tackled me. "Have you spoken to her yet? Do I have time to change?"

She stepped out into the hall, the soles of her red Vans sneakers squeaking on the hardwoods. "You have sixty seconds to change, and yes, but I will tell you on the way."

I stopped in the doorway. "Just tell me while I change."

"No. Nuh-uh. Because if I see you shirtless, we will not make it there. I'm trying to be responsible! Go!" She shooed me.

"You're not even going to step back inside, are you?"

"Nope. No, I am not." The sheer longing on her face had me taking a step back toward her. "Jake, no." She closed her eyes, shaking her head. "You're down to thirty seconds."

I ran through the apartment noting the small changes Harley had made since I was home last. She maintained that this was my place, and she was just apartment sitting until I was back in Brooklyn full time. Yet, every time I was here there was a little more of her in some corner or another. I fucking loved it. I wanted signs of her in every room, on every wall.

Once in the bedroom I dropped my bag, rifled through it to find a pair of shorts and a shirt and threw them on.

Harley was waiting patiently in the hall, well, patiently-ish. "Finally, let's go!"

I pulled the door closed behind us and threaded my fingers with hers as she made for the elevator.

"Are you seriously going to make me ask about Darcy again?" I said, pulling her into my chest as the elevator doors closed. I needed to touch her as much as humanly possible in the next forty-eight hours before I had to get back on a plane. Only for a few more months.

She hesitated, fingers curling around my biceps. "Okay, so we were leaving yesterday, and I was determined to do it before the champs because I didn't want her to think it was about that, you know?" I nodded, we'd discussed this numerous times and Harley had gone over what she was going to say every day for the last week. I wanted her to skip straight to the part where Darcy either said yes or no, but another thing I had learned about Harley in the last year was that if she wanted to tell you the full story, then you would hear the full story.

"I was kinda nervous, so after we locked up for the day, I just threw the proposal at her without explaining what it was, and she thought I was quitting."

"What?" We stepped off the elevator and out onto the street.

"It was less than ideal." She glanced at her phone then the Prius down the block. "That's our ride." We got in, Harley making small talk as we took off into traffic.

"So, anyway, she was crying, and I thought it was because she hated everything, but I was too wired to realize she hadn't actually read anything. So, then I started rambling about how it was fine if she wasn't interested and then she was all confused." She continued talking, providing unnecessary details about a bunch of things that were not actually relevant. I could watch her talk all day.

"Long story short," she said eventually, a smile twitching at the corners of her lips, "she said yes, and I officially own half a cafe. Or I will when I give her the money, but you know what I mean." The smile took over her entire face and for a second I couldn't breathe. I loved her so much my chest ached with it.

"Are you going to say something?"

"I fucking love you."

She laughed. "I love you, too, but I meant about Cream and Sugar."

"I'm so proud of you."

"I'm proud of me, too." Both of her hands came to my

cheeks. "But I don't know if I would have made it here without you, so thank you."

"Oh no, you deserve all the glory here." I paused. "I actually have some news, too."

"Oh yeah?" Her eyes darted to my mouth and back up. "Tell me."

Were my hands shaking? "You're looking at the head coach of the New York Thunder, the newest team in the NWSL expansion."

"Jake!" She pounced forward, wrapping her arms around my neck. "Are you serious? New York! You're going to be here, all the time!"

I nodded, brushing curls out of her face. "All the time."

"Wait, what's the NWSL?"

"National Women's Soccer League."

"No way! I am going to kiss Blair next time I see her."

"I'd rather you kiss me right now." It was probably the wrong thing to say, because if I started kissing her right now, I wasn't going to be able to stop. Uber driver be damned.

Harley evidently disagreed. Her arms tightened, our noses brushing and despite my hesitation at our audience—I had learned some lessons after leaving London—I closed the last of the space between us with a groan. My tongue swept into her mouth, and she whimpered, crushing me closer. She tasted like toothpaste and the slightest hint of coffee. It was always there, as much a part of her as her curls.

The driver cleared his throat.

Harley pulled back an inch and cleared her throat. "Thank you so much!" She beamed before scrambling out onto the sidewalk.

"You gotta go?" I asked and she nodded. "You've got this, Harley."

"Yes Coach," she said with a wink.

"I love you. Go get 'em."

The three finalists were lined up on the stage as the judges tallied the points from the final round. Harley was bouncing on her toes, chatting to the woman beside her. She was going to win, I was sure of it, although I was a little biased.

We all were. I was convinced that half the crowd was here for Harley, friends, family, customers. The Franklin High School varsity soccer team was in the row behind me. To my left Harley's friends, my friends now, too, took up most of the row. Darcy was beside me, gripping my arm so tight I was in danger of losing fingers due to lack of circulation. Marion Snyder, Harley's more unlikely friend, was on my right, her hand hooked through the crook of my elbow. A group of six or seven other women around the same age were in the seats beside her.

A hush fell over the crowd as the host stepped onto the stage. Darcy's grip tightened even more. I barely heard what the host said, only took in the fact that the guy on stage was second runner up. We collectively held our breath as the first runner up was announced.

"Nine Cho from Hot Press Coffee in Chelsea. Which, of course, means that this year's winner is Harley O'Connell from Cream and Sugar in Greenpoint!"

Darcy whistled so loud I had to cover one ear as the rest of the crowd roared. "That's my business partner!" she screamed, then latched onto my arm again shaking it hard enough that I feared shoulder dislocation. "That's your fucking girlfriend!"

"That's my fucking girlfriend!" I agreed, not taking my eyes off Harley as she accepted her golden trophy that looked like a piece of a coffee machine and waved to the riotous crowd in front of her. That was my fucking girlfriend, and soon I'd be going to sleep and waking up beside her. Every. Fucking. Day.

I needed to give Blair a raise.

Marion patted my forearm, and I tore my eyes away from Harley, hoping the older woman wasn't about to collapse on me. I'd never forgive myself.

I dropped my head down as she beckoned with a devious and knowing kind of smile on her face. "Now, Jake," she rasped. "I think we can do better than *girlfriend*, don't you?"

My mouth opened and closed a few times as I grappled with whether or not Marion Snyder might be able to read minds. Did she know there was a small box hidden away in one of my drawers? A small box I was tempted to pull out every time I was in New York.

"You know, Marion, I think we can do better."

"Good boy. Don't leave me waiting too long though, please. I realize it may be hard to tell, but I'm not getting any younger." With one last pat to my arm, she turned to Dot on her other side and my attention went back to the stage.

Harley was staring straight at me, smiling so wide that even from here I could see all her teeth. *I love you*, she mouthed.

"I love you, too," I said back, not that she could possibly hear me. It might not happen tonight, next week, or next year, but I was going to marry that girl one day.

ABOUT THE AUTHOR

Erin Thomson is a romance author based in (Naarm) Melbourne, Australia. Her books are full of heart, swoons and spice. When she's not lost in the pages or her latest writing project, or wrangling her two kids, you can find her in the kitchen baking up something sweet.

erinthomsonauthor.com

instagram.com/authorerinthomson

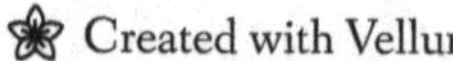 Created with Vellum